A Solitaire

A Story of Espionage in the Age of Napoleon

D.P. McCandless

© 2022
All rights reserved

No part of this book may be reproduced, or stored in a retrieval system, or transmitted in any form or by any means, electronic, mechanical, photocopying, recording, or otherwise, without express written permission of the publisher.
ISBN: 9781434855367
Printed in the United States of America

Direct inquiries to: dpmccandless@gmail.com
Follow D.P. McCandless on Facebook and on Twitter @dpmccandless

On the cover: *Bonaparte Reviewing the Consular Guard (La Revue du Quintidi)*

For Kathy,
my everlasting love

TABLE OF CONTENTS

Foreword	*3*
1. Without Appointment	*4*
2. Renewing Acquaintances	*12*
3. The Assignment	*24*
4. Preparations	*36*
5. On Enemy Soil	*47*
6. Called Into Action	*60*
7. Unforeseen Complications	*73*
8. Additional Critiques	*90*
9. Inspiration in Exile	*104*
10. Calculations and Chaos	*119*
11. The Approach of War	*136*
12. Battling Shadows	*152*
13. Portraying a Spy	*163*
14. A Faltering Alliance	*178*
15. The Endeavor's Final Act	*191*
16. Crosscurrents	*201*
17. Deliberations at Sea	*212*
18. Clear for Action	*222*
19. The Interview	*235*
20. Shattering News	*249*
21. Striking an Agreement	*257*
22. Finding the Words	*265*
Author's Notes	*272*
Recitations	*278*
About the Author	*280*

First Consul Napoleon Bonaparte

Foreword

It is the spring of 1802, and Napoleon Bonaparte commands the French Revolutionary Army, the finest fighting force in the world. He has used it to redraw the map of Europe, extending his country's influence across the Rhine and into Italy and Switzerland. On the home front, he has consolidated his power as the First Consul of France and faces virtually no opposition to any of his schemes. He is an irresistible force holding sway across all of Europe, and nations have been forced to accede to his demands in order to silence his cannons.

Major powers Austria and Russia have agreed to peace terms, and the time also has arrived for England to end its four-year-old war with the French, the sixth conflict between the old enemies in the last century. The British government needs an accord, if for nothing else, to gain time to rebuild a coalition to turn back Bonaparte. Its citizens are even more impatient for a treaty, having tired of the deprivations and the carnage of war.

With peace near, His Majesty's intelligence network is attempting to devise new means to counter France. The British seek to transform information-gathering into something more than the whispers of courtiers and coffeehouse spies, for if one thing is certain, it is that Napoleon's legions will march again. It is the outset of a modern era that witnesses the advancement of machines and weapons and the decline of monarchies and the established social order.

The Age of Napoleon calls for unconventional methods and a new kind of man. England waits for him to step forward …

1. WITHOUT APPOINTMENT

London, March 1802

Lieutenant Philip Collier strode briskly through Westminster streets with the appearance of confidence, but the facade began to crumble when he eyed the three doors on the front of Wickham House.

He selected the one in the middle, but when it would not budge, he turned and walked away, convinced that it was a signal of impending failure. On a bench some distance away, he drew a breath and settled upon the words of Daniel Defoe to appraise his life.

"I am divided from mankind, a solitaire, one banished from human society," he recited softly, recalling one of the books he had read during his long voyage back to England.

In his possession were orders received in India to return home and present himself to Lord Charles Herbert, Earl of Torrington, a man wrapped in intrigue and reputed to wield considerable power within the British government. It seemed like a simple task, but the 20-year-old army officer was a stranger to London's government district — even to his own country — after four years on the other side of the world. The larger issue was that while he was educated and intelligent, he lacked the breeding and influence of a prominent family, and the feeling of not belonging accompanied him wherever he went.

"Ridiculous," Philip mumbled to himself a few minutes later after he had succeeded in his second attempt at the doors of the impressive stone building.

His hopes sank again, however, when he found the anteroom to Lord Torrington's office filled with splendidly dressed gentlemen as well as military officers who outranked him. The growing prospects for peace between England and France were well known, and offices along Whitehall Road were swamped by men trying to establish themselves in positions before the government and the military began to thin their ranks. The competition would be fierce for a young army officer lacking both confidence and connections.

He tugged down on his uniform jacket and stood erect, trying to project his full 6 feet of height into a commanding presence. He took a deep breath just before it was his turn to present himself to a man in a plain black coat who sat behind a desk on which several stacks of papers were neatly arranged.

"And what is your purpose?" asked Westel Sparks, a dour, bespectacled man who served as Lord Torrington's private secretary and as the sentinel to the inner office.

"I am to present this packet to Lord Torrington …"

"Yes, of course, you may enter," Sparks said and turned his eyes to the stack of papers.

"Enter?"

"Yes, through that door, man," Sparks said curtly and pointed. "His Majesty's business is conducted with efficiency in this office."

Philip made his way to the doorway behind the secretary, quickly shifting his shako into the crook of his elbow. The hinges of the door were well oiled, and it flung open easily and quietly, causing him to nearly fall as he stepped into the inner chamber. Towering windows allowed the outside light to fall upon a desk where a greying gentleman sat, a tall bookcase rising behind him.

The man straightened with a start.

"My lord …" Philip began, hesitated when he noticed a figure gliding in the shadows toward the bookcase, then presented himself.

"I wasn't expecting you to be sent in, Lieutenant," Lord Torrington said, eyeing the uniform. "I was expecting a messenger from Admiral Cook, but that does not appear to be a naval uniform, unless my eyes are playing tricks, eh?"

"No, my lord, I apologize. Perhaps your secretary saw that I carried this packet and presumed …"

"Yes, I'm sure that's it," Lord Torrington sighed as he spotted the bundle. "God put Westel Sparks upon this Earth to make certain that my paperwork is completed in good order, but the man takes things upon himself. I told him to expect a courier, but he didn't so much as ask your purpose, did he? For heaven's sake!"

Philip glanced away for a moment at the third man in the room, his back turned as he ran a finger along the book bindings before pulling one from the case.

"Oh, um, Mr. Black and I were just chatting when you arrived," Lord Torrington said, then blew out a low whistle. "Let us see these papers of yours that unintentionally have been given such high importance."

He took the packet, removed some accompanying military documents and unfolded a letter that read:

Lord Charles,
I wish to recommend Lt. Philip Collier of the 33rd Regiment of Foot to you. I have found him to be an officer of extraordinary ingenuity. He is a steady man and would no doubt be of service in the endeavors of your office.
Yours very sincerely, R. Wellesley

"So you're not a courier at all, but here on a personal matter?"

"Yes, my lord, I apologize …"

"Well, nothing to be done at this point, is there? I must say, this letter from the Marquis Wellesley is most impressive," Lord Torrington said. "And how exactly did you come to the attention of the governor general of India?"

"I delivered messages that were important to his dealings with certain parties in India," Philip said, shifting his weight uncomfortably.

Lord Torrington turned the letter over in his fingers and then glanced quickly at the accompanying documents. "Well, these messages must have been *quite* important, Lieutenant Collier," he said as he read. "The governor general seems to have great trust in you."

Philip stood with his stomach churning and his head filling with ideas of how he would be perceived. Would it appear that he was trying to be coy if he offered as little information as possible? Or that he was hesitant to talk because of modesty? Or that the recommendation had been made on behalf of a crony who was expecting favors in return? He suddenly was struck by the thought that the two men in the room with him might have been gazing out the windows a few minutes earlier and witnessed his absurd failure with the door to the building.

"My lord, I apologize again for appearing without appointment," he offered, breaking the silence.

"No, no, not your fault. Sparks sometimes thinks he has all the answers, but this will allow me to put him in his place. Sending in someone without appointment? Har! I'll upbraid him with the door open, so that crowd outside will hear every last word of it. I'll enjoy that greatly, I do declare."

Lord Torrington, apparently impressed with the letter and cheerful at the prospect of lambasting his overreaching secretary, cued Philip that it was time to exit the stage before the morning's gains were unhinged by an inappropriate remark. But before a graceful request to bid his leave could be uttered, Mr. Black replaced the book on the shelf abruptly and moved from the shadow to snatch the letter from Lord Torrington's hands.

"Yes, Mr. Black, please do read the letter," Lord Torrington said after it had already been taken from him. He pushed away from his desk and pulled to straighten his waistcoat, then let out another low whistle as he relaxed in his chair.

The room was still, and Philip's stomach agitation continued. He considered why Lord Torrington had not admonished Mr. Black for grabbing the letter so rudely. Did it mean that Mr. Black was actually *his* superior, or perhaps that Lord Torrington was not a man who demanded respect? After all, he seemed to relish the opportunity to put his secretary in line, but shouldn't the secretary have known his place to begin with?

"Well, it seems that we are now aware of an ingenious young Lieutenant Collier and that he might be of service," Lord Torrington said. "Please tell Sparks how we might contact you."

"Of course, my lord, and I thank Your Lordship for his time," Philip said, blushing at the awkwardness of his own words. "And again, I apologize for my intrusion and offer my gratitude to you for having seen me."

A voice came from the bookcase as he turned to leave. "There are any number of officers with ingenuity in His Majesty's service," Mr. Black said. "What was it that made your service extraordinary?"

Philip felt his face flush as he faced the two men, and he breathed slowly to relieve the appearance of anxiety. "I carried messages from the governor's office to a particular prince," he said. "The terrain was difficult, and it became necessary to obtain help from some of the natives."

"And how did you obtain their help?"

"I made acquaintances within the native community," he replied as he examined Mr. Black's impassive face. The man's cheeks were shadowed, though he appeared to have shaved, and while his eyes were dark and had a foreign look, he bore no accent. Could he be Italian? Spanish? He carried himself with an attitude of superiority, and Philip again wondered if he were Lord Torrington's subordinate or superior.

"And who were these acquaintances?" Mr. Black asked. "I'm sure his lordship would be willing to take the time to hear your tale. After all, it apparently is 'extraordinary,' according to your recommendation. Would you like him to continue, Lord Torrington?"

His lordship sat up straight, as if he were being called to attention. "Yes, as you say, if it's extraordinary," he said.

"During the time that I acted upon the governor general's behalf, movement in the countryside was difficult because of marauding Mahrattas," Philip began. "There were merchants who took me into their confidence and allowed me to travel with them and to dress as a native."

"You dressed as a native, but you didn't speak their language?" Mr. Black asked.

"The merchants spoke English, and I dealt principally with them."

Mr. Black's upper lip curled slightly in what seemed to be a sneer. "This seems like a very difficult assignment for a young man such as yourself," he said.

Philip's discomfort began to grow as the exchange took on a tone more like a prosecution than an inquiry. He at last bristled with indignation when his credentials were the subject of skepticism.

"At the outset, I accompanied a senior officer on an assignment," he recited in the quickly delivered monotone used to address superiors in the army. "We were ambushed, and he was slain. It was my duty to continue, and so I joined a camel train of merchants traveling in the same direction. I delivered the governor's message to this particular prince and returned with the reply. We were contending with growing

French influence at the time and as a result, the governor general gave me other similar duties."

"As to these merchants of whom you speak, why did they fancy the notion of assisting you?"

"As I'm sure you know, the King's gold creates many friendships." Philip cringed as soon as the impertinent words had passed his lips, but Mr. Black paid no notice and continued with his questions.

"What sort of merchants were they?" he asked.

"Sir, they were conveying wares for the army at a forward post, and women, if it must be told," Philip began haltingly. He gauged the reaction, then added quickly, "It wasn't a proud bit of business, but I did what I thought was needed in order to fulfill my duty."

Lord Torrington let out another low whistle, his presence reduced mostly to that of a spectator. "Women? Oh, I see," he muttered. "All of those men out traipsing about, well, I don't have to tell *you* what goes on in the army."

Philip smiled and hoped that would be the end of it.

"And how did you conduct yourself with these merchants?" Mr. Black asked. "Did you insinuate yourself into a position with their business? I hear they have bodyguards, that sort of thing, in India. Did you pose as a eunuch?"

"Sir!"

"Lieutenant Collier, I am only making a jest," Mr. Black said. "You come with high praise from the governor general of India, and yet you seem reluctant to talk about yourself." He moved away from the bookcase, placed the letter on Lord Torrington's desk and took a seat in a chair beside the windows. "We can see that you are a modest young man and that you have provided valuable service to a very important government official."

"Indeed, we see this quite clearly, Lieutenant," Lord Torrington echoed.

Mr. Black grabbed the arms of the chair and leaned forward. "And now why does the Marquis Wellesley consider you to be 'steady,' as the letter also says?" he asked.

Philip's composure snapped, and he turned defiantly to face his inquisitor.

"I was abandoned, sir, do you understand? There was no detachment sent to find me, no inquiries made. Ten thousand miles from England and completely alone. And why was I considered steady? I suppose, sir, it was because I traveled through several hundred miles of enemy ground with only my wits to lead me. And I suppose, sir, it was also because I was forced to hide while I listened to the sounds of my comrade being murdered, because the message needed to be delivered. And I suppose, sir, that a man who can perform his duty with that on his conscience is somebody whom the governor general considers to be 'steady,' as he puts it."

The room again fell silent, but only for a moment.

"How did you come to be in India?"

Philip's anger subsided, giving way to humiliation as he related the origins of his service: His commission had been purchased for him, the only instance in which he had benefited from a military system that favored wealth over merit.

He was the second son of a clerk but had spent part of his childhood in the London household of Henri Espinay, *le Comte de Champeaux*, where his mother had educated the aristocrat's children. The count, who had fled France after the Revolution began, purchased Philip's commission in the 33rd Regiment, mostly in gratitude for Elizabeth Collier's patience with his indifferent sons. But the expenditure also signaled the count's determination to return the Bourbons, and himself, to their rightful places in France.

Philip's résumé had been laid bare, as if his waistcoat had been opened button by button until it revealed only a skeleton beneath a puffed-up chest. Patronage had allowed him to become an officer, and while he had done his duty in India, it had been dirty service and not the glorious action that he had expected.

Mr. Black at last seemed satisfied that the complete truth had been extracted, and he returned to the shadow of the bookcase.

"Well, young sir, you have had an interesting time so far," Lord Torrington said, taking up the conversation. "I venture to say that the Marquis Wellesley might have added the word 'courageous' to his letter. It's one thing to do one's duty, of course …" a low whistle, "but running about the foreign countryside, dressed as a Hindi and living off one's wits is quite another matter."

Philip, bolstered by the compliment, decided it was time at last to deliver closing words.

"My lord, I did only what was needed for my King and my Country. Peace might now be near, but these last years, Englishmen have not had the good fortune to select what's best for themselves. Britain often must stand alone when villainy appears, and as a nation, we *have* stood because each man has made the choice to sacrifice for the good of his Country and his King."

He had noted *Don Quixote* on the shelf where Mr. Black had been looking and concluded, "In the cause of freedom, as in the cause of honor, one can and should risk life itself."

"Commendable!" Lord Torrington said emphatically. "You've done your duty and more, and I can see that you are quite ingenious." He paused. "There's that word again. Har! Lord Richard, you have written all that was necessary here, eh?" he said, holding up the letter and shaking it enthusiastically.

Philip was instructed to return at the end of the following week, this time with an appointment to be obtained from the secretary in the anteroom. After expressing his gratitude and apologizing once again for his intrusion, he turned toward the door.

As he reached for the handle, Lord Torrington said to Mr. Black, "Well, there's an earnest young officer, very true. The King might have need of this Sir Galahad."

"Sir Galahad?" asked Mr. Black, then dropped his own reference to *Don Quixote*. "Or perhaps the 'Knight of the Sad Face.'"

"What's that? Har! You surprise me, sir. You really can be quite droll."

Philip ears burned as he realized that he might have been the victim of his own exuberance.

"Damn your eyes, Sparks, this time give Lieutenant Collier an appointment!" Lord Torrington roared, his voice carrying through to the anteroom. "Then come in here at once!"

2. Renewing Acquaintances

Philip expelled a breath as he emerged from Wickham House into the sunlight and walked down the steps past a scattered collection of soldiers, seamen and civilians who likewise were attempting to secure postwar employment in London before a treaty was signed with France. A step to the side was required to avoid tripping over one such man who sat with his face buried in his hands, sobbing and broken by whatever he had heard inside.

He tried to shake the vision of the man's heaving shoulders, but it hung before him until he finally found an open space down the street. Would he be like that some day, bawling in public over his misfortune? Or worse, would he always have nothing and therefore no wife to disappoint, no family to fail and no home to lose?

After crossing Westminster Bridge, he began to recall the details of the interview in Lord Torrington's office, oblivious to the change in the city's landscape as he walked east toward his father's home. He cut through a narrow street and into a small square filled with street merchants, where a ragged beggar hurried toward him.

"G'day, sir," the man said, drawing up close. "Would you be able to lend a coin to one that ain't done so well as y'self?"

Philip maintained his pace, lifted his chin and kept his eyes forward.

"C'mon then, sir," the man persisted. "I'm an old soldier m'self, took the King's shilling, don't you know?"

Philip pressed on until the pleading voice faded into the din of the square. At the other side, he looked back to see the beggar plying his trade on a young gentleman who had made the mistake of stopping. The eyes of the smartly dressed man searched over the shoulder of the beggar and then suddenly fixed ahead on Philip.

Startled, Philip turned and hurried away, puzzling over what seemed to be a look of recognition from someone he had never seen before. When he reached the next turn of the street, he looked back to see the young man pushing his way through the heavy foot traffic. The realization that he was being followed instantly created a griping stomach.

Sudden recollections of sinister tales about Lord Torrington's dealings, along with the encounter with Mr. Black, heightened a sense of the office's dark nature. He recalled recently reading in *The Morning Chronicle*: "We do not believe that Bonaparte can count agents here by the thousands. We are, however, far from doubting that he has some."

Philip knew that if he had just left a hive of British intelligence, then there was every reason to believe that an enemy agent would be interested in an army officer who had come and gone through the door. It likewise made sense that he should prove his mettle by evading his pursuer.

He reached another turn in the street and dashed behind a tinker's cart, removed his shako and bent down to peer through the hanging pots and piles of metal scrap. The mysterious man rounded the corner, his eyes reflecting the realization that he had lost his quarry, and his quick steps turned into a run.

Philip squatted to look underneath the cart, and a pair of legs appeared on the other side. Hesitation, a turn of the toes to one side, then to the other, and the feet again broke into a run. He raised up as his pursuer disappeared into the tightly packed traffic in the shadowed street. Philip then ducked off in the opposite direction and spent the rest of the day wandering in an effort to reacquaint himself with London and to make certain he no longer was followed. He completed a circuitous route to his father's home on Folsom Street just as the sun sank and ducked into the doorway after one last look around for anyone suspicious.

Inside, his sister Harriet chased their younger brothers with a broom as their father sat quietly in the corner with a newspaper.

"Christ on a biscuit!" Philip exclaimed.

"I will not tolerate such talk!" Robert Collier called out as he looked up.

Philip ignored the rebuke, grabbed 11-year-old Edward and 13-year-old Bartholomew by their collars and dragged them into another room. He slammed the door behind them and shouted, "Stay where you are until you can behave yourselves!"

"You will not invoke the Savior's name in such a manner," Mr. Collier stated firmly, ignoring the ruckus. "You might speak that way in the army, but I shall not stand for such language in this home."

Philip glared at his father, but Harriet averted any further discord by pulling her older brother toward the kitchen, where she pushed him into a chair and removed the cloth covering a plate of boiled beef and potatoes. As soon as his mouth became engaged with supper, she resumed her chatter from a day earlier about what had occurred during the four years he was away.

She detailed how the family cook had been dismissed after their mother's death, with the household duties unjustly falling upon her.

Philip nodded his agreement as she related how Edward and Bartholomew had received little supervision since their mother's death three years earlier, and she related their offenses against not only her, but others along Folsom Street. But he soon tired of hearing of the accomplishments of George, the eldest of the Collier children, who was away at Oxford with all of their father's expectations.

She abandoned family matters to recount how she had been entertained at several homes where the hosts had thanked her profusely for accepting their invitations. She then took a deep breath before shifting to a new topic.

"Well, you must be eager to hear reports regarding our mutual acquaintance," Harriet said as she busily concluded her kitchen work and signaled that she was about to begin dramatic commentary.

"*Eleanor*," she began, placing special emphasis on the name, "attended a poetry reading with me several weeks ago."

"What interest do *you* have in poetry?" Philip asked. "You can barely force yourself to pick up a book."

"At least when I pick up a book, it is to enjoy it, and not to simply memorize some words that I might recite when it is convenient," she shot back.

With the memory of his concluding remark from *Don Quixote* in Lord Torrington's office still fresh in his mind, Philip said nothing in reply.

Harriet smiled at having delivered a winning stroke and then returned to relating the details of the poetry reading, providing lengthy descriptions of whose heads had been turned by which young ladies, while making no mention of the works that had been read.

Philip feigned disinterest but latched onto details regarding Eleanor Vale, with whom he had exchanged letters as a young soldier far from home in India. They had first become acquainted while under the instruction of Elizabeth Collier at the home of *le Comte de Champeaux*, and she had begun writing to him at Harriet's request.

Letters from home had stopped after his father wrote to him, "Your mother has died from a weak heart and was buried," and Philip attributed it to a combination of grief and indifference from his family. But Eleanor's letters continued, and he was pleased that she responded both to his small attempts at humor and to his serious observations.

They developed an intimate style to their correspondence, especially after she began sending books and poems. Once when she complained of how her father had treated her "as an insignificant child," Philip responded with a verse from "The Thorn," which had been in a collection of William Wordsworth she had sent him.

By day, and in the silent night,
When all the stars shone clear and bright,
That I have heard her cry,
Oh misery! oh misery!
Oh woe is me! oh misery!

She wrote back, "Philip, you mock me so! I can only imagine how trifling my concerns must seem to you, so far away from home." From then on, whenever she sensed her writing contained self-pity, she would include "Oh woe is me! Oh misery!" and later "OWIMOM!" after the offending passage.

Harriet's prattle at last reached a conclusion when she announced, "You must see Eleanor."

He looked upon his 18-year-old sister and considered how her features had grown more womanly since he had last been home. People had often spoken of their resemblance: grey eyes and light brown hair, contrasted with dark eyebrows that gave them a look of intense concentration. In Philip's case, the appearance matched his bearing, but Harriet Collier was carefree and seldom quiet.

"We'll meet after my plans are settled," Philip told Harriet.

"Nonsense," she said. "We'll meet her tonight."

She explained that they were to attend a meeting of the Cockermouth Society, named after the home of Wordsworth and dedicated to his writing. In truth, it was dedicated more to the fashion that his writing implied — a modern era with romantic ideals.

They set off that evening on foot and arrived at the meeting hall to find a crowd near the steps. After a quick search for familiar faces, they slipped past and through the doors.

"Philip Collier there!" a voice called from just inside. "I welcome you back to London!"

Will Devlin, the son of a partner in the printing company that employed Philip's father, advanced with a wide smile on this face. "Your pater mentioned that you were returning, but I'd lost track of when that was to be."

"Hello, Will, it's good to see you," Philip said and pumped his hand enthusiastically. "Harriet is reintroducing me to London, whether I wish her to or not."

"Hello, Mr. Devlin, it's good to see you," she said, dropping in a lackadaisical curtsy.

Will beamed, then nodded formally.

Good God, Philip thought, he's fond of this brat.

The three of them ran through a series of topics for polite conversation: what books were to be expected in the next few months, what was occurring in India when Philip left, what Will had been doing while Philip was away, the weather in India, the weather in London, the voyage home and Philip's plans.

With a few more interrogatories and the appropriate rejoinders out of the way, Harriet began to dominate the conversation. Philip was pleased, for it allowed him to use his height to look over the large and noisy room.

He suddenly spied Eleanor in a group that stood two dozen paces away. Like Harriett, she was 18 and had changed considerably in the last four years. He watched as she listened to a discussion, but she didn't seem to be contributing her own thoughts and was oblivious to his stare.

Philip momentarily turned his attention back to Harriet's conversation, or what could have been better described as a monologue, with Will.

"... and it was the most agreeable afternoon. We all laughed so when I ..."

Philip looked again toward Eleanor, but she had turned slightly, and he could no longer see her face.

"... and I said, 'Well, why is it called politics, when it is *impolitic* to discuss it in my company?'" Harriet went on.

Will laughed heartily. "Upon my word, Miss Collier, you are delightful!"

Harriet radiated with pleasure and was silent just long enough to allow two other young men to join their small circle. She performed two more lazy curtsies before resuming her commentary.

Philip turned again to peer across the room and this time caught Eleanor's eye. He broke away and headed toward her.

"Oh, my brother has sounded the charge!" Harriet called as Philip left, then giggled, and her companions joined in with their own laughter.

"Philip, I couldn't wait for you to arrive!" Eleanor exclaimed as she reached out to take his hands. She leaned and, standing on her toes, startled him with a kiss on his cheek.

"I, well ..." he stammered.

"I had pictured you marching into the room in uniform, but I'm not disappointed. It's you."

"Harriet wished me to be in uniform as well, so that I might provide a harsh rebuke to any admirers of Napoleon Bonaparte."

"Oh, dear Harriet, that sounds just like her. Aren't you required to be in uniform?"

"I'm currently unattached."

"Why, the army makes it sound like your marital status," she said in amusement.

Philip considered her comment, along with the kiss, and his mind instantly bridged the gap from their childhood acquaintance, through their correspondence and all the way to their present circumstances, disregarding several layers of formality along the way.

"So exactly what is this evening about?" he asked uncomfortably, then fearing ambiguity, added, "Harriet said we were to discuss poetry."

"Most certainly, since the group is devoted to Wordsworth, after all," she replied, then laughed and covered her mouth. "Our speaker is …" she said and struggled to continue. "Oh forgive me, Philip, it's …" she resumed, then pursed her lips and fixed her jaw. "It's Jonathan Ransom Turgeon."

Philip had renamed the poet "Jumbled Rancid Turgid" in one of his letters to Eleanor after she had included some of his work in a packet sent to India.

He found Turgeon's work to be verbose, devoid of meaningful thought and worst of all, lacking flow in rhythm or cadence. Many of his poetic lines seemed to go on for a syllable or a word too long, and Philip decided it was a modern technique to mask the poems' shortcomings.

"Please honor me with a few lines from his poem *Casting a Glance*," Eleanor said, her eyes bright.

Philip recited from Turgeon, *"The golden grain of great array is simply too beautiful for words to be able to say …"* and then added his own creation, "but I will say these words nevertheless, even though I have already admitted in my own verse that my words are going to be inadequate to convey the splendor of the golden grain."

They laughed and then began to catch up on what had happened in London over the last four years. They also exchanged memories of one another at younger ages, mostly perceptions, rather than clear recollection of anything that had occurred between them, Eleanor having been Harriet's particular friend at the time, rather than his.

Philip expressed surprise that she could share such a close friendship with his sister. "Her personality can be oppressive," he said.

"Why, Philip, she's so dear to me," Eleanor said. "And how else would I fill in-between the lines of your letters?"

That was an unsettling thought. He could only imagine the sort of portrait of him that Harriet could paint with her words.

They soon were engulfed by the growing crowd and found themselves pulled into a conversation regarding the government's future relationship with France. While talk of peace had drifted across

London, the mood was not altogether joyous and reflected mainly a sense of relief after years of deprivation, death and discouragement.

In fact, England's standing in the world was at a low point. First had come the ignominy of losing the American Colonies more than 20 years earlier. The Revolution in France had followed, threatening to shake the foundation of monarchies across Europe. Next came the military successes of the French under Napoleon and the fear that his ambitions could not be curtailed. In some ways, the only sign that England was not in decline had been the continuing and uninterrupted success of the Royal Navy, which had allowed profitable trade to grow.

Philip could see from the crowd that the British upper classes bore little of the brunt of the times and that their lives had continued much as they would have had there been no war. The fashionable folk said they welcomed rumors of peace, mostly because they wished to visit Paris. In addition, some suggested that the future lay in the modern movement embodied in Bonaparte, who held the title of First Consul, and not in the staid British aristocracy.

A young militia major began to dominate the conversation after stating emphatically that a peace agreement was to be signed within days. London newspapers had carried reports on the discussions for months, but some in the crowd stated their doubts that diplomats would produce anything.

Philip recalled reading in *The Times* a day earlier that "the unexpected procrastinations which have taken place already do not permit us to hazard any further opinion. We can only say that those who have been the best informed on the subject have been most deceived."

He added his voice to the expressions of skepticism, but the militia officer specified in an omniscient tone a day at the end of the following week when an agreement would be signed at Amiens.

"Lord Cornwallis gave the French a deadline for concluding the matter, and they buckled," the man said. "They want peace as much as we do.

"To state the plain truth, much of the hubbub over Bonaparte is overdone," he continued. "He is ambitious, to be sure, but he is also a man of science. Why, all of the advanced scientific discourse takes place in Paris these days. Additionally, I believe his public works will allow that city to far surpass London in a few years."

Philip, eyeing the gold trim on the man's uniform, turned to Eleanor and said a bit too loudly, "Words from a man who hasn't had to leave home to fight his nation's battles."

"Sir!" the officer snapped, catching the drift of the statement.

"I apologize," Philip added quickly but with no sincerity and without identifying himself as a fellow military officer. "I simply suspect that His Majesty's officers in service abroad may not hold such a benign view of Boney as you do."

The militia officer sniffed and turned his back on him.

"It seems you didn't need to wear your uniform to become involved in debate, after all," Eleanor whispered. "That gentleman is the eldest son of the home secretary, by the way."

"Well, perhaps I should report his radical views to his father," Philip replied indignantly.

They decided to take their seats for the program, and Eleanor said she would save one for Harriet.

"You need not," Philip said. "I doubt she wishes to be seated, and I'm certain she doesn't wish to listen."

A small, balding man addressed the audience first, reciting news gleaned from recent newspapers, while adding witty asides. He spoke of the prospect of peace with France and added, "Which means we shall have more soldiers and sailors back home now, standing guard over our supplies of porter."

Philip's ears burned, even more so when he spied the militia major chuckling to show he was not offended. It was a shock to see Londoners laughing about the soldiers and sailors who would soon be begging on London's streets during peacetime. The audience's smiling faces with looks of self-satisfaction once again left him with a familiar feeling of being out of place.

At last the esteemed speaker was introduced, and Jonathan Ransom Turgeon arose from a chair at the back of the stage, swept back his coattails and pulled down on his lapels as he walked mightily to the front. He looked down for a moment, an apparent attempt to convey drama, and Philip whispered to Eleanor, "I fear he's lost some coins on the floor."

She giggled, and a woman seated ahead of them turned to glare. He winked, and the woman threw back her head and turned away.

Turgeon lifted his eyes toward the ceiling, and Philip faced Eleanor, looking upward in mockery. She covered her mouth, and he could see her shoulders quivering as she stifled a laugh.

The poet was finally ready to speak. "Words are as seeds," he began, followed by a long pause. "Our thoughts form them into gardens into which the seeds are sown."

Another long pause, apparently intended to allow full appreciation of the gravity of his declaration. "Our seeds, that is our words, are nurtured with punctuation."

Philip held his breath to stifle his own laughter, but with his mouth clenched military-discipline tight, the air had nowhere to go except through his nostrils. As a result, a snort.

"A pig is rooting about in Mr. Turgeon's garden," Eleanor whispered.

He tried coughing to regain his composure, and the woman in front delivered a bug-eyed glare.

"My pardon, ma'am," Philip whispered to her, then turned to Eleanor and mouthed, "O-W-I-M-O-M."

Turgeon continued without mercy. "Of course, in some areas of East Town, the seeds of our words sprout into weeds," he said.

The slight of the poor ended the humor for Philip, who lived not far from the area described, and he sat icily through the remainder of the poet's remarks.

Eleanor dismissed her father's coachman when they came out of the hall, saying she would prefer that Philip and Harriet walk her home, not far in distance from the Colliers' terraced house but a world away in social class.

Edmund Vale greeted the Colliers stiffly when they arrived at the family's well-cared-for stone home. He had once been a barrel-chested man, but his stomach now led the way as he entered a room.

He asked Philip how the Indian weather compared with that of London.

"Hot and dry, sir, a great contrast to cool and wet old England," Philip answered politely. "There is every reason to be pleased about returning home."

He and Eleanor met daily for the next few days, accompanied by Harriet for part of the time before she excused herself to attend to some matter she invented to give them time alone. One morning during a long walk through St. James Park, the conversation turned to his future plans.

"Do you hope to have a long military career?" Eleanor asked. "That is, do you see yourself some day as an old general, retired at his cottage and recounting his adventures?"

"It would be pleasing to know that I would live to be old, to be a general, to have a cottage and to have had adventures," he replied. "What you describe sounds like something that many officers would see as a fine outcome to their lives."

"And as for you?"

He looked up toward the barren branches of the trees on both sides of the path where they walked, the dark fingers stretching across a grey sky.

"I would like to know that what I do matters, even if in some small way," he said after giving the question serious thought.

They walked on several paces before he continued.

"When I'm old and grey, I should like to read a history of our times and know that I was present when the important chapters were written and that what I did counted for something," he said. "Does any of that make sense to you?"

"I think perhaps, yes," she said, and they walked a few more steps. "Is the military the only means for you to achieve the feeling that what you're doing matters?"

He braced as he revealed himself.

"Eleanor, as you know, I do not come from a wealthy family. I'm trying to find a path for myself, but it's perplexing to me. I would like to be happy, but I know that happiness will only come if I am able to achieve something."

She stopped and looked at him. "Philip, does your future have room for marriage and a family?"

As quickly as his mind could work, he calculated her status as the daughter of a wealthy man of business and weighed it against his own as a young army officer who was the second son of a clerk. He decided that he needed to reach a captaincy in rank and a bank account containing 500 pounds to set up a household, then recognized that wasn't the appropriate response.

He looked at her and tried to read her face, but while her eyes were wide, her mouth bore no expression. Should he blunder into a bold statement of affection? That didn't seem prudent, so he instead chose to advance his position only slightly.

"I hope to some day be able to present myself to someone as a man who can offer much," he said haltingly, then cleared his throat. "If I attend to my career, then perhaps I would appear worthy to someone."

They resumed their walk, with Philip believing his statement had gone far enough and that she would find his humility to be endearing. Generally pleased, he again looked up at the sky through the empty branches of the trees.

Eleanor looked down.

3. THE ASSIGNMENT

Philip arose early to prepare for his second visit to Lord Torrington's office, brushing his uniform carefully and hanging it to preserve the creases until he was ready to leave. Harriet served breakfast to him, but she was mercifully quiet as he ate, allowing him time to organize his thoughts. As he was finishing his meal, his father appeared in the doorway of the kitchen.

"I was not aware that the government began its work before midday," Mr. Collier said.

"It appears that they do," Philip said curtly.

"I hope that somebody is awake when you reach Whitehall," Mr. Collier said to further his jest, a hint that he wanted to know more about whom his son was to see.

Philip knew that Lord Torrington's work was secretive and significant, and he bristled at his father's attempt to learn more. He pushed back from the table, gave Harriet a kiss on her forehead and left the room without a word.

Folsom Street was dark and silent when he stepped out, adding to the unfamiliarity he had experienced since returning home. It seemed that there were far fewer children than what he remembered from the time when he had roamed these cobblestones years earlier, and the trees looked tired, as if they had given up on ever growing taller.

As he walked the city's quiet streets, he reflected upon the time he had spent with Eleanor during the past days and was generally satisfied. While he had been apprehensive about their reintroduction, he had enjoyed their time together and had been struck by her appearance. When he was younger, he had not looked upon her in the way he did now, for she then had been mostly an afterthought in the company of his bothersome sister. He found that he was very much attracted to her, and he especially favored her pleasing manner in the company of other young men. She didn't draw their notice with silliness, in Harriet's fashion, nor did she have the sort of dazzling beauty that caused a stir. She was beautiful, but in a way that other young men were unable to see because of their own shallow airs, he thought smugly.

A light mist hung over the Thames, and the familiar, unpleasant smell of the water reached his nostrils as he stopped to gather himself on Westminster Bridge when Wickham House came into view. "God sees everything," he recalled his mother saying, and he straightened his coat before approaching the building.

His steps rang on the marble floor as he marched down the hallway and came to a halt outside Lord Torrington's office. The door was locked, and it was about an hour before Westel Sparks came toward him, a frown forming in recognition as he withdrew a key from a waistcoat pocket.

Philip presented himself and stated, "I have an appointment."

"Yes, I remember you quite well, particularly the manner in which you arrived and then your hasty departure. You might have an appointment, but I shall tell you when you are to see his lordship."

As time wore on, it became clear that Sparks was making game of him, as revenge for his unannounced arrival that resulted in the secretary's upbraiding by Lord Torrington.

Philip began to stare at Sparks as his impatience grew, hoping that he would become a nuisance to be rid of. But while other visitors were directed inside the office and later left, Philip remained as the secretary worked on without regard to his presence.

Eventually, the battle of wills in the anteroom ended when Philip asked where he might go to relieve himself, receiving a self-satisfied look from the secretary. By the time he returned, another visitor had appeared. After that gentleman had been directed inside and had departed about 30 minutes later, Philip stood up over Sparks.

"See here, I had an appointment at half-past seven today," he said.

"I gave you an appointment at that time, but Lord Torrington does not arrive until nine," Sparks responded.

"And it must now be what, midday?" Philip protested.

"Don't you have a watch?" Sparks asked, shaking his head slowly in a show of disdain.

"When I speak to Lord Torrington, I shall report that I have been abused by his private secretary," Philip said but received no satisfaction from the reaction. "And I shall also mention that I have seen you dispose of several letters that were delivered to his office on this very morning. I wonder if his lordship knows that you take it upon yourself to do so."

Sparks cleared his throat and lowered his eyes. "Return to your chair," he said and left to enter the inner chamber. When he reappeared, he led Philip inside.

"Well, there you are, young sir," Lord Torrington greeted him from behind his desk.

"It's a fine coincidence that you should be here today, for I tell you in all confidence that England at this moment is concluding a treaty with France. The hostilities officially will end ..."

"Tomorrow, as I was told last week," Philip interrupted. "The agreement is to be signed at Amiens."

"What? You've been told?" Lord Torrington said, turning to glare at Sparks, who shook his head to deny that he was the source of Philip's information.

"God's thunder!" Lord Torrington exclaimed.

Philip stepped back, startled by the outburst.

"Where did you hear this? Is it the talk of every tavern?"

Sparks seated himself at a small writing table off to the side, shuffled some papers and stared ahead without expression.

Lord Torrington leaned back in his chair and drummed his fingers on the arms of his chair.

Philip straightened himself and remained silent.

"Now, that is the crux, lieutenant, the crux! This government is in the business of information, and we *pay* for information, don't you see? And yet every drunkard and every trollop in this town can apparently get the same information, *gratis*!"

Philip recalled that he had heard from the militia major at the poetry gathering that a treaty was to be signed this day. The treaty and its timing had been mentioned in casual conversation, not whispered in confidence, and he had nearly dismissed it after *The Times* reported a few days later that "negotiations for a definitive treaty will continue for some time."

"Now, where did you hear that we were to sign an accord with the Frogs today?" Lord Torrington inquired.

"It was at a social event, my lord. I assure you that it was not at a disreputable establishment, not that it makes it any less dreadful. I sincerely apologize."

"God's teeth!" Lord Torrington cried out, then looked out the window and sighed. "It's just so damned frustrating. Of course, the negotiations were common knowledge, but not the status of the treaty."

He sat back in thought for a moment. "I had no idea that you had such connections in Town," he said. "I should say that I am most impressed, although this lack of discretion in your circle of acquaintances is disconcerting to me."

Philip decided it best to let the misconception stand after briefly considering the exposure of the home secretary's son as the source of his information.

Lord Torrington whistled and again drummed his fingers. "Don't you see, this office's work is much like operating a spigot. We open the spigot, information pours out, and we try to collect it in a cup. But we don't collect it all, and the rest spills out on the ground. Anyone can have it."

Philip did not respond, as he puzzled over how the government could function if it couldn't protect its secrets.

"Don't you see?" his lordship asked, sensing lack of comprehension. "Spigot, cup, eh?"

"Yes, my lord. There's the spigot, and then there's the cup. Perhaps the spigot shouldn't be opened so far."

"What? No! We need the spigot open to its extreme!"

Philip thought it best not to engage again. "I understand, my lord, and I apologize again."

Lord Torrington waved aside his second apology. "Sparks, have you been out tra-la-la-ing down Bond Street calling out about peace?"

After a pause, Sparks replied stiffly, "No, my lord."

"Har! Well, that eliminates him as the chatterbox spilling the King's business out in the street," he said sarcastically, then returned to drumming his fingers. "Now see here, lieutenant, I've thought a good deal about you and about the Marquis Wellesley. And here's the thing: He arranged for the orders that returned you to England, isn't that right?"

"Yes, my lord."

"And he also wrote the letter of recommendation and told you to present yourself to me at this office?"

"Yes, that is correct."

"Well, there you have it then. I shall employ you."

"Employ me?"

"Oh, you may have to become accustomed to the way we speak here. We are men of business in a way. Now, what do you know of this agency?"

"Pardon me, but is Your Lordship asking what I know of this agency?"

Lord Torrington eyed him with puzzlement and nodded.

Philip cleared his throat and responded, "I *know* nothing of this agency."

Lord Torrington scratched under his chin with the backs of his fingernails. "I see that the question should be rephrased, 'What have you heard of this agency?'"

"I've heard that this agency is within the purview of the Foreign Office and that its comings and goings are, as a rule, outside the normal channels of the military, or for that matter, the government. However, I've heard nothing in the way of particulars."

What he really had heard from fellow officers in India was that Lord Torrington handled the government's affairs behind the scenes, that he had a vast network of spies and that he had piles of gold at his disposal to use in support of French royalist plots.

In fact, one of his fellow officers had complained that the government provided a better budget for its secret work than for its army to fight wars. Philip didn't see how that could be possible, but he believed the statement made a point nonetheless. None of his colleagues in India knew much about Lord Torrington personally, but that was to be expected since they were thousands of miles from the inner circles of London.

"You are correct in that we operate outside the normal channels of the military *and* the government, and yet we work *for* both," Lord Torrington said. "If you are in my employ, you need to learn to move beyond the bounds of your army training and to think of alternative means of accomplishing your goals. Do you understand what I say?"

"Yes, my lord," Philip said, imagining the fantastically clever schemes that must spring from the office. He was still uncertain of what to make of Lord Torrington, who appeared to be befuddled at times.

"You seem to have some skills in extracting information," Lord Torrington observed. "While you confess to knowing little, you are aware that England and France are signing a treaty, perhaps even as we speak."

Philip let the unwarranted compliment stand.

"It matters little. You may sit now, and we shall talk." Lord Torrington pushed his chair back from his desk, crossed his legs and pulled at his stockings as Philip took a seat in front of him. "So, Lieutenant Collier, how well do you speak French?"

"I speak French very well, my lord," Philip said enthusiastically. "I spent a great deal of time in the household of a French nobleman in Town where my mother instructed his children. I played with French children and at one time was told that I had the accent of an aristocrat."

"An aristocrat, indeed!"

"Of course, I must remind his lordship that I have spent four years in India and at sea and have had little reason to speak any language other than English."

"But you think you could get along with the French that you know?"

"Yes, I could get along very well. I could recite the 23rd Psalm in French, if that were required," he said, smiling.

"I wasn't planning to order you to a pulpit in Paris. Har!"

Lord Torrington directed Sparks to retrieve a map from a large cabinet and sat back as the secretary scurried across the room, then returned to stretch the document across his master's desk. Philip quickly recognized the outlines of Europe, but some of the boundaries differed from what he remembered.

"Is this map a current representation of the Continent?" Philip asked, then noticed a slight smile form on Sparks' thin lips.

"This office gets a new map whenever a river changes its course or some addlebrained prince sells his land to discharge his gambling debts," Lord Torrington responded brusquely. "Of course it's current!"

He rose from his chair and began to pace as he outlined the provisions of the treaty between England and France. In addition to the end of hostilities, the British were to return French island possessions they had captured in the Indies, along with Malta in the Mediterranean. Several boundaries on the map were either to be changed slightly or affirmed as well. France was to withdraw from some of the Italian states, even though Napoleon Bonaparte already had announced plans to name himself as president of the Italian Republic, which was created from territory France had conquered since invading in 1796.

Philip was waiting for a mention of anything further that France had yielded in negotiations, but Lord Torrington ended his comments on the changing European map. He then turned to the subject of trade, the principle item in the accord being that British ships would no longer harass French shipping at sea.

"On the other hand, we have received no concessions regarding the resumption of our own trade on the Continent," he added.

"Why, it seems as if we *lost* the war!" Philip blurted out.

Lord Torrington cast a long look at him and then sat down.

"That's very observant, young sir, but here's the thing: There's nobody left to fight the damned Frogs, don't you see? Certainly, the Royal Navy could press on, but who's left to conduct war on land? The Russians have begged off, and then where are we to look for support? The Prussians? The Italians? The Austrians? None of them have the bottom for it, and I can't say as I blame them. Defeat means land lost and their people watching soldiers return home with arms and legs missing. And the deaths? Why, you might lose more men on the battlefield in one day than you lose at sea in a year. You see, war on land is a charnel house, and everyone's had enough of it for now."

He leaned back in his chair and let out a low whistle. "But back to your remark. Nay, it's not much of a treaty for us, but we shall carry on as best we can."

A silence ensued as Lord Torrington fumbled to turn the map to face Philip before Sparks rose to help.

"Now," he said, glancing over at his secretary and giving him a wink, "what would you say to a tour of France?"

Philip tried to register what was said. "A tour, my lord?"

"That's right, a tour, a holiday," the second description followed by a chuckle.

"I don't understand, my lord," Philip said.

"Well, here's the thing," Lord Torrington said. "With the coming of peace, Englishmen will want to see the sights of Paris, wouldn't you say? They have been deprived of the grand French city for years, and let us say that a young military officer, currently without orders, were to visit. Why, he could see the sights just like any other tourist, don't you think?"

"I see," Philip replied slowly, though in truth he was confused.

"But he's still a soldier at heart, and so while he's entertaining himself, his interest also might be piqued by other things that he happens to observe. Are you following my line?"

"He would be looking about?"

"Yes, that's it. He sees Calais and Paris, and he takes a particular interest in roads, shipyards, military posts, or anywhere else that Bonaparte might be up to something. He might take note of such things and post a letter to an acquaintance in London."

"And you say this is to be like a holiday?" Philip asked.

"Well, perhaps I sprinkled a little too much sugar on it. After all, you'll be shot if you stick your nose a little too deeply into Boney's business, and we'll all read about it in the newspapers." He let out a laugh.

Philip shifted uncomfortably in his chair.

"Oh, I jest," Lord Torrington said. "Still, it's best to be cautious."

"And how long would I be away?"

"Why, that's up to you. You'll be acting without orders, as you recall. At any rate, you'd best be scampering back if relations begin to sour, or more likely, when you run out of funds."

"I take it that his lordship doesn't think the Amiens treaty will endure," Philip observed mildly.

"Oh, good heavens, no!" Lord Torrington barked back at him. "Boney will never relinquish any of the Italian states after preening for years over his military campaigns that won them. Nay, he sees peace only as an opportunity to rearm because he has no intention of reining in his ambitions.

"Not much conviction on our side either," he added. "British men of business will squawk like gulls at their MPs as soon as they learn that the French made no concessions on trade. So then, are you interested in taking this tour?"

"Yes, my lord, if you believe I could be of help," Philip replied. He had learned two things in the army: Don't step forward when an officer asks for volunteers, but don't turn down an assignment offered directly by your superior. The latter point came into play when the governor general of India had asked if he wished to return to England, telling him that he had "great potential" for the type of service that Lord Torrington's office provided.

"Well, there you have it then," Lord Torrington announced.

They spent the next two hours going over the map of Europe, along with names to know and some background on how the French military operated. Sparks left at one point to fetch more paper from the anteroom.

While he was gone, Lord Torrington remarked, "Sparks is still chafing over your last visit." He laughed lightly to himself and whistled.

"Allowing someone into my office while I was in conference with another gentleman, indeed. Then he compounded his misfortunes by failing to learn where you could be reached. He said you left in a hurry. Hmmmph! I gave it to him good for that, to make clear who is in charge here. The man can be, what's the word, officious? I can't have an *officious* office, don't you see? Har!"

Near the end of their discussion, Lord Torrington asked Philip to repeat what he believed he was to accomplish while he was in France, as Sparks, back at his station in the corner, took notes.

First, he was to travel along the northern coast of France to look for evidence of French invasion preparations during the time of peace. Lord Torrington told of reports reaching his desk that hinted of Napoleon's grand schemes for when war resumed.

"Boney is said to have some cock-and-bull notion of assembling a massive force across the channel in anticipation of the return of war. We have heard of activity around Boulogne, but none of these observations have involved the eyes of a military man such as yourself."

"My lord, I should point out that my service on the 33rd's quartermaster staff provided experience in military planning," Philip offered eagerly, but to little notice.

"You see, the Duke of York believes invasion to be a serious threat, and it would be good for our office to present him with evidence in support," Lord Torrington went on.

Philip's mind drifted since the duke, King George's second son, was commander in chief of the army and could provide unlimited influence on a military career.

In the meantime, Lord Torrington was ready to outline the second assignment: Philip was to observe any work around Paris that would seem to have military purposes and to, as his lordship put it, "Visit every tavern where French military officers gather. We'll hope they aren't any more tight-lipped than their counterparts in London."

Third, and this was the most important part, he was to deliver a substantial sum to a Spanish envoy, Don Martin Cristobal de Acuña, in payment for information. Such transactions could have been handled through associates within the British embassy after it reopened in Paris, he explained, but this particular gentleman wished to distance himself from such an obvious conduit for English gold.

"I'm not certain of this Spaniard's intentions, truth be told, since his country is allied with the French," Lord Torrington said. "It's to our advantage that he doesn't know you, because we don't want him to understand any more about our enterprise than he needs to."

He cautioned Philip that it might be best to complete that assignment toward the end of his stay.

"You must learn how the land lies before you go about putting gold in another man's palm," he said. "The police are everywhere, don't you see? I don't know how they can muster such large goddamned armies when they have police on every street corner in Paris."

Finally, Philip was to return to England when his funds ran short, or if it appeared that the peace was about to end.

"I thank Your Lordship for finding me up to this challenge," he said.

"The gentleman whom you met the other day expressed doubts about my employment of you, but I suspect that you may have some unique qualities."

"Do you refer to Mr. Black?" Philip asked.

"Who's that?" Lord Torrington said as he rose from his chair, walked over to the window nearest his desk and looked out, creating a striking profile as he stood in the sunlight. Philip thought that he must be contemplating something of significance to say in regard to Mr. Black.

"Gawd, there's Hazelrigg!" Lord Torrington exclaimed instead. "Why, he must be two inches broader abeam than when I saw him before Christmas. Heavens, that man can eat! If he ever invites you to dinner, you'd best bring along a cot so you can rest while you wait for him to finish."

Philip knew of no one named Hazelrigg but pictured an obese man waddling up to Wickham House. He tried to clear his head and get the discussion back on track, knowing there were unanswered questions and fearing he would not think of them until much later.

"Am I correct in saying that this Spaniard, Don Martin, cannot be trusted?" Philip asked.

"You want a cut and dried answer to that, and I can't give you one," Lord Torrington replied. "We pay in gold for many things, but not loyalty. Once the gold is gone, that's the end of it. As for Don Martin, there's little to tell. He's a fanny patter, I will say that."

"A fanny patter?"

Lord Torrington turned toward Philip with his two hands down at his side, then jerked them upward with his fingers extended in a grabbing motion.

Philip sat still, puzzled and shocked.

After an uncomfortable silence, Lord Torrington began to color. "You never know what information will help you," he said. "*That* is information I received from one of our men in Paris."

"I see," Philip said, even though he did not. If he had any further questions, he had now forgotten them, distracted by his thoughts of fanny patting and an obese man named Hazelrigg.

He was to receive what to him was an incredible sum: 150 pounds to finance his trip. "A young gentleman requires a pound per day for expenses," Lord Torrington pointed out, although Philip thought half that amount sounded like quite enough. In addition, he would be credited with his army pay while he was away.

Philip was to deliver to Don Martin one-thousand pounds in Spanish gold and Hammersley's circular notes, which served as currency for major banks of Europe.

And finally, Lord Torrington told him, "Just see what you can see. And you have no orders, is that clear?"

"And that is also in regard to when I am to return, my lord?"

"That is correct. Har! If this peace were to last, we might not see you again, would we? A young man on holiday in Paris with a fat purse provided by the government? Why, *adieu*, as the Frogs say!"

He noted Philip's confused expression and turned serious. "Make no mistake: All who come through this office must understand that this is cold-sober work, and you must expect treachery. I don't mean to say that there's evil in everyone you meet, only that everyone has his own reasons for turning this way or that when he reaches a street's end. Do you get my meaning? You get yourself into trouble when you guess which way the other man will turn, based on what *you* believe. That's the thing, don't you see?"

Philip nodded as he thought back to the rogue who had followed him from the office. "I shall begin to think outside the normal bounds, as you say, my lord," he said.

"Yes, splendid! I believe you're going to be quite useful, just as Lord Richard said. Now, have you any further questions?"

"Who will know that I'm in France, my lord? That is, would there be an *officious* clerk at Horse Guards who might inquire about me?" he asked, with a slight smile.

Lord Torrington's face brightened as he remembered his earlier comment. "If there is some *officious* army clerk," he said drawing out the key word, "who has the time to go over the rolls of your regiment and wonders what happened to a certain officer in that regiment, then he will eventually be directed to this office. Here, the inquiry will end, at the hands of another *officious* clerk." He guffawed and slapped his knee twice.

Sparks cast a steely look at Philip, who considered how long he would have to wait for his next appointment.

4. Preparations

Philip was greeted warmly when he called upon Henri Espinay, *le Comte de Champeaux*, at his London home and requested that they speak in French.

"What is this from the young man who used to call me 'Missoooor Count'?" the count said in English, exaggerating the mispronunciation from years ago.

Philip explained that he wanted to revive his language skills, which had slipped while he had been away in India.

"As you wish, I shall gladly speak in my tongue," the count replied.

After they shared memories and exchanged news of the last four years, Philip prompted the count to relate stories of his life in France. The displaced nobleman relished the opportunity, speaking fondly of his days in the Brittany region of France, which remained a royalist hotbed for years after the Revolution.

The Espinay family and some of their household servants had fled their home in 1791 after sensing the wave of horror that was descending upon their country. While he had not been threatened in the early days of the Revolution in 1789, he had become apprehensive during the period of relative tranquility that followed, when commoners no longer would give way when he passed.

"It was as if they knew something about what was to transpire," he said. "I did not need to see King Louis' head rolling across the cobblestones to know what it was."

Whether by intuition, or just luck, *le Comte de Champeaux* made his way to England with a great deal of his fortune intact, unlike those who fled later with little more than their lives.

"If I had not the sense to leave when I did, then I would be making hats or cutting shoe leather," he said callously of the Frenchmen who had been his equals but now struggled to survive in London on pensions from the British government. Still, he felt guilt that he had abandoned the counterrevolution in his native Brittany, and so he supported the royalist cause in any way that he could.

"As you know, Philippe, I chose to assist your military career because France needs brave young men to restore her to her former glory. However, I must say that I was quite disappointed when you became part of a regiment to be posted in India."

Philip dutifully thanked him for providing funds to purchase an army commission. Left unsaid was that his mother had arranged that he be an officer in the 33rd Regiment, which had become part of the East India Company's army after previous service in Flanders. Her intent was to keep him far away from Europe's wars.

"It is nothing," the count said, waving him off. "I would have helped you in any way that I could, simply because of my gratitude to your mother. She was a dear woman, and we were all so saddened when …" His voice trailed off, and he looked closely at Philip. "It must have been most terrible for you to receive word when you were so far away."

The count took him by the arm, and they began a stroll through the house. "But now is a happy time, for you are home again."

"And it appears that there will be peace," Philip said.

The count agreed, but without much conviction.

"I cannot help but think that every day that passes is another day that my nation remains in the hands of usurpers," he said. "I have not seen my home in 12 years and must admit that I long for the fight to resume."

They visited the home's large library, where Elizabeth Collier had given her lessons in Chaucer, Homer and the sciences. She had been the educated daughter of a Bristol clergyman who had come to London to serve as governess for a wealthy family and had left the position after finding a suitable match in Robert Collier. Her former employers later recommended her to Espinay as a tutor to his boys when it became clear that Robert's salary as a clerk wouldn't support a growing family. The count wished his sons to learn proper English, and so, at his suggestion, she had taken on five other children of wealthy London families, along with Philip and Harriet, to create a private day school at his home.

Philip envisioned the room where the children had sat and his mother had stood in front of a globe in the corner. He recalled how he and his sister had been in chairs against a wall and did not feel as equals to the seven other children whose parents were paying for tutoring.

Harriet was the one who had refused to accept their inferiority, striking up a friendship with Eleanor Vale, whose father had made his fortune in trade. Philip developed no lasting friendships with the other boys, especially the count's sons, who were lazy and believed themselves entitled to everything that was handed to them.

While the arrangement had benefited all of the children by creating the engagement of a classroom, it had been a burden for Elizabeth Collier. Philip's earliest memories of his mother included her lively, smiling face, while his later recollections were of a woman who was always tired and only showed forced enthusiasm when she was instructing her pupils.

The count's tour of his home ended in the kitchen, where he left Philip to visit with members of the household staff who remembered him.

Again Philip requested to speak in French, although he noted that more English servants were now in the count's employ than had been the case four years earlier. A farrier had died, he was told, and two footmen had returned to Brittany after Napoleon had declared a general amnesty for *émigrés* in an attempt to build popular support for his regime.

"The count was most displeased when they left," said Simone Jusserand, a large woman who worked in the kitchen. "He said they were ungrateful and threatened to turn out the rest of us and hire all English servants. But he eventually calmed down, and peace was restored to the house."

"Why did they return to France?" Philip asked.

"England is your home, Philippe, it is not ours," said Victor Belain, the stable master. "France would like its sons to return, but it requires money to travel."

"So France's shores are open to those who fled?" Philip asked. "There must be many Frenchmen who are taking advantage of this amnesty."

"Yes, but Simone and I have no positions waiting for us in our homeland," Victor said. "The two who left did so with money they had stolen from the household accounts."

Philip felt that his mastery of French was beginning to return as he continued to converse. He struggled with a few phrasings, but he believed that he was recapturing the sounds of the language and confirmed that he had retained a firm grasp of the vocabulary. His skills had advanced quickly as a boy in order to avoid the taunts of the count's sons, and he knew that he was speaking fluently when their teasing moved on to other subjects, such as his poor breeding or his shy nature.

As he listened to the servants, he made note of sentence construction and tried to train his mind to think in the way the language flowed. Simone asked if he would stay to eat in the kitchen that evening after the Espinay family had been served, and he agreed eagerly. He observed how the French servants ate their meal and made note of subtle differences from what he was accustomed to seeing at his family's table. In the end, however, the meal mostly revealed fingers in the food and speaking with full mouths, both of which he could have observed just as easily at supper with the younger Collier brothers.

Philip stayed late into the evening, continuing to question the household staff members about their previous lives in France, and he recited those conversations to himself as he walked home that night. In bed later, he continued to reconstruct conversations in French. "This is correct, my family comes from Champeaux in Brittany. My father one time took me to Brest to see the ships. I have never forgotten the sight of the masts, which seemed to reach to the sky. I have only memories such as these from my life in France, for I have been away for such a long time."

On Sunday, the Colliers set off for church and heard a sermon on the virtue of humility, but Philip's eyes soon began to wander out of boredom. To his right, his father's gaze was fixed forward, a look that Philip believed reflected nothing more than an attempt to appear pious. In between them, Edward and Bartholomew squirmed and kicked the pew ahead of them, and Philip wondered how the insolent pair had survived over the years without someone murdering them.

To his left, Harriet sat pleasantly, her hands folded in her lap ... with her eyes closed and mouth hanging open. Good God, you're plucky, he thought as he looked at her and for once admired her devil-to-what-people-say spirit.

Philip expanded his surveillance to the rows ahead and began to make some quick calculations. Roughly one in ten men was dozing, although Harriet seemed to be the only female. He realized that his quartermaster's duties had left an impression on him in how he naturally viewed situations through numbers.

As he scanned near the front of the church, he spotted Eleanor, and a slight turn of her head allowed him a glimpse inside her bonnet. He could see her lashes and the curve of her cheek, and he imagined her dark eyes. Edmund Vale's head was drooping, and Philip supposed that he had eaten too much at breakfast that morning. Mr. Vale was added to the calculation of those asleep.

Philip concluded the exercise and suddenly grew apprehensive and then frightened at the thought of what awaited him if he were to be arrested in France. A dank and filthy Paris prison, where he would be forgotten? Or execution at the hands of a French firing squad? Or worst of all, the guillotine?

He shuddered and opened his Bible to Psalm 71, reading to himself as he sat still and imagined God as a giant holding him in His hands.

"In thee, O Lord, do I put my trust: let me never be put to confusion. Deliver me in thy righteousness, and cause me to escape: incline thine ear unto me, and save me."

He closed the Bible and looked up to see that his father was observing and smiling approvingly. He turned away and began to pull at a thread on his coat, angry over being watched — despite the fact that he himself had just been scrutinizing others at church.

Afterward, the Collier clan was gathered outside, chatting with other parishioners, when Philip saw Eleanor, her two sisters and her parents heading toward their carriage.

"Aren't you going to speak to her?" Harriet asked him.

"They're leaving," he replied.

"Oh, El-ean-orrrr!" Harriet called out.

"Good God, is there no end to the embarrassment you cause?" Philip muttered.

"You're helpless," she responded. "You'd let the world pass you by."

He nevertheless followed her to where Eleanor stood, as her family moved on after turning toward Harriet's outburst.

"Hello, you two," she said and hugged Harriet.

"Wasn't the sermon simply awful?" Harriet complained.

Philip gaped, but Eleanor laughed. "Whatever we all may be thinking, Harriet, only you have the courage to say."

They exchanged pleasantries for a moment before Mr. Vale came over to announce that it was time to leave.

"Good day, Lieutenant Collier, Miss Collier," he said. "Are you to be home for a time, lieutenant, or is the army going to send you off to the far reaches again?"

"I am to be leaving again shortly," he replied.

"What? This is news," Harriet said.

Philip glanced at Eleanor and, seeing a shocked look on her face, smiled weakly. "I was told that I might be receiving orders," he said vaguely.

"So soon, eh?" Mr. Vale said. "They must see great promise in you, if they require your services during a time of peace." He bade the Colliers a good day, then took Eleanor's arm and led her away.

"You've upset her," Harriet said to Philip when they were barely out of earshot. "You're badly mistaken if you think Eleanor is simply sitting by the window waiting for you to walk up to her door. It might just be that another suitor arrives first. You're too slow."

She turned abruptly and headed east with the rest of the Collier family toward their modest home.

Philip lingered and watched the Vales' carriage begin to pull away in the opposite direction. It rolled for only a short distance before it stopped, the door opened and Eleanor emerged.

She approached him and curtsied, "Would you walk me home today?" she asked.

"Nothing would please me more, if your father would allow it," he replied with a bow.

"Papa held a ball last summer to announce that I have come out," she said, turning and waving to her family to continue. "Since my match remains incomplete, he has grown impatient and is now of a mind to allow his daughter to walk in the company of a young man of villainous reputation and no chaperone at her side."

A few days later, Philip again visited the home of *le Comte de Champeaux* to speak with the staff, spending most of the time with Victor, who had grown up on the Espinay lands in northwestern France.

He looked over the stable master's belongings as they conversed in his quarters, using French as he asked for names of families, bits of history about the region and stories of Victor's childhood. At one point he asked for an appraisal of his fluency.

"You sound like a native," Victor said. "However, I have been in your country for 12 years, so perhaps I do not know how a native sounds anymore. Pardon me for saying this, Philippe, but the English speak in short bits, like a barking dog. The French are more inclined to purr like a cat."

Philip returned one last time to Lord Torrington's office and received the funds designated for him, but he neglected to bring something in which to carry the valuable sum in gold and paper. Sparks shook his head in disapproval at the oversight and went to a tall set of drawers.

"I suggest that you make other arrangements, but this will at least get you to wherever you are staying in London," he said, presenting a leather bag. "His lordship had wanted to know how to contact you in Town, but that is unnecessary now, since you will be abroad."

Philip was only too pleased to have the office unaware of his humble residence. He hid the bag when he was back home, making certain that none of his siblings witnessed his activity, then lay on the bed to gather his thoughts.

The tour of France would be his chance to find the advancement he sought — with the possibility of glory. He thought of the German writer Johann Wolfgang von Goethe as he focused on a crack in the plastered ceiling. "Whatever you can do, or dream you can, do it," he said quietly. "Boldness has genius, power and magic to it."

He imagined the look on Lord Torrington's face one day in the future when he would present the information needed to bring Napoleon to his knees. A promotion surely would follow, a commendation seemed a possibility and a knighthood could not be discounted, nor could an introduction to the Duke of York. Beyond that, perhaps an audience with the King would await him.

He finally shook his head to cast aside his dreams and deal with the practicalities of his travels ahead. Lord Torrington had wanted him to leave for France as quickly as possible, but preparations remained.

Philip visited shops over the next week to make purchases for his trip, including writing supplies and a small travel chest, but his errands became hampered by his blistered feet. He had been all over the city ever since he had returned, a short period that had followed months aboard a ship, where walking had consisted only of 10 paces this way, followed by 10 paces that way.

One of his final stops was at the Fleet Street publishing house of Dunn & Gilchrist, his father's place of employment. Mr. Collier was hunched over his ledgers and frowned when he looked up to see his son drawing near.

"I had asked that you come in uniform," he said.

"I didn't want to get ink on it," Philip mumbled, although the real reason was spite, knowing that his father had hoped to impress his employers with his son's evident military success.

"I wasn't asking you to work, just to come in and speak to everyone," Mr. Collier replied.

Philip was led to an uncomfortable meeting with the partners, who seemed only mildly interested in his career, even though it was described by Mr. Collier in a lengthy, glowing account.

"You've done well for yourself in India," Hugo Devlin, one of the partners, said dully.

"I should say so," his son Will added, not picking up on his father's lack of enthusiasm for the interruption in work. "Philip has come a long way since the time he and I labored together in the shop."

"I fear my father has left out some accounts of my service," Philip said. "For instance, my extensive supervision of the digging of latrines."

The partners and Will laughed heartily, but Mr. Collier colored in embarrassment. Philip then excused himself to renew acquaintances in the company's shop, and his father led him away with obvious displeasure upon his face.

"Hey, boys, Inky is here!" shouted one of the printers when Philip was reintroduced at the building that housed the presses and the bindery. "Inky" wasn't Philip's nickname alone, but rather was given to every boy who worked at pulling apart lead type and returning it to the cases.

Mr. Collier left him on his own and returned to his ledgers.

Philip liked these men, their crude jokes and their ability to endure a hard life by being satisfied with what it offered. They asked him about India, particularly the exotic animals he had seen, and about army life.

"You like giving orders, I'll wager," one said to him, and the others laughed.

"It's all right," Philip said. "When you're an officer, nobody can say a word to you, even if you're an arse."

The men laughed again. One of them tossed him a printer's pinch, an awl-like tool for pulling apart type, and asked him if he thought he could still perform his trade. He took off his coat, pulled apart frames of type for a while and continued to chat, realizing the men were taking advantage of this interruption to find respite from their work. He examined the sharp point of the pinch and fingered the wooden handle between his fingers, then stuck the tool in a pocket when no one was looking.

As he headed through the bindery on his way out, he inquired about the books the company was printing and asked to look through spoiled copies, as he had when he was younger. He found *Grey's Natural World* and *Travels Into Several Remote Nations of the World,* better known as *Gulliver's Travels,* and took copies. It had been a productive trip, he thought to himself as he walked away.

Philip called upon Eleanor one last time before he was to ferry across to France. A servant met him at the door and showed him into the drawing room, where he sat quietly and examined decorations and paintings on the walls. While the Vales had wealth, Edmund had made his fortune on his own and not through inheritance, and he and his wife harbored no notions of superiority. They could have afforded to live anywhere north of the Thames, but Eleanor's father chose Southwark's most substantial district after his financial status was secured, in order to be near his warehouses alongside the river.

Mr. and Mrs. Vale accompanied Eleanor into the room, to Philip's surprise. He noted that she was quiet but assumed that it was discomfort over the prospect of her parents' inquisition of a potential suitor.

Charlotte Vale was a warm woman, and while Eleanor took after her father somewhat in appearance, she was blessed with her mother's countenance. Mr. Vale was not quite a gruff man, nor was he without humor, but it seemed to Philip that he was an overly busy man, always thinking of what he needed to do next to keep the machinery of his life in motion.

Mrs. Vale began to recount a time when Eleanor was a child and had lost a favorite book. There were tears from the 8-year-old, of course, but what was memorable was that she set out to cover every step she had taken since the last time the book had been seen until eventually it was found.

Philip glanced at Eleanor, who had lowered her eyes, and he could see that she was blushing deeply. He felt sympathy for her, although he thought the story showed her character and revealed nothing of an embarrassing nature.

"O-W-I-M-O-M," he said to her, and she smiled slightly.

Her parents looked in puzzlement at him.

"She was a very determined young girl, I can assure you," Mrs. Vale resumed, and was about to begin another story when Mr. Vale cut her off.

"So, do you expect a long career in the military?" he asked bluntly.

Philip gathered himself and then unleashed, at least in his own mind, his manly military wit.

"Well, sir, the prospect of a long military career is welcome when one considers the reasons why some careers are cut short," he said, smiling slightly before realizing that Mr. and Mrs. Vale didn't understand the intended humor. "I should add that I feel quite fortunate in receiving a posting, of sort, at a time when many officers are destined to be going on half-pay."

He explained that unneeded men from both the army and the navy would soon be debarking on England's shores, now that peace had come. He followed up with vague comments that he hoped would eliminate the chance for further questions regarding his own situation.

"I'm sorry I can't be more specific, but at this stage, an officer is more bound by others' wishes than by his own," he concluded.

"Well, that makes sense, I suppose," Mr. Vale said. He excused himself and his wife after a few more questions, leaving Philip and Eleanor alone.

"I'm sorry, Papa prefers such a direct approach," she said.

"There's no need for an apology. I am quite sincere when I say that it is difficult to foretell the future. I do know where I hope to be, but I fear that it would appear brash if I said with any certainty that I would get there."

"I see your position, truly. I only wish that we could turn the calendar ahead," she said and fixed her eyes on him. "But that we cannot do."

He outlined how he would be leaving soon for a destination he couldn't reveal and that writing would be difficult while he traveled.

"You must be bound for the Indies then," she said, frowning. "I hear the diseases are terrible, so you must promise me that you will take care."

He decided to allow her misconception to stand in order to avoid further questions.

"It won't be forever," he said.

"Is it really any better, if it is something just short of forever?" she asked.

Philip left the Vales' home with his confidence bolstered by the thought that Eleanor, a sensible girl, would wait impatiently for him.

He had been gone from England for four years, but this upcoming time away would be shorter and hold far greater promise.

In France, he would became the man he wanted to be.

5. ON ENEMY SOIL

France, April 1802

Philip's dreams turned into doubts during the Channel crossing and into disaster soon after his feet touched French soil. He was gazing at the nearing shoreline when he first began to question whether he should have stuck to his straightforward assignment: Travel through France as a young English tourist.

Instead, he had decided on his own that posing as a French *émigré* would make him less conspicuous and allow him greater freedom to roam. He had chosen the false identity of "Philippe Belain," using the family name of the Espinay servant Victor and inventing a life in which he had left his homeland with his family during the Revolution. Now, as a young man, he was returning to reclaim his heritage as a Frenchman.

His apprehension had grown steadily as his short journey neared its end, but his full folly was not revealed until he set foot in Calais.

"Is there any reason why you would not be available for conscription?" a clerk asked as he processed his paperwork, then rattled off a list of maladies and deformities that might disqualify him from service.

Philip said no and watched as his name was written into a roll book, fully expecting to be directed to a sergeant who would lead him off to drills with the Revolutionary Army. Instead, the clerk wrote out a new set of citizenship papers and directed him to appear at the documentation office when he arrived at his stated destination of Paris.

"You must register for conscription and apply for a passport, if for some reason you should need to return to England," the clerk had said, drawing a puzzled look from Philip. "You understand that you cannot return to England without the Republic's travel documents?"

Philip nodded as if it were perfectly clear and pursued the matter no further, choosing ignorance over the prospect of more questions. Of course, he needed no more information from the clerk because he had no intention of ever appearing at a government office when he arrived in the French capital.

A short time later, he was sitting atop an overland coach bound for Paris and reassessing his predicament. He concluded that his first mistake had been in not informing his superior of his plan, but Lord Torrington wasn't to learn of it until he received a packet that Philip had sent to Sparks just before departing. Objections might have arisen, he realized, but there had been no opportunity for the office to communicate them.

The decision had made sense to him at the time: He had developed an expectation of treachery after he had been followed from Lord Torrington's office, and he had embraced secrecy because of the loose talk about the peace treaty. In addition, he had seen his scheme as providing proof of the "ingenuity" that the Marquis Wellesley had written about.

Yet with all of that on his mind, he had overlooked what should have been his primary concern: returning to England alive. While he might have increased his chances of providing more valuable service, he had created infinitely more danger for himself, particularly if war resumed as expected.

It was lunacy, he thought, based in part upon a dream of achieving glory and in part upon the fear of failure — that someday he would be that man crying on the steps along Whitehall Road.

He rocked along with the movement of the coach as it pulled out onto the road to Paris and began to review his decisions and the resulting actions.

Good God, he thought, his contrivance had been preposterous. *My name is now Phee-leep. So ingenious, don't you see, it is French for Philip?* He loathed who he was: a pitiful numbskull, trapped in France, with no one to help him — no colleagues, no allies, no friends.

It was as if he had returned to the frontier of India, traveling alone with no signposts to lead him, no comrades to share in the danger. He had prayed that he would never again find himself in such dire circumstances, but he had opened the door and walked through on his own initiative.

And now his foolhardy plan would hang over his head until he set foot again in England.

He climbed over some bags to get to the rear of the coach's top to avoid breathing the dust churned up by the team of horses. He stared blankly at the scenery that was falling away behind, then dropped his head and muttered softly, "Experience is like the stern lights of a ship, illuminating only the track it has passed."

Suddenly, he shook away his self-pity as he remembered his purpose in France, and he forced himself to recall what he had seen since he had first arrived in Calais. He had noticed hundreds of soldiers plodding north on the road to the coast as the coach headed south toward Paris. Was this information worth risking his life to pass along? His reservations and fear overcame his great ambitions, and he formulated a new goal: to provide minimal service, with the greater emphasis on survival. Perhaps the much-coveted quality of ingenuity would outweigh the paltry results of his trip abroad.

Philip recalled that he had been influenced by what Lord Torrington had said about the government's secrets being bandied about so carelessly. That point was impressed upon him even further when he had been followed from his lordship's shadowy office in Westminster, quite likely by a French spy. He had concluded that any information that was truly secret, even small details, would be infinitely more valuable than even the most consequential information that was known by many.

He slapped a knee lightly and resolved: In a world where no one else could keep a secret, he would become a singularly valuable man.

"You like to see where you have been, instead of where you are going," the other passenger atop the coach said as he crawled back to join him in facing the rear.

Philip looked at the man, whose face and thick mustache were coated with a light layer of dust from the well-worn road as he had faced forward.

"You are clever to avoid the dust," the man added.

And you must be an imbecile, Philip thought, as he turned away from him and thought of Eleanor. Their time together had been cut short, partly because of his preparations but also because he believed that he could advance their relationship no further until he had qualified himself as a suitor. He realized that he had nipped their budding intimacy so that he could prepare more quickly for a formal courtship — one that might now never occur. He disgustedly admitted to himself that he should have listened to Harriet, who had scolded him just before he left.

"You can't just let things lie as they are," she told him. "You've been away for four years, and you don't understand that relationships must be advanced, or they will wither."

It dawned upon him that that he had bungled his affairs with Eleanor as he had with Lord Torrington. She had asked him, straightforwardly, if he had interest in marriage, but he had layered his response in shades of subtlety. Why hadn't he just said yes to her question? Then he had surprised her with news that he was leaving again. He needed to write her, but that would be difficult, perhaps even dangerous, if the French grew suspicious of an *émigré's* letter posted to England. He did have the means to pass messages to Lord Torrington, but he decided he would be damned before he would allow Westel Sparks to see his personal correspondence to her.

He slept off and on during the journey south from Calais, using his waking hours to concoct new, overly complicated solutions to his dilemma. Finally, a feeling of dread returned as the coach neared Paris.

During the long approach to the city's gates, he mopped the sweat from his brow repeatedly as he fought off the urge to leap from the coach and run away. A *gendarme* looked at his papers and asked him his business, and he answered that he had come for work. The man moved on to the next passenger without comment.

As the coach pulled away and ventured deep into Paris, Philip relaxed and reflected on how the city was a strange product of its time. On the one hand, he knew that it was the center of all things modern: science, fashion, thought and, of course, warfare. But he could see that it had grown beyond its capacity to provide a decent living for many of its citizens.

He explained to his travel mate, who introduced himself as Joseph Augier, that he was an *émigré* making his first trip to Paris and received a lengthy explanation of the city's many problems.

Jobs were hard to find, Joseph said, and the food supply was unsteady, but the citizens were calm as long as they were seeing improvements. Brigands still ruled the streets at night, but the creation of a new type of police was increasing order, while at the same time allowing the government to track and eliminate its enemies. And while sewage ran openly in the streets on its way to the Seine, First Consul Napoleon Bonaparte was now engaged in a combination of massive public projects and a flood of new art and architecture.

"It must be an exciting time," Philip observed, but Joseph just shrugged.

The coach passed dozens of men stripped to the waist and swinging picks, trailed by more men who carried shovels to pile dirt along the sides of a growing ditch.

"What are they building here?" Philip asked.

"A canal, because the water in Paris is filth," Joseph replied. "You might as well put your lips to the sewer as to drink water from the Seine. Water is brought into the city in casks, and you must purchase it by the bucket."

Philip wondered how this nation could have Europe on its knees. "So the canal will bring in fresh water from the countryside? Most impressive."

Joseph again shrugged.

Philip inquired if the canal work paid well and received a confused look.

"It is an obligation," Joseph replied.

"*Every* citizen must work on the canal?" Philip asked, fearing that he would be put to work.

"Much has changed since you were in France," he said. "The Revolution in many ways has ended, but the work of the Revolution continues, so men are obliged to help when France requires it, just as they are obliged to fight. And, of course, the burden falls mostly upon those unable to purchase their way out of the obligation."

Philip wondered if Joseph, who appeared to be five and 30 years or more, had been in the army since his comments were reminiscent of the grumbling often heard within the English ranks. He asked him of his profession.

Joseph chuckled. "Profession? You honor me. I am a wheelwright and have been to the coast, where there is much work to be done."

"Were you paid well?" Philip asked.

"As I say, men are sometimes obligated to work. I have been gone for five weeks, and I can only hope that my family has continued to eat while I was gone. But the army needed wagons, and so I was sent to Desvres. As to my pay, let me say that I would have worked less and been paid more in Paris."

Philip mentioned that he had worked in a print shop in England.

"There are a number of newspapers in Paris," Joseph said and gave directions to an area of the city where printing companies were situated. Philip pulled out a scrap of paper and a pencil from his coat and wrote down the instructions.

Joseph eyed him curiously. "You can write?" he asked.

Philip was startled by the question. "Yes, some," he replied cautiously.

"I apologize, monsieur. I thought you only looked for labor. You may find employment more easily than you suspect, and the government will not put you to work with a shovel."

Philip knew that he had made a slip. He had intended to reveal as little as possible about himself while in France to avoid opening the door to questions. Another resolution: Be more cautious when speaking.

After they disembarked from the coach, Joseph invited him to stay with his family until he could find lodgings, and he eagerly accepted the opportunity in order to save the expense of a hotel. Yet another resolution: Return to England with as much money as possible to demonstrate thrift with government funds.

The Augier family — wife Bathilde, three children and Bathilde's nearly deaf mother — seemed indifferent to their guest, but Philip nevertheless was on edge while he stayed at their apartment, one of several that had been created from a large house abandoned by an aristocrat during the Revolution. He attempted to appear nonchalant about the small chest and the travel bag he carried, even though his nerves were rattled.

Before leaving the room where he slept, he would carefully place the chest and bag in a position next to each other so he could determine quickly if anything had been disturbed. He was especially circumspect around the eldest Augier child, a 13-year-old boy named Yves, who was bright and full of questions, particularly regarding Philip's background.

"Monsieur, are you a nobleman?" he asked.

"No, why would you ask that?"

"You are a Frenchman who has returned from England. Many nobles are returning now."

"I am not a nobleman," Philip replied, then faked a light laugh. "Do I dress as one? In England, the aristocrats dress in clothes much finer than these. Is that not so in France as well?"

The boy nodded skeptically.

"In fact, young Monsieur Augier, I served a nobleman, but I have returned to France because I no longer wish to serve other men," Philip told him. "I seek to make my own way and have no man feel that he can own me."

Joseph commented cynically that he was not certain Philip would find the freedom that he sought.

"You are free to make your own way here, so long as it is the way the government wants you to go," he said.

"Papa was a revolutionary!" Yves exclaimed enthusiastically.

"He was, he was!" younger brother Pierre and sister Marie squealed in delight.

"Is that so?" Philip asked, pleased to shift the conversation away from himself.

Joseph waved aside the boy's comment. "I marched in the streets, it is true, but little more. It was an exciting time, but the trouble that followed ... I hope never to witness anything such as that again."

"Do you mean the executions?" Philip asked eagerly. "Were you fearful?"

"I was a young man with a wife and a young child, this noisy whelp here," Joseph said, pointing to Yves. "I took care of my family and kept my mouth shut, and I never felt threatened."

Philip asked more questions in hopes of keeping the conversation diverted.

Joseph had served in the army of King Louis XVI but had never gone abroad because his left kneecap had been smashed by a musket butt during training, leaving him unable to walk without a limp. He mustered out of the army as a 21-year-old in 1787, and with the carpentry skills he had learned while being put to use as an invalid soldier, he had taken up work with a carriage builder in Paris.

"I did not notice a limp," Philip said.

"The condition worsens considerably whenever the conscription threatens to begin taking older men," Joseph said wryly.

"Were you pleased when Louis was guillotined?" Philip asked.

"No, I loved the king. It was his noblemen who were to blame for the suffering of the people, and I was caught up in the spirit of the Revolution in the beginning. However, I became disillusioned after the Church came under attack."

"What is your opinion of Napoleon Bonaparte?" Philip asked.

"I believe that he has restored order, and that is good, but my greatest fear with him is that there will always be another war, and another after that. We need peace. We need to grow grain and build homes."

"Will you tell Papa's comments to the police?" Yves asked.

Philip laughed. "No, Yves, I am not a spy for the police."

"Then are you perhaps a spy for the English?" he persisted.

Joseph leaned over and cuffed the boy on the side of the head.

Philip tried to laugh without showing signs of the shock he had received from the boy's question. "No, Yves, I am not, which is unfortunate, because I know that the English pay their spies very well."

As soon as the words passed his lips, Philip castigated himself for speaking beyond what was necessary. He understood now that he would need to take even greater care that the considerable sum of money he carried was not discovered.

He eventually found lodging in the area of the city where Joseph had said he could find print shops. He took a room on the third floor of a building that housed a bakery, after being told that heat from the oven would keep him warm on chilly nights.

In his new home, he pried up boards under his cot and hid the gold coins to be delivered to Don Martin Cristobal de Acuña. He next unpacked his small chest, which had *V. Belain, Champeaux* cut into the wood on the inside of the lid, took out a package of bank notes and hid them beneath the boards under the frame of the room's only table.

Philip had acquired the chest from the servant Victor in exchange for a more expensive one he had purchased in London. He had thought the use of this old chest especially clever, lending authenticity to his new identity.

He had further asked a younger servant in the count's household, a known rascal, if he might have a French Bible to sell and received one that he assumed had been stolen from one of the large home's bedrooms. While showing signs of age, it had no writing inside the cover and Philip had penned *Philippe Belain, n. 1781, Champeaux* in ink he had thinned to give an appearance of age. He then had torn out the page that gave a publication date of 1785 and later used the Bible to document his identity with French authorities in Calais.

Philip, always in a state of self-examination, believed the chest and the Bible had helped lead him down his wayward path. Had he met early stumbling blocks after hatching his plan to create a French identity, he might have veered away. But the chest and Bible had been obtained so easily that they had provided a false sense of confidence, blinding him to any evidence that his design was flawed.

He opened *Grey's Natural World* and used the atlas to calculate that Joseph's work near Desvres was only about 15 miles from Boulogne. "Part of Boney's big scheme, eh?" he muttered to himself.

Philip hid *Grey's* and *Gulliver's Travels*, both printed in English, beneath the floorboards and made plans to purchase French books to display in his room.

With a new residence secured, Philip purchased a chicken for Bathilde to cook on his final evening with the Augiers in gratitude for their hospitality. After their meal, he asked if there was anything further he could do for them.

"Could you teach Yves to read?" Joseph asked hopefully. "He wishes to be an artist, so I am not certain he will make a good student, but I give you permission to strike him if his effort is poor, or if he fails to keep his mouth closed."

"I am certain that will not be necessary, and I would be pleased to help Yves."

"Oh, but it *is* necessary," Bathilde interrupted.

Philip smiled. "I shall do what I can. If it takes a large wooden mallet to pound lessons into his head, then that is what I shall do."

Yves scowled, and 7-year-old Pierre and 6-year-old Marie looked expectantly at Philip, as if he were about to club their older brother.

"Or perhaps we will try another approach," Philip said. "We will practice reading about art, and that might better hold his interest."

Yves smiled and looked admiringly at him.

"You may regret that you chose not to use the mallet," Joseph said, then lowered his head in shame before adding, "I cannot pay you, Philippe, but you can have supper with us before his lessons."

Philip eased Joseph's embarrassment by agreeing eagerly to the offer, seeing another opportunity to lower his expenses.

In the next few days, he walked all about Paris as he began to settle in, following Lord Torrington's instruction to "learn how the land lies." He headed off for what he believed to be about one mile in each direction, then tried to find his way back in order to draw a grid of the surrounding area in his mind.

He continued to be amazed by the filth in the streets, each one seeming to have a stream of sewage running toward the Seine, but he also was occasionally struck by the city's beauty. He might jump a puddle of muck on one street and turn the corner to behold an arching cathedral or a monument to a French victory on the next.

One day, he found himself across the street from the hotel serving as a temporary British embassy, and he considered rushing inside and begging for assistance in returning to London. However, he recalled that his assignment with Don Martin Cristobal de Acuña required that he keep his distance from Lord Torrington's agents on the diplomatic staff. To seek help also would ensure the failure of his duty.

He turned away and next found a bank to exchange his English currency and coins, then visited a clothing shop and offered to pay more for a new coat if the shop owner would throw in garments discarded by wealthy customers. To aid his appearance, he cut his hair to the shorter fashion of Parisian men, rather than clubbing it in back, and he began the lengthy process of growing a mustache.

The search for employment was a short one. A publishing house, Groussard & Co., was within 200 yards of his room on Rue de Grenelle and could be seen from the window.

The business appeared prosperous from the outside, and Philip was greeted by the familiar scent of machinery oil, paper and ink when he entered. He asked to speak to Monsieur Groussard but was told that the business had been passed to the late Groussard's son-in-law, Felix Debraux.

"Monsieur, if you please, I am recently arrived in Paris and eager to work for your company," he said upon being presented to the owner.

Debraux sat up straight behind his desk as he considered the hopeful young man. "And what abilities do you have for me to put to use?"

Philip explained that he was an *émigré* who had worked at a London publishing house.

"And what do the English know of printing?" asked Debraux, fingering the rims of a fashionable set of spectacles. He was a slight man with a mustache the width of a rat's tail, and the spectacles seemed to cover half of his face. Philip wasn't certain that he had the presence one would expect of a prosperous man of commerce and decided to play a hunch.

"The shop in which I worked exhibited none of the modern efficiency that I saw just outside your office. This company far exceeds anything I was witness to in London, but I am a hard worker and am willing to learn. And while I have been here only a short time, monsieur, I hear that *Le Journal* is the finest newspaper in Paris."

"Well, yes, that is so!" Debraux said, his face lighting up. "Napoleon Bonaparte, the First Consul himself, reads *Le Journal*. In fact, he writes dispatches for use in my newspaper from time to time."

"Monsieur Debraux, I am humbled to be in the presence of a man so close to the First Consul," Philip went on, seeing that shameless flattery was working.

"Yes, *Napoleon* is quite aware of my work," Debraux said, emphasizing the first name as if he were a close acquaintance. "We print government pamphlets here as well, including several that have been written by the First Consul's brother Lucien."

"Monsieur Debraux, you honor me with this interview," Philip said. "I am just a young man who has returned to France, hoping that his homeland still has a place for him. I know that I come from modest beginnings, but France is the one place on Earth where a man can lift himself. I am pleased to meet a great man such as yourself after such a short time in Paris."

Debraux raised his chin and grabbed his lapels. "You will find France is the perfect place for a young man such as yourself. Why, I myself come from rather modest beginnings, and yet there is a place for those of us who dare to achieve."

Or those who dare to marry the owner's daughter, Philip thought to himself.

"We will find a place for you," Debraux announced. "You seem to have ambition that will reward both of us."

"Oh, thank you, Monsieur Debraux!" Philip enthused. "I shall honor your confidence in me!"

His first duties involved mostly cleaning and oiling the presses and breaking up frames of type for the typesetters, much as he had done as a boy for Dunn & Gilchrist in London. The workers were impressed when he reached for his printer's pinch and casually began pulling apart type, and several of them later fashioned their own such devices with sharpened nails pounded through blocks of wood.

Philip saw an advantage in revealing that he could read, and he quickly added proofreading to his duties. It was difficult work, with a high level of concentration required while poring over page after page of galleys with poor lighting and occasionally unfamiliar vocabulary. He went home exhausted at night and subsisted mostly on old bread from the bakery below his room.

After a week, he took stock of his progress and was pleased that he was living like a Parisian and that his fluency in French had been enhanced by intonations and expressions that he picked up while working. He also looked more like a Parisian after abandoning the brisk, ramrod-straight gait required by the British army and walking more slowly with his shoulders slumped slightly.

In addition, he now had a good assortment of clothing to wear, allowing him to fit into whatever setting he encountered. While he believed the money was well spent, he was determined that henceforth he would live on his salary from Groussard and return to England with the rest of the funds he had received from Lord Torrington. That sum, about 130 pounds, went under the floor boards.

One night in his room, he reviewed his plans as he paged through *Gulliver's Travels* and *Grey's Natural World*, both "Published by Dunn & Gilchrist of London, England, 1802." Satisfied that he was on track, he placed a chair beside the window and looked out onto the street before reading copies of *Le Journal* that he had brought home at the end of the day.

A few days later, he began to visit the Augiers regularly at night to instruct Yves and was compensated with meals. Joseph warned him to beware of ruffians while walking home afterward, so he began to carry his printer's pinch in a coat pocket.

Philip enjoyed the meals with the family, as much for the companionship as for the food. Unfortunately, Yves had no reservations about interrupting the adults and could turn the discussion in any direction that he desired.

"Do you think Monsieur Belain sounds like an Englishman?" he asked his father during supper one evening.

Philip gulped, but then recovered. "Yves, you know that I spent many years in London. Is it surprising that I sound like this?"

"The boy's mouth runs on so," Joseph said, bouncing a small crust of bread off his son's forehead.

"What did the boy say?" asked Bathilde's mother.

"He asked if Monsieur Belain sounds like an Englishman," Bathilde said.

"Monsieur Belain is an Englishman?" the old lady asked, shaking her head.

Joseph gave Philip a sympathetic look and shrugged.

Yves turned to his grandmother and moved his mouth as if he were speaking, but without uttering a sound.

"What do you say, boy?" the grandmother asked.

Bathilde arose and slapped Yves.

"He said he is the devil!" Bathilde said loudly to her mother, who nodded in agreement.

6. CALLED INTO ACTION

Early summer in Paris was stiflingly hot, but the evenings were tolerable, and Philip allowed Yves to shorten a scheduled lesson after reading in *Le Journal* that a convoy of art — the spoils of French conquest — was arriving from Florence for a new Louvre exhibit.

They set off from the Augiers' home at nightfall and soon came upon the tail end of a massive wagon train that had taken 10 months to complete its journey from Italy. Torches and lanterns lit the way alongside scores of oxen-pulled wagons stretching across the Seine and several streets beyond.

Philip and Yves crossed the bridge and encountered a mass of humanity eager to view some of the uncovered artwork. They inched toward the front, where torches created dancing shadows on the sides of the museum to add to the spectacle.

Yves stood on his toes as workers unloaded paintings from crates on a wagon and removed them to show to the onlookers before the treasures were taken inside. A gasp followed as each work was held up to display to every corner of the crowd.

The boy asked why Florentine works were to be shown in Paris.

"Florence is under the dominion of France," Philip said.

"They have artists, but we have soldiers," Yves observed.

Next to unload was a wagon carrying a sculpture of a Greek goddess atop a heavy oval marble pedestal. The workers untied the ropes that secured the statue during the trip, then tipped it so it could be lowered into a large hand cart for transport into the museum.

"One, two, three!" they counted and lifted gingerly.

"The fools should be using pulleys," grumbled a man nearby.

The statue teetered just at the end of the wagon, and the men, unable to carry the full weight, let go and sprinted away so as not to be struck by the falling stone. The sculpture crashed to the pavement and rolled on its back, knocking over a man who held a lantern.

Glass broke and flames sprang up to cast a wide, bright glow on the startled faces opposite Philip and Yves. The light fell back after only a few seconds as the blaze was quickly beaten down, but not before Philip caught a glimpse of someone across the way who seemed strangely familiar. The face was there, and then it was gone, before he could place it.

Part of the sculpture broke off in the tumble off the wagon, leaving it with just a hand on a hip and a shoulder on one side, and with no marble arm to connect them. The crowd was silent with horror, as the workers scrambled back to their task.

The stillness was broken when a man shouted, "Why don't you break off the head and the other arm, so it will not be so heavy?" People laughed heartily as a worker made a vulgar gesture toward the man.

The accident upset Yves, and he fought back tears.

"Do you wish to leave?" Philip asked him.

"No," the boy said. "But if my work ever appears at the Louvre, I shall find stronger men to carry it."

Philip chuckled and tousled his hair, and Yves smiled back, then pulled away to squeeze between bodies for a better view.

"Hello, young Quixote," a voice to the side whispered in English.

Philip froze, his face flushing as he stared straight ahead, pretending not to hear.

"I believe that we have met," the voice said more loudly, this time in French.

A slight turn of the head revealed Mr. Black.

"Look away from me," he whispered. "I am in a difficult position and have something important for your employer."

Philip wondered what he could possess that would interest Felix Debraux, then grasped that he was referring to Lord Torrington. He felt something stuffed into his pocket.

"Your employer would want you to help me," he said and added, "You are in danger if anyone has seen us together."

Philip nodded.

"As I recall, someone believed you to be ingenious," Mr. Black said. "Now would be the time to prove that is so."

Before Philip could respond, he realized that the man had vanished. He reached into his pocket and felt a packet of papers, then stepped back from the crowd into the darkness, away from the glare of the torches and lanterns.

Something threatening could be read in every face about him as he searched desperately to find Yves. The boy suddenly tugged on his sleeve, and he jumped, but recovered to announce that they had to leave.

They pushed and dodged their way through the spectators and finally back to the other side of the Seine. Yves stopped at a wall plastered with posters and ran his finger along one to piece together the printed words.

"Today," he read slowly, "the treasures of Florence arrive at the Louvre Museum. Bear witness to the wonder."

The boy gave up after that, as the poster went on to list some of the works that were to be displayed in Paris. He peeled the paper from the wall and rolled it up, then looked back down the street in the direction from which they had just come.

"I think a man is following us," he said casually. "He probably is with the police."

"How would you know that?" Philip asked as they began their walk back to the Augiers' home.

"Papa has pointed out the police to me before. This man looks the same, with plain black clothing and a hat pulled down low so that his eyes are hidden when he lowers his head."

Philip nonchalantly stole a quick look at the man. "Did you take something when we were back at the museum?" he asked the boy with a smile. "Perhaps you have the guilty look of a thief."

Yves shook his head vigorously before realizing he was being teased. He then eyed Philip seriously, and asked, "Do *you* have anything to hide?"

The question went unanswered, and they spoke little until they reached the Augier home.

Yves rushed through the door and erupted, "We were followed by the police!"

Philip attempted to downplay the episode to the family, but the report was taken seriously.

"Sometimes it seems as if there are as many police as there are citizens," Joseph said, then questioned whether they had done anything that could be regarded with suspicion. He looked with concern at Philip. "Or perhaps you have drawn attention as an *émigré*. You were required to report when you arrived in Paris, were you not? Have you noticed anyone following you before this?"

Yves opened his mouth to speak, but Philip quickly agreed that Joseph's explanation made sense, since he had no desire to disclose his meeting with Mr. Black.

Joseph shook his head in disgust. "The faces at the top change, but the suspicion remains. Royalists, Jacobins, Bonapartists ... it is all the same. I pray that this is simply part of a police routine, but I urge you to take care, Philippe."

Philip said he had nothing to fear and soon announced that he was leaving.

He slowly stepped into the street and spied the man sitting on a crate, facing away at an angle that allowed him to see Philip from the corner of his eye while appearing to take no notice. The man puffed carelessly on a cheroot and scratched under his arm as the smoke rose lazily into the warm night air. Philip countered the feigned indifference by fiddling with his coat buttons while taking his own casual glance to the side.

The man appeared to be average in height, though he was solidly built, and Philip could see how Yves had identified him as police: He was conspicuously nondescript.

Philip turned and walked in the direction of his room, nearly two miles away in the commercial district, and his rising anxiety soon caused him to begin sweating heavily inside his collar and shirt. Doubt quickly transformed into fear as he confirmed that he was being followed, and his mind raced to a level of fright even beyond when he had been questioned in Calais.

He tried to maintain a moderate pace as he struggled with the realization that he was just an inch away from panic and with the sensation that he was about to soil his pants.

He considered discarding the papers from his pocket, but he dreaded the disgrace that would follow if Lord Torrington learned that Mr. Black's packet had ended up in the hands of French police. That bastard Black was the coward, he thought angrily, not himself. He considered running but worried that the policeman could blow his whistle and quickly find assistance in the chase.

He calmed himself momentarily by thinking back to his evasion of the man following him through the streets of London after he had left Lord Torrington's office. The heavy foot traffic had assisted him in that episode, so he would have to try new tactics on the nearly empty streets of Paris.

The street veered about 50 steps ahead, and he slowed his pace as he neared the corner. After a quick calculation, he turned and slipped out of sight of his stalker, then broke into a run, as a pair of men heading in the opposite direction eyed him curiously. He slowed again when he calculated that the policeman would be about to reach the corner and turned to confirm that he still was following.

Philip surmised that he could add more distance by repeating this ploy once more, and he would then sprint away without his pursuer seeing which direction he had gone. But just as his confidence began to grow, a thought struck him: The police would continue to look for the man who had been seen with the nefarious Mr. Black, and the trail would lead back to the Augiers.

Even if he could escape, get the packet to Lord Torrington and make his way back to England, the family would be left behind. So far as Philip knew, Mr. Black might have handed him state secrets as part of a plot that, if uncovered, would take down everyone with even the slightest connection to it.

It didn't matter if the Augiers were French. The two governments might play their games of cat and mouse, but Philip would not betray his friends.

He clenched his teeth and reached inside his pocket for the printer's pinch. He felt around the small wooden knob on the end, then turned it and fingered the thin iron spike that protruded from the wood. It was a handy tool, easy to hold, and it had been useful to a London boy whose father had put him to work pulling apart rows of lead-cast type jammed together in wooden frames.

Damn you, Father, he thought, you sent me into the army and placed this in my hand, and you must bear the responsibility for what will result.

Philip loosened his coat, fully soaked in sweat, and headed toward the nearly deserted commercial district. The area was entirely familiar from his walks, and he took a sharp turn to the right along a street that cut diagonally. He caught a glimpse of the man behind him before disappearing from view, then stepped quickly into the first doorway when he saw no one coming from the other direction. A street lamp shone up ahead, and he pulled in his feet so that his toes were not exposed in the light.

"There is some soul of goodness in things evil," he whispered.

The click of footsteps could be heard from the corner, followed by a silent moment of hesitation. When the sound resumed with a quickened pace, the die was cast. As the man drew even with the doorway, an arm reached out and pulled him back, and an iron spike was driven up through the back of his skull. The man's body jerked up straight — as if he were on his toes to peek over a wall — then went limp and disappeared into the shadows.

A short time later, Philip opened the shutters to his room and searched the sky for familiar stars, as if to establish that the physical world was in its place. His own world was upside down, and he soon closed the shutters, lit a candle and began to eat a piece of bread. When he had finished it, he brushed the crumbs off the table into a cupped hand and tossed them into his mouth. Even with no one watching, he was determined to appear nonchalant to anyone he encountered in the days ahead.

He reached into the pocket of his coat to remove a handful of coins he had taken from the man's body in the hope that it would appear that he had been robbed. He next turned to the man's papers that bore the signature of Minister of Police Joseph Fouché, and he breathed a sigh of relief that he had not murdered an innocent man. He held the document over the candle before placing it on a plate to burn.

Philip gathered himself for several minutes before reaching into another pocket for a leather bag containing Mr. Black's papers. Several pages appeared to be a French government document relating to governance of Switzerland, and Philip regretted his ignorance of European politics. Next, he found a letter, written in Spanish on four smaller sheets of paper in a flowery hand. Only an occasional word that resembled something in English or French could be interpreted.

Finally, he came upon several sheets of low-quality paper on which names and numbers in columns were scribbled.

He could make no sense of any of it, but his imagination filled in the details of a grand intrigue. This *must* get to England, he thought, and he regretted again that he had been given instructions to steer clear of the British embassy, where experienced agents would know what to do.

He blew out the candle and returned to the window, cracking one shutter to check the street below for signs of movement. Seeing no one, he opened the shutter even farther and stuck out his head for a wider view. Still no one, so he closed the shutter and collapsed on the cot with his eyes closed.

What was he? A soldier? A spy? Or simply a murderer?

Damn you to hell, Father, he thought again. He ran through the circumstances that had placed him in Paris with another man's blood on his hands. Robert Collier had sent his eldest son away to be educated at Oxford but could not afford to do the same with Philip. He had suggested the Royal Navy for the boy, but his wife Elizabeth had put her foot down because she believed life at sea too harsh. They instead had gone to *le Comte de Champeaux* to finance Philip's commission in the army, and the count had agreed enthusiastically in gratitude for her service in educating his sons. Elizabeth understood that the boy was little better suited for the army than he was the navy, but she also had no alternative, and she hoodwinked the count by finding a regiment that would serve far away from war in Europe.

Damn the army, Philip thought, as he opened his eyes and stared into darkness. He tried to convince himself that he was a soldier who had done his duty, but his mind kept returning to the sound of the metal spike cracking into the policeman's skull and the jolt from the man stiffening in his grasp. He had known of assassins in India who had taken lives in this manner, but they were professional killers, not soldiers. He briefly felt a sense of accomplishment that he had pulled off the dreadful deed without proper training, but guilt soon rushed over him again.

He tried to pray, but it was impossible, for if ever God had listened to him before, He surely would ignore him now.

When at last he fell into a sleep, it was interrupted by a dream. He was in an inn and caught sight of his mother in night clothes leaving through a back door. He followed her into another room, trying to catch up to her, but as he entered, she left through another door. Beyond that were more rooms and more doors, with his mother always too far ahead to reach. Finally he awoke, greatly disturbed.

Harriet often had related her dreams to him, in endless detail, and he would tell her that they meant nothing. But he wondered if this dream were different.

Groussard & Co. was filled the next morning with the sound of presses printing pamphlets and playbills, and preparations were underway for the next edition of *Le Journal*.

Philip worked in the back shop with the shirtless printers and put his pinch to use, methodically prying apart type and refilling the cases with lead-cast letters as the crew moved quickly between work orders. It sickened him to have the wicked tool constantly in his hand as he worked, as if as it had become permanently affixed to both his body and his soul.

That afternoon he was relieved when he was told to proofread a pamphlet that had been ordered by Lucien Bonaparte, whom Felix Debraux pointed out was "the brother of the First Consul," as if the name were unfamiliar.

While reading through the text, Philip's eyes settled upon a paragraph:

Individuals appear in certain epochs who found, destroy and restore empires. Everything bends before their ascendance. Their fortune is something so extraordinary that it carries before it even those who once imagined themselves his rivals. Our Revolution had given birth to greater events than it managed to rise in men the ability to contain them. The Revolution seemed pushed by who knows what blind force that both created and overturned everything. For ten years, we had sought a strong and knowing hand that could stop it, yet at the same time preserve it. That person has appeared.

Debraux observed him reading the pamphlet intently.

"It is to be distributed anonymously so that it is seen as evidence of a spontaneous outpouring of support from the people," he said with a wink. "The Bonapartes are clever, are they not?"

Philip pondered the pamphlet's reference to "extraordinary fortune" and Napoleon's calculated attempt to convince the French people that he alone could harness the forces of the Revolution. Was good fortune all that had made the man, or was this simply an attempt by a power-driven tyrant to falsely project his own modesty? Was his self-proclamation of greatness really any different from a king who claimed to rule by the hand of God?

His musings took his mind off his deeds from the night before as he worked late into the day, sitting alone at a table reading proofs as other workers cleaned up and prepared to go home.

Clement Thibaud, a writer who reeked of wine on most afternoons, gave him a quizzical look. "You are staying late? What is your angle?" he asked.

"Can a man not take pleasure in his work?" Philip replied.

"Well, this is a new way to gain favor! Do you no longer enjoy licking Debraux's shoes? Does the flavor no longer appeal to you?" Clement said, then added in a high-pitched, mocking voice, *"Oh, please Monsieur Debraux, may I work some more for you? And please, monsieur, no need to bother with my pay!"*

"Can I help it that it takes so long to make all of the corrections to *your* work?" Philip responded with a smirk, then added, "Besides, I need to ask to be excused for some time to attend to personal business."

"Ah, I knew there was something more at work," Clement said, pulling his coat off a hook and heading toward the door. "Well, good fortune to you then, but the wine shops await me."

Philip found Debraux in an agreeable mood when he asked to leave his duties for two weeks to visit his family in Brittany. The owner admitted that he had been pleased with his work thus far and had, in fact, been considering additional responsibilities for his newest employee.

"Perhaps I will have given that matter full consideration by the time you return," Debraux said.

"Oh, monsieur, you honor me," Philip said in the gushing tone that had first secured the job.

He was expected again that evening at the Augiers' home, but he was careful to take a route that did not include any of the streets near the previous night's events. As he walked, he tried to come to an accommodation with his own conscience, distancing himself from the cold, impassive way in which he had taken a man's life in an instant.

He finally found comfort in believing that his actions had been driven by the need to protect the Augiers, who had become an anchor in a life otherwise filled with suspicion, ignorance and fear.

Supper that night was filled with lively conversation, much of it supplied by Yves, who asked about the policeman who had followed them. He was rebuffed by Philip's explanation that the boy's imagination had been at work, and the talk drifted elsewhere.

"Is life in England that much different from here?" Joseph asked.

"No, much is the same," Philip said. "Families gather around the table in London as well, and young boys there also ask too many questions."

Yves saw that the remark was made in good humor and grinned.

"But surely life must have been better for you in England," Joseph resumed. "Are you satisfied that you made the right decision in coming to Paris?"

"You must understand that I do not come from a wealthy family and could not advance in England. I shall always be on the outside of the window looking in on the upper class. I may push my way to the front to get the best view from the outside, but they will never let me in. I have made more progress in a short time at Groussard than ever would have been possible at a London shop.

"Why, a man in a London shop with some education would be a clerk the day he took employment and still be a clerk on the day he died," Philip continued, thinking of his father. "We have a long way to go before we achieve a society such as that of France, where a man can rise above his station through his own efforts, his own initiative, his own dreams."

"Why did you say 'we'?" Yves asked. "Do you consider yourself an Englishman?"

Damn this boy and his questions, Philip thought, but recovered. "I lived the last twelve years in London and misspoke. And you, Yves, have once again proved that you have a future as a lawyer. A prosecutor, perhaps?"

Joseph stopped eating and looked at Philip. "Some of what you say is true, Philippe. I wanted to believe these things myself when I was young, but now the ideals no longer matter. I am older, and I want bread for my family. And I do not want my son, even if he is a young devil, to be sent before the cannons to feed one man's ambitions."

"What did he say?" asked Bathilde's mother.

"Joseph says that Yves is a young devil!" Bathilde shouted at the old woman, who nodded her agreement.

Yves turned to his grandmother and silently mouthed words at her, prompting Joseph to spring from his chair, grab the boy by the back of his shirt and take him outside for a whipping.

"Good, good," the grandmother said.

The chastened Yves worked diligently at his lessons that night after first being forced to read aloud Scripture regarding obedience.

Bathilde was cleaning in the kitchen as Joseph came up behind her, put his arms around her waist and pulled her back against him to rock gently.

Philip gazed upon the two and thought that he would gladly trade places with Joseph, a simple man who had everything he wanted. When he left for home that night, he walked with caution, but with less guilt over what he had done the night before to protect his friend's treasure.

He left the next morning on a two-day coach journey to Calais, where he took a room at a hotel near the harbor. The city was teeming with English visitors who had crossed the Channel for a holiday in France, so Philip took his meal privately in his room to avoid anyone who might recognize him, however unlikely that might be.

The next morning, he bundled up Mr. Black's packet and posted it with the captain of the ferry that had carried him across the Channel. He then rented a horse and headed inland to Desvres, where Joseph said he had been employed in building carts and wagons. The ride took most of the day, with occasional stops to ease the discomfort from being out of the saddle for months.

As he neared the town, he came upon dozens of men felling trees and then a sawmill constructed along a stream. From there, he followed the wagons carrying the cut planks to a huge yard where carpenters and blacksmiths toiled. It was a massive undertaking, like a giant machine swallowing the Earth, and Philip quickly began to attach numbers to what he was witnessing.

After two days of making observations during the day, and chatting in Desvres taverns with laborers and soldiers at night, Philip set out in the morning behind a convoy of carts and wagons laden with planks and spars bound for Boulogne. Late in the afternoon, he rode ahead until he found a well-rutted turn-off a mile before reaching the port city that was said to be the staging area for a French invasion. After a long wait hiding in a stand of trees, he could at last hear jingling chains, squeaking wheels, whinnying horses and talking men.

He waited in exasperation as the wagons crept slowly past him, and the sun had dropped to the tops of the trees by the time the last wagon finally was out of sight. He followed for a short distance, then turned his horse past an abandoned farm and through several fields that had been left to weeds. Just below the top of a high, gently sloped hill, he dismounted and led the horse to the crest, where his nostrils caught the scent of seawater.

Philip climbed a few steps higher until his eyes at last took in the panorama on the other side of the hill. Below stretched a long valley, with marshes surrounding a river that wound toward Boulogne's harbor and the Channel on the far horizon. The trail of wagons was just pulling into a huge yard where dozens of men were resting amidst huge stacks of planks and beams and rows of barges turned upside-down. Beyond that was a Revolutionary Army encampment with rows of tents and another assembly of workers and engineers widening the river channel and expanding the harbor facilities.

He grew light-headed with the knowledge of what he was witnessing but gathered himself and frantically led his horse into the woods. He then checked the sun's height as he reached into his bag for a pencil and a sketching pad borrowed from Yves and took a deep breath before stepping quietly back to the edge of the trees. While the barges, wagons and soldiers could not be seen by passing British ships out in the Channel, the area could be found on foot with little effort.

The notion arose that someone might have provided intelligence to Lord Torrington already, but the thought quickly was dismissed.

Philip tried to view the scene before him as if it were a landscape on a canvas in a gallery. Rather than sketch out military preparation, his papers showed trees, clouds and birds — each representing boats, wagons and soldiers in appropriate numbers.

He finished after sunset and spent the night at an inn, then dashed back the next day to the livery stable in Calais, where the hostler accused him of abusing his horse.

"You are no horse lover," the man said after lifting the hooves on the lathered animal.

"I think he will be fine," Philip responded.

"*He* is a mare, boy!" the hostler shouted at him.

Philip gave the man his coldest expression of scorn, plus a couple of extra coins, then left, muttering "clodpate" under his breath in English.

"What did you say?" the hostler shouted at him.

"I offered my apologies to the mare and said I have urgent business to which I must attend," Philip said, checking himself and returning to French.

"Idiot!" the man shouted.

Back at the hotel, Philip hurriedly packed after deciding against sending additional correspondence through Calais. Instead, he would use his time during the coach ride back to Paris to digest what he had observed. He would then put together a detailed missive that would report his discoveries to Lord Torrington. Whatever Napoleon had up his sleeve, the tyrant's downfall would begin when pen was put to paper.

"Forewarned, forearmed," Philip said to himself as he buckled his bag tightly. "To be prepared is half the victory."

7. UNFORESEEN COMPLICATIONS

While it was possible to post a letter during the period of peace between England and France, Philip had been instructed to send any sensitive communication to the office through a sympathetic priest at a Catholic church in Paris. The priest then would route the letters to an intermediary in Copenhagen, who would send them along to "Mr. Charles Puddicombe" at a porcelain warehouse at No. 22 Strand in London. The business was owned by a self-dealing Board of Trade official who was eager to ingratiate himself with someone who add access to sensitive information.

Those were the straight-as-a-die instructions Philip had received, but he had other ideas. Just before departing England, he had sent Lord Torrington a large bundle that included a letter setting out his entire scheme to travel through France as the *émigré* Philippe Belain. Included was an "addendum":

First, "Mr. Puddicombe," I will disguise the nature of my future communications to resemble that of a business agent conducting porcelain trade within France. Since my missives are to be handled by a priest, I will include commentary that is theological in nature. I shall relate my true thoughts and plans in the paragraph immediately following any reference to Psalms.

Second, I also will enclose financial ledgers that will appear to convey my transactions. A number in the top left corner of a page will refer to a page number in the copy of "Grey's Natural World" that I have enclosed in this package. Grey's contains maps of France on four separate pages. There will be a pinhole in each ledger page, and you should place said page over the appropriate page in Grey's, using the upper left corners of each to align. Then ink the pin hole, and the mark that appears on the map will point to the geographical area to which I refer.

Third, the rows of figures on the ledger should be read from top left and following to the right. The first number (pounds) will refer to the page in the enclosed copy of "Gulliver's Travels." The succeeding number (shillings) will refer to the line, and the final number (pence) to the word to be conveyed. Hence, 212£ 10s 11d in the columns would be the two-hundred and twelfth page, tenth line, eleventh word and so forth. If the first numbered column begins with a 9, then read the digits that follow as a number. I hope that our "porcelain trade" proves "profitable." Ha!

Philip began his correspondence after arriving back in Paris from Calais and soon recognized that his code was too complicated — like the rest of his undertakings. He began his correspondence enthusiastically, providing hearty wishes for the good health of "Mr. Puddicombe" and inconsequential inquiries as to the weather in London. He went on to relate that the hot winds of the past month had kept the rain away in France.

He then turned to theological matters:

Psalm 25:6-7 Remember, O Lord, thy tender mercies and thy loving kindnesses; for they have been ever of old. Remember not the sins of my youth, nor my transgressions. According to thy mercy, remember thou me for thy goodness' sake, O Lord.

That was the signal for his obscure apology that followed:

This verse provides an opening for me to beg your forgiveness for my misguided plan before embarking on this journey. It was not clear to me when I left that my course would make it difficult for me to return. However, while I have encountered obstacles, I shall continue to serve to the best of my abilities.

On another matter, I trust that you found the correspondence from Mr. B to your satisfaction. It was posted from Calais, rather than Paris, due to Mr. B's insistence that you receive it immediately.

Philip turned next to the map in *Grey's Natural World* that included northern France and the Low Countries, lining up a sheet of paper over the map and pushing a pin through it to mark Boulogne. He placed the paper on the table to label it "business accounts." Down the left side was a column of notations for fictitious transactions and the corresponding pounds, shillings and pence. He pulled out his copy of *Gulliver's Travels* and began to write in the cipher of his own creation:

214£ 1s 8d	(I)
27£ 13s 1d	(observed)
116£ 14s 9d	(from)
79£ 1s 5d	(the)
24£ 6s 3d	(woods)
93£ 1s 4d	(the)
1£ 6s 8d	(scheme)
54£ 6s 8d	(to)
41£ 15s 6d	(invade)
3£ 18s 8d	(England)
211£ 11s 7d	(period)

He was stumped momentarily when he recognized that his system did not take punctuation into account. The greater difficulty arose when he discovered that while some words were easy to find near the front of the book, he had to thumb through more than 200 pages to find the word "period" to end his sentence. The easier finds, such as common prepositions and articles, he took from later chapters to avoid too much repetition of numbers.

"I put numbers at more than 30 ships at anchor in harbor and more than 100 boats newly built," his message went on. "I put troop strength at more than 1,000 soldiers with more expected." He decided at that point to cut it off and added, "More reports to follow."

His head was throbbing by the time he finished his encryption. With all of the necessary thumbing through the pages of *Gulliver's Travels*, the relatively short message took more than three hours to complete.

He had chosen the book because he thought it likely to have most of the words needed to convey his intent, and he had grown confident of its usefulness after re-reading it during his journey from Calais to Paris. And so it was, but the exercise was considerably more laborious than he ever had imagined.

Still, he took great pride in creating a cipher that was impossible to comprehend without the letter of instruction to Lord Torrington. Watertight secrecy would be his calling card, and whatever information he uncovered would be his alone until it reached the office.

Philip sealed the letter and set off for the church whose priest was bitterly opposed to Napoleon's secular regime. He waited outside for nearly an hour before he was convinced it was safe, then slipped inside and sat in a rear pew for another 10 minutes. When the bell tower chimed the hour, he knelt at the alter and pretended to pray, then arose to find an offering box just to the side of the Station of the Cross that read "Jesus fell" in Latin. He looked both ways before inserting the letter, where the priest would find it and send it on.

Back in his room, he took out a scrap of waste paper from the shop and began three columns with headings: objectives, credits, discredits.

Under objectives, he wrote "observations" to denote his work along the coast and "delivery" to refer obscurely to the funds for Don Martin. He then added "safe return" and underlined it. Three objectives, with "observations" the only one that had been accomplished.

Under credits, he wrote "Boulogne," which was a major item, he thought, even if it was the only one. He added "stealth" to bolster this column and was about to move to the next when he remembered the encounter with Mr. Black. He added "packet" to the credits. Three items in the credits column.

Under discredits, he wrote "foolish plan," "failure to inform superior," "lack of communication" and "unnecessary endangerment." That made this list the longest of the three.

He then remembered that he had held down his expenses by earning wages and sharing meals with the Augiers. He added "thrift" to the credits, although he wasn't certain that Lord Torrington's office was all that concerned with pinching pennies.

It wasn't clear where all of this left him, but he sensed that the middle column was lacking. He held the paper over the candle's flame, then watched it burn and crumble before lying down on his cot to fantasize about bolstering his "credits."

Philip was puzzling over new ways to gain favor with Lord Torrington one afternoon at Groussard & Co., when he was approached by writer Clement Thibauld.

"Do you know why I drink?" Clement asked without allowing time for a response. "It lubricates my mind. Some men are dulled by drink, but I am fortunate in that it is beneficial to my brain. 'Only passions, great passions, can elevate the soul to great things,' " he said, raising a bottle and reciting a verse that was unrecognizable to his English colleague.

"I thought you drank simply because you enjoyed it," Philip said.

"My boy, you are too practical, because you lack the artist's vision. You fail to see the beauty, the possibilities, the emotions ..." Clement began, raising the bottle again and swirling its contents.

"... and that the bottle is soon to be empty," Philip said, finishing the thought.

"You have proved my point," said Clement, who fashioned himself as a great writer whose work at Groussard & Co. was beneath him. He had been designated as *Le Journal's* primary author of any article requiring a literary touch, with the government twaddle, police reports on Parisian crime and social news left for others, including Philip.

His colleagues simply regarded him as a drunkard, for he had bottles stashed throughout his employer's building in desks, cupboards, crates and bins. By the blistering-hot midafternoon of most summer days, sweat would soak his clothing and drip from his stringy hair to create the look of a man pulled from the Seine.

Clement appreciated Philip's knowledge of literature and arts which, although inferior to his own, still were to be admired in one so young and in such a lowly station at Groussard & Co. He casually handed him the galley proofs of an architectural criticism of the newly opened National Theater.

While Philip could understand the words, he struggled to grasp some of the subtleties. He could fathom that from the outside the building appeared "ponderous," which seemed to be a bad thing, while many of the inside details spoke of elegance and magnificence. The critique also contained numerous references to unfamiliar names, but then he was accustomed to viewing the world with only a grasp of the bare details.

"As a critic, must you criticize, or is it possible to write only praise?" he asked, taking a seat in expectation of the abuse that was to come. "I've noticed in your writings that at times you criticize, even when others find a work pleasing."

Clement raised a dismissive eyebrow. "If you see that which is inferior, then you are obliged to raise your objection," he said impatiently.

"It is an obligation then?"

The writer took note of Philip's dull expression and resumed, in quicker cadence and with higher volume. "Ignorance must not be allowed to stand. If the crowd cheers, does that make it art?"

Several printers sidled up to listen.

"But how does Monsieur Debraux feel about that?" Philip asked.

"But how does Monsieur Debraux feel about that?" Clement aped in a whiny, mocking voice. "You think I need to grovel to that weasel, as you do?"

"I don't have your wealth, so I have no choice," Philip answered.

"The hell with that!" Clement spat, then eyed the young man suspiciously. "You jab and then you sit back and await my response. I see your game: You enjoy pulling the tail on the tiger, you imp!"

"He is pulling the tail on a monkey, not a tiger!" one of the printers shouted across the room, and laughter erupted as the self-proclaimed sage of Groussard & Co. was brought down.

Clement made a vulgar gesture at the group and stomped off, but toward the end of the day he approached Philip and complimented him on adding wit to the shop.

"I am incredibly frustrated here," Clement said in a moment of humility brought on by his drunkenness. "In truth, I would prefer to have my criticism published in a literary journal. Writing for a newspaper, and this one in particular, is sometimes more than I can bear. I cannot imagine that many of our readers grasp the subtleties that I intend, and so I must paint my pictures with a broad brush, instead of the fine brush that I would prefer."

He sighed. "Do you understand what I say?"

"Perfectly," Philip replied.

Clement looked at him closely and seemed pleased that the young man was not mocking him with false sympathy. He invited him to come that night to Fraternity Hall, where wine was plentiful and conversations always lively.

Philip eagerly accepted, seeing the outing as an opportunity to gauge the mood of Parisians for a report back to Lord Torrington. He and Clement arrived early in the evening at the hall, a longtime repository for Revolutionary zeal that attracted bright minds and eloquent speakers.

They seated themselves at a table in the middle of the large, smoky room in order to listen in on various debates and oratory from their perch.

"You might want to sit in the front at the theater, but here, the middle is the best," Clement said before signaling for wine.

Philip took in the foul air — a mixture of tobacco smoke, spilled wine and sweat — and eyed the old oaken tables and chairs that didn't appear as if they could bear much weight. His ears suddenly picked up the sound of spoken English, and he turned to a nearby group of men and women in outlandish attire, far beyond the fashion that seemed to be the norm at Fraternity Hall.

"My God," he said with disgust under his breath.

"What are you looking at?" Clement asked as the wine arrived.

"Those ridiculous English tourists," Philip said, pointing as he began a bitter tirade. "Liberty, equality and fraternity are only fashion to them. Equality pertains only to those of title, and fraternity only to those with wealth. And liberty? Yes, free to live within the confines that benefit them, and only them."

Clement chuckled. "My, young Belain, you are quite the revolutionary," he said. "It appears that while you are licking Debraux's boots, you may have been plotting quietly to usurp the company."

He filled their goblets, and Philip began to drink. His head was buzzing a short time later, and he became aware of a young man standing on a chair and speaking fervently in French with a strange accent.

"Is he Austrian?" he asked.

"He is Irish, you fool," Clement said, shaking his head.

Philip listened more closely and then began to recognize the lyrical tones as those of an Irishman, but it was a strange combination with the sounds in French, and it took some time before he began to pick up the words.

"... and I, for one, would prefer to draw one breath from this smoky room bathed in freedom, rather than to draw one breath on a clear morning in an Ireland under the boot heel of England!"

Sounds of agreement rose from the room, and the group around the young man grew in numbers. Before long, a crowd was cheering lustily at his declarations regarding the tyranny of Britain.

Philip looked over at the English tourists, who were just out of earshot, laughing and ignoring the fiery rhetoric. The young Irishman continued, but in a voice that grew in volume and intensity.

"My land, for I cannot yet call it my nation, is covered by a dark cloud from the east. And by what right do Englishmen set foot in Ireland without our blessing? They hide behind the sophistry of rules and conventions of their own making. They claim to unite our isles, but they are invaders, nothing more. And by what rule of law do they govern? They govern by the slash of the sword, the bang of the musket and the crash of the cannon!" he exclaimed, jabbing the air with a finger.

"I have heard Englishmen say that we are unfit to rule our own land! I have seen them defile our church! Well, we deny London, as they deny Rome! We deny this cruel, unjustified, godless invader!"

A loud cheer erupted.

"My French brothers, I tell you that it is a merciless hand that holds Ireland in its grasp, by the throat, and not joined together with our own hand as they would have you believe. Fathers, mothers, children, all have felt more than simple oppression. Nay, violence, theft, even rape!"

The crowd shouted its scorn, and he continued.

"And the English think that we are something less than men? That we will only sit by as this occurs? We will not!"

The room roared its approval.

"I breathe! I live! I fight! And I shall die before I submit to the rule of Mad King George!" he shouted in English and pointed at the table of tourists, who raised their glasses lazily to him as if in toast.

The spectators rose and howled with their support, and Philip joined in their enthusiasm for the young Irishman.

"Who is this man?" Philip asked.

"Thomas Grant, a rebel who fled Ireland after the revolt of Ninety-Eight," Clement said loudly over the noise. He spoke admiringly of the courage and eloquence of such Irishmen who had come to France after their ill-fated uprising.

"They carry the flame that I sometimes think has died in France," he said. "They are the true romantics, although I suppose their enthusiasm comes with drinking too much."

"Well, you drink too much, Clement, but I would hardly call you a romantic," Philip observed.

Indeed, Clement drank to a state of near paralysis at Fraternity Hall that night and didn't appear at Groussard until late morning the next day. Felix Debraux was greatly displeased, and shouting could be heard behind his office's closed door before Clement emerged with the owner nipping at his heels.

"You think I cannot find another to do your work? Ha! You, monsieur, are dismissed!"

Clement stormed off to his desk, stuffed some papers into a bag and collected his dignity.

"I am a writer, not a tradesman, and I will not suffer this abuse," he shouted before heading out the door.

"No, you are a Bacchanalian!" Debraux responded in his most manly and authoritative voice.

The publisher's mettle dissolved later in the day, however, and he wandered through the shop with his hands clasped behind his back. He stopped to run his fingers through the thinning hair on top of his head, then pushed back the long, stringy strands on the sides. He then feverishly removed his spectacles, cleaned them with a handkerchief, held them up to the light from the windows, then again hooked them around his ears.

"Why is Debraux pissing in his trousers?" a printer asked Philip, who told him of Clement's dismissal.

"Please, Monsieur Philippe," the printer begged, according his young colleague a position of rank he didn't merit based on his work at Groussard, "do not tell the others about Monsieur Thibaud leaving until I can take his cognac from the paper storage." The man scurried off to find Clement's treasure trove.

Late in the afternoon, Philip was summoned to the office.

"I must ask you a few questions," Debraux began, as he rose from his chair to close the door.

"I am in a dire predicament because of what, I fear, was my own haste," he said after returning to his desk and gesturing for Philip to take a seat across from him. "As you may have become aware, Monsieur Thibaud has been dismissed. He arrived late today and in a state of drunkenness. I challenged his dedication to his job, which led to this and that, and some harsh words were exchanged. In sum, it led to this ... what is the word I seek? Imbroglio?"

"I, that is ..." Philip stammered as he began an apology for his role in the previous night's events.

"Yes, yes, I know how much you must admire Monsieur Thibaud and what a shock it must be to see your, hmmm, what? Your mentor? Yes, a mentor who, shall we say, has fallen from grace?" replied Debraux, misinterpreting Philip's attempt to explain.

He paused and pushed back the wisps of hair on the top of his head, his jitters unabated. "But you should not despair, for many a young man has seen his loftiest ideals rest upon the seemingly broad shoulders of a man with, hmmm, what? Feet of clay? Yes, a man with feet of clay."

He stroked his thin mustache nervously. "However, I must now get to my point, which is this: Monsieur Thibaud is the foremost writer employed by *Le Journal.* The others, and I tell you this in all confidence, are little more than scribes. But Monsieur Thibaud himself told me, and I believed him to be lucid at the time, that you had great promise. He said that you possessed both education and intellect."

Philip thanked him for the praise and felt his hopes rise as Debraux continued.

"I myself have watched you as well and have been pleased with your work. And so while pondering the events of today, insofar as their effects on this company are concerned, a question arose in my mind: Do I recall correctly that you had spent some time in England?"

Philip briefly related the fictitious story of his servile family fleeing France with the nobleman who employed them, receiving education in London and returning when the Bonaparte government loosened the restrictions for *émigrés.*

"Yes, now I recall," Debraux said. "So then my next question to you is this: Are you familiar with the Englishman Shakespeare?"

"Do you mean the writer William Shakespeare?" Philip asked, puzzled by such an absurd question.

"Yes, William Shakespeare," Debraux confirmed, obviously pleased with the extent of Philip's knowledge. "And you are familiar with his *Hamlet*, perhaps?"

"I have read it, but I have seen it only at a street performance and never on a stage, monsieur."

"Good fortune has blessed me this day!" Debraux exclaimed triumphantly.

He confided that Clement was to have attended the National Theater performance of *Hamlet* that evening and appraised it in a commentary for *Le Journal*.

"The First Consul himself, Napoleon Bonaparte, will attend," Debraux said, adding the name as if Philip would be unaware of the First Consul's identity.

The publisher went on to explain how it would be considered most appropriate for the newspaper to be represented at the theater, owing to the large amount of government printing the company performed. He then announced that the honor of critiquing the performance would pass from Clement to Philip, who would view the performance from the personal box of the Debraux family, or more specifically the box of his mother-in-law, Madame Groussard.

"Oh, thank you, Monsieur Debraux," Philip said in his most simpering tone. "I shall do everything to reward your generosity by making the most of this opportunity."

That evening, he was picked up by a carriage bearing the publisher and Madames Debraux and Groussard, a pair of plain, stern women. He spoke of the high regard with which the late Monsieur Groussard was held at the company he had founded and noticed Madame Debraux reach over to pat her husband on the hand. Debraux gave Philip what passed for a pleased look on the face of a perpetually agitated man.

The National Theater was much as Clement had described it in *Le Journal,* although Philip thought the outside to be grand, regardless of whether it was ponderous. The inside was spectacular, unlike anything he had seen, lit as if it were under a noonday sun to reveal sweeping colorful murals on the walls.

Philip was walking along admiring the artwork when he came come face to face with a gathering of women in shockingly revealing clothing at the foot of the grand staircase leading toward the balconies. The sleeves of the ladies' pastel gowns swept over their shoulders, but the muslin covering their bosoms was so sheer as to be nearly nonexistent.

Madame Groussard's firmly set jaw and pursed lips told what she thought of the women's revealing clothing. "Such disgrace!" she said harshly after they had passed. "They have abandoned the Church!"

Philip forced himself to avert his eyes, while Debraux cautioned his mother-in-law to lower her voice for fear of offending nearby officials of the secular Bonaparte regime. The publisher hurried them away to their seats upstairs in the family's box, which was far enough from the stage to indicate that while the publisher was a man of wealth, he was not necessarily a man of much influence.

"Prepare to stand, for the First Consul, Napoleon Bonaparte, is about to enter," Debraux whispered to Philip a few minutes after they were seated.

The theater rose as one and cheered enthusiastically as the conqueror of Europe appeared with his wife and entourage, and the curtain was raised a short time later.

Philip was amused by the inexact translation of *Hamlet* and enjoyed hearing the words in French, rather than in the stilted and archaic English in which Shakespeare wrote. He thought back to Victor Belain's comparison of French to a purring cat and of English to a yapping dog.

Philip's reading of *Hamlet* had been years earlier, but he felt fairly comfortable in following the performance. Still, he had not seen the play performed in a real theater such as this. The street performances in London were shortened productions and generally featured an abundance of buffoonery to appeal to an unsophisticated audience.

He enjoyed the first scene immensely, even though Madame Groussard continually glanced over at him with an accusing expression, as if to warn him against falling asleep. However, he later began to have reservations about the actor portraying Hamlet, whose countenance was a contrast to what he had imagined when reading the play.

Philip also was confused during Acts II and III, when some of the other actors' observations about Hamlet seemed to refer to the prince's good humor, rather than to suspicions of madness.

He wondered if it was the fault of imprecise translation, but when other speeches seemed to veer off course as well, he began to question the stage direction.

Then came the final act, with Philip expecting the Prince of Denmark's final slippage into darkness. The tone, and even some of the lines, began to veer wildly from the author's intent, and the actor portraying Hamlet took on an absurd countenance, with his jaw jutting, his chest puffed and his face fixed in determination instead of anguish.

Bewildered, Philip looked cautiously at other theatergoers for signs of their reaction, but all seemed to be watching attentively as if nothing were amiss.

His disbelief reached its height as the play ended — with Hamlet surviving and crowing over the death of Laertes. A triumphant Hamlet who survives? Why, this was Shakespeare's most tragic role!

The audience stood and cheered as Napoleon departed with his entourage, and Philip tried unsuccessfully to think of something profound about the evening to report to Lord Torrington.

As the applause died down, he became aware of a commotion in the lower seating. Several men stood with their coats off, surrounded by a group of other theater patrons who pointed at them and cursed.

"The English!" hissed Madame Groussard. "They have no manners."

Debraux, sensing Philip's puzzlement, leaned over and whispered, "The English tourists want to act as if they are Parisians, but they still behave like swine. No well-bred Frenchman would remove his coat at the theater."

From the hubbub below, Philip heard, "Go to hell, you old fussock!" spat out by an Englishman at a French woman.

"They are pigs!" Madame Groussard added to her previous comments.

The discussion in the carriage focused on the ill breeding of the English, a discourse that lasted until they arrived at Groussard & Co.

Philip thanked Debraux and the ladies for allowing him to share their company during such a magnificent evening.

"I am certain that you will write a thoughtful critique of the play," Debraux said as a coachman opened a door.

"Monsieur Debraux, the ending confused me. I do not believe that it was what the author intended," said Philip, disappointed that the distraction of the English tourists had taken away from a discussion of the performance during the carriage ride.

"Yes, you must explain all of that to our readers and leave nothing out," Debraux said. "Exploit the words and write with, what is the word I seek? Oh, yes, with zeal! The First Consul, Napoleon Bonaparte, will enjoy reading your thoughts."

Madame Groussard disgustedly reminded Debraux that it was late, as he stepped out of the carriage with Philip to hurriedly provide a schedule for having his work published in *Le Journal*.

"I will have the newspapers brought to me while I am in the country," Debraux said, then confided quietly, "The city heat does not agree with Madame Groussard."

"You will be away when I present my work?" Philip asked.

"Yes, I have left instruction for where it will be displayed in the newspaper," the publisher replied and was about to continue when Madame Groussard barked.

"Felix!"

"Yes, 'Mother,' I am coming," he told her, then turned back to Philip. "We can discuss further opportunities for you when I return."

Philip strode quickly down the street and bounded up the steps to his room, eager to put his thoughts into writing. He lit a candle, pulled the cap from an ink bottle and took a deep breath before dipping his quill. Since his previous articles for *Le Journal* had been mainly dry governmental reports, he tried carefully to follow the structure he had observed in others' writings. He had noticed in particular that Clement had used his closing sentences for summation, with a flourish at the end that would reward the reader for remaining with the article to completion.

The first two hours of work were spent putting down thoughts, scratching out inadequate phrasing and tearing up sheets of paper when he lost his temper. Praise was in order for many of the performers, of course, but the absurdity of the lead actor and his interpretation of the play could not be allowed to stand. The man had insulted every last Englishman by pouring ridicule upon the words, expressions and speeches that flowed from Shakespeare's pen into every corner of his nation's culture. By God, this misfit Hamlet would not be allowed to go unpunished for what had occurred this night!

Philip recalled an account in *The Times* of a London stage production of *The Rivals* that had been performed on Drury Lane. The lead actor, "Mr. H. Johnson," had come in for harsh criticism from the anonymous author:

His countenance should be languid, the manner melancholy and the tones whining. Mr. J's robust, florid look did not suit well, and he stormed and fretted as if he had been actuated by passionate peevishness, not by doubts about the coldness, the forwardness and the inconstancy of his mistress.

Philip's critique began to grow in intensity as he wound his way toward a conclusion, and he admired his own writing as he reread it. He believed it would be the envy of even a wordsmith such as Clement, particularly the most biting words about the lead actor, who was listed in the program as Jean-François Floquet:

Perhaps from this strutting, emboldened performance, M. William Shakespeare's tragic figure of Hamlet will be no longer be known as the Prince of Denmark, but rather will be known as the Peacock of Denmark.

Philip finished early in the morning but still arose with vigor at daylight, eager to get to the shop to continue his work. By the end of the day, he was finished and ready for the publishing process to begin.

He hovered over the man putting his words into type, detecting some annoyance on his part, which he attributed to jealousy over his sudden rise to prominence at Groussard & Co.

He also was suspicious of some snickering as his critique was proofed the next day, but he again attributed it to ill feelings directed toward a jumped-up young *émigré* who had started in the back shop and now was about to have his words published on the front page.

Philip imagined the possibility that from this point on, he would be moving permanently to the front of the building to the tables where the writers composed their articles. No more laboring with inky cast lead, no more straining of eyes to proof read others' work. Perhaps he would even be assigned to a desk — Clement's was now available, after all. His final fantasy involved moving on to a prestigious Parisian publishing house, where his writing would be bound and published, not merely stamped onto newsprint for the lowest form of reader.

His daydreams were interrupted late in the afternoon when an editor showed him corrections and asked, "Is the publisher aware of your work?"

"Monsieur Debraux accompanied me to the theater, so I would hope that he was aware," Philip responded condescendingly to a man who a day earlier had been considered his superior.

"Fine, I'll put your name on it!" the editor replied with disgust, snatching the papers and storming away.

Philip was pleased, believing that his writing was to have appeared anonymously.

The Augier family had expected him to come for a meal and Yves' lessons that evening, but he was fatigued from the previous late nights and from his daylong agitation over his work. His nervous anticipation having run its course, he fell exhausted into a deep sleep before it was fully dark outside.

The newspapers were distributed on the streets of Paris the next day, and Philip carried a copy of *Le Journal* to the Augiers' that evening. He apologized to Joseph and Bathilde for not coming the two previous evenings, blaming his recent late days at work.

"It is nothing," Joseph said. "We enjoy your company, and Yves is better behaved when you can occupy him with his lessons."

"And you even bring bread, which we can barely afford these days," Bathilde said and then told of visiting her sister on a farm outside Paris the previous week. "Her husband says his crop is failing."

Philip nodded as he recalled that the bread he brought recently had been unfit for sale. He apologized after admitting that that baker had given it to him for a sou after pulling away molded portions of loaves.

"I heard of a shop with bread that cost thirteen sous," said Joseph. "This is fine bread."

After their meal, Philip pulled out a copy of *Le Journal* and had Yves examine his critique of *Hamlet*. The boy's reading had progressed well in the few months they had studied together, and while he didn't understand everything, he was able to spot a typographical error that resulted in a misspelling. When he had finished, Philip proudly pointed out the author of the article, "P. Belain."

"So this is why you did not come to our home, because you were with your rich friends?" Yves asked.

"Yves, you are rude!" Joseph called from across the room.

"I went to the theater two nights ago and spent last night in my room because I was tired from my work," he told Yves. He blushed, for while that was true, he felt the boy had correctly perceived that he was boasting of his newfound status to a family with only one member who could read.

"Will you be visiting your rich friends now, instead of us? Will they feed you, as we do?" the boy persisted and, as often occurred, was pulled from his chair by his father and taken outside to be whipped.

"Yes, yes," the grandmother muttered to herself.

8. Additional Critiques

Philip arose early on the morning of Felix Debraux's return from the country, took a small mirror from his chest and stood near the window to carefully examine his mustache. It lacked the heft needed to make much of an impression, and he wondered if he would be better off without it.

When he had finished shaving the rest of his face, he poured the water from the basin into the bucket that served as a chamber pot and trudged down the steps to the ground floor. Along the way, he humored himself with the thought that an accomplished Parisian writer such as himself lacked a servant to carry out this chore.

He dumped out the contents behind the building and was walking back to his room when he spied a plain carriage in front of Groussard & Co. It was in the same spot when he arrived for work a short time later, but he paid little notice as he stepped through the shop's front door and grabbed his apron off a hook.

He headed toward the back, fully expecting to be led up to a permanent position at the writers' tables by the end of the day, but as he passed Debraux's office, he caught a glimpse of the publisher, his head bowed, with one hand pulling back the tendrils of hair on top of his head. A man sat across the desk from him, and another stood near the door.

Philip's imagination had barely begun to take hold when he was summoned to the office.

"This is Philippe Belain," Debraux said to the two men.

"Be seated," said the man in the chair, who like his colleague, wore a plain black coat and a tall black hat.

Philip did as requested and was shown a copy of *Le Journal,* held stiffly in the gloved left hand of one of the men. With his right hand, the man pointed a long, bony finger at the critique of *Hamlet.*

"Boy, are you the author of this?" he asked.

"Yes, monsieur," Philip replied, suddenly growing uneasy.

"What is your purpose in ridiculing a performance at the National Theater?"

Philip pulled at his collar as he struggled for a response. "If you please, monsieur, I meant no offense," he said finally.

"You ridicule a performance requested by the First Consul of France, and yet you meant no offense?" the man asked coldly with his eyes fixed on Philip, who dropped his head to reply.

"Monsieur, if you please, I have never before written anything such as this. I only looked at another such article that had been published previously and tried to duplicate the style. I apologize if you are from the theater."

The man's eyes remained on him.

"Or the Ministry of Theater?" Philip offered further, not knowing if such an institution even existed.

"Inspector Bérand is from the Ministry of the Interior, not the 'Ministry of Theater.' He is an assistant to the prefect of police!" Debraux croaked.

The publisher hastily fled the room, closing the door loudly behind him and leaving Philip alone in horror with the two men. The second one, wide-shouldered and expressionless, moved to block the door.

"What was your purpose in placing such rantings into the newspaper?" Bérand asked as he rose and began to pace.

"I only thought that I was supposed to give my honest appraisal of the performance," Philip said, looking down at the floor's planks.

"And that is your honest appraisal? That a performance requested by the First Consul, as you have written here, 'perverts the meaning of the author's words'?"

"Well, no, not precisely as you say," Philip began, pausing to gather his wits. He recalled insolent soldiers in India successfully escaping punishment by conveying earnest stupidity.

"I took a previous article, and I placed it on a table. I then underlined the different parts into categories, such as 'this is the introduction, this is the descriptive section,' and so forth. Next, when I began to write, I attempted to follow the same pattern. Is that not the correct way to write a criticism?" he asked, blinking slowly to add to his act of simplemindedness. In truth, that *was* how he had written the critique, and he recognized how ridiculous it sounded as he explained it.

"I have little interest in the manner in which you convey your thoughts," Inspector Bérand said, tugging on the black glove on his hand. "But I have *great* interest in how you are willing to share your subversive thoughts with a vast audience."

"I am confused by what you are saying, monsieur," Philip said.

Bérand ignored his response. "Who are you? Do you have other writings?"

"No, monsieur, this was my first attempt, and I ..."

"Are any of your acquaintances also enemies of France?"

"No, I know no enemies of France, and I am not an enemy ..."

"But it is clear that you *are* an enemy of France," the inspector cut him off. "You have chosen to subvert the ideas of the First Consul. It would have been treacherous enough to have spoken these words to one associate in an alley, but you have chosen to publish your thoughts and make them available to thousands of Parisians. And you certainly must understand how many weak minds you can reach by putting your thoughts into a newspaper distributed on the streets of the city. How could you possibly work for a newspaper and not realize the reach of your words?"

"You are mistaken, monsieur," Philip pleaded. "The previous writer was dismissed, and so I was thrust into this position as a result. Nobody said, 'This is what you are to do, and this is what you are to write.' I had no idea that the First Consul had requested the performance, and I assure you I had no idea that my writing would harm France."

"Oh, so you are to blame for none of this? I see how it is with you," Bérand said. "Perhaps it is your publisher who must answer for this? Is that what you are telling me?"

"No, monsieur! I regret greatly the distress I have caused to Monsieur Debraux, but you must see that I had no idea ..."

"I am to believe that this offense has occurred, but no one is to blame?" Bérand asked, taking a step closer. "Who are you? What is your history?"

"Oh, if you please, monsieur, I meant no harm!" Philip exclaimed in desperation to avoid relating his fictitious life's story, the details of which were certain to fall apart under such questioning. "I promise to return to the shop and never to write another word. I beg of you!" He began to sob as he bowed his head and covered his face with his hands.

After an agonizing period of silence, Philip heard the door close, and he looked up to find himself alone.

Philip Collier had entered France with a false identity, had slain a member of the secret police and had spied on French military operations along the Channel coast, and yet he had found his life in jeopardy because of a theater critique. He closed his eyes and prayed that his cowardly, whimpering responses had been enough to satisfy Inspector Bérand, then buried his face in his hands again, in case his interrogator returned. He shook his shoulders, trying to give the appearance that he had lost all composure, but his act was interrupted by the sound of the door opening, followed by a familiar voice.

"This is most unfortunate!" Debraux cried. "If I have lost the government's trust, I am ruined!"

Philip looked up and witnessed absolute anguish.

Debraux took off his spectacles as he collapsed into the chair behind his desk and began to pinch the bridge of his nose. When he removed his hand from his face, Philip observed a man who looked as if a gunpowder charge had exploded in his face — his eyes wide and red, strands of his hair sticking out wildly in all directions. There were no black powder burns, of course, but it was still a look of utter dishevelment.

"Monsieur, you do not appear well," Philip said. "I promise to return to the back shop and never to trouble you again."

Debraux attempted to compose himself, pressing back the hair on the sides of his head, but the strands on top remained askew.

"Yes, it would be best if you returned to the shop," he said. "Although, quite honestly, I found your writing to be very good. It is unclear to me if your criticisms were correct, however, since I have no opinions on such matters."

They sat quietly for a moment, both of them exhausted by Bérand's visit.

"I hate *Le Journal*," Debraux said finally, pausing to provide drama to his words. "Years ago, I only kept the ledgers for the company, but I was thrust into this position after Monsieur Groussard's death. I wanted to publish only the printing orders we received, and never in my life would I have sought to be in charge of a newspaper. The complaints, the pressure, nothing but nuisances.

"And I shall let you in on a secret: *Le Journal* is barely profitable," he said. Seeing the surprise on Philip's face, he added, "No, it is true."

Debraux shook his head slowly and continued, "I have wanted to close *Le Journal*, but every time I mention my feelings, Madame Groussard says, *'No, my late husband turned Le Journal into the finest newspaper in all of Paris,'* " this last part spoken in a high-pitched, cranky tone obviously meant to parrot his aged mother-in-law.

"My father-in-law fashioned himself as a public figure, and he believed that publishing a newspaper meant power, but I call it a curse. I want print orders coming and going through the door, and I want to go to my home at the end of the day without worrying about what awaits me in the morning."

Philip was puzzled. "If I might ask, why did you allow Monsieur Thibaud to write such criticism of the *architecture* at the National Theater? I would think that his writing might also have offended."

"Oh, no, it was widely known that Napoleon himself did not favor the outside of the building."

"The First Consul?" Philip asked unnecessarily.

"Yes, of course, the First Consul," the owner responded with irritation. "He preferred that the building be something more — what is the word I seek? — more ornate, you could say. The building looks like a large warehouse from the outside, as you know."

So Clement, the courageous, independent thinker, was nothing of the sort and had merely echoed Napoleon's criticism, Philip thought to himself. He apologized again to Debraux, who waved him off and told him to resume his duties in the back shop.

Philip noticed a few smirks as he headed back to his old, familiar work area.

"Hey, Belain, is your new job to clean out Debraux's chamber pot?" one worker asked, provoking laughter.

Philip still was puzzling over the day's events when his thoughts were interrupted by the sound of a familiar voice.

"I see that you barbarians have had a holiday while I was gone," Clement said as he entered the back shop.

"You have returned?" someone asked him.

"Yes, of course, I have returned, but I see that all of the bottles that I left behind are gone. Were you all so saddened by my absence that you had to drink to overcome your loss?"

The workers jeered jovially.

"No matter, I have the means to restore my supply," Clement said as he strode toward Philip. "And *here* is my salvation," he said, kissing him on each cheek. "Your attempt at writing has restored me to the good graces of the weasel Debraux."

Philip could not keep himself from smiling.

"I am here only to serve you, your majesty," he said, bowing and almost keeling over from Clement's fumes. "Is it cognac today, instead of wine? You must be quite happy to return to Groussard & Co."

"Not only have I returned," Clement said loudly as he turned about to the circle of workers who surrounded him. "My pay is nearly twofold!"

The bizarre turn of events left Philip's mind once again in a state of great confusion as he sat down that evening to pen a letter to Lord Torrington.

His message was mostly bits and pieces of news that that been published in the Paris newspapers, along with some observations from his walks around the city. He thought the report to be devoid of much value, so he stretched his mind for items to add.

In his letter to "Mister Puddicombe," he wrote Psalm 19:4, "Thou hast put gladness in my heart, more than in the time that their corn and their wine increased."

After the passage, he reported that the poor harvest had caused the price of bread to rise to 13 sous and that workers were progressing on the freshwater canal, which Joseph had pointed out one Sunday when the family had picnicked on a lawn near the construction.

He headed off in the dark to post the letter at the Catholic church, and as he returned, weighed plans to deliver Lord Torrington's funds to Don Martin Cristobal de Acuña. After that, it would be time to return to England and hope that his mission would be seen as successful.

The *Hamlet* affair died down over the next few days, as Philip returned to his menial chores at Groussard & Co. and groveled to Debraux as recompense for the distress he had caused.

He was carrying an armful of greasy rags to the back of the shop one afternoon when he heard a commotion at the front of the building. He poked his head around a corner to catch a glimpse of Debraux hurriedly ushering into his office a tall man in an amber-colored coat and breeches with a matching amber wide-brimmed hat.

Several minutes later, Philip came to the front of the building to fetch corrections for the printers and slowed as he passed the office. He was taken aback when he saw that the visitor was standing and gesticulating at the beleaguered publisher, who sat behind his desk with his palms up as if he were about to fend off a blow.

Philip had mixed feelings of pity and disrespect, with the balance tilted more toward pity after the recent torment caused by *Hamlet*. As he headed toward the back shop, he concluded that *Le Journal* must have once again brought trouble to the doorstep of Felix Debraux.

"Philippe Belain!" a voice suddenly rang out, and Philip jerked around to see Debraux waving him forward in a vision that delivered an instant chill of familiarity. Waves of nausea swept over him as he reached the office and shuffled inside.

Debraux gave him a nervous glance and gestured for him to be seated in the same chair in which he had been questioned by Inspector Bérand.

"This is Monsieur Jean-François Floquet, the greatest actor in all of France," Debraux began, his voice quavering. "I believe that he will now accept your apology."

Floquet drew up his hand to the violet scarf at his neck, as if he were about to faint.

"*This* is the writer?" the greatest actor in all of France sputtered. "Felix, what kind of writer wears an apron?"

"This *is* the writer, I assure you, Monsieur Floquet," Debraux said. "As you can see, I have moved him into a position where he can no longer cause harm."

Floquet eyed Philip, who glanced at Debraux for a cue, and the publisher gave a slight nod to indicate that it was time to speak.

"I apologize for any offense that was given. I assure you that the criticism was the result of my ignorance and my shortcomings as a writer and was meant neither to reflect a personal animosity toward you, nor to show any disrespect for your abilities as an actor."

"I see," said Floquet, who leaned on a cane adorned with a gold lion's head. "Felix ... "

"Yes, Monsieur Floquet," Debraux answered quickly.

"... you will leave us, if you please," Floquet finished.

Debraux was gone in an instant, shutting the door as quietly as he could, given the haste with which he left. The actor watched him leave and then turned toward Philip, who braced himself for his second upbraiding within a week.

Floquet said nothing and instead walked over to a window and gazed out onto the street. He tapped his lion's-head cane twice on the floor before coming back to face the cowering author of the article that had slandered him.

"Fantastic! You are an innocent!" Floquet exclaimed. "Shakespeare himself could not have penned such a plot!"

"M-m-monsieur?" Philip spat out.

"You made Napoleon the laughingstock of Paris, but the whole episode was not even intentional. This is marvelous! Ha-hahhh!" His high-pitched laugh made Philip sit up in his chair.

Floquet walked over to the door and looked through the glass to ensure that none of the workers just outside had heard him. He then turned back toward Philip, so that his face was hidden from anybody who might look in.

"Now be a witness to the greatest actor in all of France, as your foolish employer describes me," he said, flailing his arms about in random gestures and tilting his head up and down, then side to side. "All who look in through the glass will see a man in a rage, indeed a man whom they might suspect to be foaming at the mouth. Ha-hahhh! But to you, I say, thank you."

"Thank you?" Philip asked incredulously.

"Hear me now: I fled Paris as if I had been chased by wolves after that ridiculous *Hamlet*. I thought I might never return to the stage again, such was my humiliation."

"I am confused," Philip said quietly.

Floquet looked back at the door, then resumed his wild gestures.

"That performance was Napoleon's idea, an imbecilic one to be sure, and he lacked the nerve to confront me himself, such is my reputation. Instead, he sent one of his fools to tell me that I was to perform *Hamlet*, but that it would be performed as a Frenchman. This fool tells me that a Frenchman is resolute and could never falter in the manner of the Prince of Denmark. And so I was ordered to perform it as Napoleon wished. In fact, I suspect that the tyrant himself wrote some of the twisted and demented lines. Can you believe it?"

Philip could only gape.

"Well, it was a low point for me, I assure you, to hear the applause of the Philistines in that theater. Oh, I still recall that hollow sound," Floquet said in a near swoon.

The actor gathered himself and whispered, "Now, watch this." He brought his hand down quickly several times in front of Philip's face as if to forcefully bring home a point to the apparently chastened listener.

"As I say, I took to the countryside, uncertain that I could ever show my face again in Parisian society," he resumed. "But in the midst of my despair, a friend arrived from the city with a copy of your idiotic newspaper. And there I read about 'the Peacock of Denmark' and declared, 'Diogenes himself was in the audience!' Ha-hahhh!

"And not only did my performance find a cynic, but one who puts his thoughts into a newspaper that caters to Napoleon. Why, this is a farce!" he exclaimed.

He looked quickly toward the door again before returning to his audience.

"And so, I must ask you," Floquet said with a mischievous glint in his eyes. "What is your game?"

"Monsieur?" Philip said.

"You are *truly* an innocent? Why, you have turned Napoleon into the Peacock of Paris. He has suffered such a setback that I heard he wanted to have you shot!"

"What?" Philip blurted out.

"Oh, that might be an exaggeration — he threatens the firing squad every time the clock tolls — but still, he was very angry."

"A police inspector came to question me, and I told him, as I tell you, that I meant no offense," Philip pleaded. "I thought my job was to write an honest appraisal of the performance, and I had no knowledge of the First Consul's role in the theater."

"Hmmm, who was the inspector?" Floquet asked.

"His name was Bérand," Philip replied.

"Oooh, he is particularly harsh," the actor said with an expression of distaste. "But yet, here you are, and with no blood stains upon your blouse."

Philip forced a slight smile. "If his visit had not been so terrifying, I might have joined you in laughing at all that has occurred," he said.

"Now I must conclude my visit to your humbled employer. One day I shall send word for you to spend an evening with me. My friends would enjoy meeting the young man who was my salvation, for I was very poor company for a few days. Perhaps you would accept an invitation at some time in the future?"

"Yes, I suppose so."

"You don't wish to share my company?"

"Am I to be ridiculed?"

"Mercy, no, you will be toasted!" Floquet said. "Well, I must now perform the final act."

He raised both hands to shoulder height, brought them down forcefully, then stretched his arms out to the side. He turned his hands in circles before bringing them to his hips, then snapped his head forward.

"Do you approve?" he asked.

"I believe the movement of your head might have been misinterpreted by Monsieur Debraux as a sneeze," Philip said, trying to remain stone-faced.

"Hmmm, I still believe there is more to you than meets the eye," Floquet said just before he left.

A perfumed card with an ornate "F" arrived at Groussard & Co. several weeks later, addressed to "M. Philippe Belain, paragon of the literary world."

"*Le Pont Neuf,* Friday, 6 o'clock," it read.

The card was passed to Philip in the back shop, but word of its arrival gained the notice of Debraux.

"Monsieur Floquet is having a jest at my expense," Philip tried to explain, although Debraux remained skeptical.

"I must have confidence that the trouble that has followed you has reached its conclusion," he said.

"I shall be no more trouble to you, monsieur," Philip vowed sincerely.

The invitation presented a welcome diversion from planning for his escape from France. Before he could leave, he still needed to present the gold to Don Martin Cristobal de Acuña, a duty that seemed better suited to a mature agent.

Once again, he struggled with the knowledge that he was little more than a boy, and he allowed himself to hope that an evening with Floquet would provide some instruction on how to behave in Parisian society. Then, after a successful meeting with Don Martin, there remained only the need to bribe a smuggler or a ferry captain to get him across the Channel without a passport.

With his salary from Groussard, as well as frequent meals with the Augiers, Philip had managed to save enough money to buy a new hat and a fancy shirt. But as he set off for *Le Pont Neuf*, he recalled Floquet's amber-colored attire at their meeting and suspected that he had fussed needlessly over his clothing since he would only be in the shadow of the actor.

Traffic on and around the bridge was heavy, with street performers attracting small audiences and fast-talking vendors selling medicines and tonics that couldn't possibly live up to their promises. Philip took a seat on one end to pass the time and studied the bizarre sculptures on the bridge until he grew bored. He tossed pebbles into the river and was beginning to wonder if the invitation had been made in jest when a loud, clear voice rang out.

"Behold, the world's greatest literary critic!" Floquet called as he stretched out of a window on an ornate carriage, pounding on the side of the door and pointing for the driver to pull over.

He leapt from the moving carriage and ran the few remaining steps to embrace Philip, giving him an exaggerated kiss on each cheek. He was adorned in chartreuse from head to foot, this time with a scarlet neck scarf.

"Into the carriage, and we are away!"

Philip stepped up to enter the cabin but paused when he saw a beautiful woman on each side of the facing seats. Before he could go further, Floquet shoved his rump and sent him sprawling at the feet of the two. "Sorry, my boy, but we are late, and you must not be shy," he said, then let out his cackle, "Ha-hahhh!"

"I beg your pardon, madam, madam," Philip said addressing one, then the other. He took a seat beside the younger of the two women, facing the older one, whom he supposed to be only 30 years old at most. The younger appeared to be about his own age.

"It is nothing," said the older of the two, her golden hair capturing some of the day's fading sunlight. "The world is a theater to Jean-François, as you must know by now, and he has decided this evening is to be a comedy. It is he who owes the apology."

"Oh, that cuts deeply, my dear. You make it sound as if I lack sincerity," Floquet said in response, tapping down his cane, this one with a gold falcon crafted onto its grip. "I am as sincere as the day is long, although the sun is about to set."

The older woman turned to Philip and rolled her eyes.

"But where is my etiquette?" Floquet resumed. "I must introduce our players for my little play, eh? First, Philippe Belain, the world's greatest literary critic, may I present Madame Giselle deBasséville at my side, and to *your* side, may I name Madame deBasséville's *protégé*, Mademoiselle Nicollette Renouvier."

Philip blushed at his introduction, fearing that Floquet was going to make him the object of ridicule for the evening, and then leaned to kiss the hands of both ladies at Floquet's prompting.

"I was quite pleased to receive your card, Monsieur Floquet," Philip said, nodding to the women, "and I am even more pleased to see the company we will keep this evening."

"You must call me Jean-François," Floquet said. "No formalities inside the carriage, please. That goes for Giselle and Nicollette as well."

Philip didn't believe he could bring himself to call Madame deBasséville by her first name because of the combination of age, beauty and social standing. However, he thought dark-haired Nicollette might be from a lower station, like himself, and traveling in such company because of her fine looks.

Philip's eyes adjusted to the shadowed interior of the carriage as Floquet initiated small talk by asking him to relate the story of how he had come to attend the performance of *Hamlet*.

He began the tale, trying to stay with the humor with which Floquet obviously viewed it, but he soon found his eyes fixing upon Madame deBasséville's bosom. He quickly looked away after realizing that her gown was identical to those he had seen at the theater, with her bosom covered only in thin muslin.

As he told of how the heavy-drinking Clement had lost his job, he turned to Mademoiselle Nicollette instead, but found himself looking down the front of her similarly constructed gown. He next turned to face Floquet, who looked back with a raised eyebrow upon seeing the younger man's discomfort.

Philip tried to keep his eyes trained on the women's faces to avoid embarrassing glances at the bouncing, nearly exposed bosoms as the coach moved along. But when Madame deBasséville was facing Floquet to speak, Philip looked down for a bit too long and was caught when she turned back to address him. The corners of her mouth rose in a sly smile, and she let her shawl drop further down her arms.

He quickly pulled back the curtain to look outside and inquired of their destination.

"We are going to the chateau of Astrid Villemain," Floquet said. "Do you know of her?"

"The writer? I know the name only and have not read her work," Philip said.

He suddenly felt a bare foot running up the back of his leg, which he had stretched out for the ride, and faced Madame deBasséville, who gave him an amused expression. His eyes then went down to her bouncing bosom, then up again quickly when he grasped what he had done. She lifted her chin and turned her head to give him a sideways gaze. He was barely aware of the conversation, which at that point consisted of Floquet describing Madame Villemain's writing, with occasional asides to relate particular passages with a flair.

" 'Advancement of civilization requires intellectual growth and sensitivity,' " he recited from memory. " 'For the human mind to progress, it must be free of political control.'

"And so you can see why I chose to bring you along, for Madame Villemain is among those who were particularly heartened by your inadvertent defeat of the Corsican ogre's foray into the theater," Floquet added.

Philip looked at him dully, still distracted by Madame deBasséville's foot, which now rested on top of his shoe. "What is that about the ogre?" he asked, placing his hat upon his lap.

"That is Madame Villemain's own choice of words for Napoleon. She detests the man. Do you know what he asked her when they were introduced?"

Philip shook his head.

"He asked her if she breastfed her babies! Can you imagine what a woman of her stature must have thought?"

"Breastfed her babies?" Philip asked in confusion.

"Yes, Napoleon has little regard for women, except for matters of the boudoir," Floquet said with a slight nod to the ladies in the carriage. "So I suppose that this was his way to show his low opinion of her achievements. And if you were wondering why our journey seems to be extended, it is because Napoleon has banished her from Paris."

9. Inspiration in Exile

Philip remarked on the splendor of Madame Villemain's large country home, majestically lit against the darkening sky, when they reached the end of their long ride from Paris.

"Yes, quite nice, but then her husband is a banker," Floquet said dismissively. "You cannot attain this sort of wealth as a writer, if that is your intent. You instead should marry well, or at least sleep in the right bed. Ha-hahhh!"

As they left the coach behind and walked across the lawn toward the chateau, Madame deBasséville stepped up to take Floquet's arm, while Nicollette joined Philip, who offered his on cue.

"Ooh, you are tall!" Nicollette cooed.

"My mother had tall brothers," Philip replied, a truth he felt comfortable in sharing.

After polite bows from doormen at the wide entryway to the chateau, the ladies excused themselves to freshen their appearances after the long ride.

"Pardon me for asking, but there is no sense in my pretending to know how to behave in such company," Philip said. "Am I to be Nicollette's escort for the evening?"

"Mercy, no, young stag. You may roam about as you please, but I will tell you now that it was my hope that you would be *my* escort for the evening," he said, his eyes twinkling.

Philip frowned in puzzlement until the realization struck like a thunderbolt. *The man is a sodomite*, he thought to himself with horror.

"Oh, calm yourself," Floquet said quickly. "As if your countenance at this moment were not enough discouragement, Giselle settled the matter of your intentions in the carriage. My, you can be quite amorous with a little prompting."

Philip smiled weakly.

"I apologize for putting Giselle up to her caper. As she said, I enjoy a little theater wherever I go. The world is a stage, is it not?"

Floquet explained that there were no rules of comportment for the evening, but that the four companions should meet at the front entryway when the midnight hour was announced. Those who chose to return to Paris in the carriage would depart at that time, and those who had made more interesting encounters were free to do as they wished.

"You could very well find yourself alone in the carriage for the journey home," Floquet said.

"It might be just as well that I don't ride opposite Madame deBasséville again," Philip said. "As it is, it may take until midnight for me to regain my composure."

The actor chuckled. "Giselle is an excellent actress, but she suffers a woman's fate of fading beauty," Floquet said quietly in what quite likely would be his last moment of discretion for the evening. "In fact, she was deemed to be too mature to play my Ophelia."

He looked about, then continued, "Although she has a husband, she has come to find a lover to position herself for her declining years. An old general would be perfect, one with many years on the march, too feeble to launch much of an attack in the boudoir, but still possessing the pride to want a beautiful woman on his arm."

"Yes, of course, she has a husband," Philip said, nodding his head as if he understood completely. "And Nicollette?"

"She is not an actress, but Giselle brought her along because women insist on hunting in pairs." He looked about quickly. "And now it is my turn to apologize for what I am about to say, which is that they are hunting for larger prey than you."

"I assure you that there is no offense taken," he replied just as the women reappeared, and the four made their way into a large, crowded ballroom.

Philip was enraptured by the sights and sounds of the company he was to keep that evening, and his eyes passed from one guest to the next as he imagined their lofty positions. He compared his own appearance to others and was pleased that he had improved his wardrobe with a new hat and shirt.

"Is it appropriate for military officers to be seen in the company of Madame Villemain, if she is an enemy of Napoleon?" Philip asked Floquet after noting several men in uniform.

"It might be that they are old generals who still regard the monarchy with fondness, or they might follow Napoleon's orders and yet be Jacobins at heart. Or perhaps they want to be in the company of anyone favoring a new regime, hoping to advance their careers. But I suspect that it is most likely that they have come because their wives begged them to be in fashion."

"But then that begs the other side to the question," Philip said. "Why would Madame Villemain want Napoleon's generals to be guests in her home?"

"She opposes the ogre by whatever means she has at her disposal. In this case, she sent out invitations to these generals and then filled the rooms ..." Floquet said, pausing to lower his voice, "with spies."

"Spies?" Philip whispered, aghast.

"Of course, the house is full of ears. Her game is to fill these old men with wine, send beautiful young women to flirt with them, and then see what spills out. I am uncertain if much is learned one way or the other, but Madame Villemain is a woman who loves intrigue."

Philip tagged along as Floquet passed into a small room, his entry immediately bringing a halt to a loud discussion. Several people called out their compliments on his performance in *Hamlet*, at which point he turned to Philip and winked. The actor then turned with his chin jutting out to reenact his absurd appearance during the play, and several simpering women applauded lightly.

"And who is this with you, Jean-François?" one of them asked, nodding toward Philip.

"May I present Philippe Belain, who has accompanied me for this evening of entertainment," he said ambiguously, stroking one side of his chin.

Several women raised their eyebrows and smiled, while one man looked at Philip with barely veiled revulsion.

Floquet handed him a glass of champagne and led him away, whispering, "You will thank me for that. Word will soon be spread that you are my young companion, and that will allow you to pursue any woman without having to be concerned about her jealous husband or paramour. On the other hand, several *men* might pursue you."

The next room they entered seemed to be more concerned with fashion and Parisian gossip than with anything of value to Philip, who again found himself distracted by the sight of bosoms that seem to stare back at him. "Might I wander a while on my own?" he asked Floquet in an attempt to end his unease.

"By all means, out of sight, but not out of mind," he said, a remark that drew glances.

Philip chuckled at Floquet's farce and decided he didn't mind being mistaken for the actor's lover. While it would have been difficult at a London gathering, it might be advantageous to be regarded lightly at this affair. But in addition, he enjoyed the actor's good humor and decided that he didn't really care how the man conducted his life.

Philip's first attempt at conversation began with a banal comment to a wealthy merchant's wife about the cheese that had been served, and her husband joined in to mention bread prices.

"I hear that the harvest will be poor," Philip said, sharing the only bit of agricultural knowledge he possessed.

The merchant agreed and disclosed that the Bonaparte government might be forced to buy grain from western German cities because supplies of bread were running short in eastern France.

"Napoleon will not repeat the mistake of the Bourbons in allowing the people to go hungry," the merchant said. "He knows what rioting citizens can do."

Philip believed this information could enhance his earlier dispatch on bread prices to Lord Torrington, and he grew more confident in his ability as a drawing-room spy.

He drank another glass of champagne before sidling up to an industrialist complaining of his taxes paying for roads being constructed to the south and east of Paris. Philip asked of their applications to commerce, but the man scoffed, saying that the roads could only be of use for troops headed to the Austrian frontier. "It is a difficult time for a man of business who does not make cannons," he said huffily after also griping of his workers being taken for conscription.

The sound of voices more sympathetic to Bonaparte led Philip to station himself beside a large, ornate chair where an older man in uniform held court with wealthy businessmen and other army officers facing him. Giselle and Nicollette stood demurely behind him and whispered to Philip that he was General Reynard Permon.

General Permon regaled the audience with tales of successfully maneuvering his division against the Austrians. When asked his opinion of the Austrian army, he replied that they dressed better than they fought, drawing a chuckle from his audience.

"The next meeting will be even less difficult, because they now doubt their own ability to defeat us," Permon said.

"The *next* meeting, you say?" someone asked.

"I did say that, did I not?" Permon said with a wink. "A slip of the tongue. We are at peace."

He began to appraise other armies that could oppose France and listed the inadequacies of each in battle.

"What about the English?" he was asked.

"Do they have an army?" Permon said, again drawing laughter.

"The general seems to think that the peace will not last," Philip said to a man at his side.

"How can it?" the man replied. "The British trade is being squeezed and if the barbarians cannot trade, they will go to war. You do understand that they haven't vacated Malta yet, even though the terms of Amiens insisted upon it. What choice will Napoleon have?"

Philip took a canapé off a tray carried by a passing servant.

"Do we have anything to fear from war with the British?" he asked, popping the delicacy into his mouth and trying to act as if he were an eager pupil for the older man.

"Napoleon is using his time well. Work already has begun in the north, with barges piling up at Boulogne and some troops in encampment in preparation for a massive buildup next year. We'll see the Consular Guard marching across London Bridge within two years, I would surmise," the man said knowingly.

Philip gagged, a combination of his shock over the comment and his discovery that the canapé consisted mostly of chicken liver.

"Are you ill?" the man asked.

"I beg your pardon," Philip said quickly, "I am not fond of chicken liver."

His heart sank with the realization that the gist of his own meticulously coded message to Lord Torrington, the result of his daring at Boulogne, had just been laid out casually in a loud voice in a crowded room. He backed away to lean against a wall, the shock of the conversation, along with the effects of champagne, making him feel dizzy enough to nearly faint.

He imagined Lord Torrington tearing up his letter and discarding it, angered at having wasted his time with the information that had been sent to him. Why, any fool with a glass of wine in his hand could have told him that the invasion scheme was underway! He next pictured secretary Westel Sparks shaking his head in disgust as it became clear that the information was useless, then noting the amount of funds that had been wasted.

Philip tried to assure himself that the letter must have provided some details, some numbers, some estimates of strength, *something* of value, but it was a wasted exercise. Ignorance and a fanciful imagination had once again conjured up what did not exist. His initiation into intelligence was no more successful than his attempts at theater criticism, courtship or conversation in polite society. Wherever he stepped, it was with a blindfold concealing from him what others saw and easily understood.

Crestfallen, he wandered away in hopes of finding something new that might reestablish his value to Lord Torrington. Just out of earshot of Permon, a young general named Albert Chamier spoke disparagingly of the older Permon and his opinions.

"Is General Permon involved in the preparations to the north?" Philip asked a bystander.

General Chamier overheard and discounted the idea that the self-aggrandized Permon would be involved in anything vital insofar as the Revolutionary Army was concerned. Chamier also dismissed any plans for an invasion, speculating that the buildup would only serve the purpose of distracting British sea captains who were watching the coast.

"Invasion might have been a possibility a few years ago, when the English were facing riots in the streets and mutinies on their ships," he said. "Perhaps some Englishmen would have been persuaded to join in the Revolutionary zeal if we landed troops. Now, however, the British see that Napoleon has all but abandoned the promises of Revolution to pursue his own goals."

Chamier asserted that the French troops along the coast eventually would be put to use against Austria.

"Napoleon is poorly served by men who have no notion of the planning involved in combining land and sea forces. Men who took part in the Egyptian campaign say that his entire idea is absurd, especially so when we cannot even get a transport out of Brest during wartime without arousing two dozen British ships. It would take hundreds of vessels to get troops across the Channel, and they would be at the mercy of the English navy. The idea of transporting more than one-hundred thousand men, not to mention artillery, horses and supplies, is ridiculous!"

Philip was pondering that assessment when Madame deBasséville approached him.

"Don't waste your time with him, he is a bitter man," she said of Chamier. "He was a promising young officer once, but his career was done in by the Revolution, and he commands only a brigade. He is superb on the battlefield but has continually sided with the wrong person in his attempts to join Napoleon's staff."

"But Giselle," Philip said, trying to appear comfortable using her first name, "I thought the Revolutionary Army was a meritocracy."

She looked skeptically at him over the top of her fan. "Someone has to make the decision as to merit," she said, "and it helps to have friends making that decision."

Philip nodded in agreement, and they walked away to a small room where a quartet of musicians played.

They stood listening for a time, but then the actress turned to him and asked abruptly, "What do you know of English poets?"

"I know of Wordsworth and Coleridge, of course, but please do not ask me to recite," he said, fearing the exercise might reveal his impeccable English.

She smiled. "I would not, although your shyness is quite endearing. The reason for my question is that I was introduced earlier to an English poet, and I would be interested in your opinion of him."

She led Philip into still another room, where a voice rose above a small crowd.

"Do you know of this man?" Madame deBasséville asked. "His name is Jonathan Ransom Turgeon."

"Holy Mother," Philip said in disbelief as Jumbled Rancid Turgid came into view.

"You do not approve of his work, Philippe?"

"He is horrible," Philip replied, silently blessing his fortune in not having been introduced to Turgeon in London.

She frowned slightly. "My God, you make Monsieur Turgeon sound like a man who is not to be admired."

"I am sorry," he said. "It is only my opinion, and I may have been too harsh."

"Jean-François called you the world's foremost literary critic, so I must respect your opinion," she said after a moment, then smiled slightly to let him know he was being teased.

"One need not be the greatest critic to be the most outspoken," he said. "Perhaps it is best sometimes to hold back an opinion."

They watched as Turgeon stood erect, his hands gripping his coat's lapels as he explained his craft to the audience. "Words are the seeds," he said in tortured French. "Our thoughts convey them to the garden, and the seeds are, um, placed there."

Turgeon paused, as if to allow the audience time to digest his metaphorical brilliance. "Our seeds, that is to say our words, are then to be nurtured with punctuation."

Madame deBasséville turned and gave Philip a quizzical look.

"Of course, in some areas of Paris, our seeds sprout into weeds in the mouths of the uneducated," Turgeon said to some light laughter.

The poet nodded knowingly toward the actress and then began a recitation of some of his work, in English first, followed by an explanation in stilted French. He entertained a number of questions about his art — mostly regarding Wordsworth, Coleridge and other notables in England — and few about himself or his own work.

"Would you say Monsieur Turgeon is a person whose accomplishments are mostly related to the company he keeps?" Madame deBasséville asked.

"Yes," Philip replied. "There is little of him to favor."

She fanned herself and looked about. "Jean-François owes you a debt for your literary opinions, and now, so do I."

"Madam?"

"I had been introduced to this poet, and he has been quite forward," she said. "You might have saved me from making a blunder."

She walked away, leaving Philip to marvel at her emboldened attitude toward men. He knew women must somehow have their own methods of warfare when it came to the opposite sex, but her pursuit was so open, without regard for the proprieties he knew, and she left no doubt that she was a huntress.

He turned and began to stroll along slowly through hallways, eyeing paintings on the walls with an occasional side glance toward women in provocative clothing. Suddenly, a familiar voice called out.

"There you are! It is time for you to entertain our hostess."

Floquet led Philip into a small drawing room packed with guests.

"Not everyone is admitted here," he leaned over to whisper. "It is only upon Astrid's invitation, and I can assure you that any police who approach are prevented from entering."

"There are police here?" Philip gasped.

Floquet gave him a quizzical look. "My God, you are naïve, are you not? The police are everywhere, and I can imagine they have taken a keen interest in you, the way you have been flitting about like a moth near a candle."

He saw Philip's ashen face and took hold of his hand, patting it gently. "I forgot about your interview with Inspector Bérand, so I must apologize for my teasing. The police here will only report that the dashing Floquet has a new boy in tow. Ha-hahhh!"

A man in front of them turned to see who it was, and then passed the word forward. The crowd split to give way, and Floquet pulled Philip by the sleeve toward a woman lounging at the front of the room.

"May I have the honor to present Monsieur Philippe Belain, the world's foremost literary critic," Floquet announced grandly.

Madame Villemain rose, took Philip's hands in hers and kissed him lightly on both cheeks.

"Jean-François was correct, you are quite young," she said. "I welcome you with my fondest thanks for your work in *Le Journal*. It was an astounding occurrence, why, it was the talk of Paris for more than a week."

She took in Philip's confused expression and leaned forward to hug him.

"Jean-François told me you were an innocent," she whispered in his ear. "Be comfortable among friends here."

Madame Villemain led him into the center of the gathering until they were enveloped. She looked about to see who was present, and apparently satisfied, began to speak in a clear voice.

"My friends, although I have been banished from Paris, I still battle for the soul of France," she said resolutely. "Bonaparte not only means to lead us to war again, he means to wage war on our minds as well. He is a beast who would rewrite Shakespeare to glorify his quest for power. Can you imagine such arrogance? What next, Molière? Will Tartuffe become our God of War in Bonaparte's mythology?"

The room filled with light laughter and quiet comments in agreement.

"When poor Jean-François was ordered to perform, the soul of France was on trial. We knew that he could not decline or he would never again be allowed to appear on a Parisian stage," she said, nodding to Floquet. "His only choice was to perform in as ridiculous a manner as possible, and hope that Bonaparte's lunacy would be apparent.

"But when the sycophants applauded loudly, it represented a great victory for the Corsican ogre and left poor Jean-François with a gaping wound to his pride. All that he had accomplished before that moment would be forgotten, and what would be left? Not an actor, just a performing clown and nothing more."

Floquet held both hands to his breast in mock horror.

"Word reached me here through friends," she said. "They said that all Parisians who held literature, philosophy and thought dear to themselves might never recover from this assault. I myself could barely rise from bed after receiving this news."

She paused and then looked about at the faces. "But then a champion arose. From the sheets of not just any newspaper, but *Le Journal*, Napoleon's lapdog, the truth thundered across the streets of Paris. This *Hamlet* was a farce, played out by the 'Peacock of Denmark'!"

At this, Floquet took on his comical, jaw-jutting appearance as the Prince of Denmark, and the gathering broke into laughter.

"This is Monsieur Philippe Belain, who has struck a single, powerful blow for the cause of freethinking Frenchmen," Madame Villemain announced. "This is the man with the courage to speak the words that no other man dared." Men slapped him on the back, and women curtsied before him.

Astounded, Philip cleared his throat as she signaled him to speak.

"I thank you for your kindness, but I must confess that it was a moment of ignorance, and nothing more," he said and smiled. "Had I known that the police were to visit after my work was published, I instead would have dipped my fiery quill into a bucket of water to cool it off."

Men chuckled, while women gave him motherly looks.

"I understand the importance of all that has transpired, but I say to you that it was not an act of courage," he said. "I only spoke my mind."

A voice cried out, "It takes courage to speak your mind in these times!"

"Despotism stifles thought, innovation and freedom," Madame Villemain said, stepping in.

"The ogre Bonaparte possesses no qualities that we associate with the good of mankind. He has no love of literature, no appreciation of art, no sense that God has placed us here for noble purposes. He has merely his own ambition, a thirst that can only be quenched by crushing nations of people, and when that is done, by controlling thought."

Philip had seen women captivate gatherings with their beauty, their wit and a few times by wielding the power of their husband's name. But he had never beheld a woman such as this.

"Monsieur Belain is young, and he will tell you that he is naïve, but sometimes innocence is the greatest weapon of all," Madame Villemain proclaimed.

"As you recall, Joan of Arc was just nineteen when she was burned at the stake!" Floquet interjected to laughter.

A number of introductions followed, but Philip began to grow uncomfortable that his name might become too well known. He eventually excused himself and went outside to sit alone on a garden bench and contemplate the evening sky. His good humor ended when he recalled the talk of the invasion force gathering along the northern coast and knew then that his entire mission to France was a failure: beginning with the identity he had concocted all the way to his military observations that turned out to be the sort of common parlor talk that Lord Torrington scorned.

He reflected that his life seemed to be a series of waves of elation propelled by ignorance and imaginings, followed by waves of despair brought on by harsh reality. Perhaps a new flight of fancy was about to emerge, he thought, and new missteps and failures were lying just beyond that.

"Twelve o'clock!" a voice called out to end his misery.

Back in the foyer, he encountered Madame deBasséville and Nicollette, followed a few minutes later by Floquet.

"How sad, you are all alone," Floquet said when they were outside on the lawn. "I regret to inform you that I shall be staying." He embraced his companions, then turned and dashed back toward the house.

"That was not much of a farewell," Madame deBasséville said with disappointment. "I suppose that we were just an afterthought to him when he made his plans to come here tonight."

Nicollette fell asleep inside the carriage within a short time, her head dropping against Philip's shoulder. Lamps outside the doors provided some illumination as Philip faced toward Madame deBasséville, who mercifully had pulled her lacy shawl over her shoulders to cover the front of her gown. He wondered what her husband would think if he knew of her activities, or if he also took lovers.

"Madame deBasséville, whose conversation did you most enjoy this evening?" Philip asked.

"You are bold," she replied.

"No, I meant nothing," he said quickly.

She laughed. "That is a bold question, although I suspect that it was not meant in a bold manner. I must remember that there is very little nuance to what you say, for I am unaccustomed to people who say what they think."

Philip apologized, and then tried again. "Did you hear any conversation that interested you this evening?" A pause. "Is that too bold?"

She laughed again. "No, Philippe, that is a proper question, although it has a hint of nuance." She then spoke of her introductions to several well-positioned people and mentioned casually that General Permon had given his card to her.

Philip was unsure how to respond and remained silent.

"You do not feel comfortable calling me Giselle, do you?" she asked finally.

"No, I have never met anyone of your ... pardon me, but words fail me," he said. "I am not on your level in society, I should say."

"You may call me Madame if you prefer, and there is no offense taken, so long as your reason is not that you think I am old," she said.

"Madame, that is not the case," he said in a stumbling attempt at a compliment. "And pardon me again, but might I add that there was no greater beauty whenever you entered the room."

He was pleased to see her smile from across the cabin.

"And are you able to call her Nicollette?" she asked, nodding toward the sleeping girl.

"Yes, I could do that," Philip said.

"Do you like her?"

"That is a bold question," he replied.

"I also meant nothing," she said, laughing. "Nicollette is learning to make her way in society and will find a husband quickly."

"I have no doubt of that," Philip said.

"If I might ask, is there someone with whom you share feelings of affection?" Madame deBasséville asked.

He wondered if caution was in order but then decided there was little to be lost. "Yes, although I have not seen her in some time."

"Have you made your intentions known to her?" she asked.

"Not as clearly as I should have, perhaps," he said.

"Sometimes the greatest weakness in men, at least as far as affairs of the heart are concerned, is an overabundance of caution," she said. "Women need to know they are being pursued."

"That is what my sister told me," Philip said. "I did not listen to her, but I shall listen to you."

"You are a sweet boy, and I think this young lady must be very fortunate to have your affections," she said with a smile.

Philip normally detested being referred to as a boy, but this time it passed without a ripple of resentment. He decided to change the subject.

"Have you been friends with Monsieur Floquet for a long time?"

"Yes," she said ruefully. "We first acted together more than ten years ago. And we were lovers for a time, of course."

Philip was speechless.

"You are surprised, I see," she said. "You must always remember that Jean-François is an actor."

Sensing that he remained confused, she continued. "I was very young, and I believed that he was in love with me. He broke my heart, but I gave my greatest performance on the stage during that time."

"He was not in love with you?" Philip asked, wondering now about Floquet's overtures to himself.

"Sometimes I think he loved me, but in some ways it seems that he loves everyone," she replied and pulled back the curtain to look out into the night. "And if you love everyone, do you really love at all?"

"I cannot answer that."

"I know that most of all, he wants to *be* loved, but that is what all actors seek."

"I am not certain if I grasp what you are saying about Monsieur Floquet," Philip said awkwardly.

Madame deBasséville studied him for a moment and ignored his comment. "I think that you would be satisfied with one woman for the rest of your life," she said.

Seeing further confusion on his face, she added, "That is a compliment, Philippe."

He was dumbstruck by her beauty under the faint and shifting light, and he thought momentarily of revealing himself to her, showing her that he was something more than what met the eye: an enemy agent who could fill her life with adventure. It was an absurd and dangerous thought, but it had been so long since he had spoken to someone in confidence that he considered it seriously for a moment. When he returned to his senses, he realized that he had to subdue whatever desire he felt.

"You must come to my home in Paris to enjoy an afternoon sometime," she said.

"It would be my greatest pleasure," he replied, and her light chuckle left him wondering if his phrasing in French had resulted in an inappropriate suggestion. They remained silent for the rest of the trip, with both occasionally dozing off as the carriage made its way back to Paris.

Philip asked to be taken back to *Le Pont Neuf*, which left him a long walk home but avoided the embarrassment of being let out at the bakery above which he lived.

In an existence that seemed to be nothing more than a series of mistakes, he had made another. He soon noticed he was being followed, although this time by a brigand, rather than the police.

Once again, he picked up his pace to put some distance between himself and his pursuer and turned the corner on the next street. But instead of lurking inside a doorway, he ran until he thought his lungs would burst, finally reaching the safety of his room just a few hours before Paris awakened to a new day.

10. CALCULATIONS AND CHAOS

One evening after supper with the Augiers, Philip asked Yves for his sketchbook to review the lightly scribbled drawings and notes he had made while at Boulogne. The boy ridiculed the crude landscapes and said his 7-year-old brother could do better by poking a stick into mud.

Philip hardly needed another reason to feel small and insignificant.

When he arrived home later that night, he cracked open the shutters and saw his breath in the chilly evening air. He shook his head disgustedly as he acknowledged to himself that he had allowed too much time to pass after the disappointment of the evening in the country at Madame Villemain's home, where his achievements as a British agent had been laid bare.

His reporting about the French invasion had provided little that wasn't already known, so he needed something else to display his value. He knew that it would be absurd to report back to Lord Torrington that fashionable society in Paris considered him a hero, even though that apparently was now the biggest item to his credit. Could he perhaps advance the idea that he had intentionally designed the *Hamlet* critique as an act of political mischief?

Autumn was approaching, he suddenly thought, as he breathed out heavily through the window to create a pale cloud in front of his face. He considered the disgruntled General Chamier's remarks at Madame Villemain's gathering and wondered if he were correct in surmising that Napoleon's invasion plans were ridiculous.

Philip believed that while he lacked the ability to lead a company of squirrels in an attack on a walnut tree, he did have experience on the quartermaster's staff in India and, as a result, understood military planning, staging and supplying.

He placed all of his materials — sketches, numbers, observations — on the table in front of him and set out to plan how to move men, artillery, horses and supplies across the Channel from France to England.

Using his best estimates of the number of boats, barges and transport ships that could be put to use at Boulogne, plus Chamier's remarks, he went to work planning to land a force of 100,000 men.

The exercise was tedious, and Philip had to guess on a number of items under consideration. Among them was the amount of space available for loading troop barges, while at the same time avoiding the eyes from passing British naval vessels.

To calculate the loading of a barge with 50 men and the appropriate amount of supplies, he used his knowledge of packing wagons and putting a company of infantry in columns to begin a march. He then figured out the number of barges that could be shoved off at one time, using the limited available dock space in the harbor and on the banks of the river that flowed into it.

He was about to produce a preliminary estimate when it struck him that the barges couldn't all shove off at once. He thought back to General Chamier's comments on army officers planning a naval operation and forced himself to start over.

Philip worked with the notion that the river flowing through Boulogne could handle two barges abreast heading downstream. He settled on four knots for speed, although he had no true idea how fast the barges could be rowed or sailed, nor the speed of the river's current.

Good God, he thought, what about tides and wind? Ships were frequently stuck in ports waiting for the weather and tides to cooperate, so he added more calculations.

Finally, there was the "Billy the Blunderer" time, an unofficial British army rule that added 10 minutes for each hour of planned duties, figuring that something would always go wrong.

Philip found himself looking at long columns of figures, and he struggled to get them to take form and make sense. He took some coins and lined them up on the table to help himself envision the procession of vessels out of Boulogne's harbor. That brought the numbers to life, and he was finally able to finish his estimate: more than 11,000 minutes from the time when the first barge shoved off until the last one would arrive on England's shores.

His calculations told him that it would take about eight continuous days and nights to put an army of 100,000 on the field in England. And that was if everything stuck to plan without delays, an impossibility in itself.

He tipped the candle so that a bit of molten wax ran down the side, allowing the flame to grow, and he considered what he might have done wrong. His knowledge of tides and winds was limited, this much he knew, so he reduced their drag on the operation. He then dropped the numbers for troops and supplies, expanded his estimate on the width of the river channel and finally allowed that the French Revolutionary Army might not blunder to the same extent as the British.

Despite all of his adjustments, the best estimate he could arrive at was still well over three continuous days and nights.

It was an impossible period of time, even discounting the chances for unfavorable weather moving in and a slow response by the British Channel Fleet to the hundreds of vessels sailing toward England. Could the French launch at night or in fog to avoid the British fleet? It was possible, he thought, but that would only slow the operation further, not to mention increase the chances of a fiasco. Could French warships defeat the Royal Navy and permanently clear the way for an invasion? Never, he thought.

Lieutenant Philip Collier of His Majesty's 33rd Regiment of Foot was a reluctant soldier never fully tested in battle, but he was quite confident that he could report that an invasion of England, at least insofar as this one was devised, was an impossibility. Only a much smaller force could make the crossing, but it would lack the punch to do anything of consequence once it reached England. An army of 5,000 troops was not going to march on London.

He gathered up the scraps of paper, courtesy of the Groussard & Co. spoils bin, and lit them over the candle, then dropped them onto a plate. The paper turned coffee-brown, then black, and the numbers and scribblings at last disappeared. When the small flame had died, he reached out and crumbled the charred remains into tiny pieces, then took them over to the window and blew them out onto the streets of the Paris. "Farewell to your plans, Bonaparte," he said.

If France was the greatest nation on Earth, and all evidence was that it was, how could it engage in such insanity? The invasion plan was obviously Napoleon's obsession, but even if the nation were sliding toward complete despotism, why wouldn't somebody raise an objection?

Philip pondered how little he understood of the world. Politics, government, power, what did he know of any of them?

He snapped his fingers. He didn't know politics and power, but he did know *Hamlet*. And any tyrant who could turn the Danish Prince into a decisive, successful leader was someone who did not encounter objections to his follies. England had its fair share of corruption and abuse of power, but the greatest actor in England would have been hooted off a stage on Drury Lane if he appeared in such a production.

Could it be that simple? General Chamier himself had said that Napoleon surrounded himself with men who said only yes. But did the First Consul operate with such lack of constraint that he could drown an army in the Channel without any Frenchman raising a voice to stop him? Philip wasn't certain as to that, but he was convinced that the First Consul could at least assemble such an invasion force near the water's edge while his minions hoped that he would eventually come to his senses and cancel his plan.

Philip opened *Gulliver's Travels* and cyphered a message, using his conversation with General Chamier to bolster his position regarding the invasion, rather than admitting he had lined up coins on a table. Satisfied, he thumbed through his English Bible and transcribed:

Psalm 44:15 My confusion is continually before me, and the shame of my face hath covered me.

His new calculations were provided on another sheet of paper in hope that Lord Torrington could piece it together with the numbers in his original letter regarding Boulogne. "I believe these new figures will provide you a more accurate view of my accounts," he wrote. "You must trust that I am correct in what I say."

After dashing off to the church to post the letter, he sat in the dark, gazing out his window and feeling triumphant.

The imaginary ledger for Lieutenant Philip Collier, currently unattached and on leave in Paris, was finally, after all of these months, weighted toward the side of credits. Londoners never would have to fear France's buildup along the coast because *he* had managed to deduce that the undertaking was an impossibility. Napoleon would never cross the Channel.

In a world in which nobody could keep a secret, Philip believed that he had discovered a very large one that would be shared only with Lord Torrington. And for as much as he feared the unknown that lurked ahead, he knew that it now was time for him to visit Don Martin Cristobal de Acuña and conclude his business in Paris.

Appearance was paramount for his visit a few days later to Don Martin's home. This was the type of duty Philip had anticipated when he first had arrived at Lord Torrington's office: a daring Englishman delivering large sums of money to foreign agents.

No more skulking and eavesdropping by a nondescript, forgettable young man. A coolly competent, professional man was required to call at the home of an important Spanish envoy.

As he shaved, he told himself that his mustache was beginning to show promise, but after readjusting the glass, he decided the dark appearance above his lip was probably more the result of the poor light in his room. Some of the hairs were long, but there were not enough of them to impress anyone. But weak mustache or not, he still felt that he was up to the challenge of presenting himself at the fine home of an important man.

However, his nerves wobbled momentarily as he began to pry up the floorboards in fear that the small fortune he held in trust might have been stolen or had fallen through the ceiling and into the room below. But when everything was found to be in place, he gave silent thanks to the Almighty and set off in the early afternoon for the street and number Lord Torrington had provided, a location he had scouted during his first week in Paris.

Don Martin's yellow-brick home, situated in a fashionable part of the city, featured black shutters and iron trim and fit Philip's vision of where a flamboyant Spaniard would live. As with most Englishmen, he held the Spanish in low regard, seeing them as long on bluster and short on action.

He noticed a plain black carriage parked near the home's entrance as he approached, and he slowed as something began to register in his mind.

Suddenly, two men emerged through the front doors, and a glimpse of a gloved hand instantly revealed them to be Inspector Bérand and his deputy.

Philip tried not to break his stride noticeably, but he slowed enough to allow the two men to pass in front of him on their way to the carriage, keeping his head down so that his hat's brim covered part of his face.

He continued past and quickened his pace as he turned the corner and found his way to the back of the house. A woman with a basket emerged from a rear door, and he followed her to a market, where she shopped for vegetables.

He wanted to learn why Inspector Bérand had visited Don Martin, and he hoped the woman could help him, but first he needed to mask his intentions. He thought back to Lord Torrington's description of the Spaniard as a "fanny patter."

"Pardon me, but can you help me find my friend, Nicollette Renouvier, who is employed by a wealthy family somewhere near this market?" he asked, hoping that the name of his acquaintance wasn't familiar in this area of the city.

The woman, who wore the tired expression of a kitchen servant, looked up from her examination of onions and said she could not.

"I am certain you would remember my friend, Nicollette, because she is very pretty," he said.

"If she is pretty, then she would be wise to avoid my employer, because he is no gentleman," the woman said, then whispered, "One of the servants carried his child, and she was put out on the street."

"He must be a pig," Philip spat. "It is disgusting that such a wealthy man could act so dishonorably."

"He may not be as rich as it seems, for it is said that he has great gambling debts," the servant said.

It was time to strike. "That might be the least of his worries. The gentleman who employs my friend has encountered trouble with the police because of his ties to opponents of the government," Philip said.

"I doubt it is the same gentlemen then, because my employer just served a luncheon to two policemen in his home," the woman said.

Philip agreed that a meal wasn't likely to be served to police investigating the host and thanked her for helping him as he left. He presented himself a short time later at Don Martin's door as representing the wine merchants Pascal and Tardieu of Marseille, as per Lord Torrington's instructions. He gave a fictitious name, "Joseph

Bourgarel," to the doorman, who showed no signs that he was impressed with the young man's credentials as he told him to be seated on a bench in the foyer.

With his hat on his lap, Philip waited nervously until at last he was shown to a small table in the drawing room.

Don Martin entered grandly, and Philip rose and bowed.

"And how is your employer?" Don Martin asked after they were seated. "I became distressed when I had not heard from him."

"He was in good health when I saw him last, although that has been some months," Philip replied, missing the implication.

"I expected his courier earlier," Don Martin said disgustedly, making it obvious he had not been truly interested in Lord Torrington's health. "Where have you been?"

Philip, caught off guard, struggled to explain that he had suffered delays and had other duties that had slowed his progress. He wondered if Don Martin had been greatly inconvenienced by not receiving his payment, due to his gambling debts.

"I have certain arrangements with your employer," the Spaniard growled. "You will tell him that I am disappointed."

Philip had no intention of delivering that message to Lord Torrington, since he himself was at fault, so he instead tried to cut short the conversation by blurting out, "Do *you* have anything for me?"

"So like the English, completely lacking in manners," Don Martin said. "It is fortunate for you that the answer is yes, and that I still choose to deal with you, but the truth is that I wish to be rid of these." He pulled out a packet of papers from inside his coat and tossed it across the table to Philip, who gave him a quizzical expression.

"I suppose I need to explain it to you, boy, since you no doubt would be unable to discern any it on your own. These are notes and maps from a Spanish naval officer who has viewed French preparations along the coast. They are written in French, to make it simple for you, boy."

Philip took offense. "Invasion plans are nothing new, *señor*," he said.

"You turn your nose up at me, you idiot? I am handing you details of ships and troops near L'Orient, and this is your response?"

Philip's brow arched at the mention of L'Orient, and he surmised that Don Martin knew nothing of geography. How could the French launch an invasion from L'Orient on the western coast when the force would have to sail hundreds of miles through the teeth of the Channel Fleet to reach England? Did this fool know nothing of Boulogne? He eyed the Spaniard for a moment and concluded that he was witnessing desperation from a man with undisciplined behavior and unmanageable debts.

"It appears we have no business to transact today, so perhaps I should go," he said, suddenly fearful of his host's apparent connections to the French police.

"What, you have nothing for me?" Don Martin exclaimed, then exploded in a torrent of Spanish oaths.

"You have nothing for me, and I have nothing for you," Philip replied matter of factly. "Good day, Don Martin."

As he headed toward the front doors, Don Martin shouted at him. "You will not leave by the front entrance, young dog. Out the back, like a servant!"

Don Martin's doorman blocked Philip's path and then gestured to follow him down the hallway. Still angry, he began to wonder if the servant planned to rough him up when he got outside. Fine, he thought, for his blood was up and the man was not particularly large.

Instead, he was led through the kitchen and was relieved not to encounter the woman from the market. He stepped out into the alleyway behind the house and stomped back to his room, where he stewed for some time over the encounter before heading off to supper with the Augiers.

The days were getting shorter, and it was dark when he returned home, trudging up the stairs to his room, unlocking the door and placing his books on the table after he entered. He walked over to the window, opened the shutters and looked down both directions on Rue de Grenelle.

"It is a little late to be wondering if you were followed, young Quixote," a voice said, and Philip spun around. He watched as a candle was lighted to illuminate the face of Mr. Black, who was seated at the table where he had just placed his books.

"What are you doing here?" Philip asked nervously.

Mr. Black instructed Philip to close the shutters.

"Perhaps you would prefer that I was the man sent by Don Martin to beat you to a pulp?"

"What?"

"I was outside Don Martin's home when I saw you leave from the back door. He has a man who stalks visitors who are shown out through that door, but you were walking so fast that you must not have noticed."

"I suppose not. Did his man come here, too?"

"No, I bumped into him in a crowd to slow him, and he lost you, but I had seen you turn and followed you here. I had some business to attend to first and returned just a short time ago."

"I thank you for your assistance. I should have sensed that someone followed, but I was in a state of distraction at the time."

"Why do you suppose Don Martin had you followed?" Mr. Black asked.

"We had a row," Philip said sheepishly, then tried to change the focus of the conversation. "Why were *you* at his house?"

Mr. Black eyed him as if he were calculating how much information to disclose. "He was expecting a payment from your employer some time back, but it did not arrive as was intended, and it seems that his relationship with your employer has become frayed," he said, pushing the candle to the middle of the table. "Don Martin has had conversations with the French police since that time, and so your employer wanted me to reassess their arrangements. I have been watching his comings and goings."

"I saw Inspector Bérand leaving the house earlier today," Philip volunteered eagerly, hoping to avoid the disclosure that he was the reason the payment had not been received.

"The one-handed policeman has visited Don Martin several times."

"One-handed?"

"He wears the black glove because he lost a hand in the war," Mr. Black said. "How do you know him?"

"I have tried to be of service here in Paris, so I have learned many things," Philip said vaguely, feeling defensive over his ignorance of Bérand's missing hand. He thought of relating the *Hamlet* episode but decided it only would be a source of embarrassment.

"What have you learned?" Mr. Black asked suspiciously.

"Perhaps some of the same things that you learned and stuffed into my pocket a while ago at the Louvre," Philip said.

Mr. Black smiled mildly. "I should not tease you. Your employer has good words about you. Very good words, in fact. Should I tell him that you are well?"

Philip beamed with delight. "He is pleased with me then?"

"Yes, he is pleased," Mr. Black said. "I was skeptical when he sent you to France, but he was right and I was wrong, young Quixote."

"Why do you insist on calling me that?" Philip asked.

"You do not recall? You recited *Don Quixote* when we met: 'In the cause of freedom, as in the cause of honor, one can and should risk life itself.' I thought you to be a young fool at the time, the 'Knight of the Sad Face,' as Sancho Panza calls Quixote. But you are no fool."

"Your name is not Mr. Black, is it?"

"No, I use that name only when in London. It is better that you not know my name, so you can honestly say that you do not know me, no matter what is done to you."

This was an unwelcome response to the question. "If you are not English, then what country do you represent?" Philip asked.

"Again, it is better that you do not know," Mr. Black said as he rose to leave.

"But can you tell me why you are helping England? Are you being paid well?"

"There is no pay," Mr. Black said curtly at the door. "I am a patriot."

His delivery of Lord Torrington's praise had a narcotic effect on Philip in the following weeks, causing him to delay his return to England as he feverishly sought new means to please his employer. Strike while the iron's hot, he thought.

As autumn unfolded, he continued to travel around and outside Paris, looking for military activity and stopping to talk to soldiers to pick up rumors and to measure morale. He also began to delve more deeply into French politics during visits to Fraternity Hall with Clement Thibaud. He wished time and again that he had a different means of communicating with Lord Torrington, since pulling words from *Gulliver's Travels* allowed little room for subtlety.

One of his missives reported military rumors and conspiratorial talk that he heard during a visit to Madame deBasséville, who had become involved in a romance with the loose-tongued General Reynard Permon. Philip wasn't certain that any of the information was worth much, but he thought Lord Torrington might at least be impressed with the circles in which he was included.

The calendar turned to November, but he had lost track of how long he had been in Paris — six months. He had been provided expense funds for only 150 days, but his thriftiness and employment at Groussard & Co. had eliminated that from his considerations.

While his skills as a British agent were advancing, his life in France took yet another unforeseen turn when he appeared at the Augiers' home one evening after he had posted a ciphered letter to Lord Torrington.

Bathilde greeted him at the door and told him that Joseph was working late and would need to be brought his supper.

"I was hoping that you could accompany Yves," she said. "Neighbors say gangs are breaking into bread shops, and I do not want him to walk alone."

Philip and the boy set off with a small pail of stew, covered by a plate and a cloth to keep it warm during the walk. They turned a street corner and came upon a large group milling around an orator who stood atop a public well, and Philip agreed to listen if they stayed at the back of the crowd.

Shouting could be heard as restlessness grew, and Philip stretched in vain to look over the mass of people. When the sound of breaking glass pierced the chilled night air, he grabbed Yves by the collar and began to pull him away.

"Wait, blood might be spilled," Yves said loudly over the noise and twisted away to take a step back toward the crowd.

"No, we need to go now," Philip insisted.

A musket suddenly popped, followed by the staccato of more gunfire, and the crowd exploded in shrieks, angry shouts and panic.

Yves was knocked down in the ensuing chaos, and Philip covered him as a torrent of people rushed from the scene. Feet stomped on his legs and his back, and the boy showed his age as he called for his mother and wailed that they were going to die.

"You will not die!" Philip shouted to calm him, but he heard more gunfire and saw a new stampede of panicked feet dashing at them.

As they shielded their heads, Philip noticed the fleeing crowd beginning to split, like a stream splitting around a large rock. A black figure silhouetted against street lights emerged with a long iron bar in his hands, swinging it back and forth like a metronome.

"Papa!" Yves screamed.

Joseph came toward them, hitting aside one man who dared to oppose him. Even in their panic to avoid the muskets, people chose to change direction rather than challenge this demon in the street. "Stay down," he instructed his son and Philip as he sheltered them and struck another man. "It is almost over."

The sound of rushing footsteps at last died away, and moans began to be heard from the injured men and women lying in the street.

"I spilled your stew," Yves said as he tried to scrape the meal back into the pail with a broken piece of the plate. Seeing the futility of it, he started to blubber.

"Hush," Joseph said as he pressed his son's face to his breast. "We will go home now."

"Philippe saved my life!" Yves wailed.

"I know," Joseph said.

"No, you saved both of our lives," Philip said to Joseph as he fought back his own tears, feeling as if his emotions suddenly were about to be unleashed. He took a breath and felt his left foot throbbing with pain as he stood.

"Bathilde often sends my supper to me when I am late, so I came looking for Yves when I heard there was trouble," Joseph told Philip. "Fortunately, I brought this bar."

Philip's description of what had happened ignored the details that would implicate Yves as the real source of their plight because of his insistence that they see blood. The boy gave him an appreciative look before complaining of his minor injuries.

"And what of you, Philippe? Have you been harmed?" Joseph asked.

"My foot is swelling inside my shoe," he said and then buckled after trying to take a step.

As Joseph bent down to examine the foot, soldiers appeared and began to round up people who remained in the area.

"Get over against that wall," a soldier shouted, pointing a bayonet at the three.

"We were going to our home and were trampled by the mob," Joseph said. "We have done nothing."

"The police will decide what you have done and what you have not done," the soldier said.

Joseph helped Philip sit against a wall, where he grimaced from the pain and began to shiver from the cold cobblestones beneath him.

At last a young army lieutenant stopped, looked down at Philip and then spoke to Joseph.

"I saw what you did to save your boys," he said, "and I would allow you to leave, but the police wish to question everyone."

The officer left to attend to a group of soldiers dragging a limp body to a wagon. They tossed it carelessly in the back, and Yves asked if the man was dead.

"I suspect he has just lost his senses," Joseph said, and the boy seemed disappointed by the response.

"I think those two over there are dead," Philip said, pointing to a pair of fallen men, and Yves looked wide-eyed. Pools of dark blood reflected the light from torches and lanterns, and the two men lay in awkward poses that suggested neither had moved since falling to the street.

The street was nearly cleared by the time a group of men approached the three, and Philip froze when he recognized the man in the lead.

"What were you doing here?" Inspector Bérand asked them.

Philip kept his head down as Joseph spoke. "We were caught in the mêlée but had nothing to do with it."

"What he says is true," the young army lieutenant volunteered.

Bérand snapped his head around to face the lieutenant, and the younger man lowered his eyes and stepped back. "Pardon me, Inspector, I only wished to help," he mumbled.

The inspector turned back to Joseph, who stood while Yves patted Philip on the shoulder as they sat on the ground.

"This was not a mêlée, and you will not use that term again," Bérand ordered. "Now, what business did you have at this subversive gathering?"

Philip looked up at Joseph to see if his friend was showing nervousness as he told about Yves bringing his supper, but his movement caught Bérand's attention.

"What is your injury?" he demanded. Before an answer came, he grabbed a musket from a soldier and jabbed at Philip's leg with the butt.

Philip yelped. "I believe my foot might be broken," he said quietly. "I fell when the crowd rushed toward me."

"He saved my life!" Yves interjected, but he was ignored.

Bérand eyed Philip closely in the dim light.

"I know you, boy," the inspector said slowly, although the tone indicated he had not yet placed the young man's face with either a name or any circumstances.

Philip was frozen with fear, hoping the memory would not return clearly for the inspector, but then he recalled how his cowardice had helped him escape questioning the first time the two had met.

"I work for Groussard and Company," he blurted out. "I wrote a critique of *Hamlet* that made you angry."

"Yes, the boy who cried like a baby," Bérand said to his companions with a hard laugh, but then fixed his eyes downward again on Philip. "Did you tell your father of the trouble you caused."

"No, monsieur," he said and looked up at Joseph.

"Well, you seem to have the ability to find trouble. What were you doing here?"

Philip repeated Joseph's account.

"So once again your explanation is that you were the victim of an unfortunate set of circumstances."

"It is the truth, monsieur," Philip whined.

Bérand eyed him for a moment, then said disgustedly, "I shall leave your father to decide on your punishment."

Philip was elated when Joseph gave the inspector a slight nod and let the mistaken relationship stand, and the police entourage moved on with their business of sorting through the fallen members of the mob.

"What sort of trouble did you have with him?" Joseph asked Philip.

"It was nothing, ridiculous in fact," he replied, then recounted the bare details, reminding Yves of when he had shown him the *Hamlet* critique in *Le Journal*.

"You were arrested for *that*?" Yves said. "I saved that newspaper because I thought you were important."

"Maybe you should throw it away now, so it is not taken from you as evidence for my trial," Philip said sarcastically. "Anyway, I was not arrested."

"He said you cried like a baby!" Yves responded with glee.

Joseph cuffed him, then hoisted Philip to his feet to see if he could walk. Hot pain shot through his foot, and his shoulders and chest tightened as he took a step. Joseph slung Philip's arm over his shoulder and they moved away, taking every other step gingerly on the way home.

"Philippe saved my life!" Yves squealed as he burst through the door of the Augiers' home.

Bathilde rushed frantically toward them, hugging the boy and looking anxiously as Joseph helped Philip through the door. "What has happened? How were you hurt? Is it bad?" she asked in rapid succession, her voice breaking into near hysteria.

"He thinks his foot is broken," Joseph said, lowering Philip into a chair.

"How did this occur?" she asked more calmly, soothed by the unconcerned tone in her husband's voice.

"There was trouble in the street, and some people were shot," he recounted plainly. "There was a rush and Yves fell, but Philippe shielded him."

Bathilde burst into tears and bent over to hug Philip, kissing his forehead over and over. "God has sent you to us," she said, crossing herself. "Dear, sweet Jesus."

"God has sent Joseph to you," Philip said. "I covered Yves when we fell, but Joseph saved us both."

She turned to her husband and showered him with kisses as she squeezed him around the neck and shoulders. Then she brushed away tears and straightened. "I shall make you supper," she said cheerily and scurried off to feed them.

"We lost our twins four years ago, and I thought Bathilde would go mad," Joseph said in a hushed voice to Philip. "If anything had happened to Yves tonight, I might have lost her as well."

Joseph gave a description of the 6-year-old twins' deaths during a typhus outbreak and concluded, "It was the will of God."

Philip bedded with Yves that night but had trouble getting to sleep because of the pain in his foot and the boy's incessant recounting of the night's events, pointing out alternately that Philip had saved his life and that he had been accused by the inspector of crying like a baby.

Joseph was gone when they awoke, but he returned at the reins of a carriage from his shop.

"This is beautiful," Philip said of the ornate carriage after he was helped up onto the driver's bench. "It is almost a work of art. Now I know the source of Yves' abilities."

"That is pleasing to hear, but I am only a wheelwright," Joseph said. "I am more of a carpenter than an artist." He reached down behind the seat and pulled out a wooden crutch he had made that morning.

Joseph took Philip first to a doctor, who confirmed that his foot was broken and bled him to reduce the swelling. "It is fortunate that the bone broke cleanly because it is likely to heal properly without leaving you a cripple," the doctor said.

The downside was that he could fashion neither a plaster nor a splint for the injury that would both handle his weight and still allow the break to heal the way it was intended. The injury required bed rest, he said and shook his head disapprovingly when Philip insisted that he needed to work.

"He is a doctor for rich men," Joseph said after they had resumed on their way to Groussard & Co. "It is fine for his patients to lie in bed and have their servants wait on them."

Philip asked if he had paid the doctor and received a nod. "I will repay you the next time we meet," he said.

"No, I will forever be in your debt for what you did for Yves," Joseph said and would speak no further on the matter.

The injury later was explained to Felix Debraux, although the description of the circumstances was vague, out of concern for his nervous nature. He ordered Philip out of the back shop, where most of the work would have to be done while standing, and assigned him to proofreading.

"You are far more valuable to me as a reader anyway," Debraux said. "It is *your* choice to work with the printers."

"I wish to learn all details of the business, and where better to learn than at such a fine company?" he responded in his most cloying fashion, and the owner nodded approvingly.

Philip noted that there was no account of the evening of violence in *Le Journal* and asked the publisher if he wanted one written.

"Oh, I heard about it but received word that there was to be no mention of it," Debraux said. "*Le Clairon* can print it. I would love to see it shut down."

Philip knew for certain that at least two men had died the night before, and it seemed inconceivable that there would be no account for Parisians to read. London newspapers — at the very least the opposition newspapers — would relish the opportunity to recount how the government's failures had led to a public uprising.

Philip went back to his room that evening, and after a lengthy negotiation with the stairs, settled onto his cot. There would be no visits to the Augiers and no clandestine work for some time. And there also would be no escape from France until he was physically able to withstand the hardships of travel. He lay on his cot, thinking of how uneventful his life would be for the weeks ahead — that is, unless Mr. Black were again to appear from thin air.

11. The Approach of War

Philip found even the short walk down Rue de Grenelle to Groussard & Co. on a crutch to be an undertaking. Each morning he left his room and sat on the steps, making his way down one by one to the bottom, while in the evening, he relied on the crutch to work his way back up the stairs.

Alone at night, he realized how much he had come to enjoy his friends, his work and even some of his unexpected adventures while in Paris.

He also knew why: This life had allowed him to feel as if he were becoming a man, with all decisions his alone to make — for better or for worse.

Just before Christmas, he was walking mostly without the crutch when he received word from Jean-François Floquet of another gathering at the home of Astrid Villemain. The actor's carriage pulled up late one afternoon at Groussard & Co., and he emerged to make a conspicuous entrance into the building.

"Monsieur Floquet! We have the honor to see you again!," Felix Debraux exclaimed, his voice wavering with fear that there might again be a problem.

"I am here to see your young assistant, Belain," Floquet said, planting his cane loudly on the floor.

Philip limped from a storeroom, where he had changed into his attire for the evening.

"I see," Debraux said warily and whispered to him as he headed toward the door. "You are traveling in high circles."

Floquet took note of the exchange and said haughtily, "I trust that his absence will not cause a problem. If so, I can speak to … "

"Oh, no, there is no problem!" Debraux said, waving his hands. "He goes with my blessing."

After they climbed into the carriage, Floquet gave Philip a mischievous look. "That man responds easily to threats, does he not? He is extremely nervous."

"You played your cards correctly," Philip said with a smile. "In fact, I might see my salary increased when I return."

He explained the circumstances of his limp, and the actor offered a cane decorated with a gold elephant's head on the grip to assist him as he walked.

"Oh, I could not accept this," Philip said. "I am getting by quite well."

"No, I insist! Madame Villemain called a gathering to celebrate the year's end, even though this was not a good year for her, with her expulsion from Paris," he said.

"You know, I thought to myself about all that had occurred in the Year of our Lord Eighteen-Hundred and Two," he said before unleashing a recital of comments and musings as if he were performing on stage. "The high points of the year? Many, of that there is no doubt. And the low point? Why, there is no question that it was the debacle you witnessed at the National Theater. But then your appearance on the scene provided the highest point of all! And so I thought, this evening must be observed with dear Philippe. As for the cane, I have many. Do you like the elephant?"

"Yes, of course. What does it signify?" Philip asked.

"Did Giselle tell you?" Floquet asked testily. "I hear you have visited her, you wicked young man."

"Tell me what?"

"About my canes. They are my calling card, and the ornamentation is to suit my mood, or my purpose. Tonight, the trumpets blow in celebration, and so an elephant!"

"I had only noticed that you have carried a different one each time we have met. I now recall that you carried a lion when you first visited my employer."

"Yes, beware my growl. Ha-hahhh! Although given the nature of that pathetic Monsieur Debraux, a kitten would have sufficed," Floquet said, shaking his head in pity.

"And what of the falcon?" Philip asked, recalling their first trip into the country.

"For when I am on the hunt," Floquet responded suggestively.

Philip was sorry to learn that Madame deBasséville and Nicollette were traveling separately with other escorts. He was further disappointed upon finding the atmosphere at Madame Villemain's chateau to have been chilled by the onset of winter and the gloomy political scene.

He gathered delicacies from a buffet and settled into a chair with a plate as he eavesdropped on conversations around him. He heard talk that Napoleon had grown tired of British excuses for refusing to vacate Malta, which caused him to wonder why that island held such importance. He doubted that the French planned any return expeditions to Egypt after their debacle at the Battle of the Nile in 1798, although he had to admit to himself that his knowledge of the Mediterranean was scant.

He also learned that France had no intention of releasing its grip on Switzerland, as the Treaty of Amiens had set forth, and that negotiations with England to settle the matter had all but ceased. All in all, the talk was grim as to the prospects for a lasting peace, and Philip discarded his hopes for a festive evening.

While there had been a number of English visitors in attendance during Philip's previous visit, this time there were only a few. Among them was Jonathan Ransom Turgeon, who was able to draw even fewer admirers on this occasion as he discussed his inadequate poetry and limited news from London.

"I find inspiration in Paris, of course, but the threat to peace is most unsettling," the poet said. "I need to have my mind at ease in order for it to be its most creative."

Another Englishman spoke disapprovingly of his government's role in keeping tensions high in Europe, while he ignored Napoleon's part in the failing diplomacy. He also predicted a change of government in London, but Philip's only interest in British politics involved how it would affect Lord Torrington's office — and himself.

He was wandering alone through the large chateau, when he encountered Madame deBasséville on the arm of General Reynard Permon and Nicollette, who was with a cavalry officer.

"Philippe, how pleased I am to see you on your feet," the actress said, abandoning Permon to hurry toward him.

The remark caused the general to eye Philip suspiciously, and he frowned when Madame deBasséville extended her hand to be kissed by the younger man.

Nicollette did likewise, although her escort, considerably more dashing than Permon, seemed less threatened by the warmth shown toward the younger man.

They exchanged pleasantries about the length of time between encounters, and Philip had to check himself to avoid a reference to an afternoon he had spent in Madame deBasséville's drawing room while her husband had been away in Germany on a business matter. The ladies fussed over his physical well-being and laughed when he showed them Floquet's cane.

"I hope that does not mean that I can no longer depend on your affections," Madame deBasséville said, her eyes sparkling. Nicollette giggled, while General Permon appeared confused.

"I assure you nothing could diminish my feelings from our first meeting," he said, bowing toward her.

Permon looked at Philip, then at Madame deBasséville, then back to Philip, blinking frequently as he tried to make sense of their relationship.

Philip later found time alone with Nicollette and inquired about her escort.

"He is quite handsome, would you not say?" she asked. "He has asked me to marry him."

Philip wasn't certain as to why, but he felt a stab of jealousy. "I am certain the future will hold great things for you both," he said lamely.

"His family is very wealthy, and his career is quite promising," she said.

Philip had neither attribute to appeal to a young woman, and he mused that perhaps his resentment of Nicollette's beau was related to his own situation, rather than to any feelings toward her. He inquired delicately of the relationship between Madame deBasséville and Permon.

"Oh, she has tired of him already," Nicollette said, showing no sign that she was betraying a confidence on the subject. "She thinks his best days are behind him, but he suits her purposes at this time."

"Why does she think his best days are behind him?" Philip asked.

"Did you fail to notice that he is missing a number of teeth?" she replied brusquely.

Philip laughed. "Oh, that. I thought you meant his career."

"Yes, that as well. Giselle says the army has been very active the past month, and yet the general never seems to turn down a social invitation. How essential can he be to the army, if his services are never required?"

"And what of your handsome officer?" Philip asked.

"He says his services will be required when the trumpet sounds for battle."

"Does he know when that will be?"

"Oh, he thinks we will be at war by the spring," she said.

Philip slumped into a chair later and considered the seemingly unanimous opinion that war was to resume shortly. His injury needed to heal completely because he would need his physical strength to see through his plans to return to England, and he began to feel desperation over how quickly war was approaching.

Floquet came along to interrupt his thoughts and directed him again to Madame Villemain's private salon. "We are to salute the year, and you will certainly be toasted."

"*I* shall be toasted?" Philip asked.

"Your arrival on the Parisian scene was a high point of the year, and I shall insist that we raise a glass to you," Floquet said.

Madame Villemain confirmed to an incredulous Philip that his denouncement of Floquet's performance had been one of the few setbacks that Napoleon had suffered during the year.

Philip commiserated with her continuing banishment from Paris.

"It is a cruel punishment for one who is so devoted to the true spirit of France," Floquet added.

"Cruel?" she said. "Jean-François, I cannot define anything Bonaparte does by the simple word you employ. He is neither gentle nor cruel, good nor bad. Such a being has no comparison to others, and so those words cannot define him. I could call him a machine or a device, but I cannot call him a man."

"Astrid," Floquet said to her and bowed, "you are the glory of France."

Philip bowed as well, his admiration for her growing even greater.

At the end of the evening, Madame Villemain called her guests into the ballroom, where Philip indeed was the recipient of a thinly veiled tribute.

He skulked near the back as glasses were raised and was grateful that she didn't mention his name, although two men near him knew who he was and patted him on the shoulder.

Floquet himself was honored in a humorous retelling of his performance as Hamlet. He leapt forward to join Madame Villemain, then turned to face the crowd with his jutting jaw and the absurd countenance he had shown on the stage. Part of the audience hooted with laughter, while others applauded enthusiastically, apparently unaware of the circumstances.

She also saluted writers who had been published during the year, and Philip noticed Turgeon pushing up toward the front, apparently in anticipation of a forthcoming tribute. When none came, he sniffed and pushed back his hair.

"You were watching the poet Turgeon, were you not?" Madame deBasséville whispered in his ear.

He turned and smiled. "Yes, that fool expected a great woman such as Madame Villemain to take note of his insignificant work. Merciful God!"

"I am in your debt for helping me to avoid a bad arrangement with that man," Madame deBasséville said softly to him. "I was impressed when he told me that he was a friend of the Duke of York, but you helped me to see that he is insignificant."

"*He* is a friend of the duke?" Philip stammered, realizing the poet might have assisted in getting the notice of the duke, who headed Britain's military.

Madame deBasséville took his elbow and pressed up against him, the soft contours of her body creating a rush of excitement in him.

"Thank you, Philippe, thank you," she cooed.

General Permon, on the other side of her, leaned forward to inspect the amount of space between his lover and Philip. She pulled back and patted the older man's hand, which held her arm.

Philip found himself in a new state of confusion regarding French notions of romance. Was she making overtures toward him, or was this the great actress at work once again, trying to make her aging lover jealous? He knew not, but he had relished the feel of her body next to his and barely noticed as the final toasts were drunk in salute to the end of 1802.

He asked to be left off at *Le Pont Neuf* when he and Floquet arrived back in Paris that night, hoping to test his foot on the walk home. He took it slowly, and the cane helped, but his foot began to ache by the time he was halfway to his destination.

The air was frigid and the streets free of brigands, so he felt safe as he limped along until he noticed a dog pulling at something lying on the cobblestones. He crossed to the other side of the street to avoid the mongrel, but the dog looked up, growled and ran to catch him.

Philip pulled away when the mutt grabbed the bottom of his pant leg and hit it on the side of the head with his cane. The animal yelped, stepped back and showed its teeth.

"Get away, you bastard!" he cried angrily.

The dog snarled again, then lost interest and slunk away.

Philip shook his head at the absurdity of the battle between man and beast and realized how uneventful recent days had been for him. By the time he had reached the bakery on Rue de Grenelle and struggled up the stairs to his room, he was exhausted and in pain. He lit a candle and sat at the table, wrapping up in a blanket to warm himself. The landlord had told him that heat from the oven below would provide him with a cozy room during winter, but the man had lied after seeing he had a full purse.

The candle flickered as a gust of wind forced its way through the gaps in the poorly fit shutters and window. Good God, Philip thought, his departure from Paris must come soon.

Each day he had spent in the city had made sense on its own, and each week had made sense as well. But the weeks had turned into months, and he was flirting with danger in staying so long. He sat up straight when it occurred to him that his 21st birthday was only a little more than a week away in early January — or *Nivôse* on the Revolutionary calendar.

He sighed heavily and pulled out a piece of paper to reconstruct his professional ledger, first adding credits for his correspondence on the bread prices that had caused a riot and for his analysis proving that a French invasion was impossible.

Under the discredits, he wrote "Don Martin" and "delays," the latter underlined twice, once again creating an imbalance toward the bad. That brought on fantasizing about the good fortune that would need to present itself in order to shift the balance back to the good. At last fatigue set in, and he held the paper over the flame and left it to burn out on a plate.

Philip dropped onto his cot, wrapping himself snugly in the blanket while still wearing his coat and shoes. He poked out his face and saw his breath against the faint moonlight coming through the window of his frigid room. He spoke the only prayer he could recite in French.

"*L'éternel est mon berger: je ne manquerai de rien ...*" he whispered in anticipation of what lay ahead, finishing as he wrapped himself up tightly one last time. "*... et j'habiterai dans la maison de l'Éternel Jusqu'à la fin de mes jours.*"

Philip felt the effects of the long walk from *Le Pont Neuf* for a few days, but once the pain in his foot returned to just a dull ache, he discovered that he had gained strength and endurance. He finally discarded the crutch for good and began to rely solely on Floquet's cane after tying a rag around its ornate elephant's head to avoid the certain ridicule that would come from the print shop.

By mid-January 1803, he was again walking to the Augier home and learned that Yves had progressed further with his lessons than he had expected. Joseph and Bathilde had kept Yves on track, and the boy, who also had marked a birthday, his 14th, showed signs of increasing maturity.

With Yves working on his lessons after supper one night, Philip stepped outside to join Joseph, who had been banished with his clay pipe because his mother-in-law had come down with a heavy cough.

Philip was curious about Joseph's views on the approach of war.

"It will come because Napoleon wants it to come," Joseph said, the pipe's bowl casting a glow on his face. "He lives to make war, I think."

"So then it will be soon?" Philip asked.

"Who knows? What do the politicians say in your newspaper?" Joseph asked.

Philip suddenly was struck with a familiar sense of embarrassment over his own ineptitude, recognizing that he may have overlooked a valuable source of information, given Felix Debraux's allegiance to Bonaparte and his cohorts.

"I should pay more attention to politics in *Le Journal*," he admitted lamely. "I suppose that I fail to grasp the subtleties when I proofread."

"Napoleon now calls himself First Consul for Life, does he not?" Joseph asked. "He used to be simply First Consul."

Philip hadn't given it much thought before, assuming the title to be merely a formality.

He also thought back to the pamphlet that Debraux had printed for Lucien Bonaparte, which said the nation had found a "strong and knowing hand" in the form of his brother.

"Yes, that is true," he said, "although who knows what First Consul for Life means?"

"Well, how does that differ from a king?" Joseph asked.

Philip thought about it for a moment. "I suppose there really is no difference."

"And if a king wants to make war, then who stands in his way?"

Philip considered how little he had gained from his education when an illiterate man was explaining politics to him. "Do you fear war?" he asked.

The pipe glowed again.

"They will come for Yves this time, for these wars last for years and years, and he is not that far away from the age of conscription," Joseph said. "I cannot speak to Bathilde about it because I know she will go mad if anything happens to the boy."

"Is there a way for Yves to avoid conscription?"

"Maybe I should break his legs and cripple him the next time he refuses to behave," Joseph said jokingly, then turned serious. "A rich man can buy his son's way out of conscription, but I would never be able to do that."

"How much would it cost?" Philip asked.

"Impossible for me, that much I know," Joseph said.

Philip, embarrassed by his uneducated friend's superior grasp of French affairs of state, began to read *Le Journal* beyond just proofreading during the following days and sought out context when he was confused.

Both Clement and Debraux joined in the opinion that France and England were headed toward war, although the cynical writer thought hostilities were much nearer than did the publisher. When *Le Journal* reported England's final refusal to leave Malta, they both agreed that the die was cast.

Philip accompanied Clement one night to Fraternity Hall to test the tone of the rhetoric from the firebrands of Paris, but the mood was subdued and disappointing.

"The conversation is not so lively here anymore," Clement said dejectedly. "There is little reason to come, except to drink."

He downed his wine and waved for more before continuing. "After the bread riots, the police arrested many of whom I would call 'free thinkers.' The weasel Debraux refused to print a word about the disturbances in the street, even though men were killed. You were there, you know what happened."

Philip decided to change the subject. "Do the English still come here?" he asked.

"Merciful God, no, since they fear arrest. In fact, the innkeepers on the roads to Calais have been fleecing the British who are fleeing France before the war resumes. All but the fools have gone back to England."

Philip gulped a mouthful of wine. "And what of the Irishman Thomas Grant?" he asked of the young man whose speech had inspired a crowd at Fraternity Hall.

"I have not seen him in months. A pity, because he was an interesting man, to be sure," Clement replied, then leaned over and said in a hushed voice, "They say he has returned to Ireland."

"Is that so?"

"Yes, I suspect he was fed up with the Parisian scene after he discovered that Napoleon was no Revolutionary. First Consul for Life? Hmmmph!" Clement said and spat on the floor. "What modern man can believe that a lifelong appointment is anything but a return to monarchy?"

The two listened in on several uninspired speeches, but they decided to leave when a man rose to complain that the canal work still was not finished.

As he walked home, Philip cursed himself for his past delays, his indecision, his fears and even the bad fortune that had left him with a broken foot. It was clear to him that he had stayed in France too long.

Little packing was necessary because his possessions were so few, but he lightened his load even further by giving several books to Yves and discarding other items. By the middle of February, he had prepared a letter of resignation to Groussard & Co. to explain that he was joining his rediscovered relatives in the Champeaux region in Brittany. It was accepted with regret by Debraux, who in return wrote a letter of recommendation to present to his next prospective employer.

The wheels for his departure ground to a halt, however, with the arrival of a perfumed invitation from Madame deBasséville.

"An afternoon rendezvous?" she wrote and provided a time and a date that was a fortnight away. It was signed simply, "G."

Philip read and reread the note, attaching meaning to everything about it. What exactly did she mean by "rendezvous"? Was that not the way that Parisians referred to a romantic meeting between a man and a woman? And what of the very familiar "G"?

He puzzled over why he should be so hopeful, with his return trip to England so near. He was forced to admit that such an elegant and beautiful woman would have limited interest in a clumsy young man of limited means, but in the end, all that mattered was that she was beautiful and had been kind to him. He put an end to his philosophical, moral and ethical considerations and decided to go like a puppy to her, without regard to his schedule for departure.

While Debraux was normally averse to any change, he eagerly allowed Philip to extend his time at Groussard & Co., especially after being told that he had been like a father to the younger man since his arrival in Paris.

"And I could not have asked for a finer son than you," responded Debraux, who was probably blessed in being childless, given his temperament and his inability to handle anything out of the routine.

"My God, you make me sick," Clement groused when Debraux was out of earshot, then aped, *"Oh, you are like a father to me!"*

Philip laughed and went back to the presses to grab new proofs to read, but a stack of handbills with English printing caught his attention.

"Those are not to be read," a printer said as Philip reached for one.

"Why is that?" he asked the man, who had been assigned the job of printing the handbills because he was illiterate.

"I was told that it is government work and that they want only their own people to read it."

Philip acted unconcerned, but he grabbed one of the handbills and stuffed it quickly into his pocket when the printer's back was turned. Later, he emptied a bin behind the shop and then pulled out the crumbled paper from a pocket to read:

OUR BROTHERS,
You know what efforts France has made to assist you. Her affection for you, her desire to avenge your wrongs and to assure your independence can never be impaired.
After previous unsuccessful attempts, behold at last that Frenchmen arrive amongst you. They come to support your courage, to share your dangers, to join their arms in yours and to mix their blood with yours in the sacred cause of liberty.
Our triumphant troops are flying the colors of liberties across the Earth to tear up the roots of the wealth and tyranny of your oppressors. That frightful colossus is moldering away in every part. Let his property become the reward of those generous men who know how to fight and die.
Our cause is common. Like you, we abhor the avaricious and bloodthirsty policy of an oppressive government. Like you, we hold as indefeasible the right of all nations to liberty.
'Union, Liberty and Brotherhood' is our shout. Let us march. Our hearts are devoted to you; our glory is in your happiness.

The proclamation was unsigned, and Philip was confused as to its meaning.

Was this some sort of mischief to be distributed on the streets of London after the French had invaded? He felt a surge of panic that his homeland was in peril as he had been dilly-dallying in Paris, but after a short period of reflection, he realized that this interpretation made no sense and reread the bill. Were the Irish preparing another uprising? That seemed unlikely, given the failure of the rebellion just five years earlier. Still, Thomas Grant had sounded anything but mollified in his Fraternity Hall rhetoric.

Later, he scratched a correction onto a proof he was reading and turned his head to stretch his neck muscles as other possibilities raced through his mind. Frenchmen in Canada had been oppressed by

England, but this idea was foolish, he realized quickly, for why would the bills be written in English if they were for Frenchmen? He was largely ignorant of the Caribbean possessions, but he was certain the situation there didn't fit any better than Canada. India? But why would Napoleon print handbills at a Paris shop to foment rebellion on the other side of the world?

In a short time, Philip ran out of alternatives and concluded that the handbills were destined for Ireland. The French would benefit greatly from Irish unrest, for the distraction alone would be valuable when war resumed. Britain would be forced to deploy more troops on the island, station more ships along its coasts and face greater division at home after the inevitable reports of atrocities against the Irish.

He approached Debraux and vaguely referred to the handbills, but the publisher said, "I chose not to look at them, and neither should you. My belief is that the less known, the better."

Philip worked late into the evening until he found himself alone in the building. Rummaging through the clerks' work, he found a ledger book that he thought might contain the information he needed. The entries were chronological, and he easily discovered the one he had sought:

Order 634: M. Claude Audibert, Ministry of War, 5,000 handbills
Completion date: Ventôse 25
To be delivered to: First Brigade, Second Division, Gen. Jean-Pierre Marconet, L'Orient

He scribbled the details onto a scrap of paper, then grabbed his coat and cane and headed out the door. A leisurely stroll brought him to a circular plaza, where he rattled the cane along the iron rails of a fence before taking a seat on a bench.

Philip's cheeks suddenly flushed and began to burn as he considered that the handbills were to be shipped by mid-March to L'Orient, a port city that could provide an easy departure to Ireland. He recognized that he had made a colossal blunder months earlier in rejecting the packet from Don Martin that detailed French military operations at L'Orient. The purpose behind the handbills likely had been within his reach at that moment but had vaporized in his fit of indignation directed toward the Spaniard. Good God, he thought, he had compounded his error by failing to deliver gold to Don Martin, likely turning the man into an enemy.

All of his inadequacies shone before him like the front of the National Theater. He had turned the trip to France, "a holiday" as Lord Torrington had put it, into a fool's escapade. England had been in need of a reliable man, but a nincompoop had taken the assignment. His eyes began to flood as he recalled how time and again he had fallen victim to his own inadequacies. But this time he had failed not just himself, but England and everyone he knew.

"For want of a nail, the shoe was lost," he muttered and wiped a sleeve across his face as his nose began to run.

Over the next few days, he continued to anguish over the harm he had done to his country, along with his own career, and conjured up ways to atone for his error — or at least to cover his tracks. Finally, he came to a decision: Even though Don Martin had called him a "young dog," he would grovel before him to get his hands on the L'Orient packet.

But first, Philip needed to finally end his employment at Groussard & Co. and spend an afternoon with Madame deBasséville. He had considered calling off the visit in the midst of his crisis, but he yielded to the prospect of once again touching her hand, seeing her laugh and breathing her perfume.

He was shown into a drawing room at whose center was a table arranged with silver service, china and a vase bursting with early-blooming crocuses, a welcome sight after walking through the slush-filled streets of Paris. He suddenly suspected that this was not to be the intimate meeting he had anticipated, a fact that was confirmed a short time later with the arrival of a handful of acquaintances from the theater. He settled into the notion that this was to be something less than a romantic affair, but his disappointment disappeared when the hostess appeared.

"Our final guest, Jean-François, is to be here soon, but I wanted to prepare you for his arrival," Madame deBasséville began. "You may not have heard, but he has been ordered into the countryside to perform and will be away from the city for some time. I am uncertain if he can survive away from Paris, so I have invited all of you to bring him cheer before his departure."

A commotion outside provided notice that Floquet had arrived, and when a servant opened the doors to the drawing room, the great actor entered, bowed deeply and then stood tall with his arms spread wide.

"My friends, my friends!" he said grandly. "Could there be a more beautiful day than this?"

Madame deBasséville leaned close to Philip's ear and whispered, "This is so strange. I spoke to him but a few days ago and feared he would leap into the Seine."

As everyone took seats at the table, Floquet leaned his cane — this one with a gold fox's head for a grip — against a wall behind his chair. He confirmed that he had been ordered to Nantes, where a new theater was to be dedicated to Napoleon Bonaparte. "I might as well appear on a stage in Mauritius," he sniffed.

"What are you to perform?" he was asked.

"*Oedipus the King*," Floquet replied. "One of Napoleon's minions, with whom I have become all too well acquainted, tells me that our glorious leader favors dramas that show decisive leadership. And what could be more decisive than killing your father? The Corsican sees great symbolism in the arts, as you are all well aware, a misguided notion in the wrong hands."

His fellow actors were aghast over this further assault upon their craft and took turns expressing their outrage, but Philip eyed the cane, along with the pleased look on Floquet's face, and laughed out loud.

"I suspect that Monsieur Floquet has constructed another triumph for the stage," he said. "Something sly, I would say."

The actor's eyes brightened as he shook his finger at Philip as if to scold him.

"It is true that I was disheartened at first. However, later I thought to myself, 'Since I am performing in the countryside, why not present *Oedipus* in a form that the peasants will comprehend?' " he said, then glanced about the table at the quizzical looks. "The actors will be dressed as barnyard animals for this performance. Jocasta, the mother of Oedipus, is a cow, Tiresius a pig, and so forth."

"And you, Monsieur Oedipus?" Philip asked.

"Why, I shall be an ass," Floquet said seriously as he turned toward him. "We leave in two days, and perhaps you would like to travel with me for your encore as a critic? I am certain that the greatest minds of Nantes will be unable to understand the meaning of my performance. Why, they'll probably throw vegetables onto the stage to feed the animals."

"It would not be the first time that vegetables were thrown at you on stage," Madame deBasséville quipped.

Floquet ignored her, turned to the other guests and said, "Because of this young man, I can endure yet another insult. Philippe Belain restored me after the last time Napoleon launched an incursion onto the stage, and the government dared not risk such a folly again in Paris.

"I shall suffer this in Nantes, however, because the peasants could not possibly know the difference. In fact, they might be quite pleased with the performance, especially if the actors make barnyard noises at dramatic points. Either way, I will not be subjected to humiliation in Paris."

As the gathering was concluding later with farewells and embraces, Philip caught a private moment with Floquet.

"You mentioned that I might travel with you, and in truth, I myself am leaving Paris, bound for L'Orient to see my family," he said.

"If you are traveling west, then you must join us on the journey," Floquet replied enthusiastically. "It will be an adventure!"

12. Battling Shadows

Asking Don Martin Cristobal de Acuña for essential information about L'Orient seemed like chasing a feather in the wind, but Philip had no alternative but to try. He once again pulled up the floorboards, extracted the gold and bank notes and set off for the yellow-brick home.

The Spanish envoy's doorman frowned slightly when he opened the door one rainy afternoon to again see the wine merchant "Joseph Bourgarel," but he nonetheless showed him to the drawing room.

As he stood waiting, Philip reviewed his plan to leave Paris with Jean-François Floquet, the sound of drips from his wet cloak onto the marble floor heightening his sense of urgency.

Don Martin finally entered with a sour expression, accompanied by a tall man with a long face, sideburns and a goatee, the look of a tough from the streets of Paris whose work required a menacing appearance.

"I had hoped to have an audience alone," Philip said, growing even more apprehensive.

"You will not decide how we are to meet," Don Martin snarled. "You are an insolent young dog, and if you displease me, my associate will provide a lesson in etiquette."

Numbed by the threat, Philip proceeded cautiously. "I wished to reintroduce our business arrangement," he said. "I agree that our last meeting was not successful, and I had hoped that we could restore the ties between my employer and yourself."

"Your *employer*," Don Martin spat, "needs to know that I am not a man to bring to anger and that the price for relieving that anger is quite high. Do you understand what I say?"

"Yes, and I shall make certain that he understands as well," Philip said, suddenly worried that he lacked the funds that would win back the Spaniard's favor. "The reason for my visit is to see if you still are in possession of the information from L'Orient."

Don Martin seemed confused at first by the request, but then cast steely eyes upon him.

"Oh, I see that you do not know everything there is to know, and so you come back begging like a little dog."

Philip lost his composure. "I apologize for thinking that perhaps we could do business," he said, "I apparently was mistaken."

Don Martin's companion made a move to block the door, but the Spaniard waved his hand to stop him. "Wait," he said and walked over to a small desk by the window, scribbled on a card and passed it forward: "Convent of St. Bertin, 11 o'clock."

The doorman again showed the back door to Philip, who cautiously stepped out into the alleyway and looked both ways to see what awaited him. The rain and the approaching night combined to heighten his fears as he fumbled in his pocket for the printer's pinch.

"Where are you, you bastard?" he muttered to himself as he cast side glances for Don Martin's villainous associate.

He stepped slowly away from the alleyway and crossed the street, cautiously eyeing a pair of men who stood beneath an awning over the entrance to a tobacco shop. Convinced that they were the Spaniard's thugs, he approached them and asked for directions to the convent of St. Bertin, gripping the pinch tightly in his left hand while making a fist with his right as he prepared to strike first. However, the men barely turned to face him and provided the instructions without either of them making a threatening move.

Philip returned to his room and nervously awaited his appointment at the convent. The prospect of danger rose in his mind as the time passed, and his expectations of success dwindled. Weighing against the doubts, however, was the need to follow through with the meeting to exhaust all chances of obtaining information on L'Orient.

The rain had ended by the time the cathedral's bell tolled ten o'clock, and he soon was striding quickly toward St. Bertin along wet, deserted streets enveloped in a light fog. The street lamps produced a soft glow in the thick air above the street and cast ominous shadows around every corner. When the convent came into view, he slowed and quickly sidestepped into a doorway across the street to survey the scene.

It had seemed a strange place to meet, but now the reason was apparent, for the convent had been abandoned, a Catholic casualty of the Revolution. While Napoleon had made half-hearted attempts to bring the church back into some role for his own purposes, religion had already suffered a mortal blow among the upper classes: It simply wasn't fashionable, and some parishes and abbeys in Paris had been unable to survive.

Philip's thoughts were interrupted by the sound of footsteps, and he caught a glimpse of a figure approaching with his head down, then turning down a side street.

He realized that he had been sloppy in letting his guard down, and he stayed back in the doorway for a few more minutes to survey the walled convent with its gated entrance.

Every instinct he had developed in his secret service told him that it was a mistake to enter through the iron gate in the front, but he could not shake the belief that he had no choice. He had turned Don Martin toward the French and impetuously rejected vital information that might reveal Napoleon's plot against Ireland. Whichever tipped the balance — the desire to do what was right or the need to cover up his mistakes — did not matter in the end, only the calculation that he must push ahead.

His stomach churned in fear as he crossed the street and found that the gate's lock was broken.

He gently pushed one side of the iron bars to slip in quietly and disappear into the shadows inside the wall.

Philip surveyed the pitch-black courtyard with a mind unable to hold an idea for longer than a split second before another alternative appeared. He crept slowly along the wall, searching for any movements or noises. He stopped when his eyes finally began to adjust to the dark enough to spot a stone well and benches beside an overgrown garden.

His ears perked at every tiny sound that came from the night until his nerves pushed him beyond his capacity to stand still any longer. He stepped quietly toward the well but froze when a voice called out in an urgent but hushed tone from the blackness beyond. Confused momentarily by what the man had said, he then grasped that it was "Bourgarel," the name he had given at Don Martin's door.

He edged toward the voice that had come from the arches of a covered walkway beyond the well and reached into his pocket to clutch the pinch.

"Why have you taken so long?" Don Martin hissed as he emerged from a dark archway with his hands stretched out to show he was unarmed. "We must trust each other if we are to ..."

A figure exploded from the side, and Philip instantly raised a hand to block a knife coming down toward him, the blade tearing into the skin and glancing off as he fell to the ground.

Just as suddenly, another figure emerged from the blackness, wrapped a forearm across the attacker's forehead and pulled it back. A new blade emerged in the dim light, this one longer and more frightening as it came fully across the throat, nearly severing the head of the attacker in one swift motion.

Don Martin began to run toward the gate, but he had taken only a few steps when he was grabbed from behind. The long and dreadful knife drew back like a pump handle, then plunged the full length of its blade under Don Martin's ribcage and upward. His killer held up the rigid body and shook it on the blade before letting it fall hard onto the stones.

Philip looked back at Don Martin's thug and saw a spreading pool of black blood in the faint light, then collapsed onto his hands and knees and retched. He turned his head back toward the body of Don Martin just as his killer put a boot onto the dead man's buttocks and withdrew the knife from his back. The man lifted the Spaniard's arm and wiped blood from the blade on the sleeve of his coat.

"Are you well, young Quixote?" a voice asked in a loud whisper, and a quick explanation followed.

The men who had provided Philip with directions to the convent were associates of Mr. Black who were watching Don Martin's house, and they had suspected that something was amiss when Philip left through the back door without being followed. They informed Mr. Black, who deduced correctly that Don Martin had set a trap.

"But if you knew Don Martin's intentions, then why did you give me no warning?" Philip asked after he had risen to his feet.

"I received word only this evening and went to see you as quickly as I could, but you had already left. I caught up to you when you reached the convent, but I wanted Don Martin to think you were alone, so I slipped in through the back. I admit that it was a close call, but you are well, no?"

The man's voice was agitated, not cold and dispassionate as before, and the slightest of accents could be detected.

"You are an Italian!" Philip whispered triumphantly.

"You are clever, young Quixote, I give you that, but not clever enough to have avoided a knife to your throat a moment ago," Mr. Black said.

"I owe you my life," Philip stammered, nearly choking with the release of emotion. "I am in your debt, sir, and I shall trouble you no further regarding your identity."

Mr. Black looked at Philip's hand, which was drizzling blood onto the stones, and pulled out a handkerchief to tie around the wound.

"The knife glanced off my palm," Philip said. "It feels more like a bruise, and the cut does not seem to be too deep."

"We must leave this place," Mr. Black said after bandaging his hand.

Philip confused his meaning as he looked down at the nearby blood and vomit in the courtyard and agreed, "Yes, it is a disgusting sight."

After a hesitation, Mr. Black replied, "I mean that the police may be near, for Don Martin draws much attention wherever he goes."

"Yes, of course," Philip said with embarrassment.

Mr. Black rifled through the clothing of Don Martin's henchman to find a pistol inside the man's waistband. He eyed it carefully before handing it to Philip, then instructed that the same be done with the Spaniard's body.

Philip dragged Don Martin away from the puddle of blood and turned it so that the lifeless eyes looked away. From inside the braided coat, he removed another pistol and a leather purse, but no papers regarding L'Orient. He stood up straight and sighed heavily with the understanding that the meeting at the convent had been pointless.

He stooped again to pat the front of the dead man's breeches and discovered a watch. After momentary guilt about becoming a thief, he took a hardened look at the body and remembered who it had been.

"The little dog will be able to tell the time now," he said as he snatched the watch.

Mr. Black spat on the ground next to the Spaniard's body and crossed himself. "He planned a murder at a holy site, and I take pleasure in ending his life before he could crawl off to a priest to confess his sins," he said. "Enjoy the ninth circle of hell, Don Martin."

They hurried to the rear of the courtyard and climbed through a broken-out window and into the black interior of the convent. A glance back revealed lights bouncing along on the buildings beyond the outer walls.

"Don Martin has been followed, as I guessed," Mr. Black said. "He undoubtedly planned to kill you, take your money and then curry favor with the police by claiming he had trapped a dangerous spy."

They crept slowly and blindly through the building, crunching glass and stumbling over broken boards until they reached a door to a side street that stood slightly ajar.

"You know that war is near?" Mr. Black asked Philip.

"Yes, I had been planning to leave Paris the day after tomorrow."

"Good, I would be most unhappy if you were to be arrested. If you travel quickly, you should be able to get back safely to London."

"I believe I have some new and vital information to report," Philip volunteered. "It involves …"

Mr. Black cut him off. "You must not tell me, just as you must not know my business. Take your information with you and get back to England."

"I have some complications in returning," Philip blurted out and explained that he lacked papers to travel. "I am unsure if I can get past the authorities on the coast."

"I suggest then that you visit Calais and find a wine smuggler to carry you across. Just jingle your purse, and one will appear."

Philip cleared his throat. "I am going to L'Orient, not Calais," he said.

"L'Orient, why? Oh, young Quixote …" he said, his voice trailing off.

"I must," Philip insisted.

"Your work is not finished? Perhaps you should abandon it."

Philip shook his head in disagreement.

"I know few men with your courage," Mr. Black said.

"Courage?" Philip asked.

"I take small steps because I am cautious," Mr. Black said. "But you are daring, and you take long steps. You recall that you came in through the front gate tonight, while I sneaked in through this back door."

"That is not courage, sir," Philip said. "I am only a young fool."

"You are wrong," Mr. Black said emphatically. "You knew the danger of coming here, but still you came, because you believed it was vital, true? You may end up dead, but it will be your courage that does you in, not your foolishness."

Philip accepted the compliment silently, with the shame of knowing it was undeserved.

"We must part now," Mr. Black said as he pulled back the door far enough to peer out into the side street. "Which way do you wish to go?"

Philip gestured toward the back of the convent, and Mr. Black stuck one foot through the doorway and paused to look both ways.

"Good luck to you, Sancho Panza, and thank you," Philip said.

"And to you as well, young Quixote," Mr. Black replied with a slight smile, then raced away quietly without looking back.

Philip took a deep breath and removed the pistol from his right pocket. It was too dark to see if it was primed, but he pulled back the cock anyway, then reached down to secure the pinch in his waistband.

With a quick look both ways, he edged down the side street, glancing back to see shadows from lantern lights still dancing behind him. He hoped that Mr. Black had made it away safely as he realized that he had chosen the safer path to the back of the convent.

As he crept quietly along the side of the building, he ran his bandaged left hand along the bricks to steady himself. When he reached the corner, he stopped to take a deep breath as he prepared to dash away, then took his first step and gasped.

Inspector Bérand advanced into his path, followed by a young *gendarme* a few paces behind him.

"Halt!" Bérand ordered instinctively, then instantly recognized the startled face under a street lamp. "You? I know you!"

Philip raised the pistol, pointed it at the inspector's stomach and squeezed the trigger.

Click, followed only by the sizzle of a flint putting a spark to damp powder.

"You!" Bérand exclaimed angrily, as he reached in an attempt to wrestle the pistol away while the young *gendarme* stood frozen with disbelief behind him.

Philip pulled out the second pistol and pushed the barrel into Bérand's ribs. The inspector's only hand was already in use, and his eyes widened with the recognition of what was to come. The trigger was squeezed, the hammer clicked and the second pistol exploded in fire and smoke.

Bérand was knocked back two steps, then regained his bearings and looked down at the smoking powder burns on his coat. He opened one side to reveal a small, dark circle on his white shirt that began to spread, and he reached behind as if to scratch his own back. He glanced at Philip for an instant before his eyes rolled up in his head, his knees buckled and he collapsed onto the street.

The shocked *gendarme* bent down toward the body, and Philip dropped both pistols, grabbed the printer's pinch from his waistband and lunged forward. The weapon barely pierced the young man's neck, but it caused him to lose his balance and fall to a sitting position. He quickly scrambled back to his feet and ran away.

Philip was so startled that he momentarily considered giving chase, but he regained his wits, picked up the pistols and fled in the opposite direction. Whistles began to blow a short time later, but the police accompanying Bérand were too slow and confused to give chase.

The planned departure from Paris with Jean-François Floquet was still another day away and no longer an option. The police would be scouring the city in the morning for the man who had killed one of their brethren, and the young *gendarme* with Bérand surely would recognize him if their paths were to cross again. Riding in the actor's carriage would require passage through the city's gates, further increasing the chances of arrest.

Philip earlier had worked out a contingency plan to leave Paris through an unfinished canal, and the idea remained clear in his mind. Packing was a hasty affair, with quick choices on what to bring and what to leave behind. He put coins and a few bank notes into his coat pockets and was stuffing the rest of his funds into a hidden pocket inside his travel bag, when he remembered Don Martin's leather purse.

He sat down and stared in disbelief after emptying thousands of francs in gold coins onto his cot. Recovering his wits, he began to sort the paper and discovered what appeared to be recordings of enormously high debts. Philip saw now that the Spaniard had been desperate for the English gold to pay off gambling losses, and the meeting at the convent had been just a pretense for robbery and murder, not to deliver information about L'Orient.

Philip put the records of debt to the flame, returned 2,000 francs to the purse and stuffed the rest of the money into the travel bag. There was little time to reflect on his departure from the room that had been his home for nearly a year — just one last look around, and he was out the door, down the stairs and into the street. On his way to the unfinished canal, he veered off course for one final stop at the Augiers' home.

He knocked lightly on the door, but when no one came, he began to tap on the shutters on a side window.

"Who is it?" a voice came from within.

"It is Philippe. I apologize, but I must talk to you."

The door opened a short time later, and Joseph appeared in night clothes to invite him in.

"No, I came to say goodbye. I must leave Paris tonight."

Joseph went back in, then returned wearing a heavy coat. "Why must you leave now?" he asked as he closed the door behind him.

"I have encountered trouble, but I must not concern you with it," Philip explained

"Is it the police? Is it that kind of trouble?" Joseph asked.

Philip hesitated. "Yes, but you must not be alarmed."

"Yves thinks you are a spy," Joseph said. "Is that so?"

Philip was so dumbfounded by the question, he could only nod affirmatively.

"Are you a royalist?" Joseph continued, registering no surprise at Philip's admission.

"No. My God, Yves thought I was a spy?"

Joseph told his son's version of seeing Mr. Black pass something to Philip at the Louvre on the night that the art convoy arrived from Florence and of the policeman who followed them afterward.

"I could never understand why a royalist would labor in a print shop, but if you are not a royalist, then you must be a Jacobin," he said. "Napoleon has abandoned the Revolution."

"You must know only that we believe in the same things: peace and justice."

Philip reached into his coat and pulled out Don Martin's leather purse containing 2,000 francs. "Is this enough to keep Yves out of the army?"

Joseph looked inside. "Yes, but I cannot accept this," he muttered.

"If you refuse, then I can never repay you and Bathilde for your kindness," Philip said. "I love you as my own family."

Joseph embraced him and kissed him on both cheeks. "Then I accept this gift from you as I would from my own son. Bathilde was right: God has sent you to us."

Philip vanished into the night, moving like a wraith as he sprinted from one patch of blackness to the next, always away from the sounds of police whistles. He stepped into the narrow space between two buildings facing a plaza and watched wide-eyed as the jiggling lights from police lanterns came toward him and then veered away.

He put down his belongings, took off his cloak and wrapped everything into a bundle that he looped over Floquet's cane and hoisted onto his shoulder. After a deep breath of the cold, damp air, he darted across a lawn to an excavated stretch of unfinished canal. He slid down the side to the completed brickwork at the bottom and cursed as his foot stepped into standing water, the runoff from the evening's rain.

After removing his shoes and stockings, he set off at a slow pace that limited the noise of splashing, until at last he reached a wall near one of the western entrances to the city. He climbed up to peer over the lip of the canal and spotted a gate where one sentry stood while another leaned against a wall sleeping.

The sky was already starting to lighten, and there was no time to fret over whether capture or freedom waited on the other side of the wall where the canal entered the city. He slipped back down into the water and waded slowly into the black tunnel beneath the wall, emerging on the other side to see shapes moving along the road leading into Paris. The sound of ox-drawn wagons' jingling chains meant that traffic from outlying farms was approaching.

Philip gathered up his belongings before climbing on his belly toward the top of the embankment, then scrambled to his feet and ran toward a stand of trees a quarter-mile away. When he was concealed, he returned the stockings and shoes to his freezing feet and looked back at the soft lights glowing above the city's dark walls. A faint trail of footprints showed in the frost on the grass where he had run.

The end of one journey, he thought, and the beginning of another.

13. PORTRAYING A SPY

Philip overcame shivering exhaustion to put nearly ten miles of countryside between himself and the city walls by midday. His wandering eventually brought him to a village where a blacksmith gave him directions to the road to Nantes, and he took a room at an inn south and west of Paris at nightfall. He arose early the next day, sore from head to toe from fending off a knife blade with his hand, wading barefoot through freezing canal water and lugging the bundle slung on his cane over his shoulder. But after a sponge bath and a full breakfast, he felt reasonably fit for the new day.

He climbed a small hill with a good view of the road from Paris and sat down under a large tree to read a copy of *Le Clairon* that a traveler had left behind at the inn. The rival of *Le Journal* reported First Consul for Life Napoleon Bonaparte's pronouncement that the English were leading the world inexorably toward war with their refusal to leave Malta.

While Philip didn't fully comprehend the subtleties of the newspaper report, he sensed that the article was skeptical of the French government's claims that it must maintain troops in Switzerland, a sticking point for the British. He reflected that Felix Debraux might have been correct when he predicted that *Le Clairon* would be shut down eventually.

Just before 11 o'clock, an ornate carriage emerged from distant trees, and Philip scurried down the hill to the inn. A coachman climbed down and beat off the dust from his clothes, straightened his coat and opened the carriage door solemnly. A stockinged leg stretched out and lowered onto the step.

"Make way for the world's greatest actor," Philip announced loudly.

"Philippe, this is quite unexpected!" exclaimed Jean-François Floquet, who wore a bright red scarf to accent his sky-blue coat, trousers and hat. "I had understood you to say that you would join me before we departed from Paris."

"I was forced to change some of my arrangements, but I had hoped to find you on the road," he answered vaguely. "Are you traveling alone?"

"I *was* traveling alone, and it was quite dull," Floquet said with a pout as they walked toward the inn. "Well, perhaps you can explain it all to me inside after I am served coffee."

Philip provided an unconvincing explanation of how he had been mistaken about the arrangements of their departure and had left a day earlier in the belief that he had missed the planned rendezvous at the National Theater. He said that he recognized his error later and decided to stop at the inn to wait.

Floquet inquired about his bandaged left hand and was informed that it was cut by broken glass while packing.

"Well, that is an interesting account, no doubt," the actor said and tapped his cane, this one decorated with a horse's head. His tone left no question that he was skeptical of the story, and Philip colored with embarrassment that his lies had been so obvious.

The discomfort between the two lingered until they had been on the road for some time, but just as easy conversation was beginning, the coach began to slow. Floquet drew back a curtain to see what was happening.

"Some soldiers have closed off the road and seem to be searching a wagon up ahead," he said. "Well, if war is nigh, then I suppose we must resume this sort of nonsense."

Philip peeked out the window on his side and saw two soldiers talking to a man driving a wagon laden with barrels, while other uniformed men sat on tree stumps or lay on the ground.

Their relaxed, careless attitudes did nothing to avert his immediate sense of alarm.

"Monsieur Floquet, I believe that my presence may be a threat to you, and so I must leave now," Philip said, his voice cracking slightly.

Floquet eyed him seriously. "Are you in trouble?"

"Yes, and I must apologize for bringing it upon you."

The actor again peered out the window as the carriage pulled forward and turned back with a worried expression.

"It is too late, they are coming this way," he said. "Allow me to handle this matter."

Before Philip had a chance to reconsider, an older army officer with slumping posture opened the door to the coach and stuck his head inside to examine the passengers.

Floquet had moved over to drape an arm around Philip's shoulders, and he fingered a button on the front of the younger man's shirt.

"Oh, you startled me," the actor said, feigning surprise. "There was no announcement that anyone was about to enter the cabin."

"My apology, monsieur," the lieutenant said with little feeling as he looked at Floquet, then at Philip and then at the disposition of the two. A look of distaste came across his face.

"Are we to be delayed?" Floquet asked in a whiny tone. "I am Jean-François Floquet, and acting is my profession. I am en route to a performance personally requested by Napoleon Bonaparte, if you must know, and this sort of thing is quite upsetting to me, and to my friend here as well."

The lieutenant looked at Philip, who nodded weakly and smiled, then asked Floquet of their destination. He stepped back down after hearing that they were bound for Nantes.

"You may continue without further delay," the lieutenant said dully and closed the door without requesting documentation from either of them. He could be heard speaking in a barely subdued voice to the soldiers under his command, and laughter followed.

As the coach pulled away, Floquet remarked, "Now tell me about this trouble you have found, for you know how I enjoy intrigue."

Philip, forced into providing at least a partial explanation, admitted to having engaged in espionage, believing that he would find sympathy from one who so detested the Bonaparte government. He also acknowledged that he had encountered trouble in Paris that had forced him to flee, while skipping over the events at the convent with the hope that news of the slayings of a Spanish envoy and a French police official had not yet spread through the city.

"Are you a royalist?" Floquet asked.

"I prefer not to reveal my cause because it would endanger you further to know details of my comings and goings," he replied.

"I admit it seemed like a strange question, even as I asked it," Floquet said. "After all, why would a royalist get ink under his fingernails at a print shop? So then, are you a Jacobin?"

"My cause is simply to avoid arrest and nothing more. Please, monsieur, I would prefer to say no more, for your own safety."

Floquet sat back with a finger on the point of his chin. "Here I sit, traveling on the road with a dangerous spy."

"I shall leave you as soon as it is possible, to avoid having you implicated in any way," Philip said seriously.

"Nonsense, depend on me to assist you in any way that I can, although I am not a courageous man and you must not ask too much of me."

"You wish to help me?" Philip asked.

"But of course I will help. This trip is going to be an unexpected pleasure."

The carriage arrived at a roadside inn in the afternoon, and the theater company's convoy pulled in several hours later. Floquet introduced Philip as a writer and friend whom he had brought along from Paris, and as usual, knowing looks and nods followed.

After dinner, the theater company's members munched on candied nuts and drank wine in the inn's tavern as they discussed their upcoming production.

Nantes was to proudly provide most of the cast for the performance, since the National Theater in Paris had sent only the main actors, along with some workers and materials to assist in staging.

The Ministry of State also had volunteered the services of Jacques Pinault as stage manager to ensure that the government's wishes were carried out by the petulant leading actor.

It soon was obvious that Pinault had received no word of the intention to perform *Oedipus* in a barnyard setting.

"Now as I see it," Floquet said, tapping his fox-crowned cane on the floor as they began to discuss the performance, "we must be as subtle as subtle can be."

Philip tapped his elephant-crowned cane on the floor to echo his support. "Yes, I can see that, and I concur, but to what degree? That is *my* question," he said adamantly, playing along in his role as the writer. "Pardon me for saying this, but our Nantes audience will not be nearly as sophisticated as Parisians, and I would not want them to miss out on the meaning that we wish to convey. After all, the First Consul himself has requested this performance."

"I appreciate your caution," Floquet said, tapping his cane on the floor again as he appeared to be plotting out his next move. He reached beneath his chair and pulled out a bound copy of the play.

"Now, here is an example of the effect we will be seeking," he said, thumbing through the pages until he came to one that had been marked. "This is a crucial scene that will put forward our course. Follow me here, for this is Oedipus speaking to Tiresius."

The others looked at him thoughtfully.

"Oedipus says, 'Despite your grey hairs, you still must learn what chastisement such arrogance deserves.' And so by playing off the author's own words, we see that by reference to grey hairs, Tiresius is best portrayed as a horse."

"A horse?" stage manager Pinault inquired quietly, but was ignored.

"I see, Jean-François," said the actor who was to play the part of Tiresius, signaling that he was in on the plan. "Now after such a harsh rebuke, would it be appropriate for Tiresius to lift back his head and shake it, much as a stallion would if perturbed?"

"A stallion?" Pinault asked.

"That is precisely where we are going, and I thank you for your insight," Floquet said, still paying no attention to the manager sitting beside him. "Now, allow me to continue, for next the Chorus chimes in, 'To us it seems that both the seer and you, Oedipus, have spoken angry words. This is no time to wrangle, but consult how best we may fulfill the oracle.'"

Philip jumped into the conversation. "There are two options for the Chorus, which is to be made up of sheep, for what could be more obvious? They could adopt a monotonous tone and thereby achieve the desired effect of the flock's sound, or they could deliver their lines plainly and bleat when finished."

"Sheep?" Pinault asked, and reached across to take the play book.

"Is it out of the question that the Chorus do both?" Floquet asked.

"Well, that gets back to my question, Jean-François, which involves the *degree* of subtlety," Philip responded arrogantly. "Are the sheep costumes and the droning sheeplike voices enough, or must the Chorus also bleat when finished?"

"I believe in the actor's craft, Philippe," Floquet said. "And since the Chorus will be composed of local actors, I believe we should leave this question to them."

"But I must protest, Jean-François," Philip argued. "What of the writer's craft? Such serious consideration surely should not be left to *local* actors."

Floquet bristled at this supposed insult to his brethren. "They may be only local actors, but they are actors nonetheless, and they are the ones who put their pride and their names before the audience. They cannot hide in their seats in the dark."

"And is your point that the writer hides?" Philip responded in mock anger.

Floquet adapted a tone of forced patience. "See here, my friend, my point is only that the actors must be able to perform with enthusiasm. They must have the freedom to seek the best elements of their parts. You must not take away their ability to decide whether to bleat. Why, that is their last bastion of creativity!"

Philip nodded in ascent and reached nonchalantly for a handful of candied nuts. "Fine, your point is taken," he snipped.

"What is this talk?" Pinault interjected. "I know nothing of horses and sheep."

Philip and the actors turned and looked incredulously toward him. Madame Léger, the actress who was to play Jocasta, Oedipus' mother, looked at the others and then smiled sympathetically at Pinault.

"We are performing the play *pro bestia*," she said soothingly as she reached over to pat his hand. "Communication within the National Theater is embarrassingly poor, and it now occurs to me that you never took part in all of the planning. It is an outrage that you were not included, but we of course had no role in deciding who participated. Still, I apologize for all of us, for it is the height of rudeness."

Pinault was obviously charmed by the actress, who patted his hand again and then left hers on top of his. He nodded to accept the apology but persisted. "But what is this *pro bestia*?"

Floquet sighed as if his patience was nearing its limits, then explained that it was common in the Ancient World to perform plays in animal costume to enhance the experience for less educated audiences. "And need I mention that *Oedipus* is a play from the Ancient World or that Nantes is much less sophisticated than Paris? The conclusion seems obvious. Or must I spell it out further for you?" he asked.

"No, I see what you are saying now," Pinault answered meekly. "In truth, this is my first experience with the theater. I can pledge to you that I am fully competent at managing the wagon train and providing resources to make your performance a success. And I enjoy the theater, I assure you of that.

"Still, I confess that my most meaningful professional experiences are not in the arts, and so I shall defer to your judgment in such matters."

"Well, we have full confidence in you, of that there is no doubt, and we are pleased to have your full confidence as well," Floquet said, slapping the man on the back. "In fact, I would go so far as to mention that if you happen to have any experience from a farm, please feel free to contribute to our performance."

Floquet tapped his cane on the floor to signal that the discussion was concluded, and Philip tapped his cane to signal his agreement.

"Were you mocking me with your cane?" Floquet asked after the meeting concluded.

"Why, not at all," Philip replied. "I believed that it would enhance the presumption that you and I are of the same mind."

"That is quite clever of you," Floquet said seriously. "A brilliant little piece of staging, I would say."

As they were making their way to their room, they passed a table where several drunken farmers engaged in a loud conversation.

"Hay will bring a good price again with the war," one said.

"War has resumed?" Philip interrupted.

"Yes, so they say," the man said, pointing to a group of soldiers at another table.

After Philip and Floquet returned to their room, the actor ordered his footman to bring brandy and cigars for them to share at a small table.

"War overshadows the importance of *Oedipus*," Floquet said after blowing out a smoke ring and sitting back in his chair. "We need to discuss *your* drama."

Philip crushed out his cigar and sipped a bit of brandy, which he enjoyed only insofar as they provided him with the illusion of sophistication. "I am sorry, Monsieur Floquet, but as I said before, it is in your best interests that you know no more."

"I recall you saying that, but the situation has changed, and we need to share confidences," Floquet said. "I am aware of royalist plotting in Paris, and Napoleon is frantic to arrest everyone with any whiff of sympathy. Because of some of my own personal ties, I may need to protect myself."

"Do you mean to say that *you* are a royalist spy?" Philip sputtered.

"No, I am an actor," he said indignantly. He paused, allowing his statement to achieve its desired effect, then added, "But our mutual vulnerability requires trust between us."

Philip naturally felt uncomfortable with the offer because of his conviction that his value as an agent was based on his singular ability to keep secrets. But fearing there was no alternative, he agreed.

"Good," Floquet said. "My own intrigue involves Madame deBasséville."

"*She* is a royalist?" Philip asked, aghast at the thought.

"No, she is an actress," Floquet scolded him. "But she shares a bed with one."

"I see," Philip said. "I have never met her husband."

"Not *him*," Floquet said impatiently. "I refer to the fossil, Reynard Permon."

Philip sat silently to ponder that one of Napoleon's own generals was a traitor.

"Permon remains loyal to the Bourbons, for it was they who advanced his career when he was younger," Floquet explained. "I do not understand such things, of course, but I have been told that he was a general who knew which way the wind was blowing during the Revolution, and that he has served the consular government for the same reason.

"More recently, *le Comte d'Artois* enlisted Permon and several other generals who were resentful of the jumped-up little Corsican," he continued and then leaned forward. "However, I fear Permon may have misjudged the situation."

"Who is *le Comte d'Artois*?" Philip asked.

"Mercy, what kind of spy are you?" Floquet snapped. "He is the king's brother, of course, and he runs the most substantial spy ring in Paris."

"The king's brother, yes, how foolish of me," Philip said, his confusion increasing by the minute. "You must forgive my upbringing away from France. Will General Permon be arrested?"

"Anything is possible," the actor said. "My only concern is for Giselle, and myself, of course."

"Do you think Madame deBasséville is in danger?"

"She is only a woman, so perhaps she will not be implicated. Still, Napoleon frightens me greatly for he is a beastly man without a shred of civility."

Next came Philip's turn to spill out his story, which was abbreviated and only partly true. He did not admit to being British or to using an alias, but instead retold his story of growing up in a nobleman's household in England, then emigrating back to France to seek a better life.

He admitted to passing along information regarding military preparations that he had stumbled upon and was pleased that Floquet seemed to show no interest in such mundane concerns. He said that he feared having been exposed in Paris and was seeking refuge in L'Orient, where he believed that he had family. There was no mention of Ireland or of the murders of a police inspector and a Spanish envoy at a Paris convent.

Floquet accepted the story. "Well, there you have it," he said. "We are desperate spies."

Philip smiled. "We are ridiculous spies."

"Nevertheless, we are partners in this intrigue," Floquet said. "Is that agreed?"

"It is agreed, on the condition that no one else is to know of my situation," Philip said. "As you can tell by my ignorance of *le Comte d'Artois*, I really am not part of the shadow world, and I worry greatly over having my comings and goings known."

"Why, Philippe," Floquet said with a smile, "I shall protect you as a jealous lover, if that arrangement does not embarrass you."

Philip gave his ascent to continuing to pose as the actor's young companion and writer.

"Remember," Floquet said, pausing, then continuing grandly, "men like me are so discreet in love, that you may trust their lasting secrecy. The care we take to guard our own good name may fully guarantee the ones we love. So you may find, with hearts like ours sincere, love without scandal, pleasure without fear."

Philip looked at him dully.

"Merciful God, that's *Tartuffe!*" Floquet bellowed. "What kind of writer are you?"

The actor delayed their departure the next morning while he engaged in an extended conversation with the innkeeper's wife before handing her a letter. He barely spoke during the last leg of their journey, but the instant he stepped down from the carriage in Nantes, he began demanding that he be shown to the new theater where he was to perform.

"Shabby," Floquet said, looking out from the stage. "Hopelessly shabby."

Stage manager Pinault tried to calm the actor as a contingent of Nantes dignitaries appeared to welcome the great actor and his entourage.

"You will recall that you are here to dedicate this new building," he pleaded.

"This theater, if that is what you call this hovel, would be confined to the back streets of Paris," the actor sniffed.

"Please, Monsieur Floquet, I beg of you, you must be discreet in your comments," Pinault said desperately as the Nantes' leading citizens came up a side aisle toward them.

"I am an actor," Floquet said indignantly, then turned and put an arm across Philip's shoulder. "My writer will provide me with my lines."

Pinault turned frantically toward Philip and again pleaded, "Please, Monsieur Floquet must not offend."

Philip tried to appear deep in thought for a moment, then said, "I am most delighted to have reached your beautiful city and look forward to sharing the pleasure that only the theater can bring."

Floquet shook his head in disgust at the line, to the horror of Pinault.

"Welcome, welcome!" said a short, squat man bounding up the stairs to the stage. He introduced himself as the mayor of Nantes, eyed the colorfully attired Floquet and bowed. "You must be our most honored guest, Monsieur Floquet."

"I am most delighted to have reached your beautiful city and look forward to sharing the pleasure that only the theater can bring," the actor said in a loud, clear voice that carried to the back of the building.

The city's officials beamed with pleasure, and Pinault's shoulders heaved with relief as polite conversation began.

"Quickly, Philippe, a line," Floquet whispered after announcing he was going to his hotel, and Pinault looked hopefully toward the supposed writer.

"We part company now, but we will meet again in the magical glow of the theater lights," Philip whispered back.

Floquet walked past the mayor to the edge of the stage and delivered the line with a hand extended toward the nonexistent audience.

They were introduced to the local cast members the next day to explain Floquet's vision of *Oedipus pro bestia*. The actors' heads bobbed as if the entire concept made sense, for who were they to argue with the greatest actor in all of France?

When the question of the Chorus arose, Pinault advocated the use of the dull tone without the bleat.

"The audience of Nantes is far too sophisticated to require such a simple device as a bleat to drive home the message," he said with assurance.

The local actors nodded approvingly at the compliment, and with that, the rehearsals began.

Philip, his role in the production diminished, walked the streets of the city trying to plot his journey to L'Orient while worrying about the increased danger with the resumption of war. After lengthy consideration, it was clear that his only hope was to enlist Floquet's help.

He arrived back at the hotel before rehearsals had ended and lay on his bed for more than an hour pondering how to approach his friend with a request to put his life on the line in the game of espionage. The sound of footsteps in the hallway, followed by an obsequious servant's voice, signaled the actor's return.

"Monsieur, I beg your forgiveness for what I am to ask," Philip began after Floquet's footman had left the room. "I have withheld parts of my story in an effort both to maintain secrecy and to protect you, but now I fear that there is no choice but to enlist your help in my dangerous business."

"Oh, yes, proceed," Floquet said with enthusiasm as he seated himself.

"I am about to tell you of a most dangerous plot that Napoleon is about to spring and request your assistance in learning the final details that will allow me to foil his scheme."

"Why, then you truly are a spy," Floquet said, suddenly sounding cautious. "Are you certain that I can help?"

"I request that you accompany me to L'Orient, where I believe that your fame would allow us to meet with some of the notable citizens, including certain high-ranking military officers."

"Merciful God, Philippe, you want me to spy on the army? I would not know the difference between a cannon and a tree stump!"

"No, your part would only be as a social conduit for my activities, and you would be shielded at all times from suspicion. Surely you must see that I would not place you in unnecessary peril after all of the kindness that you have shown me."

The actor sat back uneasily in his chair as Philip spun the story of the handbills bound for L'Orient, along with the bits and pieces of military information that had led him to suspect a planned invasion of Ireland.

Floquet nodded slowly as Philip spoke, and the younger man reflected that it was the first time he had seen the actor exhibit an honest, sincere response to any situation.

"This is very serious indeed," Floquet said. "What do you believe to be the outcome of such an invasion?"

"I believe that England will commit itself fully to eliminating France from the Isles," Philip began. "And while the English are doing that, I believe that Napoleon then will unleash war on the Continent."

"And what of Ireland?" the actor inquired.

"England eventually will slaughter the French soldiers and restore Ireland to its dominion. Then it will exact great cruelty upon the Irish rebels for having joined with the French."

"And you believe that Napoleon would send French boys to their deaths in Ireland, simply as a gambit for his greater designs?"

Philip nodded. "What he might consider a gambit is in truth the creation of yet another battlefield to set aflame before he returns to his true game, which is the Continent," he said. "By tying down the English in Ireland, he can march his armies elsewhere in search of more conquests."

"Yes, my heart at this moment tells me that you are correct, for he is a man without honor, without feeling," Floquet said. "My God, nobody would win in this outcome."

Philip took his cue. "France does not win, because what is a nation, if not its people?" he said. "Does a flag or a golden eagle on a staff define a nation, or is it the mothers and fathers who will lose their sons? Barbarity, plunder and death represent the nation of Bonaparte's creation."

He continued forcefully upon seeing the actor's serious expression. "How can that be a victory for France? Only Napoleon wins, because he exists simply to make war."

Floquet pondered the words before uttering, "Philippe, I love France."

"As do I, never more than now. In my mind are our families, our friends and all the Frenchmen with goodness in their hearts. Think what Napoleon will do their lives. Think of what he will do to their sons who must march to war. Think of the glory of French theater, art and music forced to exist in a nation in which they are subjugated by a tyrant. *These* things are France, monsieur, not the man who calls himself 'First Consul for Life.' "

"Then you are convinced that we are not traitors if we try to stop this scheme by Bonaparte?"

"I cannot answer that for you, only for myself, but what I ask is not to betray our own soldiers on the battlefield. It is quite the opposite: to prevent them from dying on yet another battlefield."

Floquet nodded for him to continue.

"Still, to take action against such a tyrant requires a close examination of one's very soul, of the nature of loyalty to nation versus loyalty to mankind and reverence to God. I can take such action, monsieur, because I know what is right for me, but you alone must decide what is the nature of your loyalty to France. I have made my case to you, but you alone can make this decision."

Floquet reached into a wooden box and extracted a cigar, which he struggled nervously to cut and light. He drew in the smoke and blew it out slowly, and Philip considered whether the actor was actually searching his conscience for a response, or merely trying to recall a dramatic scene he had performed on a Parisian stage.

"I agree with you that Napoleon is a terrible man, and I also believe you to be righteous in wanting to see this plot of his undone," Floquet said, then paused to consider the burning end of the cigar before continuing. "I am a brave man only in the sense that I can stand up before hundreds of people and pretend to be something I am not. But does acting really require courage, or is it cowardice that leads me to wear a mask because I fear that people will see me as I truly am? What if they detest me? What if they see me for what I am, and they say, 'So this is Jean-François Floquet. I cannot stand the man.'"

The actor's face seemed to fall as he spoke, draining it of its normal exuberance and taking the appearance of some unfamiliar, older person.

Stunned, Philip tried to intercede. "You fill a room when you enter, monsieur, I have seen that. You are a great man, that is no act, and that is all I seek to summon from you. Monsieur, what are any of us when our confidence is removed? Surely, we all drop our masks at times and are revealed, but look at what is left of us, compared to you at even your lowest moment. You command attention wherever you go, and you are still the greatest actor in all of France. But what is left of me, what is left of the rest of us, when we remove the mask that we show to the world? A few random qualities, but in sum, what do they amount to? I admit that I am nothing."

"But you *are* something, Philippe," Floquet protested, suddenly distracted from his own self-pity.

"I am not," Philip said. "But even so, I know that I must stop this thing by pulling together what little intelligence and courage that have been divined to me and doing what is right. And if I do, then perhaps I might prove that I *can* be something."

"My boy, you *are* something," Floquet insisted again, his face beginning to tighten back into a semblance of its normal appearance.

"Not unless you help me," Philip pleaded. "Please, monsieur, I beg of you to consider my request with the understanding that the danger arises not from lurking in shadows, but only from your association with me and from the knowledge of what I have told you."

The actor arose and flung open the shutters as if to allow the tension of the room to escape. He drew on the cigar and blew a long trail of smoke into the evening air, then turned back toward Philip. "You say the danger lies in my association with you and in the information that you have told me?"

Philip nodded.

"Then it seems as if I am in danger at this moment, and it matters little what my conscience tells me," Floquet said. "I am already a spy, am I not?"

14. A Faltering Alliance

After two weeks of rehearsals in Nantes were completed, Floquet persuaded Jacques Pinault to arrange a special visit to L'Orient so that the actor could be allowed to breathe the sea air to alleviate his problem with dry lungs.

"What are dry lungs?" Philip asked when he heard of the ploy.

"I have no idea, but members of the *bureaucratie* rarely ask questions, unless the problem involves a document to be signed," the actor said. "He likewise ignored the fact that the open sea is a simple boat ride down the Loire River from here."

Pinault had taken to heart his role as the stage manager and pushed back the opening performance of *Oedipus,* insisting that everything must be perfect for the Nantes audience. He also put together an itinerary for the actor's announced trip to L'Orient, including visits with local dignitaries and a performance one night.

"I did not inquire about local actors to assist you," Pinault said.

"That will not be necessary," Floquet sniffed. "I am quite capable of mesmerizing an audience on my own."

The actor fussed mightily before the trip, and Philip saw little of him until their carriage was about to leave.

"What have you been doing?" he asked as Floquet appeared a full hour after their appointed time of departure.

"I had some personal details that needed my attention, if you must know," he responded testily.

Philip apologized for asking and was surprised when Floquet accepted seriously, rather than with the usual careless wave of the hand.

They sat silently for much of the trip, as both attended to their own concerns. Philip finally broke the silence by sharing his plan: The actor would request that they be given a tour of L'Orient and, acting upon cue, point out certain areas of interest that would require a closer look.

"Yes, I see that this is very clever," Floquet said.

"No, it truly is not, but it is the best I could do," Philip replied and tried to downplay the danger. "I shall not commit my observations to paper while I am with you, in order to limit your risk. Still, by implication at least, you will be perceived to be involved in anything associated with me."

Floquet looked out through the coach window onto the countryside. "I believe that you may count on me for more help than that. We are partners in this endeavor."

The trip to L'Orient did nothing to bolster their confidence. A cold, driving rain began shortly after they left Nantes and had not relented by the time their exhausting ride ended in the dimming light of the late afternoon the next day.

No one was on hand to greet them as they arrived at their hotel, which Floquet declared to be barely adequate.

"This city, if that is what you would call this slag heap, falls far short in the area of courtesy," Floquet said inside the hotel's doorway as their belongings were carried past them.

"Well, city officials might not have known when to expect us," Philip said, trying to ease his agitation.

"Pinault handled the arrangements, and I cannot imagine that he neglected such a detail," Floquet said as he sat down disgustedly in a chair by the door.

Philip quietly informed the hotel manager as to the importance of his guest and requested that word of their arrival be passed to the appropriate people. Later, a small, thin man knocked at Philip's door and presented himself as an adjunct to the city's mayor.

The man apologized for the lack of an official greeting, saying he had believed they would not arrive until the following day because of the storm. The mayor had been busy preparing for the actor's arrival, he said, but he hoped to make amends by hosting them at dinner.

"I suppose that will do," Floquet said grudgingly when told.

They ate with the mayor in the hotel's dining room, along with a dozen men of commerce who spent much of the meal grousing about the resumption of wartime restrictions.

Floquet cast a sly glance at Philip, then took over the conversation, mixing a combination of complaints about their difficult journey with the latest gossip from Paris and occasionally tossing in a question about the war and its effects on the city.

"There is a hill nearby where you can see the English ships out in the bay," the mayor offered.

"Oh, is that so?" Floquet replied, nodding knowingly to Philip.

The merchants agreed that all things considered, they had benefited from the French government's designation of the city as the nation's chief naval yard. The main difficulty during wartime had been the port's proximity to England and the limits that the Channel Fleet had placed upon commerce. They looked with envy upon Marseille, whose limited military importance allowed it to develop into a smuggler's paradise.

After several toasts, Floquet began to regain his social bearings, inclining his head humbly as the mayor and the city's leading citizens complimented him and thanked him for coming.

Floquet in turn heaped praise upon their city, particularly its beauty, which Philip knew to have been observed only from inside the coach during a driving rain.

"The splendor of L'Orient is even beyond what had been described to me," Floquet declared, as Philip coughed into his napkin.

While the arrangements were being made for the following day's tour of the city, Philip edged near the actor and said quietly, "I fail to recall your remarks about the city's splendor during our arrival."

"Why, it is a lovely city," Floquet insisted.

"The mayor's flattery has improved your eyesight."

Floquet tapped him affectionately on the chest with his cane, a gesture that caught the eye of several of the men at the table, and Philip assumed that word would spread quickly of the relationship between the actor and the young writer.

After the evening's farewells, Philip and Floquet sat in stuffed chairs near the fire in the hotel's great room and again shared cigars and brandy. As they discussed their strategy for the following day, the sound of carriage chains could be heard outside, followed by shouts that rose above the incessant sound of the rain.

The hotel's manager was hurrying toward the entrance to investigate the disturbance when a dark, dripping figure glided through the door.

"If you please, it is late, and we can accommodate no more guests," the manager said.

The figure bent over to allow the rain to drip off the cloak and onto the rug beside the doorway, then bent back to throw off the cloak's hood. A pile of light golden hair emerged.

"Oh, my God, I am sorry," the manager stammered.

"Giselle!" Floquet exclaimed.

"Madame?" Philip asked in disbelief.

"I am sorry, my boy, you should have been told," Floquet said out of the side of his mouth as he looked ahead, smiling.

"Told?" Philip said.

"Yes, I wrote to Giselle regarding our endeavor, in very vague terms of course, and asked that she join us. I was forced to leave instructions for her in Nantes when she had not arrived before our departure to L'Orient."

With that, it was apparent that the confidence between the two regarding the "endeavor," as the actor insisted upon calling it, had been breached.

Philip stood to the side, stewing over the unraveling commitment, while the hotel's staff found accommodations for the newly arrived guest.

But the ice in his countenance began to melt when he looked again at Madame deBasséville, as striking in a dripping heavy cloak as she had been in the glory of Paris fashion. His objections faded with the sight of the room's light falling upon her hair and the color returning to her cheeks as the fire's warmth reached her.

"Yes, here we are, the three of us," he said at last, and they retired to Floquet's spacious room to discuss their plans.

"I impress upon you the need for prudence," Philip lectured his two cohorts after the door was closed. "I must be blunt in telling you that your normal circle of acquaintances places no great importance upon discretion. However, you must understand that my life is forfeit should I be revealed, and your association with me could result in great danger for yourselves as well."

"Are you a royalist?" Madame deBasséville asked.

Philip winced.

"Ha-hahhh! That was my question as well!" Floquet exclaimed.

Philip realized he hadn't heard that silly laugh since they had joined in their "endeavor."

"My allegiance is not important," he said.

"He is quite slippery as to that question, and as to whether he is a Jacobin," Floquet butted in. "But, Giselle, I tell you that his motives are pure and that he has the courage to see us through."

Madame deBasséville turned to Philip and looked closely into his eyes. "I see that it is so, and I am at your service." She curtsied with a solemn expression.

Philip was mesmerized momentarily before regaining his senses to spell out Bonaparte's plans for Ireland to her.

"Many of the details escape my grasp, Philippe, but your sincerity does not. I know Napoleon to be a brute, and all of this fits in well with what my friends tell me of his ambitions. The man means to export chaos to every nation in Europe."

Philip took her "friends" to include General Permon and was pleased to receive any bit of affirmation of what he had concluded since stumbling upon the handbills.

She shared the news from Paris regarding the war's resumption. It mostly consisted of parlor talk, but Philip was taken aback when she mentioned that the police had imprisoned a number of English tourists who had ignored the drumbeats of war, including Jonathan Ransom Turgeon.

"He was a dull man, of course, but I wished him no ill will," she said.

Philip felt a sickening dread in his stomach, although it was more for his own safety than for Turgeon's.

The three decided that the next day would begin with the crucial tour of the city to glean every military detail that was at hand, particularly along the harbor area. In the evening, they would attend a reception, where Madame deBasséville would use her considerable charms to learn any meaningful gossip the city had to offer. The following evening would be the performance at the city's theater, where additional morsels of information might be obtained.

Floquet expressed disappointment that he would not have a greater role in the intrigue.

"But you are the reason we are here, so what bigger part could there be than yours?" Philip asked.

The actor's face revealed little satisfaction.

The next day, they rode through the streets of L'Orient with the mayor, a local merchant and a ship owner in an open carriage in chilly, blustery weather. Philip took note mentally of the taverns and inns on the waterfront and imagined smugglers and other nefarious characters whose help might be needed for his escape. While they did not draw near to the French Navy at anchor, he could still count five large warships from a distance, along with a number of smaller vessels.

Floquet clumsily took the lead when the carriage turned away from the harbor.

"I have heard that the view is quite fine along the River Scorff," he said to the mayor, a ploy to gain access to an area where Philip had suspected troops would be encamped.

"Is that so?" the mayor replied. "I would have thought you would have preferred to see our famous architecture."

"No, I insist that we see the river," Floquet said, then glanced deviously at his companions.

Madame deBasséville rolled her eyes.

While Philip had nothing but gratitude for everything the actor had done for him since they had first met, he was annoyed by the actor's shortcomings in this new role. Floquet operated at a high level of social competence when he was in a comfortable setting, but he was ill-equipped to take one step outside his familiar world. God had given him everything as an actor, but he exercised his craft in life at the expense of good judgment.

While the army seemed to have taken over the area on the city's north edge, the three purported spies were disappointed to observe little that was out of the ordinary. Hopes for any great discoveries were further dashed when they were told that they could not continue past a well-manned barricade.

Floquet protested to the army captain blocking their way, then winked at Philip.

"I am sorry, monsieur, but you may not proceed without written orders," the captain said.

"Well, the mayor is right here in the carriage with me," Floquet argued. "What more authority could you need?"

"Monsieur Floquet, I believe that we may go no further," the mayor said diplomatically.

"No, we will not be treated so rudely!" Floquet insisted.

Philip jumped in, fearing further attention from the soldiers who were witnessing the actor's tantrum. "Madame deBasséville is quite cold, and so perhaps we should return to our hotel. I believe we have seen all that we need to see."

"Yes, Jean-François, I am chilled to the bone," she said.

Floquet gave them a satisfied look and let the matter drop until they were back in his hotel room with the door closed.

"Well, that went extraordinarily well," the actor proclaimed as he slung his coat over a chair and rubbed his hands briskly in front of the fire.

"Do you mean the scene you created that almost got us arrested?" Madame deBasséville asked.

"I was merely playing my cards, but you apparently failed to grasp the situation," Floquet said dismissively. "Philippe, did *you* think it went well?"

Philip pulled up a chair and took a seat facing out the window. "It went as well as could be expected, I suppose. I am uncertain what we are seeking, but whatever it is, I fear we have yet to find it."

"But did you think I overplayed my hand with the soldiers?" Floquet asked, eagerly seeking approval of his actions.

"I believe you handled the situation in the best way that you could imagine," Philip said absently as he looked out onto the harbor in the distance.

"He is being polite, Jean-François. You were ridiculous," Madame deBasséville said, then added mockingly, *"Oh, I am so important, take me to your secret army places. I am the world's greatest spy, as well as actor."*

"That is so like you, Giselle, jealous unless every eye is fixed upon you," Floquet responded, then pirouetted across the floor and mocked her in return: *"Look at me, everybody, look at me!"*

"Please, monsieur, madam," Philip begged, but the bickering continued.

His disappointment in Floquet grew, and he soon found himself witnessing a shrill side to Madame deBasséville that never before had been exposed. His hopes sank, and he stared vacantly out the window, weighing the incomplete pieces to his puzzle.

As the warring continued behind him in the room, he became aware that Madame deBasséville's voice and attitude were growing in strength, while Floquet's were shrinking. The victor was becoming apparent, as was the fact that the actress was unleashing some pent-up fury from old wounds.

"Giselle, you will withdraw that immediately, or I will consider our friendship dissolved!" Floquet shouted after a particularly nasty insult.

"I will not!" Madame deBasséville responded vehemently.

"That is enough! I will hear no more of this!" Philip barked, startling the combatants into silence. "How can you speak to each other in this way? Do I need to remind you of what we are trying to do here, that a few minutes ago we were friends willing to risk our lives together? I would rather see Napoleon sink Ireland into the ocean than listen to this for another minute!"

They pulled back their claws and hung their heads.

"If we are to continue, it must be together," Philip resumed, lowering his voice. "I have placed you both upon pedestals, for you are what I can only hope to be. But this bickering? For the love of God, I can see such behavior in the streets or in a slop shop. This endeavor requires that which sets you apart, your greatness, not that which makes you common."

Floquet apologized and bowed toward him, then took Madame deBasséville's hand, held it up to his face and kissed it.

"Pardon me, Philippe. Pardon me, Jean-François," she said meekly, then began to cry.

"No, we also need no tears, only strength," Philip said. "For me, that means clear thought. Monsieur, we need the diversion of your grandeur. Madame, we need your unfailing charm."

She smiled back at him through her wet eyes.

"We are together, or we are nothing," he said.

Their hopes were restored that evening when they arrived at the reception to find a military contingent in attendance, offering the promise that the "endeavor" could perhaps still bear fruit.

"I believe our fortunes have changed," Floquet said confidently as he scanned the uniforms in the large social hall.

The mayor came forward and introduced L'Orient's dignitaries, then ushered them through the buzzing hall toward three extravagantly decorated tables at the front.

As the mayor began to explain the evening's order of events, Philip noticed the medals, braid and puffery of high-ranking army and naval officers at one of the three tables. Floquet's voice interrupted his thoughts.

"Monsieur, I would be most appreciative if you could seat me with our men in uniform," he said to the mayor. "I wish to offer my support as they prepare again to undertake the responsibility for defending our glorious nation."

Philip glanced at Madame deBasséville, who looked back helplessly.

"Perhaps might I join Monsieur Floquet at that table?" Philip asked desperately.

"No, no," the mayor said. "We would like one of you at each table."

And so the plan was in tatters, just as the evening was beginning.

Madame deBasséville, who shared company with one of Napoleon's generals and could charm her way past the defenses of the military men most likely to have information, was assigned to a table of local government officials and their wives.

Philip, who could best comprehend any important military information, was seated with merchants, manufacturers and ship owners.

And Floquet, whose expertise was confined to the theater, fashion and gossip, was seated among a table of high-ranking officers with whom he shared nothing except self-aggrandizement.

Philip barely paid notice to what was said by his dinner companions, his attention frequently drawn to the sound of Floquet's incessant voice at the other table — signaling that little information was being passed while the actor dominated the conversation.

When the meal had concluded, the mayor stepped to a rostrum decorated with colorful bunting and introduced each of the three guests. They stood and acknowledged the audience's polite applause.

Philip, introduced first, was unaware that he was considered to be a dignitary, but Pinault had been thorough in his preparations and had identified him as a heralded writer from Paris. It was a ridiculous thought, since the only literary works he had produced had been the ill-fated critique of *Hamlet*, along with his contributions to the script of *Oedipus pro bestia.*

His mind was still wandering after the introductions of Floquet and Madame deBasséville, when the mayor's voice suddenly rose in volume.

"At this point, might we impose upon our guests to speak briefly to us about their craft? Monsieur Belain, if you would be so kind as to begin the presentation for us?"

Applause broke out, and Philip took a sip of wine in an attempt to stall while he searched for something to say. He stood and bowed to the audience and walked slowly toward the platform, where the mayor greeted him and vigorously shook his hand.

He had never spoken before such an audience and could feel small beads of sweat beginning to form on his temples. As the applause died down, he cleared his throat loudly and began by thanking the city for its warm and generous welcome. He then remarked on what he, Floquet and Madame deBasséville had seen thus far on their visit and how they hoped that the rest of the trip would likewise be enjoyable.

"But Monsieur Belain, we are most eager to hear more about your craft," the mayor called out from his seat. "What can you tell us about your devotion to writing?"

Philip stood silently for a moment, then reached for the only response that came to him.

"Our words are like seeds," he began, mimicking Jonathan Ransom Turgeon. He sought out Madame deBasséville's table and caught her eyes twinkling in amusement.

"Our thoughts carry them into a garden, and it is there that the seeds are sown," he continued. He looked about the room, then to Floquet's table, where the actor sat with his hand under his chin and a finger on his cheek in an expression of feigned admiration.

"Our seeds, which is to say, our words, are nurtured with punctuation," Philip said and drew back to take in other faces, seemingly captivated by his absurd remarks.

At this point, it was time to toss in a bit of Turgeon's dull humor.

"Of course, in some areas of L'Orient, particularly down by the harbor, our seeds sprout into weeds," Philip said. The crowd laughed heartily and only quieted down after many of them had traded their own jests with each other.

Warming to the response, Philip set off on his own.

"Now you might say to yourselves that a writer has all of the responsibility for the garden," he said. "But this is not true, for it is the forces of nature that do the real work.

"The writer merely lays out the design with which the garden may grow. But then, he must sit back and allow the actors to make his work bloom. It is these forces of nature who are the *sine qua non* in the garden. And now, may I present to you, Madame Giselle deBasséville, for she is the sun, and Monsieur Jean-François Floquet, who is the rain."

The audience roared and lifted their hands high to applaud.

Madame deBasséville arrived at the platform first, and Philip bowed to kiss her offered hand. "If that dreadful Turgeon had your way with words, he would have had me," she whispered, and the young man blushed deeply.

Floquet arrived a moment later and waved to the crowd with both hands above his head. He also bowed to kiss Madame deBasséville's hand, then turned to Philip and hissed, "Why was I not the sun?" He turned back to the crowd, smiling broadly, then dropped his head humbly before taking one hand from each of his friends to lift in triumph.

"Your speech was quaint, Philippe. You really do have a fertile mind," he said, then dismissed him back to his table.

With the citizens of L'Orient quiet once again, Floquet began his address, using Madame deBasséville only as a prop for his comments. She smiled warmly and remained behind him as he spoke, and Philip suspected she wished to push him from behind so that he would fall from the platform.

Soon after the event concluded with Floquet's final remarks, Philip found himself surrounded by a strange collection of people who professed to be either admirers of his work or budding writers themselves.

His eyes searched for Madame deBasséville, who had been joined by the ladies of L'Orient, interrogating her about the latest gossip and fashion from Paris. He smiled when he caught her eye, but she returned a look of concern that told him that she likewise had learned nothing of importance.

He quickly glanced in the other direction and spotted Floquet lounging back in his chair to strike a manly pose with a cigar, nodding knowingly several times as if he understood the discussion at his table.

If it had been Paris, the night would have continued for hours, but it was time for the festivities to wind down in L'Orient. Philip and Madame deBasséville moved with the mayor toward the entrance of the hall in an attempt to salvage something from the evening.

They finally spotted Floquet striding toward them in the company of some of the same military officers with whom he had been seated.

"My God, what a fool," Madame deBasséville said quietly to Philip. "He will begin to wear gold braid on his coats now and expect to be called General Floquet."

"Do you think he could make sense of what was said at that table?" Philip asked hopefully.

She looked back at him skeptically. "Can you be serious? You know his limitations."

"Giselle! Philippe!" Floquet exclaimed as if he hadn't seen them in weeks. "I shall bid you good night, for I have been invited to the gaming tables. But we shall see each other in the morning and discuss our ... " he said, with a dramatic pause, "endeavor."

He exited without a chance of resurrecting their plan, his head thrown back in wild laughter as he disappeared through the doors and into the night.

Philip returned to his room and lay in bed staring at the dancing shadows on the ceiling as the lamp's dimmed light flickered. The more he considered the evening's events, the angrier he became with Floquet, and he imagined the nonsense that would flow from the actor's mouth the next morning. Everything was theater to him, and now he was portraying a spy.

Too furious to sleep, he climbed from the bed and pulled out his travel bag to check and recheck its contents. Tomorrow was the performance, but he had not even bothered to ask Madame deBasséville what she and Floquet had prepared for the audience. All he could think about now was how to find his way out of France.

The delays, the excuses, the fears, the wandering mind that could not crystallize a plan, none of that mattered any longer. He would be compelled to step into the darkness and learn his fate, either as a man who would make a difference, or one who would be no more.

15. THE ENDEAVOR'S FINAL ACT

Philip was still in a foul mood the next morning when he heard Floquet's voice in the hallway outside his room. Next came the familiar cackle, followed by what sounded like a witty closing remark and then footsteps leading away.

A loud knock came a short time later.

"Philippe, come quickly," Floquet ordered as he flung open the door and gestured for Philip to follow him to his own room. At the window, the actor pointed down to an empty carriage in the street at the front of the hotel.

"Very nice," Philip said. "Is that our means of travel today?"

"No, look," Floquet said in exasperation.

A portly figure in blue emerged at last from the hotel's entrance, the gold epaulets on his shoulders visible from the window above. His large bicorn hat, festooned with ostrich feathers, dipped as he stepped into the carriage.

"Very nice, I hope you had an entertaining evening," Philip said flatly.

"Oh, the man was a complete bore, although the feeling was in no way mutual," Floquet said devilishly.

Philip, already annoyed with the actor, for the first time felt revulsion toward him, as the conflicting images of Floquet courting the affections of both men and women appeared in his mind.

"I am pleased that you are able to continue your escapades, although it might have been more beneficial for me to sit at your table last evening," he said sarcastically. "I might have understood what was said."

"Philippe, are you angry with me?" Floquet asked in surprise but received no response. "Well, I believe that may subside when you hear what I have learned."

"What is that?"

"Oh, what am I thinking? Giselle must join us!" he crowed. "She can't be expected to absorb everything, of course, but I believe she might enjoy some of my techniques."

Madame deBasséville entered the room a short time later in no better mood than Philip. Floquet had the two of them sit while he stood to spin his tale, beginning with the table talk at the reception.

When she responded acidly to his first piece of information, Floquet was taken aback.

"Why, Giselle, I have only just begun my report. But never mind that, let me tell you what I have learned from General Cheaulier, who departed from my room not ten minutes ago."

"The man who just left?" Philip interrupted.

"Why, yes, of course."

"That was an admiral, not a general."

"Admiral, general, it makes little difference," Floquet said nonchalantly.

Philip covered his face with his hands.

"You idiot!" Madame deBasséville snarled, then unleashed a string of oaths that shocked Philip.

"That is so unnecessary, Giselle," Floquet resumed. "The point is *what* I have learned."

"What can you have learned when you fail to even discern the difference between a general and an admiral?" she asked, then arrived at the point of her anger. "You knew the plan was for me to take the lead last night. If any information was to be learned through intimate conversation, it was to have been learned by me!"

"Oh, so that is the problem, as if that had not been clear enough before," Floquet shot back. "Philippe and I are trying to save our nation from the ravages of Napoleon, while you are more concerned with whose head you can turn as you enter the room."

She unleashed a new torrent of curses, then added nastily, "What would you know of Napoleon? I have shared a bed with one of his generals while you have been prancing about with doormen and dowagers."

Floquet was wounded by this cut and turned away in embarrassment. "I am sorry, Philippe, Giselle is correct," he muttered at last. "You must forgive me, for perhaps I am an idiot."

Philip sensed that the actor might be near a breakdown.

"Jean-François, we are in this together," he said quietly. "However, you must remember that we had made plans, and they have been altered. So now we will fortify ourselves and continue, is that not right, Giselle?"

Her clenched teeth began to loosen, and at last she sighed. "Yes, of course. Jean-François, we are all very concerned with this endeavor, and you were trying your best to help," she said. "There is nothing to forgive."

Floquet straightened his coat and regained his confident posture. "Very well," he began. "This was no easy task, for the man insisted upon discussing his views on Voltaire. After that, he began to expound upon the theater. Merciful God, such a windbag."

Philip pulled out his watch and noted that it was after 9 o'clock. The three of them were to be at the theater by 6 o'clock that evening, with the performance at 7:30 and socializing afterward. He fought a feeling of panic as he pondered how quickly and smoothly everything needed to transpire, both for the endeavor and for his departure from L'Orient. Then there was the matter of hiring a boat to carry him out to a British naval vessel in the Bay of Biscay.

Floquet continued. "… and I said to him, 'Well, that is all well and good, but if the play were to end there, it would no longer be a tragedy, would it?' This stopped him in his tracks, and from there I began to cast my nets, if you get my meaning."

Philip imagined himself ridiculously stumbling about in a dark, sinister waterfront tavern, no better equipped to succeed than Floquet had been with Admiral Cheaulier. Whom would he approach, and what would he ask? *"Pardon me, would you direct me to a smuggler, if you please?"*

"… I hoped at this point to keep him interested in the conversation, and yet I felt that it might be good to raise his level of discomfort," Floquet went on.

"Discomfort? What on Earth are you talking about?" Madame deBasséville interrupted.

"Yes, discomfort, that is precisely the word I intend. For at that point, I am thinking that he might let down his guard. Do you see now?"

Philip paid little attention to either of them as he continued to plot his escape from L'Orient.

"… and I said to him, 'Laurent,' for I thought the use of his first name would add to his discomfort, he being someone who is used to hearing 'Admiral This' and 'Admiral That.'"

"But you thought he was a general," Madame deBasséville interrupted again.

"Must we cover that ground again? I am trying to tell the story, and my ignorance of these insignificant military ranks has no bearing here."

She let out a small sigh.

"At any rate, I said to him, 'Laurent, how essential can you be when your ships never leave port because of the English blockade.' Ha-hahhh!"

Philip looked over at Madame deBasséville, who seemed to be listening intently. Floquet noticed Philip's glance and asked, "Are you able to follow this?"

"Yes, of course," he said.

"Well," Floquet resumed, "I remind you that this is a man who has been trying to impress upon me his knowledge of Voltaire and the theater for well over an hour, and here I have unseated him. I have struck at the very heart of his pride with this business about leaving port."

Philip went back to his own thoughts.

"So this is the point where he puffs up his chest and says, as if to prove himself to me, 'I am no landlocked admiral, monsieur,'" Floquet said, then paused to consider his own words. "Well, I suppose you are correct, Philippe, for I now recall that he did say that he was an admiral. How forgetful of me, but then we have all been under such duress during these past days."

"Please arrive at your point," Madame deBasséville said.

"I am about to do just that and, if you please, do not interrupt again," Floquet said.

"At any rate, he says, 'I am no landlocked admiral, monsieur, and I shall be leading my squadron out of Brest within a month.' To which I respond without concern, 'Oh, is that so?'"

She interrupted him yet again. "At last we get to the point. Philippe, are you listening to this?"

Philip, who had been barely paying heed to what was being said, snapped to attention. "What was that?"

Floquet gave him a cross look and then resumed his story. "So I say to him, 'Oh, some rehearsals at sea?' And this fills him further with indignation, and he says to me, 'The squadron will leave Brest, and the action could be quite heavy as we dart up the coast to Boulogne. Then I gave him a look of worry and expressed my best wishes for his safety. But in order to ease my concern, he then added, 'You need not fear, for it is merely a ruse.'"

"A ruse?" Philip asked, now quite interested.

"Exactly," Floquet said, delighted that both members of his audience were at last captivated by his story. "It is designed to draw the English fleet away while the true intention is obscured."

"And what is the true intention?" Madame deBasséville asked.

"Why, to sail a second squadron out of L'Orient, of course!" Floquet announced triumphantly. "To quote Voltaire, 'I have made only one prayer to God, and it is a very short one: O Lord, make my enemies ridiculous. And God granted it.'"

Philip sat up and digested what he had heard before firing questions at Floquet, who, incredibly, had answers.

When would the French ships leave Brest? In about three weeks, as soon as the wind and the tides were favorable. The plan was for the English to see the ships slipping away from Brest and redeploy their frigates from the L'Orient blockade to join the Channel Fleet in giving chase to Admiral Cheaulier.

When would the invasion force leave L'Orient? After receiving word through land signals sent from Brest to L'Orient.

While the admiral had revealed only that a squadron would sail due west out of L'Orient, it was obvious to Philip: The French ships would sail into open water and then set course north for Ireland.

"Jean-François, this is unbelievable news!" cried Philip, rising to his feet and pumping the actor's hand in congratulations.

"*He* has provided something of value?" Madame deBasséville asked in disbelief.

Philip responded affirmatively, and she jumped up to kiss Floquet all about his face.

"Giselle, please do not embarrass our young man," Floquet said.

"You do not embarrass me," Philip said quickly. "I admire your willingness to share your bed in order to help our cause."

"Share a bed with that lout?" Floquet bellowed, crossing his arms in a resentful pose. "My God, what do you perceive me to be?"

"What kind of question is that to ask of Philippe?" Madame deBasséville snapped. "From you, of all people, someone whose affections change with the wind."

Philip's mind was tossed as he sized up Floquet, but as with many such considerations, he surrendered to his own lack of expertise in yet another area — the boudoir.

He returned the conversation to the French plot, obtaining as many details as he could, but Floquet's limitations quickly became apparent again. The actor had understood the gist of the plan because of the cleverness and the subterfuge involved, much as he could follow a story that was told within the dialogue of a play. However, he had no interest in or knowledge of troop numbers, types of vessels and the rest.

It didn't matter. Philip knew that he now had all that he needed.

Floquet and Madame deBasséville at last excused themselves to begin their preparations for the evening's performance.

"And then, Philippe, we will turn our attention to the farce we have planned in Nantes," Floquet said as he was about to leave.

"I am afraid that I must leave after your performance tonight," Philip said.

"You are not returning to Nantes for *Oedipus pro bestia?*" Floquet asked with surprise.

"No, I must get to sea."

"To tell the English?" Madame deBasséville asked.

Philip hesitated before nodding in agreement.

"He only wishes to undo Napoleon's villainy against Ireland," Floquet said. "He is as loyal to France as any man can be."

Later, after the three had adjourned to their own rooms, Philip became aware of a commotion in Floquet's room, where the actor had been noisily ordering a servant to move the large trunk that had been brought along from Nantes.

A loud discussion could be heard later, elevating into an apparent quarrel punctuated by Madame deBasséville's voice.

It was a silent ride to the theater later, with Floquet and Madame deBasséville making it clear that they were preparing themselves for the performance. The mayor greeted them at the entrance, and the actors left Philip and headed backstage.

"Do you know what Monsieur Floquet has prepared?" the mayor asked.

"I am afraid that I do not," Philip replied.

"Are you not his writer?"

Philip checked himself. "Yes, but he was adamant that this was to be a special evening, and his selection was to be a surprise."

The mayor beamed with delight as he took the young man's elbow to lead him to a seat among dignitaries in the theater's front row. A master of ceremonies began the evening with a long-winded speech extolling the honors that had been bestowed upon their guests from Paris. He at last announced that France's most famous actor would perform selected readings and conclude with a scene from Act III of *Hamlet*.

Philip slumped as he thought of having to sit through another French butchery of Shakespeare, but Floquet was a different man during his readings, nothing like the one who had unleashed the ridiculous performance at the National Theater in Paris. This time, he was subdued and contemplative, a contrast to his lack of restraint in life, and when he left for a brief intermission, the audience buzzed in anticipation of his return.

He reappeared in costume, accompanied by Madame deBasséville, to seemingly recreate through *Hamlet* their own personal drama that Philip had witnessed.

"How have you been during these many days, my lord?" asked Madame deBasséville, appearing as Ophelia.

"I humbly thank you for asking, quite well," Floquet replied.

"My lord, I have your gifts that I have longed to return," she said. "Please receive them now."

"I never gave you anything," Floquet said dismissively and turned his back on her.

"My lord, you know very well that you did. And with them the words so sweetly spoken, to make the gifts even more valuable. Take them back. For to the noble mind, such fancy gifts are worth little when the giver proves unkind."

"Ha! And were *you* honest?" Floquet asked as he turned quickly back to face her.

"My lord?"

"Were *you* fair?"

"Whatever do you mean?"

"That if you were honest and fair, then your honesty would allow no discussion of your beauty."

"But my lord, does beauty have any better partner than honesty?"

"Yes, this is true, for the power of beauty will more easily transform honesty from what it is to a poet than the power of honesty can transform beauty to him. This was always a paradox to me, but with time it has become clear," Floquet said, then hesitated. "I *did* love you once."

"Indeed, my lord, you made me believe so," Madame deBasséville said sadly, looking down at the stage.

"But you should not have believed me. I did *not* love you," Floquet contradicted himself emphatically, but without a trace of emotion.

"Then I was the one who was deceived," she said to him and fixed on his eyes with a meaning that Philip alone in the audience understood.

The scene ended with Floquet's exit and Madame deBasséville's final words about the demise of the man she had loved.

The audience was frozen for a moment and then erupted as it rose to its feet. It had been an extraordinary evening, and Philip now knew that Floquet's reputation was no exaggeration. He joined the ovation, beaming with pride that he could call such a man his friend. The actor was no longer the Peacock of Denmark, for he had performed with all measure of greatness.

A large bouquet was presented to Madame deBasséville, whose tears had left streaks on her heavily powdered face, and she smiled down and nodded toward Philip. Floquet returned to the stage and accepted the enthusiastic applause with humility, in what might have been his finest acting of the evening.

The three arrived back at the hotel just before midnight and exchanged embraces and kisses in the courtyard outside as Philip prepared to depart. They stood in a circle holding hands and vowed that what they had done in support of the "endeavor" was important enough to justify placing each of them at risk.

"If there is to be credit given, then you must take the lion's share, Philippe. Giselle and I shall gladly accept our accolades quietly," Floquet said.

"For the love of God, have you no sense?" Madame deBasséville cried. "Why would he want credit? Credit would get him shot!"

"Some day, the world will settle itself, and I promise that everyone will know what you have done," Philip said soothingly, trying to head off a new row.

"But how will we know if you have succeeded?" Floquet asked.

"Permon will know what has occurred," Madame deBasséville said. "He loves to tell such tiresome war stories, but this time I shall make a point to listen."

Finally, Philip announced it was time for him to leave, and he expressed his regrets over missing the performance of *Oedipus pro bestia*.

"Ha-hahhh!" cackled Floquet. "That will be a night to remember!"

Philip fidgeted as he gathered up his belongings into a large oilcloth bag.

"You are trembling," Madame deBasséville said.

"My fears make the first steps difficult," Philip said.

"You told me once that you had affection for someone," she said. "Would you do this thing for her?"

He nodded half-heartedly and tried to picture Eleanor's face.

"Do not think, Philippe, act. Risk everything for the chance to see her again."

She grabbed him by the shoulders and pulled him near to her. "Look into my eyes," she said.

He relaxed a bit as he stared at the actress and at last began to recall some details of Eleanor. The sheen of her black hair pulled back behind her head and tied in a ribbon. The mournful eyes that shone when she had first seen him after his return to London. It was more of a list of her traits than a clear vision, but it would do.

"I can see her," he said.

Madame deBasséville leaned up toward him and kissed him on the lips.

"Do this thing for her. When you are frightened, whisper her name," she said softly and then kissed him on both cheeks. "And do this thing for me as well. Be the man who would risk *everything* for me."

She pulled away, and Philip wondered if he could walk on his wobbly legs. He didn't know if she was acting or not, if what he felt was only a fantasy, but it didn't matter.

"I shall risk everything for you," he responded obediently.

"Merciful God, Giselle, your vanity exceeds even my own," Floquet said as Philip turned away and headed down the dimly lit street toward the water.

16. CROSSCURRENTS

Philip took one last look over his shoulder at the two figures silhouetted in front of the hotel's lamps and thought he saw Madame deBasséville lift a hand one last time before he turned down the street toward the quay.

The spring air was crisp and the sky clear, and his footsteps seemed especially loud on the empty street's paving stones. Lights flickered in the distance from inside weathered buildings along L'Orient's waterfront as he approached two sentries at the beginning of a walkway along the sea wall.

He slowed to gather himself and prepared to show his papers.

"Eleanor," he said to himself, then added, "Giselle."

The soldiers noticed him coming and ended their conversation, and one appeared ready to unsling his musket.

Philip pulled back his shoulders to accentuate his height as he neared the soldiers, waved and cheerfully greeted them.

The men nodded but said nothing, and he continued at a steady pace, the clicking of his footsteps accompanied by the sound of small waves lapping up against the seawall.

He at last arrived at a large, noisy tavern and entered cautiously, took a table toward the back and scanned the collection of roughnecks as he was served fish stew and wine. It didn't take long for him to grow impatient while waiting for an opportunity to present itself.

When the tavern keeper came to take away his bowl, he cleared his throat and asked, "Where do you find a woman around here?"

The man looked at him. "*You* want a woman?"

The months of experiences that had led Philip to feel as if he were becoming a man evaporated in an instant, and he was a boy again. "Yes," he croaked.

The man pointed to a staircase. "Up there. Speak to Claude."

At the top of the stairs stood a one-legged man in a filthy striped shirt with a cudgel in his hand, and he pointed to a doorway at the end of the hall.

Philip took in the reek of spilled wine and perfumed water as he pushed aside the curtain to the room and took a seat on the bed to wait. Several minutes later, a young woman entered and began to untie her bodice. "Please, sit beside me," he said, holding up a hand to stop her. "I only wish to talk."

She shrugged. "You still will pay me?"

He nodded, and she sat, eyeing him carefully. "Tell me what is wrong," she said and began to stroke his hair.

"No, I want to ask you a few questions."

"About how I became a whore? Are you a priest?"

"No, I just have some questions."

At that point, she insisted that they discuss her fee and requested five francs, which Philip considered a bargain if he found what he was seeking. Still, he had never before struck a deal with a tavern prostitute, and he suspected the price was exorbitant.

"What about two?" he asked.

She accepted quickly, and he realized he still must have overpaid.

"I need to get to sea," he said. "Can you point me toward a smuggler with whom I might travel?"

"Where are you going? I know a captain who is making a run to America for sugar."

"I just need to put out to sea, so the destination is of no concern to me," he said.

"Then why not go out on a fishing boat?" she asked. "The crew could put you ashore somewhere along the coast, if that is your intent, so long as the distance is not too great."

He couldn't explain his situation any further, so he accepted her advice and gave her another franc when she took him to the top of the stairs and pointed to a fat, bearded man slumped in a chair at a table where several heads rested face down.

"That is Bouilly. Any smart fisherman would be asleep now, instead of drinking, but I doubt you are looking for a smart man," she said.

He thanked her and as he began to head down the stairs, she grabbed his arm.

"Are you a thief?" she whispered.

He said nothing.

"It is all the same to me," she said. "You look more like a priest."

Philip approached the table and dropped his bag on the floor.

Bouilly turned his head slowly toward him, his bulging eyes red and wet as he struggled to focus on the young man standing before him.

"You are Captain Bouilly?"

The man straightened in his chair, belched and nodded to acknowledge that he was.

"I am seeking to go out with a fishing boat in the morning, and I shall pay," Philip said, while wondering if the captain was capable of making sense of even this simple arrangement.

"Yes, my *Brigide* will take you," Bouilly finally said and provided slurred instructions on how to find his lugger before dawn.

Philip checked his watch and took a room at the tavern for a few hours of sleep before he departed.

He pushed the bed up against the door so that no one could enter without waking him, then reached into the oilcloth bag and removed the pistols he had taken from the bodies of Don Martin and his henchman. He primed both and shoved them inside his coat pockets, then took the printer's pinch and stuck it in the bed frame so he could reach for it in the night, if necessary.

He lay down and stared at the ceiling, leaving a candle burning so he could occasionally check his watch while he spent the night in a familiar state — alone, confused and afraid. A thought occurred, followed by another: This would be his last night in France, or perhaps his last night on Earth.

Just after 4 o'clock, he paid a boatman to row him to a large lugger identified in flaking paint as the *Brigide.* Not a soul was awake when he tossed his bag over the side, even though bells rang, feet scrambled on planks and voices called out from other boats along the anchorage in L'Orient harbor.

Philip snuggled up against a rail and waited patiently in the chilly morning air as the *Brigide* slept on, gently tossing in the water. A hatch finally opened well after 5 o'clock, and a man emerged on deck, scratching his crotch and then his stomach. He stepped back in surprise upon spying the young man rising to his feet.

"What are you doing here?" the crewman asked.

"Captain Bouilly has agreed to my passage," Philip said, gripping a pistol inside his pocket.

"Passage?" the man said in a surly tone. "This is a fishing boat."

"Nevertheless, he agreed last night that he would take me out with you today."

"Jesus, that worthless drunkard," the man muttered, shaking his head. He inquired of the price and suddenly became more enthusiastic. "Fine, boy, the tide and wind are on our side."

Other crew members came out from below and began to perform their chores, some of them moving slowly and rubbing their eyes as they prepared to make sail. The stone anchor was lifted in surprisingly quick fashion, considering the crew's unimpressive appearance and that it was acting without guidance from its captain.

Philip introduced himself to the mate, an agreeable younger man named Matthias.

"You are paying, eh?" Matthias said, then added after he heard the price, "Would *you* like to take us out?"

Philip cleared his throat. "I am no seaman. We would end up on the rocks."

"Suit yourself, but with the bargain you have struck, we can go wherever you wish."

"Out to sea, that is all," Philip said, recognizing that, as with the prostitute, he had overpaid for Bouilly's services. He uncocked the pistol in his pocket and removed his hand to take hold of the railing as the boat swung around and headed toward open water.

With the sky lightening behind the boat, Philip took in a deep breath of chilled sea air and looked out onto the dark water ahead. He steadied his legs as the *Brigide* pitched while creeping down an inlet past rows of lime-washed houses rising up the hills and tall naval ships at anchor. Suddenly, the lugger rolled to starboard, causing him to lose his balance and nearly fall.

Matthias laughed as he shifted the tiller. "You were truthful in saying you are no seaman."

"What happened?" Philip asked.

Matthias banged a pipe on the rail to clean out the previous night's residue, shoved in some fresh tobacco with his thumb, and then asked Philip to light it.

"It is the crosscurrents," he said and explained how the swells from the Bay of Biscay bounced off a headland leading to the inlet.

"Sailing out in a boat this size is no easy matter. There is the wind, which you can hold up your finger to gauge, and there are the tides. Both can be understood and overcome, but the crosscurrents are their own master. One minute you think you are sailing out to open water, and then they push you back into the harbor. Another minute you think you are going to be broken on the rocks, and a crosscurrent delivers you to safety."

"What are you supposed to do?" Philip asked.

"You let them do the work until you find the one that will help you. But always you must know that they are the master."

"I understand," Philip said, but only insofar as he knew how capricious forces seemed to control his own life.

Captain Bouilly finally appeared on deck at 8 o'clock and declared it a foul day, but his crew ignored him.

"Who are you?" he asked Philip, prompting Matthias to turn his head to stifle laughter.

"We met in the tavern last night, and you agreed to take me to sea," Philip said.

"And you are paying, yes?" Bouilly said, rubbing his beard and searching for some shred of a memory from the previous night.

"I am paying, yes," Philip said.

Bouilly looked at Matthias for a sign that the deal he had struck was satisfactory, and when the mate nodded, he said, "Matthias is taking you where you wish to go?"

"He is," Philip said. "Out to open water."

Bouilly belched and seemed unconcerned, leaving Philip to conclude that his price must have been much greater than what the crew could have earned by casting its nets this day.

They sailed at a steady pace west by southwest for most of the morning until the coastline disappeared from view. Bouilly announced just after midday that they had gone far enough and instructed the crew to lower sail and cast the nets over the side.

As Philip watched the men at work, he continued to wonder if the captain was taking advantage of him. The amount of money mattered little, since it was not his own, but he resented that something about his countenance allowed others to view him as someone who could be cheated easily.

Bouilly sidled up to him with an expression on his face that was difficult to read.

"We are where you want to be," he said. "We might as well fish, so long as we are here."

Philip found Matthias and asked him if they would encounter other ships.

"Are you looking for an English ship?" he asked and caught the surprise on Philip's face. "Then we are where we need to be."

"How do you know I am looking for an English ship?" Philip asked.

"One of the men said many English were caught in France when the war resumed," Matthias said.

"You think I am English?" Philip said.

"It makes no difference," the seaman said casually. "We sell fish to the English captains."

Time passed slowly but pleasantly for several hours as the crew sat back and worked their nets. Bouilly spent most of the time leaning against the tiller with a pained expression, but after 2 o'clock, he began to grow agitated, and shortly thereafter the tops of masts appeared to the west.

"Coming our way?" Philip asked.

"No, headed southwest," Bouilly said.

"What type of ship is it?"

"Probably British. She wants to avoid being caught on a lee shore."

Philip hesitated, since his nautical knowledge was limited, and then asked for an explanation.

"The wind has changed," Bouilly said. "If she stayed on her previous course, her crew would be forced to spend the night in L'Orient."

"Can we follow?" Philip asked.

Bouilly spat over the side. "No, we will head back to port," he said and pointed toward a line of clouds along the northwest horizon foretelling that a squall was on the way.

"We must not go in," Philip said quickly. "I shall pay you double our bargain."

The captain sized him up and spat again. "I agree to stay out, but I cannot chase an English ship. We are too slow."

The crew nervously watched the clouds coming toward them as they continued to fish. When the first gust of cold air blew across the deck, several men crossed themselves, then looked back with irritation at their captain.

Bouilly impressed Philip with his seamanship as he put the bow into the wind, and by nightfall the wind had slackened as the rain arrived. The crew members disappeared down into the hold to be fed, and Matthias handed him a tarp to cover himself as he remained on deck. The wind strengthened again as the night wore on, and the boat began to heave and roll clumsily, as waves occasionally washed over the deck.

"Eleanor, Giselle," Philip whispered through his chattering teeth.

The storm had passed by the next morning, and the crew's mood improved with the realization that they had survived the hazards of the previous night and that their pay had been doubled. But as the second day dragged on, they grew restless again as they became aware that the English ship that Philip was seeking must have been blown far off course.

In the late afternoon, Bouilly announced that they were headed back to L'Orient and could not be dissuaded by the offer of payment for a third day.

"I would stay out, but the men have decided that you are bad luck," the captain said.

"We must remain at sea," Philip insisted.

"I told you, no more," the captain said and began issuing orders to make sail.

Philip pulled the pistols from his pockets.

"I am sorry, but I cannot allow you to return to port," he said.

Bouilly looked at him in disbelief. "What do you mean by this? You must have shit for brains, boy!"

Philip pressed his point by lifting the pistol and aiming at the captain's face. "Captain, I say again that I am sorry, but we must remain at sea until we find a British ship."

Matthias and the other crew members gathered behind their captain, but Philip quickly pointed the second pistol toward them.

"I apologize for drawing these weapons, but you surely see how desperate I am," he said.

Bouilly unleashed new insults, along with a vulgar gesture, but to Philip's surprise, the crew seem amused by the situation.

Matthias stepped forward with a hand raised.

"Be careful with those pistols," he said. "We will go along with you, and you do not need to shoot anyone. You will pay for a third day, yes?"

"You have my word," Philip said.

"What good is your stinking word?" Bouilly bawled. "You have a gun pointed at my head! If I get the chance, you will go over the side and swim home."

Philip waved the pistol again at the captain, who raised his hands to show he wanted no violence and then disappeared down the hatch. When he returned near sundown, it was apparent that he had spent his time below with a bottle or two of wine. Glassy, red eyes shone from his weathered face as he popped out to look over the deck. When he saw Philip, he appeared to remember why he had gone down to begin with and unleashed a new string of oaths before turning to speak to his mate.

Matthias approached, squatting about ten feet away so as not to pose a threat.

"You are willing to pay for us to continue?" he asked again.

"I said that I would," Philip said, growing increasingly tired and agitated.

"Bouilly wants to get back even more now, because his wine supply is running short, but the rest of us are agreeable, so long as you pay and the weather is favorable."

"I shall pay," Philip repeated. "I apologize for my actions, but I must find a British ship."

"While the captain has become difficult, the rest of us are used to being out to sea for days at a time," Matthias said. "The English pay well for our fish because their men tire of salt beef and moldy biscuits, so this will work well for us. But I warn you, Bouilly has a vicious temper when he is denied his drink."

Philip's outlook grew ever bleaker as the day wore on. When the sun began to drop below the horizon, he made his decision.

"Drop sail and then everyone go below!" he shouted at Bouilly, pointing the pistol to emphasize his command.

The crew suddenly was less sympathetic and grumbled as they rigged a sea anchor before going down the hatchway. When the last head disappeared below, Philip walked over and looked down to see if anyone was left on the steps.

He quietly closed the hatch and pushed an oar under the railing to jam it tight.

It took several moments before the crew noticed.

Bouilly's voice could be heard bellowing.

"And what happens if there is a storm?" he shouted, while other muffled voices carried up through the deck, but Philip chose not to respond.

An hour later, Matthias called quietly through the hatch and told him that he had sacrificed the goodwill of the crew.

"I am sorry, Matthias," Philip said. "I feared I would fall asleep during the night, and nothing can be left to chance."

There was silence for a moment, and then Matthias said, "If the weather becomes rough, you will let us out immediately, yes?"

"I have no desire to go down with this boat," Philip told him.

"Eleanor, Giselle," he whispered before nodding off.

Fortunately, mild weather lasted through the night, and he awoke to the sound of small waves lapping against the hull. Checking the priming in the pistols to be certain the powder was dry, he returned one to his pocket and kept the other in his right hand as he released the crew.

Bouilly finally appeared after 11 o'clock, and his appearance made it clear that he at last had exhausted the supply of drink in his cabin. His skin had a greyish cast, and his eyes, while red as always, also appeared to express great pain coming from either his head or his gut.

"You shit brain," he snarled at Philip. "I shall have your head if you drop that pistol. Remember that."

"Captain, I apologize, but you must be able to see my position. You will be compensated for your trouble. But I warn you, I have checked my pistols this morning, and my powder is dry."

Bouilly hacked, then spit a disgusting glob that just missed Philip's feet.

The *Brigide* continued to drift until the wind began to freshen from the southwest in midafternoon.

"Now we will be forced back to port," Bouilly said, rubbing his hands together.

Philip cocked his pistol and moved toward him quickly. The slow-witted captain was stunned by the sudden move, allowing himself to be grabbed, turned and forced to the deck with a pistol's barrel planted behind his right ear.

"You will order the crew to take us out farther," Philip said coldly.

"Jesus, Mary and Joseph!" Bouilly bellowed at the crew. "Raise the sheets and take us west!"

Philip released him and took a seat on the deck as the lugger tacked on a westward course. He rubbed his eyes and realized that he hadn't eaten or slept soundly since commandeering the boat and considered how he had nearly blown apart a man's head in cold blood.

"The Lord is my shepherd, I shall not want ..." he began.

"Hey, you stinking bastard!" Bouilly suddenly shouted, pointing toward the horizon. "There is your ship, now pay us!"

Philip could see nothing and suspected a trick as the captain pointed to an empty spot on the Earth's rim. But the drunkard's eyes could see what he could not, and within an hour the bow of a British frigate could easily be seen cutting through the sea toward them.

Philip fired a pistol into the air as the ship approached, and it dropped sail. When it had pulled to within 100 yards, a lieutenant hung off a ratline with a speaking trumpet and called, "What boat there?"

Philip gave his silent thanks at the sound of an English voice and made his way to the *Brigide*'s bowsprit, grabbing a line and summoning all of his concentration to shout in English: "Sir! This is the French fishing boat *Brigide*! I beg your assistance! I am a British army officer!"

"You say that you are a British officer?" the naval lieutenant asked when the frigate was close enough to forgo the speaking trumpet.

"Yes, I was caught in France when war resumed," Philip said, choosing to provide no more detail until he was in a secure location.

"You are English?" Bouilly asked, but Philip ignored the sound of the French voice behind him.

"We are sending a boat over for you," the lieutenant said.

Philip was smiling broadly and waving when he was hit across the back of the neck by a club swung by the irate captain of the *Brigide*.

"You English turd!" Bouilly yelled as Philip fell off the boat's side and into the water.

17. Deliberations at Sea

At sea, spring of 1803

Philip flapped his arms in the water long enough to stay afloat until an oar struck him in the head. Two seamen pulled him by the collar and lifted him into the frigate's jolly boat, where he collapsed, took a few deep breaths and then hung his head over the side and retched.

Cheering rang out from the naval vessel above. "That's the army for you, needing the navy's help again!" a voice called, and laughter filled the air.

"Silence!" another voice boomed.

Philip was rowed to *HMS Valiant* and helped up the side until he gathered enough strength and dignity to climb the final feet unassisted and onto the deck to present himself.

"First Lieutenant William Edney at your service," the waiting officer replied. "The captain sends his compliments, and he would be pleased to see you in his cabin, if you are fit."

Philip felt the knot on his forehead where the oar had struck him, and he removed his hand to see a smear of blood on his fingers. He shook himself to regain his senses and asked if his bag could be retrieved from the deck of the *Brigide*.

"That should be easy enough," Edney said, handing him a handkerchief for his wound.

A midshipman led the dripping, coughing visitor down a stairway and toward a door where a red-coated marine responded to their appearance by pounding the butt of his musket into the floorboards and snapping to attention.

"Might I request that we meet alone?" Philip asked after he was announced to the captain, and the midshipman left, closing the door behind him.

Captain David Terwillerger sat behind a sturdy oak table with charts and papers before him, his work interrupted by the visitor. He rose slightly from his seat to take note of the drips of seawater around

Philip's feet, then sat down again heavily, with a slight frown on his face.

"I am Lieutenant Philip Collier, recently of the 33rd Regiment of Foot, and I am in possession of important information."

"You're an *army* lieutenant," said Terwillerger, a professional-looking seaman with thinning hair and wrinkles around his eyes from years on deck. "All right then, Lieutenant Collier, what is your information?"

"It is a long and difficult explanation, but I have uncovered French plans to invade Ireland and provoke rebellion."

"Is that so?" There was a long pause as Terwillerger pushed his work to the sides of the table top to clear a spot directly in front of himself.

The cabin's air was stuffy, and Philip was again feeling ill. "Captain …" he got out before bending over to retch. "I'm sorry, sir, it's the seawater I swallowed, you see …"

"Corporal!" Terwillerger called to the marine at the door, and the redcoat appeared with the midshipman behind him. They both looked at Philip, then the mess on the planks, and then at the captain.

"Mr. Smythe," he said to the midshipman. "You are to put together a party to clean this immediately."

"I am to put together a party for cleaning," Smythe repeated slowly, then added, "immediately." However, he failed to move immediately and only did so after the captain waved him away with a disgusted look.

"What good is it to repeat the order, if you don't act upon it?" Captain Terwillerger asked under his breath, then addressed Philip as if an explanation were in order. "Thomas Smythe has connections in the Admiralty, so I am stuck with him."

The marine corporal, on his own initiative, pulled up a chair for Philip to sit before the captain.

Smythe then returned with six men, clearly more than enough for the job, and they quickly finished their work so that at last the conversation could resume.

"He'll probably make post-captain before Edney," Terwillerger said absently after Smythe had left, then checked himself. "Now, I shall hear what you have to say."

"Sir, would you like me to relay my information in its historical sequence, or should I get to the nub quickly?" Philip asked.

"The beginning is a good place to start, what?" Terwillerger said, chuckling at his own little jest as he poured two glasses of claret.

Philip began his tale by recounting his assignment from Lord Torrington.

"One of Lord Charles' men, eh? I've heard you're a clever lot," the captain said and continued to weigh in with his thoughts as the story progressed.

Philip explained how he entered France posing as an *émigré*.

"Hmmm, don't believe I've heard of anything quite like that. You're an officer, you say?"

Next came the observation of the preparations near Boulogne for invasion of England, its mention designed to impress Terwillerger with his credentials.

"Splendid work there, splendid."

Philip recounted that through his acquaintance with a Parisian actor, he had met French military officers who had discounted the chances of a successful assault on England.

"A bit unorthodox, and dangerous I should think, but you kept your ears open, and that's all to the good."

Philip then told vaguely how he had happened upon the handbills bound for Ireland and handed his copy to Terwillerger to examine.

"Deuce of a piece of good luck, I must say."

He was then forced to flee Paris with the war's approach, he continued, and accompanied the aforementioned actor to L'Orient to complete his espionage work.

"Seeing it through to the finish, excellent."

Philip explained almost by way of apology that he was uncertain what means Floquet had used to learn details of the plot from Admiral Cheaulier, owing to his own confusion over French love matters.

"Oh, I see. Well, I'll reserve judgment on the man."

And finally, there was the escape on the fishing boat and his rescue by the *Valiant*.

"Extraordinary, from start to finish, really," Terwillerger concluded.

Philip had emptied his glass of claret by the time he had finished and was feeling much improved when they arrived on deck. He sheltered his eyes from the sunlight and noticed the pathetic figure of Captain Bouilly under guard with his hands tied behind his back and his head bowed.

Lieutenant Edney stepped forward to report to Terwillerger that Bouilly had struck Philip with a club and nearly killed him.

"We'll give him a trial," Terwillerger said. "Striking a British officer is a capital offense at sea, and I'll make no allowance for the fact that you were not in uniform." Bouilly looked about nervously as the conversation continued, and at last Philip broke in.

"Captain, this man fairly contracted to take me to sea, but a disagreement arose as to how long we would stay away from port. I believe he may not have been entirely in the wrong in wanting to regain command of his boat from me."

"You commandeered his boat?" Terwillerger asked in astonishment.

"What I would take leave to suggest is that Lieutenant Collier is the one who should hang, for piracy, that is," Edney interjected with a smile, then stiffened when his captain gave him a cross look.

Terwillerger rocked on his heels for a moment.

"Sir, I could not have escaped without this man's help, and he is still owed payment for carrying me to you," Philip said.

"I see, then release him," Terwillerger said, ordered his purser to pay the debt and turned to Philip. "Your information is certainly worth the King's coins."

Philip asked to speak to Bouilly, who still looked unsettled as he was being taken to the side of the ship for his departure.

"Listen to me," he said in French, "You could be hanged for striking me, but I convinced them to release you upon the condition that the payment go to Matthias and the crew."

"But it is my boat!" Bouilly protested.

"I can pass along your objections to the frigate's captain, if you would prefer, but look around you. There is no shortage of rope for a noose."

"No, I agree!"

Philip called out the terms to Matthias and the rest of the *Brigide* crew, and they cheered heartily.

Philip was assigned to a cabin in the *Valiant*, where he changed his clothing and rested as he waited to join Captain Terwillerger and his officers for dinner. As he lay swinging in a hammock, he felt completely at ease for the first time in a year and began to imagine the roomful of admiring navy men who would greet him at the captain's table that evening. However, Terwillerger barely referred to Philip's actions in France during his remarks at dinner, and while he used glowing terms to describe the young man's bravery in escaping enemy soil, he revealed nothing of what had been reported earlier about L'Orient and the invasion of Ireland.

The officers at the table leaned in to hear their guest's commentary on the conditions in France and the morale of the enemy, and he obliged them by telling them mostly what he thought they wanted to hear. When he was finished, Terwillerger announced that the frigate would deliver their guest to Admiral Kenwyn Voss aboard his flagship, *HMS Mercury*.

The men around the table exchanged side glances to acknowledge that they had been correct in suspecting that something was afoot when the *Valiant* had changed course earlier.

"The admiral might have his own take on your story, owing to the fact that he's Cornish," Terwillerger said of Voss, and the officers nodded knowingly.

Philip had no idea what that implied and instead turned his attention to the meal, which included a platter of recently butchered beef and onions. The officers thanked their captain for his generous dinner invitation before attacking their plates, and the expressions of gratitude increased as bottles of claret were opened. Two of the younger midshipmen became stone-faced drunk and began to question Philip regarding details of his career.

"Have you seen much action?" one of them asked.

"Only a little in India, but nothing really to speak of," he replied.

"Well, you might be of use in a scrap," the midshipman said.

"I would hope to be," Philip said in an attempt to convey manly modesty, though in truth he wished to be set down on the shores of England without seeing any action at sea.

On the morning of his third day aboard the *Valiant*, he was awakened in his cabin with the news that they had joined the Channel Fleet off the northwest tip of France. He sprung to the deck, shading his eyes to find the sea around them filled with ships, and walked over to stand beside Lieutenant Edney to take in the majesty of the Royal Navy. Signal flags raced up and down the lines, while Midshipman Smythe slowly scratched out the message on a tablet before at last announcing that the captain was summoned to the *Mercury*.

Philip tried to mimic Terwillerger's stoic expression as they were rowed toward the admiral's flagship. The *Valiant*'s seamen were dressed smartly for the short trip to Voss' three-decker and stuck to business with crisp oar strokes and no chatter, obviously handpicked men who would do nothing to discredit the frigate and her captain.

A boat ferrying another captain drew within a half-cable's length away, and the *Valiant*'s coxswain said in a low, harsh voice, "Look smart now, you whoresons!" The oars dipped and rose with increased precision, barely causing a splash as they pulled with even more power and speed.

Philip was impressed and smiled at Terwillerger, who continued to stare ahead without expression. His admiration for naval fanfare increased as the *Mercury's* boatswain piped aboard the visitors, and they passed the silent and disciplined lines of the large ship's assembled company.

Admiral Voss' cabin was the size of a drawing room in a fine London home, although the table was inadequate in size to handle the assembled group of more than a dozen ships' captains. Several tried to nudge their way forward so that they could have an elbow at the table, but others gave up and simply pulled their chairs to the rear or stood.

Terwillerger alone was assigned a particular spot at the table, which he took matter-of-factly, and pointed to a chair beside him for Philip. The captain retold the story of the planned French invasion of Ireland, embellishing a bit on the younger man's accomplishments to provide an altogether flattering presentation.

Voss remained silent throughout, as his captains uttered "admirable," "impressive" and other appropriate remarks. When Philip gave his account, the admiral seemed to ignore everything except insofar as it pertained to naval operations. Voss pulled out a chart of the inlet to L'Orient's harbor and asked about the placement of French ships.

Philip did his best to point out where warships had been anchored, their disposition to merchant and fishing vessels, and the location of the troop encampment. "The larger vessels are nearest to the mouth of the harbor," he said. "I would assume that owes to the shallower water as one proceeds further in."

"You've done fine work, Lieutenant Collier," Voss complimented him. "Now, since you sailed out of that harbor, is there anything worth mentioning?"

Philip recalled the explanation of the crosscurrents and pointed to the spot where the water seemed to move with a mind of its own.

"If I may, sir, I would point out that the fishermen who took me out said to ride the currents where they took you, and not to fight them," he said. "I am not a seaman and do not pretend to know anything of a nautical nature, but I remember those instructions."

"Understood, lieutenant, and I thank you. Now, gentlemen, let's crack this nut," Voss said, turning to his captains. He unrolled another chart, weighing down the corners with an ink bottle, a table clock and two bottles of wine.

Philip could barely distinguish the features on the map, with depths, shoals and the like noted along the coastlines. Neither did he grasp much of the naval jargon, although he could at least follow that there were two schools of thought.

Voss said nothing as the sides made their cases. The first plan was put forth by a one-eyed captain who advocated sending every available ship straight into L'Orient harbor with guns blazing, blasting the French vessels as they lay at anchor. He received little support for his plan, which was short on subtlety and whose success was threatened by gun emplacements at the mouth of the inlet.

"I ain't about to piss down my breeches over some damn Frog fort," he said in a gravelly voice.

"Well, sir, I hope you are not implying that my objections are an indication of cowardice," one of his opponents countered angrily.

"Gentlemen, I will not tolerate this sort of confrontational approach," Voss interjected. "Any man who cannot remain civil in our discussion will return to his ship and simply await my orders."

"My tongue bested my brain, admiral," the one-eyed captain said in apology.

The second plan involved waiting off the coast until the French ships came out, then swooping down to engage them.

There ensued a long and complicated discussion of winds, tides and uncharted waters that made Philip drowsy, and he began to look over Voss' cabin for things of interest. He found a bookcase and searched for titles he recognized, but most of the covers bore names of scientific or geographic journals, so he turned his attention to a small portrait of a woman that had been nailed to a beam. It seemed that the woman's eyes were looking at him, so he tilted his head to see if the effect continued. He then noticed that the woman was quite homely and appeared to be cross-eyed, and he thought she had a face that would keep a man at sea.

Voss' voice suddenly intruded on his thoughts. "Lieutenant Collier, do you disagree with that?"

"No, admiral, I do not disagree," Philip said quickly.

What he had not disagreed with was unclear at first, but he soon realized that it was to the assertion that the time to act was short.

According to the chronology that Admiral Cheaulier had set out to Floquet, the French operation could begin in a little more than a fortnight. Meanwhile, Voss made the point that the uncertainties of weather and the time-killing machinations of the Royal Navy would not allow for more ships to be added to his command.

"The reduction of the fleet during peace has left us shorthanded and unable to accomplish everything we'd want," Voss said and heard bitter agreement from his captains.

"Those poxy bastards in London ..." one officer began but stopped when Voss gave him a stern look.

The British admiral had to consider whether his force was large enough to take on the French fleet coming out of Brest — Admiral Cheaulier's ruse to pull the British away from L'Orient — and still be able to destroy the invasion squadron that would follow out of L'Orient.

It was one or the other, Voss said, and total success for the task at hand — preventing the French from reaching Ireland — was the only acceptable outcome.

That led him to a third plan, which was to leave the strength of the fleet near Brest to allow for a major engagement should Cheaulier come out, but detach a squadron of five ships to L'Orient, where the captains would send in marines to wreak havoc in the harbor and prevent the French force from leaving.

"Gentlemen, we must keep our focus on protecting Ireland and nothing else," Voss said. "I admit the prize money is tempting should we engage the enemy outside both Brest and L'Orient. Why, we could all retire to the countryside with what we could make with our captures."

Philip noted the grim faces at the table. The army looked with envy upon the navy's system of selling off captured enemy vessels and doling out the proceeds to the crews. The captains, of course, received the lion's share, but the admiral also would receive a large piece of any prize captured by ships under his command. Voss potentially was throwing away thousands of pounds for himself by sending a raiding party into L'Orient harbor rather than engaging with the French in the open sea.

Nevertheless, Voss announced his selection of the third plan and immediately sensed that it was not the favorite. "Blake," he said to the one-eyed captain, "you have never turned down a chance for action. Do I have your support for this last proposal?"

Blake's mouth was set, but he nodded his reluctant agreement.

"I thank you, Captain Blake, and you may remain with me outside Brest, should Admiral Cheaulier and his fleet come out to meet us," Voss said.

"My gunners'll take his bloody head off," Blake growled, his mood suddenly improved by the knowledge that he would stand the best chance of seeing a battle at sea.

"Terwillerger, you will command the operation at L'Orient," Voss said next. "You know those waters best, and it was you who brought this matter to my attention."

"I am honored, admiral," Terwillerger said humbly. "I request that Lieutenant Collier be allowed to accompany me. He knows of these crosscurrents in the inlet, so his help would be invaluable."

All heads turned to face Philip.

"Lieutenant Collier has faced perilous duty for a year now and deserves to return to British soil, rather than to go gallivanting about on the ocean with a pack of cutthroat seamen," Voss said with a smile. "But I shall put the question to him."

"I would be honored to accompany Captain Terwillerger," Philip said after a slight pause. "I wish to see Boney's insidious plot foiled."

Later that night back aboard the *Valiant*, he swung in his hammock and managed to concoct several clever responses that might have allowed him to proceed to England without delay. He might have said that he possessed too much valuable information to risk being lost at sea. Or that he was under personal orders from Lord Torrington and would need permission before acting under the Navy's command. Or that his health was failing and that the sea air worsened the condition.

If only one of them had popped into his head at the right moment, he could have avoided action, but now any mention of such excuses would hint of cowardice. He had no choice in the matter, for he was going to war.

18. Clear for Action

Philip was sorting through his bag when a tap came on the frame of his cabin. He quickly put away the purse stuffed with money as the curtain was drawn back and Lieutenant Edney entered.

"I have splendid news," Edney said, his face aglow. "I am to command the lead boat, and you will accompany me."

"I couldn't be happier for you," Philip said, aghast that he himself would be in the lead boat.

Edney looked down at the contents of the bag spread out on the planks.

"Say, why would a lubber such as yourself have a marlinspike?" he asked.

"This?" Philip asked, picking up the printer's pinch. "Why, it's a tool used in a print shop."

"I'll be damned, a bit smaller than a spike, but very much the same," Edney said.

"The hands use theirs for getting the knots out of rope, untangling wires and such," he went on. "Yours is smaller, but it could do the same work, I believe. You have worked in a print shop?"

Philip suspected that like most officers, Edney was a gentleman from a wealthy family and had never known work.

"Yes, I have labored," Philip replied curtly.

A few years earlier he might have tried to disguise his background, but he had abandoned the need to pass himself off as a gentleman. He had ambition and sought wealth, but after a year in France with its notions of merit and advancement, he nearly regretted returning to an aristocratic world in which he would never fit in.

Edney showed no reaction to the comment, however, and took the pinch from Philip to examine it.

"I have seen the hands use these as weapons," he said. "Deep, painful wounds without a lot of bleeding. Usually not fatal unless they're stuck in the right spot, so I suppose that's why the men fight with them. They can go below the waterline to settle their quarrels, and the survivors don't show the signs of the scrap."

"Is that so?" Philip replied absently.

"Nasty things, and you can imagine getting one in an eye, or in the heart or the liver. Why, you'd find a dead body with just a few drops of blood, and you'd be hard-pressed to find the wound. I'd suppose if a man did it right, he could kill someone, and no one would know quite how he died," he said, putting down the pinch. "Dastardly weapon, I must say."

"Quite."

"My, Collier, that's a fancy cane," Edney said next as he picked it up by the elephant's head. "Life in France must have been to your liking."

"It was a gift from a friend," Philip said. "I have never lived better than I did in Paris, at least at times. Of course, it was always while keeping an eye over my shoulder."

"Did you fear arrest?" Edney asked.

"Very much so, if my identity as a British officer was revealed. I used a different name, you see."

"Oh, yes. That's strange for an officer to be in disguise."

"Strange?"

"Well, you would know better than I would regarding the army's rules for such business," Edney said, though with a tone of lingering doubt.

"Yes, it was quite different from anything I had expected," Philip said, missing the implication that his actions might have breached officers' unofficial code of conduct.

He later went up on deck to pass the time and escape the confinement below, taking a spot alone on the quarterdeck so as not to be underfoot. The *Valiant* and the other ships in the squadron had taken six days to return to L'Orient because of foul weather, but the wind had slackened and the skies had become fair.

The delay had mattered little since they had planned to wait for a new moon to provide them cover of darkness for their mission into L'Orient harbor.

He looked out on the waves, choppy but not threatening, and considered if the action ahead would be a test of whether he really had become a man during his time in France. While he wasn't certain of how his performance of the past year would be judged by others, he at last had begun to satisfy himself by facing his fears and acting alone without direction.

His accomplishments might have seemed even more substantial if men no longer called him "boy" when they addressed him, he thought with disgust.

His musings ended with a start as the ship's bell rang out, and he sprinted to the steps leading downward, reaching the captain's cabin for a scheduled meeting just ahead of Edney and Midshipman Smythe.

Terwillerger began his presentation by solemnly noting that the captains of the other four ships in the squadron were laying out their plans to their officers at the very same moment.

Each of the five ships was to contribute a launch and 20 men to the enterprise, along with kegs of gunpowder and other supplies that he listed. The boats would be set down outside the view of the L'Orient's outer fort two hours after sunset and would make their way into the harbor without use of sails, to avoid being seen.

Even though there was a new moon, the crews were to take the further step of darkening their faces with boot polish, and the ships' marines were to remove their white cross belts. The oars were to be wrapped and muzzled to limit the noise, and a flogging was promised to any man who spoke once they were within 1,000 yards of the fort — provided he returned alive. Finally, the officers were ordered to return with as many men as they could, and under no condition were they to endanger their complement of seamen for one or two who might be left behind.

Terwillerger concluded by voicing his regrets that he could not join them, his expression showing that he was sincere.

Philip always had been amazed at the Navy's ingenuity. He had read reports in the *Naval Chronicle* from officers who had pretended that their ships were damaged and close to surrender, then uncovered their cannons and boarded the enemy vessel after it drew near. Naval officers had also frequently led parties on shore to capture forts and destroy enemy supplies, and their reports often were so fantastic as to read like fiction.

The army, by comparison, was slow, clumsy and less adventuresome — and lacking in the glory that accompanied the navy's success.

He was confident that Edney was up to the challenge, but he feared Midshipman Smythe might falter if asked to perform anything beyond his duty to simply assume command if the first lieutenant were incapacitated.

The captain invited Philip and his officers to dinner that night, but only one glass of claret was served to each, and that in a solemn toast to the night's success. Some commanders preferred their men drunk to ease their fears, but Terwillerger said he wanted seamen who had their wits about them. He shook each officer's hand solidly as he bade them good night.

Philip returned to the deck to watch the preparations and was surprised that crew members seemed jovial, apparently pleased to have something to relieve the tedium of the sea. As the sun began to fade into a bank of clouds on the western horizon, Philip closed his eyes for a silent prayer, then returned to his cabin to prepare. He sat down to write to Harriet.

Dearest Sister,

The reason for this missive is that I am about to embark on hazardous duty from which I might not return. It is my hope that you will know my fate before you have opened this letter, so as to avoid the cruelty of learning of my death upon its receipt.

I have been away for so long that in many ways it is difficult any more to feel part of our home. I am filled with fine memories of our childhood, and I apologize to you for the times when I was cross or distracted in your presence.

There should be a considerable sum of money that comes from my account. If you have questions regarding its whereabouts, please inquire with a certain Lord Torrington at Wickham House. I believe he will know how to handle the matter and should feel a debt to you because of my service for him. This sum is for you alone and should help to secure your future as a dowry. You may show this letter to Father to confirm my intentions.

Enclosed is a letter for you to deliver to Eleanor. Perhaps some small portion of your grief over my passing will help to restrain you from breaking the seal.

I pass along my fondest wishes to you. I ask that you also to do the same to our brothers and to Father in the hope that I will be remembered in tender thoughts in the years to come.

Your loving brother, Philip

He then turned to the second letter.

E —

If you receive this, then you will know that I am not returning safely to England's shores. The past year I have been away on hazardous duty, the details of which I was unable to disclose to you. Forgive me for my silence, for I am aware that you must have had questions as to my intentions. I wish you to know that during moments of my greatest fears, you were in my deepest thoughts in ways that I never could have expressed had I been standing before you. I told you once of a desire to know that what I had done was important and that it had made a difference. I rest with that knowledge, but what haunts me during this threatening time is that I shall never be able to say the words that convey my feelings toward you. Be assured that I held you in my highest regard, with the hope that we would share a life together.

— P

He enclosed the second letter sealed within the first, which was addressed to Harriet and fixed to his bag, to be found if he did not return.

Back on deck, he stood alone beside the rail to take one last look out on the final signs of light disappearing on the western horizon. He wondered how his family would react to the word of his death and hoped that the messenger would deliver the news of his demise with embellishment. His name then would be spoken with reverence up and down Folsom Street, and small boys would point to the home where the hero had lived and take turns pretending to be "Lieutenant Collier" when they played their games of war in the street.

"Gentlemen," Terwillerger said, interrupting his reverie. Officers and crewmen came together and dropped their heads as the moment of departure had arrived. Their captain removed his hat and tucked it under his arm before opening a Bible.

"They that war against thee shall be as nothing, and as a thing of nought," he read. "For I the Lord thy God will hold thy right hand, saying unto thee: Fear not, for I will help thee."

He concluded: "In God's name, we undertake this, our duty, and give thanks for the opportunity to once more serve King and Country."

"Amen," the men said in unison.

It was a long row to the harbor of L'Orient, with the *Valiant*'s crew leading the way for the four other boats. Oarsmen pulled slowly and methodically until the war party neared the inlet leading past the fort, which was illuminated by torches burning inside its walls.

"From this point on, we will have complete silence," Edney instructed the men in a quiet, self-assured voice. "A double ration of rum to you when we return, but a flogging to any man who breaks the silence."

The British launches entered the inlet in line, with the *Valiant*'s men continuing to take the lead as they passed the fort. L'Orient's harbor lights finally came into view, and the scene grew more ominous as they caught sight of dozens of French warships rocking at their moorings in the distance.

Edney nudged Philip and whispered, "I believe our boat might have done this job alone. I don't know why this enterprise required one hundred men."

Midshipman Smythe edged in to listen, but Edney said nothing more.

The lieutenant motioned the coxswain to steer to starboard, then pointed to an unlit fishing boat that resembled the *Brigide* as it lay anchored away from the French navy's vessels. The *Valiant*'s boat bumped up against the side, and a second followed a few seconds later.

British sailors and marines piled onto the deck and subdued and gagged two men they found sleeping. Edney led a group down the hatchway and after a few muffled cries and sounds of scuffling, he emerged to declare the vessel secured.

The rest of the boats pulled alongside, and crewmen began to carry aboard barrels of black powder, first to the bow and then below deck. One cask of whale oil was emptied into the hold, and another was spread onto a pile of canvas on the deck. Finally, a group of British seamen passed the gagged French fishing crew over the side and into the launches, while another group raised the anchor to allow the lugger to drift.

Edney gathered the officers from the other launches on the lugger's deck to discuss their plan.

"Do you think the wind would carry us across?" he asked, pointing to the line of French warships that lay at anchor. "That would be the simplest way."

Two of the younger and more nervous officers declared that it would be easy to rig a sail and secure the tiller to let the boat go on its own. But the most senior lieutenant spoke last and gave his opinion that the lugger would have to be rowed at least part way to ensure that it would reach its destination.

"That's it then," Edney said.

Crewmen threw up lines from the launches to secure to the lugger, while Edney had the mainsail raised.

"We shall tow it to within two cables' length, at which point I shall set the boat ablaze from below," he said when their work was finished. "At one cable's length, all boats but mine may cast off their lines and head back to their ships. The *Valiants* will see it in to make sure that the deed is done."

"Don't take it any farther than you need to," the senior officer cautioned Edney. "It doesn't have to be perfect to be successful."

"I appreciate your concern, and I do hope to meet you back in the bay to toast our success."

The other officers shook hands with Edney and wished him well in hushed, solemn voices before climbing back into their boats.

"Do you want me with you?" Philip called up from the *Valiant's* launch, hoping his offer would be refused.

"Nay, the army can't help with this one," Edney replied. "Mister Smythe, please accept assistance and counsel from Lieutenant Collier."

Philip sat hard on the bench as the oarsmen strained to get the lugger quietly moving across the harbor toward the row of French warships.

His watch showed in the faint light from the harbor shore that it was a little after 2 o'clock.

As they pulled nearer, sounds could be heard from some of the French vessels and from the faraway inns along the wharf, but nothing resembled an alarm. They drew to within a cable's length, reaching the most hazardous part of the operation.

When Philip looked back at the lugger under tow to see if Edney had gone below, he became aware of the oarsmen panting from the exertion of pulling the larger vessel's weight.

"Qui êtes vous?" someone suddenly called out, and he whipped his head around to spot a small boat being rowed in a perimeter guarding the warships.

Philip could hear shuffling and whispers from the other British launches, followed by the sounds of hammers being pulled back on muskets, and he wondered if the noise had carried to the Frenchman who had issued the challenge.

"Je posséde des orders de Amiral Cheaulier!" Philip shouted back authoritatively in the direction from which the call in French had come. There was no response, and Philip quietly instructed the six marines in the middle of the boat to point their muskets in the direction of the French boat.

"On my order, one ... " Midshipman Smythe whispered.

"No, we must draw as near as we can," Philip told him.

After two more oar strokes, a French voice again asked who was coming, just as flames from the lugger's hold cast a glow upward to illuminate the single sail that had been raised. The surprise was over, and several enemy voices sounded the alarm.

"Fire!" Philip called, ignoring the fact that Smythe was in command.

The marines' muskets spit fire, followed by less disciplined sporadic shots from the other launches.

"Tell the others to head off now, and we'll take it in," Philip ordered Smythe, as the sounds of footsteps on the decks of the French ships carried across the water.

"Cast off and return to your ships!" Smythe called out in a high-pitched attempt at command, and the other British boats fanned off and away.

The *Valiant*'s men pulled on alone, watching enviously as their fellow tars left them.

"Row as if your lives depended on it, boys!" the coxswain barked, the need for silence gone.

French seamen could be seen scurrying with muskets as the burning lugger advanced toward them, and a shot soon rang out. Just then, the fire spread to the fishing boat's deck and began to rise into the sky, illuminating Edney as he steadfastly manned the tiller.

"Shouldn't we cast off now?" Smythe asked desperately.

"No, Mister Edney will give us the word," Philip said.

More French muskets began to pop, and the balls could be heard whizzing overhead and splashing harmlessly in the water.

"Keep down! The bastards are firing at Mister Edney, but they'll be aiming at us soon enough," Philip told the oarsmen.

The *Valiant*'s marines fired again, clearing the nearest French frigate's rail for a short time while also calling attention to the launch. The musket balls soon began to plunk into the water, and a British sailor shouted out in pain as he was hit.

"Now! Cast off!" Edney finally shouted, and the crewmen on one side raised their oars to allow their mates to complete the turn.

"Jump!" Philip shouted to Edney as they peeled off and away.

"I need to see it in a few more yards!" Edney called back.

"God bless you, sir, and abandon ship!" a crewman yelled.

The launch passed the stern of the lugger as it headed toward the mouth of the harbor, but Edney stood firm at the tiller as he drew closer to the French warship, a black figure alone amidst a hellish wall of flames.

"Sweet Jesus," Philip whispered to himself in admiration of the man's courage.

With the lugger still 50 yards from the nearest French vessel, Edney finally turned and headed toward the rail but disappeared as an explosion tore apart the bow.

The men aboard the launch turned away instantly from the blinding light, and several *Valiant* sailors cried out as their ears were hit by searing pain from the sound of the blast. When they looked back again, they saw the lugger still afloat and plodding toward the French warships as the burning debris from the explosion fell on their decks and ignited.

A second explosion came a moment later, this one from below, lifting a section of burning planks high into the air as the lugger bumped up against a French warship and began to spread its havoc. The crew in the *Valiant*'s launch sat silently, momentarily forgetting that their own lives depended upon them pulling on their oars to escape.

"Oarsmen, pull!" Smythe squeaked.

"No," Philip said, "we mustn't forget Mister Edney."

"But Mister Collier," the midshipman pleaded. "Captain's orders were to return with as many men as we could."

Philip said nothing and scanned the water for signs of the lieutenant.

"You don't understand the Navy," Smythe persisted. "If we lose our seamen, we can't fully man the ship. Mister Edney is probably gone anyway, and we can sail without a first lieutenant but not without our seamen."

"No, we must wait for him," Philip insisted.

Smythe cleared his throat and tried to deepen his voice. "See here, Mister Collier, I am in command, and I ..."

Philip whipped out the printer's pinch from his waistband and put the point between Smythe's eyes, which popped open with the sight of the metal tip and shone through his blackened face in the light of the burning ships.

"Look here, you pampered little squint, you don't ever abandon a man," Philip barked, then added for emphasis, "Never abandon a man!"

"But our orders ..." Smythe whined before wisely cutting it off.

Philip turned to the coxswain and pointed to a spot in the water. "You, get us over there. We are fetching Mister Edney, or we will join him in Hell. Is that clear?"

"Very clear, sir!" the coxswain snapped back, enthusiastic at the prospect of ignoring his midshipman, and the men pulled hard to turn the boat about and toward what might be their own demise.

Philip stood to scan the water for a sign of Edney and was about to regret his own rashness when he heard Smythe mumbling about a mutiny. But just then, he spotted a head bobbing in the water and ordered the launch in that direction. It arrived just as Edney was going under.

"I cannot feel my left arm," Edney said calmly, as they pulled him in. "I fear it is gone."

Philip examined the shredded and bloodied sleeve and found a charred but solid limb inside.

"No, your arm is still with you," he told him.

The oarsmen turned once again and pulled feverishly toward the mouth of the harbor, working beyond what could have been expected after their labor of the last few hours.

"With Mister Edney's compliments, go to Hell!" a crewman shouted back at the French ships as they rowed out of musket range.

French soldiers stood on the fort's parapets watching the burning ships, too distracted to notice the launch being rowed past them. The *Valiant's* sailors continued to dip their blades quietly as they headed out to sea.

The launch began to pull to the side suddenly, and the coxswain admonished the oarsmen for falling off in their efforts.

"It is only the crosscurrents," Philip explained. "Go with the current and allow the oarsmen to work at a slower pace."

Smythe heard the instructions and muttered, "Now he thinks he's a naval officer."

The crosscurrents did their work, and at last the boat was out of range of the fort and plunging into the swells of the Bay of Biscay with its sail raised and its oarsmen allowed to rest. It was a long, but triumphant trip back to the *Valiant*, especially so after several more large explosions were heard behind them, sending raging flames even higher into the night.

Four British ships rocked in the Bay with noisy sounds of jubilation rolling from their decks as their crewmen returned, but the *Valiant* was silent as its men scanned the water for their own. The minutes passed slowly, and seamen bit their lips raw as they feared that their mates would not return.

When the launch finally came into view, the call went out, "What boat there?"

Before the necessary reply was given, someone aboard the *Valiant* shouted, "It's our lads!" and a roar went out from the deck. Captain

Terwillerger turned sharply and disappeared below, allowing the break in discipline to run its course.

"Give three cheers for Mister Edney!" the coxswain shouted as the launch bumped up against the *Valiant,* and the crewmen obliged loudly.

"And three more for Mister Collier!" another man called out, and they obliged again. There were no huzzahs for Midshipman Smythe, however.

The men who had gone into L'Orient's harbor were issued their double ration of rum as promised and, after the festivities died down, were allowed to sleep through their next watch.

Philip declined an offer of brandy when an exuberant Captain Terwillerger later welcomed him to his cabin. Instead, he asked about Edney.

"He is up to his shoulder in some sort of smelly salve," the captain said, "but the ship's surgeon says it will save his arm."

Terwillerger said *HMS Valiant* would remain at station off L'Orient and requested that Philip board another ship to carry the official report of the night action to Admiral Voss, and then to the Admiralty in London.

"It would be my honor!" Philip exclaimed.

"The admiral might want to submit a separate report to explain his own actions," Terwillerger said. "I doubt he had the success we experienced."

The captain winked and added, "But then that's rather typical of a Cornishman, don't you think?"

"I suppose so, captain," Philip said, again having no idea of the implication.

"There is another matter, however," Terwillerger said sternly.

Philip's stomach flopped. "Captain?"

"There is the matter of your conduct regarding Midshipman Thomas Smythe."

That little toad, Philip thought.

Smythe had reported the foray's success to Terwillerger and included in detail the actions of the overreaching army officer who had taken part. He omitted any mention of his own weakness and didn't press the issue of the crewmen's failure to follow his orders, apparently realizing that his command to leave Edney behind might not be seen in the best light.

"Do you deny your personal abuse of Smythe in front of the men and your countermanding of my direct order that he was trying to execute?"

"No, captain, I do not, but ..."

"And do you deny physically threatening him during the action?"

"No, sir, I do not. But if I might explain?"

Terwillerger waved him off.

"Discipline is everything at sea, Mister Collier. The men who witnessed your actions have lost their respect for Mister Smythe, and the word of what you did will spread to every man jack on this ship, sir. Is my meaning clear to you?"

"Yes, Captain, but I'd like to explain."

The captain held up his hand.

"The men love Mister Edney, and now they think you're a bloody hero for bringing him back alive. But your actions have cast Midshipman Smythe in a poor light and might very well have undermined the morale of this ship."

"I apologize, Captain. I didn't comprehend the repercussions and was only trying ..."

"I assured Mister Smythe that his complaint about personal abuse would be passed along to the highest authority, and that would be your Lord Torrington, I believe. Do you object?"

"No, Captain," Philip said, his head bowed. "I believe that you are justified, of course, and I apologize most sincerely."

"I can imagine Lord Torrington will take very seriously the personal abuse of a midshipman," Terwillerger said solemnly. After a second, his face broke and he guffawed. "Of course, what good is a midshipman, if not for personal abuse?"

Philip could hear the captain's laughter continue as he walked away to his cabin. He dropped into his cot but struggled to get to sleep as he reveled in the excitement of the night's events. One final thought was on his mind as he drifted off: Let no one call me a boy ever again.

19. THE INTERVIEW

London, spring of 1803

Philip's confidence was sky high when he left *HMS Valiant* and was diminished only slightly by his later meeting with Admiral Kenwyn Voss aboard *HMS Mercury*. The admiral read Captain Terwillerger's report and then wrote his own for Philip to carry forward to London.

The success of the mission into L'Orient's harbor was evident in the fact that the French fleet had never left Brest: The invasion of Ireland had been prevented, and so there had been no need for the French ruse that had been planned in the Channel. That meant no action, no glory and no prize money for the ships under Voss' command.

"Word of the action at L'Orient apparently reached Brest quickly because the Frogs remained in port," said a subdued Voss, his disappointment evident. "I had hoped that our timing would work out that we could get both jobs done, but a bird in the hand, eh?"

"Yes, it was wise to ensure that the invasion of Ireland be stopped," Philip offered enthusiastically.

"Yes, perhaps the Admiralty will see it that way as well," Voss said, but his voice betrayed the hopefulness of his words.

Philip was put ashore in Portsmouth, where he boarded an overland coach for London. He reflected as he rocked along on the ride that it hardly seemed as if he was returning home after having been settled in Paris for a year. Still, he looked forward to reporting his success to Lord Torrington and to seeing Eleanor's face when he announced that he would like to meet with her father.

His financial situation was secure after meeting with an agent to deposit a shocking sum that included the bounty he had taken from Don Martin's body, even subtracting the 2,000 francs he had given to Joseph. He also had retained well over 100 pounds from the funds he had received for expenses in France and decided he even could pinch a bit of that, since Lord Torrington hadn't expected him to return with much of it anyway. As for the matter of the British gold originally intended for Don Martin, Lord Torrington would not be aware that he had never made delivery, and Don Martin wouldn't be telling him. In the end, he felt little guilt over any of it, believing he had more than earned every last pence for his service and that the government would never miss it.

Philip headed off to Wickham House as soon as he arrived in London, walking with self-assurance through Westminster on his way to Lord Torrington's office.

Westel Sparks looked up over the tops of his spectacles and took a moment before showing a sign of recognition.

"You? There had been no word, and I had presumed that you had come to an end."

"Well, the surprise shows on your face," Philip said smugly.

"What surprises me is that you were gone for months longer than was expected."

Philip ignored the remark. "In addition to my business with this office, I have an important dispatch for the Admiralty. Perhaps it would be best for me to return another day."

Sparks' hesitation gave the signal that Philip had won the battle of incivility. "I shall announce you," the secretary conceded, but he remained in his chair.

Philip played his trump. "You may convey this packet to Lord Torrington, and I shall await his summons," he said, taking the seat nearest to Sparks in the anteroom.

The fastidious secretary delivered the bundle, then returned to his position and began to fuss over a stack of papers.

Philip pulled out his watch and checked the time, then snapped it shut loudly so that Sparks would know that he now was in the company of a man with a timepiece. When the secretary glanced up, Philip returned the watch to his pocket with a flourish.

It was a long wait, but when Lord Torrington opened the door and spotted Philip, he smiled broadly as he waved him into the office, then beckoned for Sparks to follow.

"Oh, my gracious, you look like a Frenchman," he said as they shook hands, noting Philip's trimmed hair. "The army will wonder what has become of you."

"At one time I had a mustache as well," Philip said as he took a seat across from Lord Torrington while Sparks took his station at the small writing desk in the corner.

"Well, it was a good hunt, an excellent hunt!" Lord Torrington began. He reviewed the portion of Philip's report that had dealt specifically with events from the time he had left L'Orient and informed the Royal Navy of the French plans to invade Ireland. "Your work and the results were magnificent."

Philip beamed and nodded.

"We had received reports of troop activity in L'Orient over the past year, of course. The French are building a large shipyard there, as I'm sure you well know."

In fact, Philip had caught a glimpse of the works down by the harbor but had never investigated further, so he chose not to cast doubts on his abilities as a military observer.

"We had taken it to be merely an encampment to protect their assets," Lord Torrington said. "We also, of course, have knowledge of French sympathies toward Irish rebels, but putting the two together, nay, that had not been done. Agents inside France have subsequently confirmed that Bonaparte's plans were exactly as you revealed and that the Corsican was most displeased to have his plot unhinged. I congratulate you most heartily, Lieutenant Collier."

Philip nodded again and glanced over at the impassive Sparks.

"But as to another matter, the dispatch from Admiral Voss was disappointing, I must say," Lord Torrington resumed. "He was prudent, I don't argue that, but he didn't make hay with the French fleet in Brest, did he?"

"I believe that he wanted to ensure that the invasion of Ireland was thwarted at all costs," Philip said. "In addition, I understood the admiral to say that the Channel Fleet had been diminished considerably during the time of peace."

"Well, that is so, but a little boldness might have allowed him to catch the Frogs in the Channel and gotten him a pretty penny in prize money, I might add."

"He seems to be a good man," Philip said in Voss' defense.

"I'm certain of that, and it might be taken into account. Still, he won't have much support from those under his command. All of his captains were cheated of their prize money, don't you see? The Admiralty wants a certain amount of recklessness, so long as you succeed. But succeeding modestly with caution? The Royal Navy probably would have preferred that he had sunk the French squadron off Brest and let the invasion of Ireland go on as planned. It then would have been the army's concern to drive the French out of Dublin."

He let out a low whistle before concluding. "Nay, I fear that Voss may have made a hash of it, in the Admiralty's view. All in all, very typical of a Cornishman. Pour some pebbles into a pot and call it a stew, what?"

"To be sure, my lord," Philip said flatly, still puzzling over previous slights voiced about Cornishmen.

Lord Torrington leaned back in his chair to gather his thoughts.

"I come from a long line of navy men, don't you know?" he said. "My great-grandfather, also named Charles Herbert by the way, fought the French off Beechy Head in 1690.

"While he took on a superior force and performed admirably, he nevertheless could not claim victory because our ships retired at the end of the day. The French fleet was damaged severely and limped back to port, but that was no matter to the Royal Navy. He was court-martialed and acquitted, but he was never again given such a command."

"That doesn't seem fair, my lord," Philip said.

"Fair? Well, that's the navy for you," Lord Torrington said brusquely.

Lord Torrington gazed out the windows for a moment. "I suppose it all sounds quite sad to hear it, but when it's your own family, that's just the way you know things."

"After hearing the treatment that your great-grandfather received, it's difficult to hold out much hope for Admiral Voss," Philip said.

"Voss?" Lord Torrington asked with a puzzled look, then recognition that he had drifted off topic. "Oh, yes, not much hope for Voss."

He concluded his comments on the naval action without mention of the personal abuse of Midshipman Thomas Smythe, to Philip's relief.

"We'll await word on what becomes of all of this, but it appears that you've done quite well for yourself," he said. "Now, I believe we need to review your service over the last year. There are a number of odds and ends in that regard."

Philip felt a sense of foreboding from the phrasing and glanced over at Sparks, who seemed to have a look of anticipation upon his normally cold and expressionless face.

Lord Torrington issued a strong rebuke of Philip for not clearing his plan before heading off to France under the false identity of Philippe Belain.

"You had the simple instruction to visit France as an English tourist, not to pose as something you were not. I'm not saying that sort of thing is never done, you understand," he said of living in Paris under a false identity. "The point is that I needed to know, because I tell you frankly that I would not have approved, young sir. A British officer wandering about like a gypsy, what?"

Philip apologized and explained his thinking, but Lord Torrington resumed his criticism.

"I'm likewise not denying that it turned out for the best, nor am I saying that it wasn't clever. I'm saying that you took unnecessary risk without informing me. I must know these things, young sir," he said, rapping the desktop with his knuckles for effect. "It's essential!"

Seeing that the younger man was appropriately chastened, he moved next to Philip's observations around Boulogne.

"We have received much the same information from other sources, but your detail was exceptional." He paused. "And sending your findings to us by using that book, what was it?"

"*Gulliver's Travels*," Sparks interjected.

"Yes, you *would* know," Lord Torrington said, then erupted in laughter. "That was a tedious piece of work to decipher, was it not? Numbers, pages, maps, even Scripture! Har!"

"Additionally," Sparks inserted with a tone of irritation, "your handwriting is most egregious."

"Now, Sparks, that's enough," Lord Torrington scolded his secretary.

Sparks ignored him. "I was so pleased when you at last decided to forgo articles, such as 'the' and 'a' in your messages," he said sarcastically. "How clever of you to realize that they were unnecessary to the information that you were relaying."

"God's thunder! What a laugh whenever I'd toss your letters onto his desk!" Lord Torrington exclaimed, shaking his head in amusement as he turned to Philip. "Writing down this, looking up that. Har! Why, one time when I hadn't heard from you for some time, I accused dear Sparks of snatching your letters before they reached my desk, just so he wouldn't have to decrypt them. I had to apologize to him when the next one finally arrived and I learned of your injury. An apology to Sparks, can you imagine that?"

"No, my lord, I cannot," Philip said.

"Har! Too bad this final report today didn't require that kind of work," Lord Torrington continued. "Then you could have observed Sparks' agitation in the flesh as he pored over the pages of *Gulliver's Travels.*"

He laughed heartily and added, "*Gulliver's Travels,* indeed!"

Philip smiled weakly, and his face colored.

"But here's the rub!" Lord Torrington went on relentlessly. "We have codes, don't you see? Why, they're perfectly simple to use. But that creation of yours, well, only Sparks knew how to make sense of it. Sparks could have decrypted *ten* letters in the time it took for one of yours!"

He roared in laughter again, and his face turned a bright red as if he were choking.

"Twenty," the secretary corrected his lordship. "It took until after midnight to untangle the first communication that you sent."

"I know that codes are used, of course," Philip said, scrambling to recover. "However, I hadn't done that sort of thing before and thought it might be presumptuous to ask."

"Well, you would have been told, had I known what you were up to," Lord Torrington replied, suddenly turning serious.

"With what was supposed to have been done, the simple posting of letters at the church would have sufficed. That was an earlier wartime arrangement, so it would have been quite secure during a time of peace. The priest sends our mail to a man of business in Copenhagen, and without the seal being broken, I might add. The messages travel from there to the porcelain warehouse in Town, which is owned by a member of my club who is eager to strengthen his ties to well-placed people in government.

"I'll admit that a code might have been in order with the details you were providing, but again, that was unexpected," he added.

The sun was beginning to sink behind the building on the facing street, and Lord Torrington ordered Sparks to find some refreshments so that they could continue their work.

"He doesn't approve of me, does he?" Philip asked after Sparks had gone.

Lord Torrington had gone over to the window and was looking out onto the street. "Hmmm, that's very odd," he said as he observed something out of Philip's view, but he didn't finish the thought before turning back. "What's that you say? Nay, Sparks probably doesn't like you, but little matter."

Philip was feeling his moment of triumph slipping away. The interview had begun at the height of success but had fallen away since, first with the upbraiding for his secret identity, then with the ridicule of the code of his own device. He sat unenthusiastically as they moved on to his letter reporting General Albert Chamier's doubts as to an invasion of England, along with the figures proving that the invasion was not feasible.

"Now that was a fine piece of work," Lord Torrington said. "Your intelligence was quite detailed, and I must compliment you on gaining the confidence of the French military."

In truth, Chamier had only been overheard in a social setting and was never introduced to Philip, who used the Frenchman's name to attach more importance to the report. Neither had the general provided the detail in the intelligence.

"Your letter regarding this disaffected General Permon also was extraordinary because it fits in with our plans to strengthen the French royalists' hand in finding support from Napoleon's military," Lord Torrington said. "I commend you for the way you insinuated yourself into the French high command."

Philip chose silence over an explanation of how that occurred and pivoted to ask if the British army had been informed of his actions.

Lord Torrington returned to his chair and pulled on the whiskers on the sides of his face.

"The Duke of York and Horse Guards are not aware of your mission," he said. "I'm afraid that because of your age, you might not understand all of the dealings within your government."

"My lord, it seems that I don't understand *any* of the dealings regarding *anything*."

"Oh, don't be so hard on yourself because you'll learn these things in time. At any rate, after your departure — you'll recall that England and France were at peace at that time — this office's finances were put on the butcher's block, if you get my meaning."

"Butcher's block, yes," Philip agreed.

"Where before I had tens of thousands of pounds for my use, I then had merely thousands. Do you follow?"

"I believe so, yes, the butcher's block."

Lord Torrington, sensing that Philip was not seeing the picture clearly enough, went on. "Decimation, that is my point. A decimation of this office's finances, is that clear?"

"Yes, of course," Philip said, this time with a tone of assurance that would allow the discussion to continue.

Lord Torrington explained the situation as he had seen it: The Peace of Amiens was a matter of convenience and not a lasting solution to the conflicts between England and France. Unfortunately, political opportunists in London had chosen to cut funds available to the military and to his office, under the guise of fiscal prudence. The only threat holding politicians in check had been the longstanding fears that an invasion of England was in the cards.

"I needed to mine the hysteria, so to speak, by passing along what was known about Napoleon's plans. But I couldn't very well include your analysis that the entire thing was nothing more than some cock-and-bull scheme that would never bear fruit."

Neither spoke for a moment before Lord Torrington broke the silence. "Your information will be passed along to the Duke of York and the army, but at the appropriate time. I assure you that your superiors then will know of your actions, in some form at least."

Philip understood only that he shouldn't count on any patronage from the duke. The workings of government were confusing to him, and he had no desire to learn more about why politicians would be cutting funds when war obviously had been waiting around the corner.

It also was inconceivable to him that the nation would be so subservient to personal ambitions, and he pondered how the nation's leaders walked the fine line where self-interest bordered upon treason as they advanced the causes of both war and peace for their own gain.

Sparks returned with tea, cold beef and bread, and they sat and ate quietly for a time. Lord Torrington suddenly held up a piece of bread.

"Why, this is the perfect example of what I mean regarding deployment of funds," he said and took a bite.

Philip and Sparks sat equally in confusion until the bread had been chewed and swallowed.

"One of the neatest bits from your reports was word of the bread prices in Paris," Lord Torrington resumed. "You see, the noblemen and courtiers I normally employ would never think to tell me something of that nature. Nay, they inform me about who is sharing a bedroom with whom, who needs money to pay gambling debts and so forth. But when have they ever purchased bread?"

Lord Torrington recalled Philip's letter telling that the poor crop in France had resulted in loaves of bread selling for 13 sous, a terrible price for the citizens of Paris. That had sprung a plan: Word was passed to a Frankfurt merchant, who saw the opportunity to purchase grain from men of business in German cities near the French border. When the Bonaparte government came calling, desperate to feed its people and discourage unrest, the merchant held out and worsened the French distress before eventually selling the diminished supply of grain at an exorbitant price. So the Frankfurt trader made a fortune in the squeeze, and the French paid dearly for what they got.

"I didn't expend a farthing from this office to create the whole mess, I merely sent word to this gentleman in Frankfurt of how he might turn a profit. Money that isn't wasted is money made, if you follow my drift."

The story became even more fantastic. Lord Torrington went on to explain the repercussions of the unrest over the bread shortage during a time when Bonaparte's finances were hamstrung.

"Your work fit in nicely with other mischief we've created to burden Boney's finances. Here we are now, beginning a new war and he's scrounging for funds. As you know, he's been forced to sell an enormous piece of land to the United States. That will eliminate the

French threat from the Americas, because they've already been pushed out of the Caribbean by the slave revolt."

Lord Torrington related how the French had been defeated in Hispaniola and Bonaparte had sent his brother-in-law, Charles Leclerc, to regain control of the island. But the fever had nearly destroyed the force under his command, and Leclerc himself had died. The debacle had forced Napoleon to abandon his plans to extend his domain into the New World.

"I'm not saying the price of bread did the trick by itself, but you can't discount the effects," Lord Torrington said. "That damned tyrant needs everybody under his heel, you see, so that when his people get out of line, he must act at once. He witnessed what happened to old Louis in the Nineties when he didn't respond quickly to the rioters, and he won't repeat that mistake. Didn't Boney deal quite harshly with those in Paris who raised their voices over the price of bread?"

"Yes, that is so," Philip said, realizing that he had been injured in a *mêlée* of his own making.

Lord Torrington sat with a pleased look on his face. "Buying up German grain, a neat bit of business, to be sure."

They spent additional time discussing the mood of Frenchmen and their views on Napoleon, the war and the way their government attended to their needs.

"I'm not entirely certain how the majority of the people feel about Bonaparte," Philip said. "He's regarded as heroic by some, even a latter-day Caesar. But the conscription is not popular, nor is the diminution of the Church's importance. I also would say that he faces some opposition among the educated and the cultured."

"Yes, I see. And what was the motivation of this actor who assisted you?" Lord Torrington asked.

"I believe it was a sense that the arts would be subjected to the government's decree," Philip replied. "He also considered me a friend and knew that I shared his opposition to Bonaparte. He was instrumental in helping me to escape Paris."

"Hmmm. You know, of course, that your false identity as an *émigré* actually would have tended to arouse suspicion, rather than provide cover."

"Yes, my lord, I am quite aware now that it was a mistake."

"Many of the networks inside France are operated by *émigrés*, in fact. Mostly Royalists."

"So I've been told."

"You might have visited our embassy in Paris for assistance, since much of the staff is employed by this office."

Philip said he believed that he was supposed to steer clear of the embassy because Don Martin Cristobal de Acuña wanted to avoid contact with official British sources.

"Well, that matters little, now that the Spaniard has gotten himself killed," Lord Torrington said. "Danilo Ruggiero informed me how that filthy cur betrayed you."

Philip puzzled over the name for a moment before it occurred to him that Ruggiero was the man he knew only as "Mr. Black."

Lord Torrington offered cigars to Philip and Sparks, both of whom declined.

He reached down into his desk and pulled out one for himself, then placed on his desk a wooden device with a blade on one side. He held the end of a cigar under the blade and tripped a lever. Nothing happened. "Damn it!" He fumbled again with the lever, and the blade cut more than an inch off the end of the cigar, leaving shreds of tobacco dangling from the severed end.

"God's thunder!" he bawled.

"Rather like a guillotine, my lord?" Philip suggested lightly.

"Not at all, *those things* get the job done," Lord Torrington grumbled, oblivious to the jest. He tossed the mutilated cigar into a basket under his desk and pulled out another. Again he tripped the lever, but nothing happened. He began to shake the device, but Sparks arose to take it away. The secretary placed it on the end of the desk, confiscated the second cigar and neatly trimmed off the end, then handed it back to his employer before returning to his station in the corner.

"Well, the damned thing only works when it feels like it," Lord Torrington concluded as he lit the cigar over a candle.

He inquired further about Jean-François Floquet, but Philip remained vague on many of the details concerning their friendship and chose not to reveal that he had labored in a print shop — a story bound to produce only more questions and further embarrassment.

"So I gather from your description that this actor was a molly, is that correct?" Lord Torrington asked bluntly.

"No, my lord, I did not intend such an implication, although that was what I believed to be the case at the outset," Philip answered, then coughed to allow himself time to briefly compose his thoughts.

"The truth is that Parisians, both men and women, were a constant puzzlement to me insofar as their intentions," he resumed. "Men's advances toward women, men's advances toward men, women's advances toward men, it was all a world that I could not fathom. I understand those implications no better now than when I first arrived in Paris."

"Well, you won't find the answer to such questions in this office!" Lord Torrington exclaimed with a hint of indignation. "Isn't that right, Sparks?"

The secretary remained silent, and Lord Torrington cast a look of disdain at him for failing to come to his aid.

"On another matter, you say that you were questioned by the French secret police," he resumed.

"Yes, by an inspector named Bérand."

"I know of Bérand, an assistant prefect who has been a thorn to us in several matters," Lord Torrington said. "You will be pleased to know that he was murdered on the streets of Paris."

"It was I who shot him," Philip announced, not taking time to consider the effects of the admission.

Lord Torrington cocked his head. "You *assassinated* a police official?"

Philip scrambled to recover, explaining his encounter with Bérand after escaping the trap at the convent of St. Bertin with help from "the Italian," hoping to confirm Ruggiero's nationality.

He left out many details of his dealings with Don Martin, including his own refusal to pay the Spaniard for intelligence, which had precipitated the ambush.

"Ruggiero said he had helped you out of a tight spot, but he made no mention of the crowning touch."

"Mister Ruggiero was not present when I encountered the inspector. I was forced to shoot him in order to escape," Philip said, then registered the reference to "the crowning touch."

"*You* killed Bérand? I declare, that is most interesting," Lord Torrington mused, then released a low whistle. "Upon my word, Lieutenant Collier. I have heard nothing to match that. I am flabbergasted. After all that you've accomplished, *and* an assassination to boot?"

Philip smiled pleasantly and glanced over at Sparks, who sat expressionless and apparently unimpressed.

"It is fantastic!" Lord Torrington exclaimed, thumping his desk, then tugging lightly on his wig, which had slid off-center. "I tell you now that the continued existence of this office was in great doubt, but you have helped to restore it. Why, the return on the pittance you were given, it cannot be ascertained!"

Philip considered whether this was the point at which he needed to account for the funds he had been given for his expenses and for Don Martin.

Instead, Lord Torrington sprang from behind his desk and came around to shake his hand enthusiastically. "You will continue to be a great asset to this office, of that I am sure!"

"I am to remain attached then?" Philip asked.

Lord Torrington's brow lowered. "Does that not please you?"

"I'm not certain that the work suits me because good fortune plays a larger role than I would prefer," he explained lamely.

"When Bonaparte is eventually defeated, it will be by men with luck, don't you see? The ones that lack it will not be around to see this business through to the end. You're correct that luck plays its part, but that is so with everything."

"But it plays a larger role than I would prefer," Philip repeated. "I have been laid low so many times that it defies belief."

"But you persevered, and you succeeded. Is that not the essence of good fortune? Why did you continue if failure was so close at hand?"

Philip bit his lip and reflected on what had pushed him forward during his worst moments. Ambition? Perhaps. Love of a woman? Often. Love of country? Certainly. The fear that he would die as nothing, without ever having made his mark? Always.

"Please be assured that I am ever so grateful for what you have done for me," he said after an awkward silence. "This duty just might not suit me, that's all."

Lord Torrington seemed severely wounded by this turn and stepped away to draw on his cigar. When he turned to speak again, it was to announce coldly that Sparks would arrange a return appointment.

"We shall see how you feel about things at that time," he said, abruptly closing the interview.

20. Shattering News

Philip arrived at his father's home on Folsom Street late at night and began to unpack alone in the kitchen, his mind awash with emotions and numbed by fatigue. It finally seemed as if his yearlong ordeal was at an end, but he did not experience a feeling of relief.

He looked down at his clenched fists, and images began to form of the weapons his hands had held and the blood and burnt gunpowder that had covered them. He unclenched them and held them straight out with the palms down, watching as they began to tremble beyond his control.

"Are you well?" asked his father, standing in a nightshirt in the doorway.

Philip immediately dropped his hands and nodded.

"You have been gone so long that we didn't know when you would return," he said. "Will you be staying?"

"I don't know," Philip answered without looking up, as he reached into his bag on the table. "I can find other quarters if it is a burden for me to be here."

"You are welcome to stay," Mr. Collier said meekly and, receiving no further response, returned to his bed.

Philip arose late the next morning after his father had left for work and his brothers had headed out into the street to engage in the day's mischief.

Harriet prepared his breakfast and tea while interrogating him about his activities of the past year.

His vague answers didn't satisfy her.

"You don't offer much," she said. "Will you be staying longer this time?"

"I hope so," he answered and began to make hints about his future plans still needing some attention. He believed that his sister would sort through his comments and volunteer information about Eleanor, but she did not.

"There are some people I must see," he said, at last eliciting a response.

"Well, if you're asking about Eleanor, I will remind you of my guidance before you left," she said sharply.

"Which was what?"

"That you were too slow."

He felt dread over what he believed he was about to hear. "Whatever do you mean?"

"She is engaged to be married."

The news hit Philip hard. The blood rushed to heat his face as he struggled to maintain his composure. He pulled his watch from his pocket and returned it without registering the time.

Harriet studied him.

He picked up his fork, but with no food before him, he placed it back on the table and pulled out the watch again.

"Why do you need to know what time it is?" she asked. "Didn't you hear what I said?"

He nodded.

"She is to marry Mister Eustace McGiver, a business associate of her father," she said. "The man is over 40 years old. It's the most awful thing."

"If it's so awful, then why is she marrying him?"

"What choice does she have, Philip? Her father has no sons, and he wants his daughters married. He is a man of business, not a matchmaker, and he wants the business of marrying his eldest daughter concluded. Eleanor has been 'out' now for nearly two years, which to her father means an unfinished transaction that requires a lower price in order to complete it."

"And in order to strike his bargain, he would have her married to a man in whom she has no interest?"

"You act as if you are so far superior to the rest of us because you have traveled all over this Earth, and yet you have no sense of society."

She went to the stove and returned with a plate of sausages that she slammed down on the table before stomping off.

Philip stared at the plate with his hands folded in his lap as he tried to make sense of everything.

He had risked his life continually for over a year, and his reward was to gain the stature and financial stake that he thought was necessary if he were to court Eleanor. He had known no such success as this in his life, no such satisfaction and no future so bright as it had been just ten minutes earlier. But now he was left to ponder the end of his triumph.

He confronted the likelihood that his feelings and expectations about Eleanor had all been just another of his elaborately constructed fantasies. Doubts arose about her, and he hardened his heart to what she was so that he could brace himself for her rejection. Was she truly beautiful? Perhaps he had deluded himself because she was the only woman whom he had thought he could claim. Was she bright, or had he been so starved for contact from home that her letters to him in India had conveyed more meaning than had really existed? Did she truly feel affection for him, or had he been her only alternative to marrying a 40-year-old business associate of her father?

The questions and doubts whirled in his head. Perhaps it had been a relationship that existed only in his own mind, he thought, the dream of a woman who loved him folded into an imaginary world in which status and wealth did not matter.

The sausages were cold by the time he finally ate them.

"As I live and am a man, this is an unexaggerated tale. My dreams become the substance of my life," he said to himself and was startled to find that Harriet was back in the kitchen.

"You don't need some silly passage from a book to show you the way," she told him. "You need to be bold."

Philip said nothing but finally rose from the chair and went into the parlor to sit, looking at some of the personal items that decorated the Collier home. A table clock, with one of the hands bent by his older brother when he was a small child. A small painting of a country home with blooming roses. Silhouettes of his parents cut from black paper and affixed to the cover of a book filled with mementos of their marriage.

He had not looked at the book in years, but he crossed the room and picked it up. Inside was a letter from his grandfather granting the hand of his daughter Elizabeth to "Robert Collier, a legal clerk in London." The letter listed personal items and funds that were to accompany his daughter into her new life. It was a cold, emotionless document that Philip thought must have pleased his father.

"A woman deserves something more than that in a letter," he said quietly to himself.

He snapped the book closed, then went to his chest and took out his uniform to dress. He bent back the small plume on his shako so that it stood straight and was preparing to place it on his head, when Harriet came into his room.

"You look ridiculous," she said in disgust. "You have creases going in every direction imaginable."

She took his uniform jacket from him and steamed it over a kettle until the folds were no longer visible, then pressed it and returned it to him. He thanked her as he worked on the buttons, and she gave him a kiss on the cheek.

"Women like men who are bold," she repeated.

Philip pulled on his great coat as he stepped out into the cold, rainy morning, not knowing where he was going as he followed the water running along the curbs until he eventually stood beside the Thames. He watched the river passing by and tried to find meaning in everything that had transpired.

He considered his jumbled existence: heading one direction, then another, then yet another until none of it made sense — and with not even a hint of which way to turn next. It was not a tragic life, for he had known some who had found far more disappointment and even calamity. It also was not an easy life, for he had seen the way that wealth and patronage had created a more direct path for the fortunate few. It was mostly a confusing life, of that alone he was certain.

His mind drifted back to a similar time spent gazing at the Seine.

His year in Paris was to have been a building block in his life, but what would be the final result? If nothing else, he knew that he would not be like his father: beaten, submissive and without dreams, shaped by his own inability to take the risks that might lead to success. Mr. Collier had abandoned his plan to become a barrister and taken his position at Dunn & Gilchrist because he considered it a safer route to provide for his family.

But the year in Paris had proved to Philip that he could not be a man of compromise, for his own brash notions would mean that his life would be all — or it would be nothing. Perhaps his triumphs in France would shape his destiny, and he would be blessed with fortune, comfort and respect. Or perhaps he had balanced his dreams too heavily upon the love of a woman, and his life would be molded by the resulting bitterness.

He pulled the printer's pinch from inside his coat, eyed it briefly and then threw it into the Thames in an attempt to unburden his conscience and prepare for what lay ahead.

Shivering, he drew in his coat and turned away, wandering only by intuition until he reached a familiar street corner. He jerked around hard at a sound behind him, and a familiar sensation of fear gripped him at the thought that he had once again let down his guard. A sudden recognition that he was again in London made him shrug with the knowledge that the sounds of a city street never again would be something to ignore.

Philip crossed the street to the Vales' home and stood at the door, hoping for a pleasant invitation to come in from the rain. But he didn't recognize the servant who answered and was forced to provide an awkward explanation of his purpose. A long wait in the foyer ensued, until voices could be heard down the hallway, followed by the sound of footsteps on a staircase in the rear of the house.

The servant returned to announce Eleanor's arrival, and she appeared in a drab bluish-grey dress, her face drawn. He bowed stiffly, and she dipped her shoulders to return the greeting, then pointed silently toward the drawing room. She took a seat on one side and he on the other, a wall formed by the coolness and distance between them.

"I was not aware that you had returned," she said. "Harriet had not informed me."

"I only arrived home last night, and she did not know until this morning," he said before providing a vague explanation of where he had been for the last year. "I often thought of writing to you, but the circumstances would not allow it. For that, I apologize."

"If the circumstances would not allow it, then there is no need for an apology," she replied.

Philip plunged into the topic on his mind.

"I've learned that you are to be married."

She did not respond immediately, appearing to gather her thoughts. "That is true."

He cleared his throat. "Is this to occur immediately?"

She looked at him hard. "Fairly soon, I suppose. There are considerations."

He struggled for what to say next, and after a lengthy pause, he asked, "Might I be a consideration?"

"Yes," she said in a voice just above a whisper.

"I know that my absence has not advanced my position during this past year," he began. "I had hoped that our time together last year had created some understanding of what I intended."

"I'm not sure what you mean."

"Did not our time together create a certain … affection?" he asked awkwardly.

"I believed that it did on one of our parts, but it was unclear as to the other."

Philip took his time trying to determine what she meant before responding, "I believed it to be clear on my part as well."

"*You* may have believed it to be so, but it was not clear to *both* parties."

It seemed to him as if their spoken sentences needed to be written down, then connected with lines and arrows to provide meanings and implications. His attempt to be more direct bordered on rudeness. "And this man you are to marry, is the affection clear to both parties?"

She let out a small cry and rose to walk toward the windows.

"Why couldn't you have written me, even once?" she asked with her back turned to him.

"As I said, circumstances would not allow it."

"What was I to do?" she asked, her voice rising with emotion. "Was I to wait until I knew your intentions? And when were those intentions to be conveyed? Was I to know the next week, the next month, the next year? When?"

"I thought you understood my position."

"I did not."

"I realize that now, and I apologize," he said. "Still, I don't see how you could not have had at least an inkling of my position."

"And is that what a girl is to cling to, an *inkling*, when she is presented with an offer of marriage from another? Was I to tell my father that he must decline the offer because his eldest daughter has an *inkling*?"

"I was not in a position to offer anything more at the time, surely that must have been clear."

"It surely was not."

"How could I possibly have discussed courtship with your father a year ago? I had no position, no prospects."

"Papa liked you, and he would have heard what you had to say. My God, Philip, I told you that he had an extravagant ball for my coming out. It was a mortal embarrassment to him that it had been nearly two years without an offer for him to consider."

"And he would have considered my intentions?"

"Yes, he thought you had promise."

"That was not clear to me."

"If you had spoken to me, I would have told you that."

"My God, Eleanor, my family is beneath yours, and I thought an offer to your father was barely possible. And how could I be confident? After all, a beautiful young woman is likely to have many suitors."

"You are calling me beautiful?"

"You are."

"I have always thought myself to be plain," she said flatly.

Philip rose and drew nearer.

"My silence and my absence were misjudged, I can see, but is a marriage arranged by your father the chosen alternative?"

"If that is the life I must lead ..."

"Eleanor, I needed to achieve something before I could speak to your father, and I undertook an endeavor that would allow me to reach that goal. I have faced great hazards and done things I never dreamt I was capable of doing, but you were always in my thoughts."

"That was not known to me," she said weakly. "How could it be?"

"I thought you understood what I was about," he said, then gathered his strength. "I believe that extraordinary people are needed for these extraordinary times. That is what I would try to be for you.

You don't want someone who's ordinary, do you? Is that what you want, to live an ordinary life with an ordinary man?"

"Philip, how could I possibly comprehend everything that's been rattling around in your mind for all these months?" she cried. "I've been here, I've been alone, and it's been torment!"

She burst into tears and began to sob.

Edmund Vale suddenly appeared in the doorway, having heard the commotion. He looked at his daughter, then at the young man who had disrupted his home.

"Lieutenant, you must leave now," he said calmly to Philip.

"Yes, sir."

Philip was on his way to the doorway when he stopped, reached inside his jacket and pulled out the letter he had penned aboard *HMS Valiant* as he had prepared to meet his end. He handed Eleanor the letter — the farewell that it was intended to be.

Mrs. Vale scurried off to get his coat and shako, then returned and handed them to him. She grabbed his arm and squeezed it tightly.

"Philip ..." Mrs. Vale said plaintively.

"He must go, my dear," Mr. Vale said.

Philip walked out the front door, down the steps and into the street.

Behind him as he trudged off in the rain, a curtain was pulled back to reveal a fallen face, an open mouth half-covered by a handkerchief and finally a wail that couldn't penetrate the glass to reach him.

21. Striking an Agreement

Philip's temper ruled the Collier household after he received the news of Eleanor's impending marriage, and his wrath fell upon his father and Harriet. They in turn unleashed their anger upon the undisciplined younger brothers, Bartholomew and Edward, who were not accustomed to such harsh treatment and were outraged to experience it.

Each verbal blow rippled through the family, with the sound of loud voices reaching a peak before cold, silent incivility. The periods of quiet eventually became too much for the younger boys to stand.

"Why don't you go away again?" Edward hollered at Philip over supper one evening. "Things were quite well enough with you gone."

"You need your ears boxed, and I'm the one who will do it if you don't shut your mouth!" Philip barked back at him. "You're rude and an embarrassment."

"Philip, that is quite enough of such talk," Mr. Collier said.

"And what about them?" Philip said, gesturing toward the two younger boys. "You let these two run wild. Mother wouldn't have allowed it."

"That is enough, I say," his father responded. "You have brought an inharmonious air to our home."

"So you're putting your foot down with *me*? And what are your plans for these two? The army? They'll be flogged to the bone inside of a week."

"Philip!" Mr. Collier shouted, standing above the table.

The son arose and stared his father back down into the chair, then stormed out of the kitchen as Harriet cried for them to stop.

Philip was repacking his chest later in the evening when the door flew open. He quickly gathered up some of the more suspicious items and tucked them away as Bartholomew came in and stood beside him.

"What are you hiding?" he asked.

"Why don't you leave me in peace?" Philip retorted.

"Say, what you got this for?" Bartholomew asked next, picking up the elephant-head cane from the floor.

"Do you have any idea how ignorant you sound whenever you speak?" Philip said in yet another question that was not going to be answered.

"You think you're a dandy gentleman, don't you?" his younger brother countered, twirling the cane in his fingers.

Philip tried to take it back, but Bartholomew stepped away and began to strut about the room, leading each step with a fancy motion of the cane.

"Get out of here, you barbarian!" Philip snarled as he snatched away the cane, then used it to strike a sharp blow on his brother's backside.

"Ow!" Bartholomew yelped.

Philip had been a patient tutor to a boy about this age while in Paris, but he had no such inclination toward his own unruly brother in London. He grabbed the boy by the shoulders and shoved him out the door, slamming it behind him.

Time passed slowly in the days before his next appointment with Lord Torrington, and Philip spent as many hours away from home as possible.

He often took long walks with no purpose other than the hope that he would return to find that his letter had swayed Eleanor into convincing her father to break her engagement. When no word came either by post or from his sister's tongue, his thoughts turned to considerations of the man he would become and whether the pain and humiliation washing over his life eventually would recede to leave deep scars etched upon his soul.

Despondency turned to anxiety when at last the day of his appointment at Wickham House arrived. As he set off in full uniform, the idea of employment with Lord Torrington seemed more agreeable in the wake of the disappointment over Eleanor. If nothing else, he acknowledged to himself that he would like to be away from London. Sparks looked up as he entered and presented himself, then down again without comment.

Philip settled himself into the familiar discomfort of one of the stiff oak chairs, wondering why Sparks would now believe that he again had the upper hand in the anteroom. The previous meeting had established his worth with Lord Torrington, and it seemed odd that the secretary would treat him once again as just another of the visitors to be herded like sheep into a pen.

After an hour, timed precisely since he now had a watch, Philip asked if there were some reason for the delay, since no other gentlemen were waiting.

"Lord Torrington will see you when he is available," Sparks said.

Philip began to work on the words to unleash on the bespectacled man, but just as he was about to deliver an appropriate insult, Sparks instructed him to enter the inner office.

Lord Torrington sat solemnly behind his desk and began to speak before Philip had extended his courtesies. "I have received reports regarding the action in L'Orient, in addition to some unexpected news from Ireland."

"My lord?"

"The news from L'Orient is exceptionally good. One French frigate was destroyed in the navy's raid, three other warships burned and badly impaired and several more damaged. There's a shipyard there for the repairs, but they won't be putting out to sea soon, of that much we're certain. All to the good."

"And the news from Ireland, my lord?"

"Apparently there was an attempt at rebellion in Dublin, but of course it failed miserably without French support. While that is favorable for us, Thomas Grant has been arrested and surely will be hanged. He was a rebel, but an exceptional young man nevertheless and correct in saying that England would never honor its promise of emancipation. Shameful thing on our part really. It was the King's doing, as you know."

Despite this intimate disclosure of his own views, Lord Torrington seemed otherwise more reserved than he had been at previous meetings, and an uncharacteristic formality filled the room. Philip began to ponder why he had not been offered a chair as his lordship continued to speak.

"In summation, Lieutenant Collier, you have done extraordinary work for this office," Lord Torrington said and leaned back in his chair.

"Perhaps the French are onto something, that this is the beginning of a time without kings, when a man's worth is determined by his deeds and his character and not by his birth. You are young, Lieutenant, but perhaps you are a man who embodies such a notion, who can find a place in a new epoch." He sensed Philip's confusion, then added, "I am telling you that you might be the very man for such times, and that I and others of *my kind* need men such as yourself if we wish to steer the future."

Silence.

"I must have you."

"My lord?"

"This office is the vanguard for every effort to defeat Bonaparte, and it needs your services. That much is certain, and it must be apparent to you as well."

"My lord?"

"At times in the past, we employed men who were not sufficiently intelligent or adequately educated to understand the information we were seeking. An eavesdropper in a tavern might overhear military conversations, but he generally would lack the grasp of what he was hearing. We would learn far too late that he had become aware of things that might have helped us, had they been passed along in the first place. Do you follow?"

"Yes, my lord."

"We also have employed gentlemen who traveled in the highest circles, but their plots rarely bore fruit. And the motivation for these so-called gentlemen? Money, of course. Power? Yes, that too. But love of country? Hardly. That sort of business has had its successes, but it's expensive to do the deed, if you follow."

"Yes, my lord."

"*You,* young sir, are able to put together the pieces of a puzzle and yet seemingly with the ability to avoid notice. Somehow, you are an invisible man. I could go out into the hallways of this building and ask who has passed this way, and how many would mention you?" Lord Torrington asked, then looked at him with piercing eyes. "But I see you very clearly."

Philip silently reflected on how his most important discoveries in France had come during times when nobody would have been aware of him. He had been nothing more than a laborer, the sort that no one in a position of power would consider to be of substance or a threat. He truly had been invisible, like a germ infecting blood, and the world would never know that a plot to invade Ireland had been unhinged by a man whose fingernails were blackened by ink as he pried apart blocks of leaden type. He was about to agree to employment, when Lord Torrington resumed.

"Still, despite your success, I confess to not knowing precisely how you operate," he said. "It's strange how you go about things, that's all I can say."

Philip had been prepared for a compliment, and he bristled at the remark. "My lord, doesn't the fact that you find my methods 'strange' mean that I'm not what you need?" he asked. "Doesn't it suggest that you could find someone more suitable? Perhaps I am not the right man for the job."

"Let me see if I can make a comparison for you," Lord Torrington said, looking about the room. "Ah, let us say that this office needs to be reorganized. Why, I can have the burly man come in to move this heavy desk, while I can have a lighter man move the chair, and I can have a meticulous man do the dusting. Don't you see? Each to his own purpose?"

Philip shifted on his feet and said nothing.

"Like the furniture, don't you see? One moves it, another dusts it?"

The analogy further confused Philip.

"My lord, as I told you during my previous visit, I'm not certain that this sort of work suits me," he said.

"Oh, but it in fact does suit you, and extraordinarily well," Lord Torrington replied emphatically. "I accept your assertion that there is good fortune involved, and I don't deny the peril that you face, but I admire your ability to conquer the unknown and have confidence that you will continue to succeed.

"You see, there were no charts that warned of pitfalls here and pratfalls there, and yet still you persevered and prevailed. You simply can't unroll a document that outlines all of the contingencies that could possibly transpire, don't you see? *Somebody* has to step into the unknown and be the one to chart the course."

Silence again.

"Don't you see? I need nimble men, ones who adapt, who recognize the danger that England faces and will put their love of country above all other concerns."

"Is Your Lordship telling me that I cannot return to my regiment?"

"Nay, I shall not tell you that, but here is what I shall tell you," Lord Torrington said, pulling out a paper covered with scribbled notes. He held it out far from his face, then drew it closer to gauge the proper distance from his eyes, and finally began to speak in the calm, flat tone of a court bailiff.

"First, if you remain with this office, you will be brevetted immediately to the rank of captain. If you instead wish to return to your regiment, then a captaincy would be available to you only when a vacancy occurs. And as you well know, the commission would need to be purchased."

Hearing no response, he resumed.

"Second, if you agree, then you will receive your captain's salary from this office, in addition to expenses that you might incur. I have learned from your agent that you have deposited a sum well in excess of one-thousand pounds in an account. I by no means need to know how you returned from France with such a sum, do I?"

"No, my lord," Philip said quickly, not wishing to explain that his failure to deliver gold to Don Martin might have swayed the Spaniard to the French cause. Neither did he wish to admit that the sum in his account also included what he had rifled from the dead man's body.

"Fine then," Lord Torrington said, looking hard into his eyes.

"Third, Signor Ruggiero believes that you are in his debt, and he is disposed to make use of your services," he continued. "He has made inquiries in Paris and believes that your name has not been connected to the death of Inspector Bérand. In short, you could return to your previous station as a young *émigré* in Paris, with a full purse and no encumbrances."

"I am to return to France?"

Lord Torrington placed the paper back on the desk and looked up. "Is Signor Ruggiero correct in his belief that you are in his debt?"

"Yes, my lord, I most certainly owe him my life," Philip said and fingered the healed knife wound as he stood with his hands clasped behind his back.

Lord Torrington glanced down one last time at the paper.

"Finally, there is a most unpleasant matter that I must raise."

"My lord?"

"After you left for France last year, a second letter arrived from the Marquis Wellesley, this one addressed personally to me. Why it came so late after your arrival here, I do not know, but the governor of India has much to keep himself occupied, of that you can be certain."

"A second letter, my lord?" Philip asked.

"Yes, and in this particular one he detailed more fully your service to him in India. He confirmed, of course, much of what you had told me and expounded upon a number of other points. In a way, his second letter provided a glimpse into much of what subsequently has transpired during the last year.

"Lord Richard said that you were very much on your own for a time in India as well, although not by your own design, as was the case in France. He said that you likewise performed very valuable service there, in some ways nearly as extraordinary as that of the past year. But in India, as in France, there was the question of an army officer surreptitiously traveling about, appearing to be somebody he was not."

"I am confused, my lord."

"*Some* believe that a gentleman does not behave in that manner," Lord Torrington said, with emphasis on "some," and he paused to let his comment sink in. "In short, it seems that your fellow officers believed that your actions had compromised your honor. Lord Richard wisely sent you back to England, fearing that you would be ostracized if you remained with your regiment and that your career would be stained. He was quite grateful for your service, of course, but he didn't want you to incur abuse over what you had done."

"I understood my return from India to have been a reward, my lord."

"All one and the same, much as it is now."

"Yes, my lord," Philip responded, his mind dulled by the consequences playing out before him.

"Very well then," Lord Torrington concluded. "I may count on your services?"

There was but one reply: "Yes, my lord," he uttered, less in triumph than in defeat.

Lord Torrington folded the paper that contained his notes and slipped it into the belly drawer of his desk. "Please let Sparks know where you can be contacted, *Captain* Collier. That matter was neglected when you appeared last year. I sent a man after you, but he reported that you disappeared into the vapor of a rookery south of the river."

Philip blinked stupidly, dazed by yet another random turn: An office courier, and not a French spy, had followed him after his first visit to the office a year earlier. That episode had instilled in him an expectation of treachery that had led to his ill-fated decision to create a false identity for himself. Everything he had suffered through — and accomplished — had been set in motion by his penchant for misjudging situations.

Lord Torrington eyed him closely. "We shall meet again soon, I trust?"

The agreement had been struck. Not written by pen in clauses, sentences and paragraphs, but laid out clearly nonetheless in implications, understandings and obligations.

22. Finding the Words

In the days after his meeting with Lord Torrington, Philip no longer burdened his family with anger and resentment. He instead spent most of his time quietly gazing out a window for long periods, only responding to questions put to him with brief, simple answers. As often as not, he would be away during supper and return late at night without a word to his father or siblings. His natural restlessness had been stilled by the unavoidable path that lay ahead.

Should there have been elation that he had achieved promotion and advanced financially? Or should there have been despair that he was to resume an imperiled existence? Neither emotion would fit him now, for if life were to be a game of chance, then he had seen only the very next throw of the dice. He was to step again into the world of the unknown and the unexpected and, as always, he would try to find his way alone.

The Times carried an account of the action at L'Orient harbor among its reports on the resumption of war, but the article included no context for the affair and gave the credit for the operation's success to Captain David Terwillerger of "the appropriately christened *HMS Valiant."*

Philip later obtained a copy of the *Naval Chronicle* and was pleased to read a more comprehensive report that Terwillerger had submitted, passing along proper credit to Lieutenant William Edney. But he gasped when his eyes fell upon praise of Midshipman Thomas Smythe for his rescue of the heroic Edney.

Well, Philip thought, Terwillerger obviously knew which side of his bread was buttered, for the mention of the well-connected Smythe would sit well with the Lords of the Admiralty and at the same time allow the young snip to be transferred to a more prestigious vessel. An undeserving advancement to be sure, but at least the *Valiant* would be rid of him.

Also within the pages of the *Chronicle* were mentions of the promotion of Edney to commander of the sloop *HMS Greyhound* and the transfer of Admiral Kenwyn Voss to duty in Portsmouth harbor, a sad step down from commanding the Channel Fleet.

Neither *The Times* nor the *Naval Chronicle* drew any connection between the action at L'Orient and an intended invasion of Ireland, nor was there any mention of a daring young army lieutenant who had provided assistance. Philip was unmoved. The military couldn't very well expose its sources of information, and he had become an outcast whose actions would have been an embarrassment to the army. While he still existed to serve the needs of the government, Horse Guards would never wish to acknowledge that a British officer had shed his uniform and lowered himself to spying.

Philip arose early one morning as his father prepared to head off to Dunn & Gilchrist and announced that he would be leaving again soon.

"Where are you bound this time?" his father asked.

"I cannot say," he told him.

A silence followed that lasted through most of breakfast. At last Mr. Collier spoke, instructing Philip to accompany Harriet on an outing with Will Devlin, the son of one of his firm's partners.

"There will be the three of us then?" Philip asked.

"Your sister is not permitted to travel into the country alone with a young man, even if it is young Mister Devlin. You will honor my request?"

Philip agreed, and Mr. Collier left without another word.

Harriet had been uncommonly quiet as she scurried about in the background during the conversation. Philip thought it odd, since it would have been more in character for her to have sassed her father regarding the need for a chaperone or to have hectored her brother into committing to the outing. As he finished his breakfast and was about to leave the table, she swooped in to freshen his cup of tea, then patted him gently on the shoulder.

"What are you about?" he asked.

"I thought you should like a second cup to fortify you for the day," she said pleasantly.

He sat and looked at the steaming drink, knowing that some sort of foolishness was afoot, but not caring enough to ask what she had in mind. Later, however, he caught a slight smirk on her face as she folded a cloth to hang over the back of a chair, and his disinterest ended.

"That's enough then. What is this about?"

"What can you mean?" she asked sweetly.

"What have you planned?"

A pause followed as she performed another kitchen duty with far more diligence than was normally shown, then delivered a curt reply. "We are going to the Vales' country home for the day."

Philip stared at her, then let out a French curse that he had learned from Yves.

"What did you say? You know my French is not good."

He said nothing.

"We were invited, and you promised Father that you would accompany me, so the matter is settled."

"I am not wanted there, so why would you include me?"

"That is where you are wrong. You were invited, by Mrs. Vale herself."

"Why on Earth … is this the result of your meddling?"

"You will recall that you promised Father that you would go," she repeated, sealing the orders.

Will Devlin was an agreeable companion on the trip in his father's carriage, although Philip grew tired of his fawning over Harriet, which prompted giggling and talking that added to the annoyance. He also was surprised that while he was away, Will's interest in his sister had increased to the point where he would accompany her on this occasion.

Harriet raised the subject of music, mentioned in passing that she was accomplished on the piano forte and then launched into a strong opinion on a musical composition. Much to Philip's relief, the carriage just then pulled around a bend to reveal the Vales' stone cottage with dozens of people gathered on the lawn.

Mrs. Vale came immediately to the carriage as it pulled into the yard.

"I am so pleased that you have come," she said to Philip, ignoring Will and Harriet.

"My father asked me to accompany Harriet and Mister Devlin," he said in explanation.

Harriet darted off in search of friends, and Will followed in her wake.

Philip added quietly to Mrs. Vale, "I hope that my appearance isn't cause for awkwardness at such a pleasing event."

"Philip, you are most welcome. Eleanor looks forward to seeing you."

He was momentarily stunned, but then recalled that Mrs. Vale had seemed reluctant to let him leave during his last tumultuous visit to her home. He had wondered many times during the days that had passed how his conversation with Eleanor would have concluded had Mr. Vale not entered the drawing room when he did, or if he had not silenced his wife when she had begun to speak.

Mrs. Vale pointed him toward the lunch that was about to be served, and he began to walk in that direction, trying not to appear as if he were alone.

His path eventually took him within earshot of Harriet's chatter just as he spotted Eleanor making her way through the guests. He turned away to listen to his sister's discourse, or what could have been better described as a monologue, with Will.

"... I was thinking that the day couldn't possibly be any better, but just then Mr. Russell interjected his thoughts ..."

Philip looked again toward Eleanor, who had stopped to speak to someone before resuming her way toward him.

" . . . and I said, 'Well, why is it called politics, when it is *impolitic* to discuss it in my company?'" Harriet went on.

Philip cringed, having heard her witticism a number of times before, but Will laughed heartily. "Oh, Miss Collier, you are captivating!"

Harriet's face shone with delight as she looked about to see if she had attracted any other admirers.

Philip was considering an acidic remark, when a voice came from behind.

"Philip, I am so pleased that you could come," Eleanor said.

He turned and nodded stiffly, and when his eyes lifted, he detected strain upon her face.

"I hope the day finds you well," he said, then blushed as he realized how ridiculous he sounded.

She seemed to study his face for a moment, causing him momentary discomfort, but then he looked directly into her eyes. Suddenly, there seemed to be a recognition of what had been, and she broke into the smile that he had tried to remember when he had been alone and afraid.

"Will you walk with me?" she asked.

They strolled along a long wall that led around the boundaries of the Vales' property, finally coming to a halt in a grove of fruit trees. The conversation was warm, though insignificant, and finally Eleanor leaned against a tree to face him in an inviting pose.

Philip cleared his throat and asked uncomfortably, "Is your Mister McGiver not in attendance today?"

"He and Papa are in Town with their business."

Philip looked about and saw no one. "I apologize again for my behavior. I, that is to say, I wish …"

She reached one hand up behind his neck and pulled him forward into a long kiss.

"I know now," she said. "I read your letter."

"My letter?" he asked absently.

"The one you passed to me after Papa asked you to leave. You were in great peril when you wrote it, were you not?"

"Yes, I was afraid it was to be the last letter I would ever write," he said, recalling his feelings as he had penned the few words before leaving on the mission into L'Orient's harbor.

"It will not be the last," she said, then took his hand. "What would you have told me, had you been standing before me at the moment that you wrote it?"

He cleared his throat again. "I would have told you of the high regard that I have …"

"Would you have told me that you loved me?" she interrupted.

"Yes," he said quickly but with little confidence and almost as a question.

"This is what I had dreamed," she said. "I have hoped upon hope that we could have a life together, and while you were away, I searched for your face in every star."

"But what of Mr. McGiver?" Philip asked. "There must be matters to be settled."

She reached over and placed the palm of her hand against his chest. "I know what is here, and that is all that needs to be settled."

"But what of your parents?"

"It was Mother's idea to invite you today. She doesn't want me to settle for a marriage of convenience."

"I see," Philip said, although her mother's defiance of Mr. Vale surprised him.

"And Harriet was involved as well," Eleanor added.

"Harriet? Good God, that girl has no bounds!"

"Philip, she told me that the only way to know if love is true is if you are willing to toss away everything in its pursuit. And I am, without hesitation."

"I recall that your mother said you were a very determined little girl."

"Papa will say the same thing soon." She took his arm as they resumed their walk but dropped her hand when they approached the other guests.

"This has all happened so suddenly, and there are many things that we need to discuss," Philip said, stopping. "I shall be leaving again, and soon, I suspect."

"I know that, Harriet has told me."

"Must she be involved in everything? I so resent her meddling."

Eleanor took his hand and patted it. "I know that you must go again, but I shall wait for you."

"But we must marry immediately, before I go," he insisted.

"If we can, but if not, I shall wait. And you will write to me."

Philip thought about all that had occurred in their relationship, including the whirlwind events of the last few minutes.

"I was constantly confused while I was away, but now that I've returned, well, I thought my doubts would end."

"Were you confused about me?"

"I was confused about everything: where I was going, what I was doing, when I would ever find happiness."

"One can be confused and still be happy."

"One can?"

"Yes, of course. You mustn't think about things so much. Just keep your mind on the task at hand."

"But I fear that is my shortcoming, because I can't keep myself from pondering questions that have no answers."

"But what is it you want?"

"A life that's more than just a collection of dreams."

"Philip, you simply need to learn to accept that life is utterly confusing, and it will always be so."

Following Eleanor's advice to keep his mind on the present, Philip awkwardly reached for her hand and bent over to kiss it.

"I love you," he murmured after raising back up. "You were my beacon when I was lost."

Eleanor burst into tears and embraced him, no longer caring if they were seen together.

His joy matched hers, although his feelings were less an emotion than they were pride. He would have envied another young man who had Eleanor on his arm, but it was *he* who had captured her heart.

The simple words, "I love you," had unlocked a strength within him, and he felt as if his dreams were within his grasp. And he *did* love her, even more than he had before he had said it.

"What are you thinking?" Eleanor asked him.

He looked up at the sun's rays pouring through the trees and tried to extract something tender from William Wordsworth to recite. He thought of how he had conquered seemingly insurmountable odds on his own, and so he searched for a passage from *Robinson Crusoe*. He thought of how he could find peace with his father, and he was reminded of the Prodigal Son. He thought of the war that would need to be fought in Europe, but while he knew *Henry V* would be appropriate, he finally abandoned his search through the written words he had stamped upon his mind. At that moment, it dawned on him that a recitation would not be adequate.

He turned to look into Eleanor's glistening eyes and squeezed her hand.

"I cannot now find the words that define everything I hope our life can be, but I know that they will come to me."

Author's Notes

A Solitaire is a work of historical fiction — with a heavy lean toward fiction — that tells of the early steps in British secret service through the eyes of a young agent.

My research relied heavily upon Elizabeth Sparrow's *Secret Service: British Agents in France, 1792-1815,* which details the rise of England's clandestine network in the years after the French Revolution. Some of the characters in the book are based on the people who charted a new path for intelligence gathering in the late 18th and early 19th Centuries.

William Wickham headed England's Alien Office, which initially was created to handle displaced French noblemen after the Revolution. These disaffected *émigrés* provided the office with a bountiful source of men willing to engage in work to overthrow the Revolutionary government.

The mission also served as the perfect cover for other activities that followed, allowing the British government to scheme against France under the guise of resettling "refugees."

Wickham's covert actions even escaped the notice of many in his own government. Sparrow wrote, "The existence of the Alien Office was never a secret, but the full extent of its activities was known only to the few who worked there. Not even (Prime Minister William) Pitt was informed."

The office and its successes allowed espionage to become institutionalized and elevated its importance in the war effort. By doing so, Wickham created the foundation for modern secret service as his agents grew to become something more than "spies," a label that originally had been used to describe lurkers, eavesdroppers, tattletales and gossips. Wickham no longer was with the Alien Office during the period of this book, having been named chief secretary of Ireland, but his spirit lives on as Lord Torrington. The "Wickham House" referred to in this book is a fictional creation that was named in tribute to the spymaster.

The Alien Office's efforts primarily involved the disbursal of gold to obtain information and to advance plots intended to lead to Napoleon Bonaparte's downfall. But while much of Britain's work was carried out by high-born aristocrats, Wickham also turned to unconventional means. For instance, he employed an 18-year-old clerk, Charles Flint, in some of his secret affairs — including numerous trips inside France — and was pleased with the results.

I wondered while reading Sparrow's book how Flint came to learn his trade when obviously no training manual was available. He also lacked the social and family connections that might have helped him in an arena that required admittance into fashionable drawing rooms. It seemed to be almost comical that such a young man would succeed and a certainty that he had stumbles along the way. And so the character Philip Collier and his employer, Lord Torrington, were hatched. His lordship is a fictional creation based on the extinct peerage of Arthur Herbert, first earl of Torrington, and not on John Byng, the actual Lord Torrington of the period.

Were Flint's ideas shaped by literature and poetry, much as today's young people are influenced by dialogue from movies and lyrics from pop music? Did he find it necessary to quote literature in order to keep his young, restless mind on track? Surely not, but that is the case for Philip, who relies upon Defoe, Shakespeare, Cervantes and the Bible to help point his way. Flint likewise did not concoct his own cipher based on the pages of *Gulliver's Travels,* an exercise that I can confirm required more than three hours to encrypt Philip's first message.

A Solitaire largely follows actual events, with context of the time provided primarily by *Napoleon's Wars: An International History* by Charles Esdaile. Additional material comes from the newspaper archives of *The Morning Chronicle* and *The Times* of London and of *Le Moniteur Universel* of Paris, fictionalized in the book as *Le Journal* of Felix Debraux.

Scholars of this period will recognize that some of the chronology of 1802 to 1803 — particularly French invasion preparation — was rearranged a bit in order to accommodate the story.

A number of characters — in addition to Philip and Lord Torrington — were drawn from important figures in the period during the Peace of Amiens. However, only a few actual individuals from the time are included, and then only by way of reference and not as characters in *A Solitaire*.

Napoleon Bonaparte ruled France, of course, serving as First Consul and Consul for Life during this period and later as emperor. He not only dominated the nation militarily, but most other aspects of life as well, including the theater and the arts.

An example of Bonaparte's interest in the theater can be found in a letter to Minister of Police Joseph Fouché in 1805: "I read in a paper that a tragedy on *Henry IV* is to be played. The epoch is recent enough to excite political passions. The theater must dip more into antiquity. Why not commission Raynouard (a French dramatist of the period) to write a tragedy on the transition from primitive to less primitive man? A tyrant would be followed by the savior of his country." Oddly, Bonaparte believed the audience would see him as the savior, rather than the tyrant.

His censors also on occasion rewrote the dialogue and plots of plays to fit his views, although his tinkering with the premise of *Hamlet* in this work is fiction. Additionally, Bonaparte expressed admiration for *Oedipus* because of its show of decisive leadership, though not for the fictional performance *pro bestia*.

The Corsican Ogre, as he was often called by his enemies, changed the nature of theater in France, with state companies becoming increasingly common and their actors employing texts that had been approved by censors. By 1807, most small theaters in Paris had closed, limiting the chance that anything heard on the stage would offend the emperor. François-Joseph Talma was France's greatest actor during this period, but unlike Jean-François Floquet, he was loyal to Napoleon and didn't resent the government's interference with the theater.

Bonaparte likewise had a profound effect on religion while attempting to bridge the divide between France and the Catholic Church from the days of the Revolution. However, the ties created under the Concordat of 1801 allowed the government to keep the upper hand in the arrangement and did not provide for the return of land the church lost during the upheaval of the 1790s. The secularism of the time left religion out of favor with the ruling elite, and public morals did not return to the pre-Revolutionary standards. The immodest style of gown worn by Madame Giselle deBasséville and other ladies in the book was in fact the style in Paris at one point.

References to other important figures of the time are worth brief explanations.

Marquess Richard Wellesley served as governor of India during this period and was the brother of Arthur Wellesley, the Duke of Wellington, who commanded the 33rd Regiment of Foot in which Philip served in India.

While the infamous Minister of Police Fouché is mentioned, he actually had been dismissed in July of 1802 and reinstated at a later time. He devised a system of paid spies who reported to prefects of police, such as the fictional Bérand, or sometimes directly to himself. The name Fouché today is associated with treachery and villainy.

Samuel Taylor Coleridge and William Wordsworth were leading literary figures of the time and greatly admired in society during the early part of the 19th Century. Jonathan Ransom Turgeon, who was not greatly admired, is a fictional character, and it is good fortune that you will not find his poetry in any collections from this period.

Other historical figures are presented in spirit. Elements of the writer Germaine de Staël and the Irish rebel Robert Emmet were turned into the fictional characters Astrid Villemain and Thomas Grant. Several quotations attributed to Madame de Staël and to Emmet were included verbatim in the book's dialogue, simply because I was unable to match the words that actually sprang from their own pens and tongues. Bonaparte did, in fact, insult Madame de Staël by asking about breastfeeding her children, and she in return frequently described him as a loathsome creature.

Emmet fled to Paris after a student rebellion in Ireland in 1798 and discussed Irish independence with Bonaparte, but he eventually returned to his homeland disillusioned by what was occurring in France.

Fears of a French invasion of Ireland were real. The *Dublin Mail* reported in 1803: "It is extremely probable that Bonaparte may attempt a descent in Ireland, if not in the expectation of final success, yet in the hope of giving occupation of our troops, and to occasion expense and embarrassment to the country by aiding and supporting the disaffected. … He may think that comparatively a small number of troops would create a powerful diversion and be able to maintain themselves till they had occasioned the loss of many lives and the desolation of one part of the empire."

But perhaps because a French invasion led by General Louis Lazare Hoche had failed in 1796, a second one was never attempted. The wording on the handbill that Philip finds at Groussard & Co. comes from an actual poster the French had printed for Hoche's attempt.

With no French assistance in 1803, Emmet went ahead with an ill-fated insurrection that amounted to little more than a Dublin street disturbance. At trial, his stirring speech for Irish independence concluded: "When my country takes her place among the nations of the earth, then, and not till then, let my epitaph be written." He was convicted and his boundless passion extinguished when he was hanged, drawn and quartered as punishment.

The dates of the Peace of Amiens and the resumption of war were shifted slightly to fit the plot. The two nations did suspend hostilities for a year, during which time England's defense budget, like Lord Torrington's, was cut severely. When the war resumed, it lasted for more than a decade until Bonaparte's eventual defeat.

The Battle of Trafalgar in 1805 eliminated once and for all French plans to invade England. Lord Nelson's defeat of the combined French and Spanish fleet thwarted Bonaparte's scheme to take control of the Channel and allow his troops to cross over to England.

Some historians question whether France ever really intended to invade England, seeing the planning as just a ploy to stoke the fears of the British. Bonaparte wrote in 1803: "If the English want to make us jump the ditch, we will jump. They may capture a few frigates or a few colonies, but I will strike terror in London, and I prophesy that before the war is over they will weep tears of blood." On the other hand, while discussing the possibility of invasion in another letter, he wrote that the time from the "giving of the order to its execution there must be only an hour or two," among the many logistical considerations that the French would never be able to overcome. Further confusing the matter are the deposed emperor's later memoirs, in which he occasionally rewrote history to present himself in the best light. While the assemblage of troops of the Grande Armée near Boulogne never set foot on English soil, it eventually was put to use against Austria.

Whatever France's invasion plans entailed, England shuddered in 1803 as it looked across the Channel. The hysteria in London during this time was evidenced by a cartoon depicting the Corsican Ogre tunneling beneath the water to enslave Britannia.

Philip Collier could have sized up what lay ahead by turning to Shakespeare's *Henry V* to express his thoughts: "In peace there's nothing so becomes a man as modest stillness and humility, but when the blast of war blows in our ears, then imitate the action of the tiger."

D.P. McCandless

Recitations

Chapter 1: "I am divided from mankind, a solitaire, one banished from human society." —From *Robinson Crusoe* by Daniel Defoe.

Chapter 1: "In the cause of freedom, as in the cause of honor, one can and should risk life itself ." — From *Don Quixote* by Miguel de Cervantes.

Chapter 4: "In thee, O Lord, do I put my trust: let me never be put to confusion. Deliver me in thy righteousness, and cause me to escape: incline thine ear unto me, and save me." — Psalm 71:1-2.

Chapter 4: "Whatever you can do, or dream you can, do it. ... Boldness has genius, power and magic to it." — From *Faust* by Johann Wolfgang von Goethe.

Chapter 5: "Experience is like the stern lights of a ship, illuminating only the track it has passed." — From *Table Talk* by Samuel Taylor Coleridge.

Chapter 6: "There is some soul of goodness in things evil." — From *Henry V* by William Shakespeare.

Chapter 6: "Forewarned, forearmed. To be prepared is half the victory."— From *Don Quixote*.

Chapter 7: "Only passions, great passions, can elevate the soul to great things." — From *Philosophical Thoughts* by Denis Diderot.

Chapter 11: L`éternel est mon berger: je ne manquerai de rien ... et j'habiterai dans la maison de l'Éternel Jusqu'à la fin de mes jours." — *Psaume* 23:1-6

Chapter 13: "Men like me are so discreet in love, that you may trust their lasting secrecy. The care we take to guard our own good name may fully guarantee the one we love. So you may find, with hearts like ours sincere, love without scandal, pleasure without fear." — From *Tartuffe* by Molière.

Chapter 15: "I have made only one prayer to God, and it is a very short one: O Lord, make my enemies ridiculous. And God granted it." — From a letter by Voltaire.

Chapter 18: "They that war against thee shall be as nothing, and as a thing of nought. For I the Lord thy God will hold thy right hand, saying unto thee: Fear not, for I will help thee." — Isaiah 41:12-13.

Chapter 20: "As I live and am a man, this is an unexaggerated tale. My dreams become the substances of my life." — From a letter by Coleridge.

ABOUT THE AUTHOR

A Solitaire is the first fictional work of D.P. McCandless. Topics of his nonfiction include World War I, World War II, Vietnam and the Cold War, and his areas of research include the CIA, the history of policing and the political career of Hubert H. Humphrey. He has edited more than 25 books, whose subjects include World War II, the Cold War, investor Warren Buffett and the presidency of George H.W. Bush.

Direct inquiries to: dpmccandless@gmail.com
Follow D.P. McCandless on Facebook and on Twitter
@dpmccandless

Printed in Great Britain
by Amazon